Unknown Country

Book 3

Light Of The Home World

Sequel to

Light Of An Alien Sun

By

Gregory J. Saunders

Unknown Country, LLC

Original Artwork by Andres Rodriguez
Cover Design by Gregory James Saunders

First Printing
All characters appearing in this work are fictitious. Any resemblance to real persons, living or dead, is purely coincidental.

Library of Congress:

LCCN: 2008928888

ISBN: 978-0-6152-0757-5

PUBLISHED BY UNKNOWN COUNTRY, LLC

www.gregoryjsaunders.com

Printed in the United States of America

Light!

Distant. Alien. Human.

Each a description from the books of Unknown Country, and each entwined one to the other.

For Vi-t-ry it is a search, as much for self as for home. A journey of awakening and rediscovery. To bathe under the strange and alien Light From A Distant Star. One that illuminates and watches over a race known as human.

For Niloc-al-teal, the Light Of An Alien Sun shines down upon him. Streaming, life giving radiance, flowing down from the one under which he was born. A clansman, a thinker and warrior; unaware of his history, his duty, or his legacy. Great loss drives Niloc, pushing him toward a destiny in the service of an alien being. One who is strange and unknown, and yet as familiar as the stars above the clansman's head. His is a journey of self discovery and that greatest of all tests; faith.

For Lt. Colonel James Macintosh "Mac" Crowe, the only sunlight he wants to see is a quiet sunrise on Earth and from his own sun. The one called Sol. That, however, is a few thousand light-years distant. Instead, the shipwrecked astronaut has become the central figure in an ages old legend. One dreamed up on an alien world he never imagined existed. To some he is the slayer of a god. To some a friend, and for others a leader. But to Niloc, Mac is nothing less than the Light Of The Home World.

Light! Distant, and Alien and Human.

I hope you enjoyed the stories as much as I enjoyed creating them. Happy reading.

Gregory J. Saunders

I started this project a few years back thinking, *How hard could it be?* Three books later I know. If you call yourself an author, you have my respect. This one is for my sons, Colin/Niloc and Dean/Den'al, And for my loving wife Jeannie and her eternal patience and faith. And to all of you who read and proofed and kept me going, particularly my sister Melinda. To all of you I give my undying thanks.

Books By

Gregory J. Saunders

Unknown Country

Book 1
Light From A Distant Star

Book 2
Light Of An Alien Sun

Book 3
Light Of The Home World

Zahir
A Novella

Visit
www.gregoryjsaunders.com

Prologue

On the planet Mith Sul-Anroth (Five Months Earlier)

Darkness enveloped the priest as he sat cross legged on the bare stone floor, a floor as bare as he himself, for what he faced he would face just as he'd entered the world; naked. The room in which he sat was bare as well. Large, cold and devoid of light except for a single hole drilled through the granite slab that served as a roof. A hole no larger than the third finger on one of his two left hands. Dim light shown down from a dawn that was not yet fully born and the priest stared up at it. Unblinking. Waiting. Just as he had since the mid of night. As he would until the sun reached its zenith and stabbed a fiery finger into his forehead for a single though interminable instant. An instant of vision and foretelling. The priest, known by his people as the True Leader, did not feel the cold of the floor as it crept through his skin, nor the cramping of muscles long unmoved. His body screamed the need of water. Both to quench his thirst and to purge his system of waste. Yet these were worldly concerns and of no consequence. For the True Leader had lost his god.

Riding low in the sky and visible by day or night, Dracoolus was the eye of god that saw and watched over them all. The one constant in an otherwise chaotic world, and never had it wavered in all the histories told by all of the True Leaders who'd gone before.

Until two nights ago. It was then that god's eye flared an angry blue, flashing his displeasure down upon the True Leader and his people. Many voices screamed in dismay, and more than one pale body lay crumpled and broken beneath the Caves of Life, having thrown themselves from the precipice in despair. Then

Dracoolus had blinked furiously many times before closing tight his eye. In an instant, the light of god was gone.

Yes, worldly matters would be of little significance for the priest until he brought Dracoolus back. Found what had displeased the deity and righted that great wrong. He sat the floor in a trance. Waiting. Outside the stone building his people gathered in their multitude, waiting in hushed silence lest they disturb the vision, each watching the heavens for the return. No cloud marred the sky and no breeze stirred the dust, the silence a pall that seemed to dim even the sun which climbed painfully slow towards its zenith.

The change in the chamber was not subtle. One moment the priest was statue still, the next, writhing and screaming in agony upon the stone. Spittle streaming from his mouth and urine splattering uncontrolled across the chamber. The single beam of light had tracked across his forehead then struck his right eye, releasing the trance and bringing the real world back into focus. The pain was excruciating, and it was the pain that brought the revelation to life.

The Hall of Visions was built like the lodge of a beaver, and when the priest emerged it was head first through a small hole, appearing as if from the birth canal. He stood on shaky legs staring up at the heavens and the unseen hole where Dracoolus should be, seeing nothing but light green sky. He did not remove his gaze as he sent his mental command directly to the brain of every being kneeling in the valley. The True Leader received his revelation, though as a result of simple deprivation or true divine intervention, no one would ever know. Nor would it matter. He pointed across the mountains which lay purple and jagged in the distance, the granite towers erupting from the plain like rotten teeth bursting through putrefied gums. Every being there nodded in agreement, and with that order, the Army of the Chalgu began to move.

Characters in Order of Appearance

(Sul-Anroth, Niloc's World)

Lt. Colonel James Macintosh "Mac" Crowe (Commander of the Atlantis, Shipwrecked)
Payload Specialist Susan "Sue" Rael (Astronaut on the Atlantis, Shipwrecked)
Dr. Demitri Karkov, Russian Scientist (Space Station Unity, Shipwrecked)
Jehkal warrior of Clan Paliece

Saber (Alien cat mentally connected to Mac)
Niloc-al-teal warrior and sole survivor of Clan Sar-too
Dr. Rebecca Carver, British Scientist (Unity, Shipwrecked)
Captain Cameron "Cam" Mitchell (Pilot of the Atlantis, Shipwrecked)
Den'al warrior of Clan Paliece

Shumak, Wilderness Commander of the People

Altil, True Leader of the Chalgu

Mograth, headman of Aranu Warren Kilkeep

Rahkal, Brother of Jehkal and warrior of Clan Paliece

Hatchik-al, warrior of Clan Grouw-sul

Peri'ackt, Chieftain the reptilian People

Sil-casus, Oot of the Fist (Corporal), Chalgu warrior

Eneri, warrior of Clan Cal'dil
Chief Solonar of Clan Briss'y, Valley of the Moon
Chief Zukal, of Clan Paliece, Valley of the Moon
Solonak, Son of Solonar

Chapter 1

(The Present!)

Fire in the stone hearth crackled and popped, the glow throwing contented shadows about the darkened room. Bookshelves overflowing with well known friends stood as silent sentinels, and the smell of fresh split pine and a hint of wood smoke perfumed the air. The man sits in a well worn and ratted recliner, dressed in his most comfortable evening attire, allowing one of those friends to paint images of far places and incredible adventure on the vast canvas of his minds eye. No other illumination casts its glow over the room as he prefers to read by natural light alone.

Outside his window a storm rages. The tempest combining with the careful staging of the room to reflect the story and lend a touch of suspense. Lightening flashes and thunder rumbles, rattling the panes of glass in competition with sleet and wind, but these sounds were distant and barely heard over the cries of fog bound sailors echoing from the black script that flows before his eyes. So real the weaving of the words that the smell of brine and the damp cold of clinging fog cause him to shiver.

A broken spar slaps the water as the ship bobs and rolls slowly in the swells, her shifting weight creaking her storm weakened timbers. The sound a physical groan from the disabled vessel, as if she too hears the distant waves crashing against a reef. Hidden stone daggers that would tear out her heart and plunge her terrified crew into the abyss of icy dark. Suddenly, the roar of a foghorn sounds on the wind, and the faint stab of light from a tower on the headland pierces the gloom, giving the promise and illusion of safety. If only her rudder had not sheared! If only her sails were not hanging in tattered ruins, shredded in the violence of a winter storm. The sailors have stood a chance then. Instead, the waves and current would have their way. Bent and broken, the captain could only watch and pray as his one true love was pulled mercilessly toward her death. Her proud belly bared to the mercy of the rock. Only one chance could stay the butcher's hand, one desperate chance... He turned the page.

Concentration momentarily broken, a new sound impinged upon his consciousness. The crash of waves receded as the storm outside grew, and within the storm, the cry and yell of sailors was replaced by a distant scream. Hideous, full of pain and very real! A sound drifting on the wind, compelling in its need and so familiar. The hackles on the back of his neck dance as the scream echoes briefly then dies away. Staring hard at the glass, the scream sounds again, this time closer, yet shredded by the wind. Fear and dread freeze him to his seat, eyes wide, staring at the window with certain trepidation.

Sleet turning quickly to water ran in rivulets down the fire heated glaze. Outside, momentary flashes of lightening create a strobe of the darkness, silhouetting the limbs of the old oak tree in the yard. Wind whipping the barren sticks gave the appearance of so many grasping fingers, reaching and pawing.

He heard another cry, different and closer. This one not of pain, but of the hunt and its ultimate success. A cry he'd heard before in another life, familiar and terrifying. Yet the true memory of it proves elusive. Outside the tempest rages on, building itself to a climatic pitch even as the scream of terror and the cry of the hunt sound once more, almost as in union. Whatever they were, they were in the yard outside his den. This is where the hunt would end and still he was rooted to his chair.

By shear force of will he drives himself to move despite the fear that invades the room like the thickening fog in his now forgotten tome. His movement comes in slow motion, moving as if fighting a great and invisible current. Yet need compels him! Outside someone was in great and dire need. He feels their desperation. Their primordial fear.

Overcoming the forces that hold him he stirs, the book in his lap ignored, falling to the stone floor, cracking its spine and spilling a hundred pages across the floor. He rises on leaden legs, and just as stands erect a face is pressed, cheek and ear, outside against the pane of glass. Staring in horror, a silent cry escapes him. It is a familiar face that slaps the glass, and it slowly distorts as pressure pushes it against the windowpane. Raven hair, stringy and wet frame her face, her terror driven tears competing with the rivulets. Wide eyes look inward, beseeching him, and still he's rooted. Now fully paralyzed!

He stares, not able even to tremble or shake as a hand slowly snakes around her neck. The movement languid as if from a loving caress. Thin fingers, long and tipped in black nails, curved and sharpened too pointed claws score the ivory skin, drawing lines of bright red. Her eyes widen further. Suddenly, a visage rears into view. Hideous and alien! Huge eyes glow from under a hood of rotting skins, glittering as they stare in at him with certain and knowing alien intelligence. The scene is a physical blow, and his gorge rises along with an elemental wail inside his head.

Rebecca! he screams, reaching for her. The gleam in the alien's eyes intensify, and a mouth bristling with sharp yellowed teeth yawns wide, moving relentlessly toward the unprotected throat. Stricken, he watches as the woman he loves mouths his name, pleading silently for him to save her, *Mac!*

"Mac!"

He jerked as if he'd been slapped and swung wildly at the hand that shook him. Then he moaned once more before his eyes snapped open.

"Wake up, Mac. You're having a nightmare!"

Startled from his sleep, the vestiges of the night terror quickly slipped away, only to be replaced by his even stranger reality. He groaned and rolled over to face his savior, payload Specialist Susan Rael.

"Jeez, Mac! You were thrashing about like something was attacking you. You ok?"

Lt. Colonel *Mac* Crowe, late of the star ship Atlantis – no one could call the marooned and wrecked ship, after what it had been through, simply a space shuttle – rubbed his eyes against the alien sunrise. A sunrise which bathed a fantastic, yet empty and devastated city in its strange green glow. His voice, when he spoke, was gravely and raw, which described exactly how he felt.

"Yeah, Sue! I'm fine." As fine as one could be sleeping under an alien tree, on an alien buffalo skin, in the middle of an alien winter. Hungry, cold and still bone tired, summed up his situation. He shivered again, as much from the dream as from the weather. "I'm fine."

The woman who stood over him bore little resemblance to the emotionally broken astronaut who'd crashed landed on this planet so many months ago. One of the five that survived. Now, she looked…? She looked like a survivor. Wild blond hair spilled out from under a fur hat, and she wore a fur poncho that wrapped her like a sack. A fur that never covered any animal on earth, and cut from a beast Mac himself had killed. Her face was dirty and fatigued and without a trace of makeup. She looked exactly as her ancestors must have several hundred years ago. Oddly enough, she was developing a fierceness and self-assured attitude reserved for those few who survive great peril. And killed to do so.

"I don't suppose you woke me for coffee and donuts?"

"Nope! But we have some lovely tubers, a few nuts and some mostly rotten fruit. Maybe chase it with some nice fresh snowmelt."

"Well! And here I thought this would be a bad day."

Not even a chuckle from her. In fact, because of his history of blanking out on them, she was looking *very* concerned. "Seriously, Mac. You we're practically screaming. Must have been some dream."

Yes, some dream indeed, and an explanation he had no wish to pursue at the moment. He changed the subject, "Where's Jehkal and Demitri?" He scanned the makeshift campsite, surprised the clansman would venture any further from the fire than he could heave a feather. The clans, and it seemed all the peoples of this world, shunned the area they found themselves in. A place they called the Rayattl! It was an area around the ancient city, or maybe the city itself, into which no one would venture. An area clearly marked by a line of sun bleached skulls mounted on poles of various lengths. They stood as a warning to the curious or unaware. A line which Jehkal could not have crossed on his own, his primitive superstition driving the fearless warrior into bone freezing terror just sighting it. He had crossed though, but only after suffering an incapacitating head wound and, virtually unconscious, was dragged over the line by Demitri.

"Foraging," she said.

Mac raised an eyebrow in disbelieving question.

Sue just laughed, "I know. Jehkal wouldn't move from the fire until Demitri called his manhood… well Clanhood, into question. Even then it took Demitri holding his honor to the great Drakil," she rolled her eyes, "Over his head."

Mac cringed at the thought. The clansmen believed Mac to be the embodiment of what they called the Drakil-at'sakaal of legend. A bigger than life figure described in an ancient prophecy! A verbal myth handed down generation to generation by clan holy men. A legend which was about the only item the clans could agree on. That and warring upon each other. Supposedly Mac was going to deliver them into a better life. Some joke that was. He and those with him were no better than beggars. Hunted beggars at that.

"Well, Mac, I guess you being a living breathing prophetic fulfillment has some benefit after all." She was almost wistful, staring off into the trees.

"Maybe they can find something to eat that has some blood in it." Mac said. Equal parts hunting and gathering was how they made their living now, but Mac preferred to be the consummate carnivore, preferring the hunt over the gather anytime.

"Not likely! Here they come."

Mac caught movement through the low brush. From his position on the ground the view was surreal. Narrow leafed brush, bright red fading to blue, the summer color changed to fall on this planet, framing blue evergreens and the green sky beyond. Enter from center, two figures which couldn't be more dissimilar. Yet so alike. Demitri, tall and dark, beard now full and richly black reflecting every inch the Cossack of his Russian ancestors. Dressed in animal skins over the ripped remnants of his NASA coveralls issued so long ago for his fateful stint on the International Space Station. Demitri carried one of the bows they'd made from scratch. Alien wood and alien animal gut for string! He also sported a long spear tipped with a sharpened heat tile salvaged from the wrecked Atlantis. The shuttle that lay buried under tons of dirt in an alien arroyo many miles and months behind them. Demitri could easily pass for Ivan The Terrible, though a calmer and more centered man you could never meet. It was the man's long morning shadow that provided the contrast and similarity.

Jehkal! Warrior of Clan Paliece and resident of the planet Mac found himself on. A place named Mith-Sul-Anroth in the native tongue, and a word that meant *earth*, or home, or mother. Mac simply shortened the sound and called it Myth. Less than a year ago, he would have said he 'believed' in life on other planets, but that belief was really only a factor of the educated mind. He couldn't conceive of a Universe so vast, with so many billions of stars and planets, yet only Earth held life! Nonsense. But even this belief was sprinkled liberally with skepticism.

That all changed the day satellites began disappearing from orbit over Earth. Firm proof of life elsewhere came as a rude and painful shock to him and the world, resulting in the loss of fellow astronauts and friends. Now, here he was the alien on an alien planet! And one who could call the same was walking into their campsite with food for his breakfast.

From a distance Jehkal would pass for an old west vision of a fierce Sioux warrior. Long dark hair past his shoulders with many colored strings woven in that danced as he walked. Tanned hide shirt and pants, not buckskin, but an animal known as a Shart, the true buffalo on this planet. At least this small portion of it. As Jehkal drew close, any kin to Earth began to fade. He looked human in all proportions, if you could overlook the dual thumbs that characterized his race. The ritual scaring of his cheeks bore no resemblance to any seen on Earth, drawing the eye to an over wide face and bright alien eyes that glimmered like molten mercury. Jehkal was a clansman. A would be leader of his tribe and up till now, a pain in the ass! Still, Mac felt blessed to have him around.

The other *friendly* aliens were with the rest of his team, and Rebecca. The woman from his nightmare. Even now the memory of the dream made him shudder. Was she safe? Were the others? Cam and Niloc? Den'al? There was only one way to find out, that was through the strange connection he had with his pet alien cat. Mac had rescued the kitten after its mother and siblings were killed by another of the saber toothed beasts, and somehow unexplainable by him, he and *Saber* had a mind link. One to the other. A link which allowed Mac to actually *see* though the cat's eyes. When connected, Mac would go into a coma like trance and see everything the cat saw, and Saber had sent Mac warning of impending attacks from their enemy, the Aranu. He now had to amend that to enemies, because they had another race to contend with that seemed just as brutal as the Aranu. They were known as the People. Mac had ordered Saber to go with the others of his group as their protector. This was after they were separated in a three-way battle with the reptilian *People* and the hideous Aranu. A more brutal world he couldn't imagine.

Mac and his group needed to know how fared the others, so, after he had eaten he would try and 'link' with Saber and find out. Great concentration was required for him to forge the connection, and that would be difficult at best with hunger boring a hole in his stomach.

Jehkal slapped a fist to his chest in salute as he stepped into camp. "Good to see you awake my Drakil!"

The alien's first greeting of the morning did little to brighten Mac's mood. He didn't need any fawning this morning. Too much had happened for him to feel anywhere close to being anyone's savior. Still… He refrained from the retort that nearly burst from his lips. Jehkal was part of them now, part of their team, and critical to their survival. Mac would do what he must, even if it meant playing along with a tragic farce. He returned the greeting in the clansman's own language, using the hand signs they'd developed as backup.

"Morning, Jehkal! I hope your hunt this dawn was successful."

Jehkal's face clouded and his eyes lowered. If there was one thing the brash young man hated, it was failure. Especially failure in front of his Drakil! Mac smiled inside at his discomfort, though he was careful to keep the humor from creasing his face.

"My apologies, Drakil. I have naught but some Kassa root. As for meat, we were unsuccessful."

"Not to worry, Jehkal!" Mac smiled through the grit in his mouth and a ten day growth of beard. "I'm hungry enough to eat… even Kassa root!" Was that relief he saw in the young warrior? How hard to grow up in a world where failure could mean excommunication from the clan, or even death at the hand of chieftain who felt he'd been crossed, or disrespected, or perhaps was having a bad day. Mentally dismissing him, Mac looked to Demitri and switched to English.

"How about our friends? Given the fact we're still here..." He let the thought hang.

Their "friends" were the reptilian warriors of the People. A race Mac never knew existed until they were chased right into their laps by the Aranu. And the Aranu were worse. Hideous only began to describe them! The humans had killed several, and they resembled the bulging eyed aliens from the Roswell incident, though not cute in any way. They were deadly killers that had harassed and attacked the humans repeatedly.

Yesterday, a battle between the three parties left Mac, and those standing around him, separated from the rest of his team by a mêlée of battling Aranu and the lizard warriors. It also left them on the inside looking out. The People would not cross the line of skulls into the Rayattl, nor would they let Mac go free. Yesterday at dark, a guard line was strung along the entire perimeter as far as they could see. A perimeter which supposedly surrounded the entire ancient city. Mac had no idea if there were any holes in the perimeter and they could see only a small portion of it, but finding out was job one. Somehow they had to escape and get back to the others.

"Not much change." Demitri sounded as tired as he looked. The Russian spoke American English far more precisely than any native, though that precision was wearing off with his time around Mac and the others. Americans all, except Rebecca. Her accent was British precise and eloquent.

More interesting than the Americanization of the Russian was the fact the humans had begun integrating "Clan Speak" into their own everyday speech, most times without even realizing it. Instead of root, it was jar-root for the tuber they were so dependent on. Instead of sword, it was the clan word clav'l, and instead of horse it was skeel, the name of the mounts the clans rode and herded. He figured that after a few years the English/Can languages would merge, but that was in the future. A future Mac certainly hoped to see but was very much in doubt of at the moment. Demitri politely cleared his throat. Mac's mind had wandered again.

Demitri continued, "Except they seem intent on carving up that big beast that was after you." He raised an eyebrow at Mac. "I've never seen anything like it."

The beast was what the People called a Hydral. As big as four or five elephants! An animal which hunted by stunning the nervous system of its victim, much like a jelly fish stuns its prey, yet far worse because this animal didn't need to touch you. It could stun you with a look at a hundred yards and could swallow a VW whole. Even more disconcerting for Mac, this particular Hydral seemed to be hunting him exclusively, yet its intervention in yesterdays battle may have actually saved their lives. Mac wondered if he alone had the mental connection to certain animals on this world. No one else seemed to be afflicted or influenced by it. And why? First Saber, now a Hydral? *What next,* he thought, *those damn ugly squirrels? I'd hate to have them following me around.* Yes, the Hydral was a surprise that turned the fortunes of war. The battle yesterday claimed the lives of many of the People, and an unknown number of Aranu. A fact that was certain not to have endeared the humans to either of those races.

"Do you want to hear the rest of it, Mac?"

Damn, he thought. At least two minutes had slipped by as he once again wandered, amazed at how fatigue was playing with his head. "Sorry, Demitri. Don't tell me. They're going to mount its head on a pole and add it to the Rayattl!"

Mac was kidding, but Demitri frowned and became even more serious. "Not only *that* head."

Mac's mouth rounded in an 'O' as the ramifications struck him. "All of them?"

"Yes. Aranu, their own warriors, and the big one! Decapitated. Shoved on a sharpened stick and added to the line. The head of the beast they just drug over and left in a wide spot between two poles." The big man sat down heavily as if the simple barbarism of it all was too much.

"I saw them cut the head off one of their own, Mac. Just whacked at it until it came free. They threw the body up on a pile of other corpses, then took care of the head." Demitri was unconsciously rubbing his neck. He looked up, his stare boring into Mac. "There were none of ours!"

"I know, Demitri." He said it softly because he'd seen that it was the truth. Seen through Saber that none of 'theirs' had died in the battle.

The others were not so certain. The Russian clearly wanted to believe in Mac's ability, but none of them, clan or human alike, truly believed in his mental connection to the cat, or its reliability. How could they. Earth man connected mentally to an alien saber-toothed lion! Mac told them yesterday that he'd *seen* the others escape through the eyes of Saber. Described it in detail. Demitri wanted to believe and wanted confirmation, but all he could get, all any of them could get, was Mac's word. He would believe because Mac was a rational being not given to fancy, and not broken despite all they'd been through. He would believe because he'd actually witnessed the 'connection' more than once. But his doubt could not help but linger. Even Mac's promise to try again left them with mixed feelings. Would he succeed? Would it matter?

"If they were in trouble or imminent danger, I'd know." Mac knew he would. Saber had warned him of impending danger time and time again. Like lightening out of the blue, Saber would project a vision into him mind. A vision so real Mac could feel it. So real, because it was; a real time visual directly from the cat, and when it grabbed Mac and took him in, it blocked out all else.

The connections, up until yesterday, were initiated by Saber. But yesterday, in the midst of battle, Mac called and connected to the cat on his own, by his own will. Only once and very quick, and just long enough to command the cat to look after Rebecca. Look after Cam, Niloc and Den'al. No news was good news, and today he would try again. He would search out the cat with his mind and confirm the others still lived and were safe. Then…? Then they would go about seeking their escape from the Rayattl, and from the reptilian People.

Saber ghosted through a forest that seemed almost primordial, dodging in and out between the roots of enormous trees that had never known the axe. The cat moved with the same effortless grace of his Earthly cousins, yet his vision was closer to that of the canine. Through a combination of his eyes and a highly developed nose, the world was seen in the vibrant palette of scent. Dull gray mist, the smell of the living wood, flowed from the boles of trees, swirling in eddies in the soft breeze or settling to the ground in the cool near frost of morning. The aspiration of soft evergreen leaves a much brighter gray tending toward white.

Darker variations represented the unique smell of each different plant, the deeper blacks emanating from the world of fungi. All as distinct in scent as the shape would be to a human eye. Through this rainbow of grays, an enticingly bright swatch of blue swept down the center of a path. The blue a signpost of a warm blooded animal well known to the cat and the slowly dissipating trail signifying his next meal was only moments away.

Other trails of color painted a living and vibrant world. A world with far more information than could ever be gathered by the two legged animals Saber found himself attached to. Saber's mother and sibling were killed when he was only days old, an incident which should have spelled his death. But a fortuitous and unlikely event had prevented that particularly unwelcome outcome. Mac stumbled upon the nest shortly after a large male, not Saber's sire, had attacked and killed his family. Saber, the runt of the litter, was deep in the underground lair and the only survivor. Then along came Mac and small cat had been confused. But he was also strangely attracted to the man. Part of that attraction was because Mac had raided his mother's body, taking parts to make strings for their bows. Her scent had been strong on the man and this compelled the kitten to follow him. Later, the attraction became much more.

Saber's species relied heavily on telepathic communication. Except when the mothers denned, the cats hunted in small packs, utilizing their mental ability to incredible advantage over any prey. Prey that included the top of the local food chain, clan, Aranu and the People.

Had Saber been more than a beast, he might have considered his connection to Mac an anathema. Would possibly have ruminated on why he felt no similar bond to any other in Mac's group. Only Mac himself. Might have considered possible feelings of jealousy, because others of his kind felt the same growing connection to his master, though mostly they fought against and stayed away. But Saber didn't have those thoughts; he was after all, simply an animal. Yet he was an incredibly extraordinary animal! With sharpened instincts created within him, and within all his species, by genetic engineers in ages past. Saber was not merely a cat; he was the descendant of semi-intelligent body guards of the Collective elite, the master-race! His ancestors and theirs were marooned here, left behind by the war that had destroyed all vestiges of civilization on this world, and very nearly all other life as well. With no one to control them, the cats had gone back to the wilds and reverted to more instinctive ways.

Unknowingly to Mac, his simple act of touching the kit with the scent of the mother clinging to him, closely paralleled the bonding process employed by a Collective Master to seal his animal body guard to him. A bond which was as much technical as physical and certainly not the magical manifestation the clansmen thought it was. Such was the amazing technology of the Collective that the cellular sized robotic nannites, originally implanted in Saber's ancestors, continued to re-manufacture themselves and pass down within the genetic mix of every successive generation, completely unchanged from the original. As Mac stroked the kitten, many of the millions of nannites literally jumped ship, passing through the dermis of the cat and into his hand where they quickly spread out and began to multiply. They now coursed through his body, and once established, created a link to their brothers in Saber and bonding the two in a connection that could be broken only by death. The nannites, after having transferred to Mac, quickly satisfied themselves that he was the new Collective Master. They strayed no further, no matter who touched Saber. Not that many willingly did, the cat was truly Mac's.

Saber felt his master in the far distance. There was no call, simply a presence, and with his orders firm, watch and protect Mac's pack, he would continue to do just that. That same pack lay sleeping just over the crown of the hill behind him, and the only danger he could detect anywhere near them was a wounded Aranu warrior left behind by its own pack as they fled the battle yesterday. Wounded, but not currently stirring and Saber would make sure it never moved again. After breakfast!

Niloc-al-teal sat in a cold camp, slowly chewing dried meat and contemplating the turns in his life and the gravity of his duty. Niloc was an unattached clansman. Orphaned young by a clan he didn't know and adopted by Clan Sar-Too, but unattached to them by marriage. Unattached he would forever remain. He was the last surviving member of that same clan, for the Sar-Too had been utterly destroyed by the Aranu at the beginning of spring, just as they were migrating to their summer pastures. A truly and utterly tragic event, but one that was preordained by his god. At least that was how Niloc saw and justified it, for had the Aranu not destroyed the Sar-Too; Niloc would have never been driven forth to his destiny. He would have never discovered the 'One' known as the Drakil. Would never have become his guide. His teacher and protector.

Though to be fair, it was the Drakil who had been sent by god to discover and rescue the last of the Sar-too! Fate and god, fickle and mysterious. Even now god made his task most difficult, but Niloc knew that to fulfill a prophecy required nothing short of faith, and it was Niloc's faith that was now being tested.

Circumstances had fallen far beyond his control, and Niloc found it necessary to abandon his Drakil. Abandon him or die because the two parties were separated by an army of the People battling to the death with a war band of the Aranu. As he watched from the dubious safety of the forest edge, Mac/Drakil had fled beyond Niloc's protection. Fled into the Rayattl, a haunted place shunned by all who knew it. Death and worse than death awaited any who dared venture beyond the line of skulls. Yet the Drakil had dared! The ancient words decreed it would be so! *Lost to darkness he returns!* is how the passage read. The Drakil must be discovered, which had occurred in the spring, then be lost, which had also occurred, only to return again to the clans. Niloc's current agony, current test of his faith, was whether the Drakil really would return! Could anyone escape the Rayattl? Again and again Niloc chanted he had memorized so long ago, the words that held so much mystery and so much promise;

In the mists of time beyond seeing
Comes an age at the end of an age
Winter of the people draws near
Enemies more numerous than Clan or Council
Swarm the lands where none may hide
Demons, Despair and the Reaper walk the abandoned road
Filling the hollows with maimed and dead
Clan young quake and moan, crying for mothers who answer no more
And war and death and famine reign or'e the land
Yet the brink of extinction is not the end
Salvation comes
By darkness before the lost small wanderer

A pillar of flame descending the heavens
Announced by thunder
A savior appears, an army in his van
The Drakil-at'sakaal
A Greater Kraagen on his banner flows
With the serpent at his feet
Lost to the darkness he returns
A great warrior, to stand forth and lead victories charge
His enemies quail and fade away
A new age from the ashes springs
The long climb from darkness is nigh
With prosperity and life following as a wave from great tide of change

Yes, he decided for the hundredth time. *Yes!* The foretelling was unshakable. Too much of it had already been revealed. Much remained dark, but too much; war as they had never seen, the lost moon, the Kraagen, the new ideas brought by the Drakil, all pointed to this being the time. The human known as Mac was the long awaited Drakil! It had to be. If only…

Silently Niloc cursed himself for his weakness of faith, and for his other shame. Across the small clearing lay the others of his party, two humans and one clansman. A clansman of the hated Paliece who was now more than a friend, he was a war brother. Unheard of, and in Niloc's mind, further proof of the Drakil and the prophecy.

Near him was a human male, also a protector of the Drakil. His true name was Cam and he was fierce and loyal. Many enemies had died by the hand of Cam and this same human had rescued Niloc not once, but twice. Niloc was twice debited!

Finally, his eyes flowed over the last of his charges, a human female named Rebecca. The Alt-sul (mate) of the Drakil! Her name, her shape, her very essence stirred him. To his eternal shame she stirred him. It was not enough that she was of a different race. A race which lived farther away than he could possibly conceive. If his faith would allow it, on a different world. A world which glowed under the light of an alien sun. No, that was not enough to bring him dishonor. Niloc's hidden shame was that he was stirred by the Drakil's own woman! Even as watched her she awoke, and he quickly averted his eyes lest they betray him.

Shame and shaken faith! It would take great strength and devotion if he were to survive, yet survive he must, for it was up to him. Up to Niloc, the councilor! Niloc the guide! It was up to him to reveal the unfolding legend to all the clans. He now firmly believed it was his destiny to leave the Drakil behind and go to the clan lands. Bring them the Drakil's woman as proof. He must prepare them for Mac, prepare them for change. Niloc had no idea that destiny, and perhaps his god, had other plans.

Shumak, Captain of a wilderness patrol for the army of the People, and defacto, if not physical, captor of…? Of what exactly he didn't know. Thoughtfully, he looked over the killing field where his Chieftain's son, an august individual known as Peri'il, had died. Killed by a dart of some kind before he could even come close to his enemy. That same dart Shumak now held in his hand, personally hacked from the body of the man he considered a fool, and an artifact which possibly held the key to Shumak's own survival. It was Shumak who had led the attack which took Peri'il's life, and his father, Peri'ackt, would demand payment in kind as penalty for failure. Usually that would mean forfeiture of all Shumak's worldly possessions, including his head. Now? Possibly this dart, and the description of those who wielded it, gave Shumak his chance. A slim chance, but as a gambler that was all he needed, and one he would gratefully grasp.

Instead of accompanying Peri'il's body back to Slsilakx, the center village, as custom dictated, Shumak would send an honor guard with a vivid description of Peri'il's incredible heroism. Included in his report would be word of an Aranu/Clan alliance and the terrible here-to-fore unknown race which led them, and this dart as proof. Spun well and Shumak would live. Possibly even tasked to lead an army to crush this threat! Spun wrong? Shumak turned his mind from there, he would not contemplate failure.

The very fact that Shumak would not abandon his post and accompany the body lent gravity to the nature of the menace. At least he hoped this was the message conveyed. To help his cause, word would be spread by a courier racing ahead of the honor guard. Word that Shumak held a leader of this new race, the killer of Peri'il, in virtual prison inside the shaman's line around the

Rayattl. *Yes!* he thought, *'Inside" the forbidden ground, where not even the Elders dared go!* A place the clansmen and this new race, for some mysterious and arcane reason, were desperately trying to reach before the Hero Peri'il, almost destroyed them.

That thought brought a rise of bile to the back of his throat. Peri'il the Hero? Hardly. Peri'il the unmitigated fool! Peri'il the arrogant and insufferable! He cautioned himself to hold his thoughts lest his tongue or face betray his true feelings. Shumak steeled himself and nodded to his second in command, Liss'atl. "You have your orders!" he barked.

The big golden body in front of him shimmered as the reptilian snapped to attention. Shumak placed the dart carefully, almost reverently inside a skin sheath. Placed it as if his life depended upon it. Which it did.

"Take this and the body to Peri'ackt. Give the counsel as we discussed and return here with orders!"

Liss'atl slapped his golden scaled and massively muscled forearm over his hearts in a grave salute, his voice deep and gravelly, "Yes, Commander! Look for my return in five turns of the sun." The subordinate looked his Commander directly in his golden brown eyes and deep dark reptilian pupils. An unprecedented and dangerous move for an inferior, considered an insult or challenge, yet in this case it meant something far different. It meant agreement and understanding. "I will not fail!"

Shumak knew he would not, for Shumak's chance was Liss'atl's. They would live or roast together. All of them would. The life of every warrior under his command would be forfeit if the actual *truth* be told!

Shumak contemplated the cost. How much he would owe this Under-Captain when this deed was done. It was a personal point of honor with Shumak that he not be in the debt of anyone, and it would be even worse with the possibility of blackmail. Shumak may have to kill Liss'atl in the near future, a thought that bothered him not at all. But that was a ridge that must be crossed much later. For now, Shumak sat and watched as the procession wound its way up the flank of a hill, his eyes never leaving it until it was lost in the trees upslope.

A golden escort followed the body of the dead son of Peri'ackt, which was mounted upright on its Thalk as if he still lived. An honor befitting a Royal. To further his cause, Shumak rolled a large piece of hide from the Hydral and mounted it as a trophy behind Peri'il. The lizard like body of the Thalk practically disappearing under a load of dead warrior, animal skin, and many the weapons gathered from dead Aranu. Far, far more than Peri'il deserved. Far more than Shumak cared to give, but little enough when balanced against one Wilderness Commanders precious life.

Shumak smiled for the first time in days, exposing purple gums bursting a dual row of pointed teeth. The gods gave little and cared less, so Shumak had cast the dice, but of course, only after weighing them carefully in his favor. Now the cast was done, the dice were rolling and it would be days until he saw how they settled.

Shumak cast these unpleasant thoughts from his mind and turned his attention to a more immediate problem. That of capturing these strange new beings held in a prison of which he held no key and for the first time he wondered. If the lowly clan could tread where all feared go, possibly Shumak could follow!

Chapter 2

Mac drifted somewhere between reality and the first dreams of sleep while laying on a mat of soft leaves, smelling their bruised skin. A most pleasant aroma, mingling with moldering earth and the damp detritus left under the small tree where the lay. His ears heard too much as he tried to ignore the nervous movements and breathing of others around him. The soft rush of the breeze. The songs of alien birds. Mac tried his best to ignore it all and concentrate on only one thing. Saber!

Saber! he called repeatedly. Nothing. Concentrating harder, *Saber.* Nothing. He pictured the cat in his mind and called again. *Saber!* Nothing! Mac sighed and tried again, and again, and came close to despair as still nothing happened. He felt the cat. Felt him out there somewhere, but couldn't bridge the gap. Did not know how. From a distance, he felt impatience flowing from Demitri and Sue in waves. Felt Jehkal's stare as if it burned. Felt it all and tried to ignore it. Wanted to tell them to go away and leave him be, but could not. They had to witness this. Had to believe. He sighed and tried once more, *Saber!*

Suddenly, his perception shifted. The turmoil behind his eyes calmed and changed into a single picture. Sound ceased and Mac knew he was seeing as did the cat. Though he could not know the image was translated into a vision his mind could understand by the tiny robots. A vision of dense forest with incredibly large trees and ferns of varying type filled his view. A dead and half eaten animal lay on the ground before him and the coppery taste of blood stained his tongue. *Saber,* he called, *Take me to Rebecca!* The vision swung as, without question, the cat abandoned his meal and moved quickly through the undergrowth. Mac felt a moment's vertigo as the world swung and the vision blurred, very nearly breaking his concentration, but instead he prevailed further sealing the bond.

Briefly, he thought about this incredible connection as Saber ran down the trail. Thought it odd he could taste as Saber tasted, yet could hear nothing of the cat's world. Vision was in black and white, and there was absolutely no tactile sense other than what was in the cat's mouth. Out of body was a description that fit, but he felt there could be so much more. If only he could learn.

His drifting thoughts were interrupted by a vision which nearly stopped his heart. There before him sat Rebecca. Disheveled, teary eyed and weary, yet alive and well. Tentatively, she reached toward him/Saber. She mouthed a word he couldn't make out, then he could taste the musky salt of her skin when Saber licked her hand. Again she mouthed a word and this time he knew it, *Mac?*

He knew it was a question by the look on her face, and he was so surprised he shook. Like a slap the connection was gone. His current world rushed back with all the sounds and smells, and the itchy feelings of a filthy body. Gone was Saber, and gone was Rebecca. His eyes snapped open and he croaked a whisper, "They're ok!"

A cold camp greeted her as she awoke. Awoke to the feeling of eyes upon her, then catching the look Niloc tried to hide as he quickly glanced away. She sighed inward. It was a look most men cast at an attractive woman. Some sly. Some shy. Some surreptitious, and some blatant. Something all women experienced to some degree, and either glowed in the admiration, tolerated it, or hated it, depending on whim, circumstance, attitude or a million and one other factors unknown and unknowable by those who cast them. But she would never enjoy it when she was filthy, cold, hungry, and many days without a bath. Then again, she didn't know how she should feel, given the admirer was an alien born on a planet hundreds of light years from her own. She'd seen the looks Cam gave her. She longed for the looks Mac gave her. But sometimes she flushed warmly at a single look from Niloc. In many ways he was a dream! Tall and dark. Masculine in every way. Chivalrous and polite to a fault, yet a true savage, ready to kill without hesitation. She sighed again, putting the thoughts away for another time.

Cam smiled as she stood to stretch out the kinks left over from the night. He handed her a large leaf plate filled with roots and nuts, "Grubs for m-lady?"

She rolled her eyes. Cam could find humor anywhere, and loved to poke fun at her being what he called, "Proper British." Most times she would have played along. Now, the loss of Mac and the others hurt too much. She gave him a wan smile, "Thank you."

"Welcome." She knew by the sudden change in look and demeanor there was something else coming. "You know, I've been thinking more about this, Rebecca."

She didn't have to ask what he was talking about. It's the same thing they'd talked about last night, and much of the day yesterday. She was so very weary of it. She merely looked at him and his good humor evaporated.

He pushed on anyway, "We've shaken the Aranu. We need to circle back like I suggested yesterday. If Macs' really safe behind those skulls, we need to be there too. We'd be safe as well."

She sighed, not yet ready to fight this battle. It was too early and she was just too beat and weary to think clearly. "I don't know, Cam." She didn't, literally. Though it was her paramount desire to be back with Mac, other confederations weighed heavily upon her. Niloc insisted they go as well, but not to Mac, to the clans. He was positive Mac and the others were safe, and that 'this' was how it was supposed to be. She didn't at all believe in Niloc's prophecy bullshit, and she was torn, unable to make a decision. She certainly didn't want to bring more attention or harm to any of them, and marching back into the People's territory seemed foolish. But that way lay Mac. "I just don't know. Niloc…"

"Screw Niloc!" His voice was loud, and even though Niloc and Den'al couldn't understand his English, they understood the subject of the debate. Both just sat there; Den'al with his Paliece braided hair drooping past his face and staring at his leather boots like a kid ignoring bickering parents, and Niloc politely looking just slightly away, no doubt re-formulating his own arguments.

Cam pushed on with a dark glance at the Sar-too. "We know his position. I'll leave him behind if we have to. Hell! I'll leave you if I have too!"

She looked at him, horrified. "Don't say that, Cam. Don't you ever say that!" She didn't scream, but it was close. "We must stay together. We're all we have left."

Cam was torn between grabbing her in a big reassuring bear hug and slapping some sense into her. *Doesn't she realize what was at stake here?* Yet the rational side of him knew she fully understood, even more so than he himself. The tears growing in her eyes as much as anything else shut him up and he looked down in frustration, formulating another approach. An approach which lay stillborn when Rebecca suddenly stiffened and stared. "What is it?" he asked.

She gave no answer, but he looked where she did, seeing Saber moving through the undergrowth. There was a change in the cat that was unmistakable. He was making a beeline towards her; fresh blood still staining his muzzle as if he'd just dropped a kill. There was no cat-like circling. No drifting eyes or sniffing the air. No slinking tail. Just an intent stare right into her eyes, and for a brief moment Cam wondered if Saber was going to attack. He reached for his sword and grasped the hilt just as the cat stopped, folded his back legs and sat. Still staring at her, but unquestionably non-threatening.

Rebecca knew in an instant. Knew it in her soul. "Mac?" she questioned softly, gently reaching out a palm. Saber continued to stare, but grazed her skin with his tongue.

"Mac?" she asked again.

Like a switch being flipped, the connection dropped and Mac was gone. Saber went back to being a cat. He dropped his eyes and slunk off, probably to finish whatever he was doing prior to being interrupted.

Rebecca burst out in a sob, reaching for him as he left, "Saber, come back! It was Mac. He was there. Saber!" But the cat neither acknowledged nor turned and was out of sight in moments.

"Cam. You saw it! Mac was there?" Her last plea was a search for confirmation.

He stared at the brush where Saber ghosted away, a single fern gently waving the only evidence the cat had ever been here.

"I'm not sure what I saw, Rebecca." No lie, he wasn't, but he saw a way to use this to his advantage. In a stronger voice, "But I think you're right! I think he was reaching out, trying to contact us." Her face lit up with this declaration, and he cursed himself for the asshole he was, "Yes! I think so, and I'm not sure why, but…"

"But what?" She needed an answer. Emotionally drained, she needed something.

He stood and moved over to her, taking the hand Saber had just licked, "But I think this proves what I've been saying. We need to go back!"

Her face lightened, but she was saved having to answer by Niloc who interrupted speaking in the clan language, "It is as I told you, Drakil-Alt-sul." This was the proper address for the woman of the Drakil. "The Drakil and the Kraagen are becoming one. He has sent Saber to watch us over us upon our journey."

In that moment, Cam's temper got the best of him. He'd listened to Niloc preach on and on about his prophecy and his precious Drakil. Listened and argued the many hours after they'd abandoned Mac. Cam was ready to go back, and die if he needed to, trying to reach his Commander and friend, and the only thing that had stopped him was Rebecca's pleading. That and the Aranu who chased them. He'd talked until he was blue in the face, and now, when he had Rebecca leaning his way, Niloc butts his alien ass back into it. And because he was emotionally on the edge, and feeling great guilt at having fled in the face of danger, he broke.

Cam reached for his sword and drew it in a blinding flash, swinging in an arc towards the alien's torso. Cam didn't mean to harm, just wanted to drive Niloc back, but the stroke flew with deadly intent anyway. Yet quicker that any human and quicker than Cam could imagine, Niloc's own blade was there, parrying the blow, the contact shocking his arm hard enough to numb. The sound of metal on metal echoed loudly in the small clearing. Slowly it died away, leaving the two blades locked and leaving the two staring at each other from just a breath away, and across a huge gulf now separating two friends.

On Cam's face was a combination of shock and dissipating anger now bordering on fear. On Niloc's, shame and sorrow. Shame that he'd rose in anger at one of the Drakil's house, even if in self-defense. Better if he had let the blade sink home. Sorrow for himself and for Cam who had been brothers in battle, together shoulder to shoulder in a great cause had destroyed their enemies. Had Cam been a warrior of the clans, one of them would now die. In that moment, Niloc considered how best to disengage; to bow out without blood being shed. He was saved that duty by a scream from Rebecca.

“Stop! My God! Stop!” Everyone froze, even Den’al who’d drawn his sword but stood well away from the combatants, not sure where his loyalty should lie. Rebecca was shaking and staring up at them, a pleading on her face. “Is this what’s to become of us. We strike out at each other?” The tension bled out of Cam first, and with his release Niloc stepped back.

“I’m sorry Niloc.” Cam said. “I just…” His apology or whatever it was to become, died with the low cough from the bushes. Saber’s warning, followed quickly by a horn sounding in the distance. Someone else had heard the ring of steel or Rebecca’s shout, and it was Den’al who recognized the call.

“The People have found us!” He turned to the distant noise, trying to do the impossible. See through the forest. “Do we stand or flee.” By his tone, it was clear he wished to stand and fight. His brother had been killed by the Aranu just a few days before, and he’d been alternating between consuming grief and the verge of berserker rage. It was not to be.

“We flee!” Rebecca barked the order with steel in her voice. Her mind was made up. For now at least they would continue the race against their pursuers. She would believe in Mac and Saber, and she would allow Niloc his belief as well. Allow it to take and guide them, at least for now. Without thinking she’d just taken command of their little group.

Chapter 3

A gentle hill covered in tall grass burned brown and stiff by frost and late fall sun overlooked the village. Early morning light left the bottom of the valley in shadow, brightly lit treetops contrasting with deep almost black shadows beneath their limbs. A single long hall, thatched in grass harvested from that same hill, belched blue smoke from its top and the occasional inhabitant from the entrance. Log corrals held large animals, and snarls and fighting emanated from a pit, though what caused the noise was unknown.

Down wind the smell of the place was horrid. Burnt meat and rotted meat competed with the midden for dominance of the breeze. Just outside the hall, a lone sentry drowsed beneath the limbs of a tree that only partially concealed him. Twelve warriors, fifteen females and seven young rounded out the total inside, while three more warriors had left the village prior to daylight traveling towards the east.

On the hill the grass moved slightly and unnaturally as the observer watched the unwary observed, his long spear lying beside him. Fifty nine of his brothers stood just over the lip of the hill, awaiting his report. Satisfied with the scene below, he whistled softly twice. A sound which should have alerted the sentry, as it was the call of a bird never seen on this side of the great mountains. The sentry did not and continued his bored stance. Had he looked up the hillside he may have seen the tall grass wave. Might have given some warning. Instead, the war party reached within a stones throw before one of the corralled animals gave a single surprised snort. By then it was far too late.

Sixty warriors rose as one and silently charged forward. The sentry, his reptilian eyes going wide in horrific disbelief, barely managed a strangled cry before three spears pinned him permanently to the tree, unlucky enough to be the very first of the People to die at the hand of a new invader. Only then did the eerie silence erupt into the chaos of battle. The bird calls changed to throaty yells and gnashing teeth as the full weight of a Chalgu battle group fell upon the hapless outpost. Religious fervor drove them and mercy was not a word they knew.

The fight was quick and brutal; all in their path speared and hacked to death, including the Thalk. The Parth in their pit were left alive to feed upon themselves until the last one starved. Such was the way of the True Leader. An army was a hungry beast and it demanded meat. Great hunks of bloody fodder were gathered from this battle, but not of Thalk or Parth! Only one kind of meat was fit to feed a Chalgu army on the march and it was stripped from the bodies of the enemy dead, and the better that enemy fought, the better the food. Sixty warriors attacked the hall, and forty-seven walked away; the People were a worthy opponent indeed!

A single hour later, Altil himself, True Leader of the Chalgu, entered the village. He cast his gaze across the charnel ground and pronounced it conquered, then sat himself in the center of the wreaked hall, where his warriors brought him the heads of the vanquished. One by one, he split them with a crushing blow from his ceremonial ax and pulled forth the halves of bloody brain. Each he searched with all his senses. He sniffed the gray mass. He searched the patterns and swirls of the frontal lobe. He listened to the slow drip of blood as it splashed at his feet, and he tasted the essence of each. A single bite before pronouncing it clean, then passing it to his warriors. Meat could be roasted, but the brain must be eaten raw.

The True Leader sighed in disappointment. The one he sought was not here, Altil could not sure The One was even of this race. *The search must continue and The One must die.* It was the mantra that carried them over the mountains. Only that event, the death of The One and the ritual consuming of his brain, could make right what was wrong. Could bring back the True Moon and the God within. The army followed the True Leader, and the True

Leader followed a streak in the sky. One witnessed soon after the night his god was lost, and one that burned in his mind like a branding. The legends foretold it. He began the ritual chant, and was quickly joined by the members of this small part of his host. Each hearing Altil's mind and responding in kind. *The One has come. The One must be found. The One must die!*

Mac crawled up the small rise pausing just at the top, lifting his eyes just enough to see the killing field from the day before. Much of it was etched upon the paths of his grey matter, and much of it was only vaguely remembered. The mad flight from the Aranu and bursting from the forest into the trap laid by the People was vividly clear. He worked through each step. Their sudden plunge from trees and into the clearing, desperately trying to out pace the screams and spears of their pursuers. The shock at seeing the humanoid reptilian People for the first time, and realizing they were as much or more the enemy than the hideous hide covered Aranu. Mac traced their mad race across the field to where his mount had died on its feet after having been wounded by an Aranu spear, throwing him and Jehkal to the ground just short of safety. Then the attack of a small troop of reptile warriors that had split from the main battle. It was a near thing as they shot and killed one and the others of the group inexplicably halted their attack, surrounding and protecting the one who'd fallen. *Someone of consequence? Probably,* he decided. His mind placed the bodies where he remembered them. Crushed grass was all that remained, but these things he remembered with vivid clarity. Then the behemoth had entered the fray, continuing its stalk of Mac himself. From there the details got real fuzzy.

The beast stalked him was a terror whose weapon was a mental sting not unlike a stingray. It had stunned him with a glance, knocking him senseless. Of all the beings battling on the field that day, only him. Only he was affected by that malevolent gaze. *Why? Some relation to Saber?* He could not know. After that the battle continued without him, and without Sue, Demitri and Jehkal, because they all had been able to escape into the Rayattl. But continue it had and the proof lay below, just as Demitri described it.

In the field, the reptiles slowly rendered the huge carcass of the beast, carving it down to manageable pieces; he assumed for food. The head, hard for him to look at even now without a shudder of revulsion, decorated the line of skulls along with the rest of the dead. *What motivated these beings? Savage and superstitious.* None of the reptile warriors came near the line of skulls, though many watched it.

His world, the modern world of Earth, couldn't prepare them for this kind of superstition. The savagery he could understand. He'd seen it and even participated in it. War was hell, and undeclared wars, the kind he'd fought in a former life, were even worse. But understand his enemy he must. That was the task which brought him here, and the more he watched, the further from that knowledge he got. He watched the reptiles march back and forth in front of the line of the Rayattl, never coming near except to add a new skull, and that with what could only be described as a ritual warding of evil.

Jehkal was little help. He couldn't, or wouldn't, tell them why the Rayattl was bad, just that they must avoid it at all costs. Yet here they were, in the poisoned ground where everyone feared to tread. *Let the People watch the line,* he thought. *Let them watch till they rotted.* Mac would find another way out.

Today they would begin exploring the ruins behind the security of the skulls. They would see for themselves whether the city held death or, as Mac suspected, only the bones of the dead. It was time to discover the many clues to the history of this place, this city and this planet. He also suspected they would find their means of escape. With a last look and sigh of disgust, he pulled back from the hill.

Mac turned toward the city and looked at Demitri. "You think Jehkal's heart can take this?"

The big man laughed, "We carried him over the line. I will carry him to the city if I have to!"

Mac looked at him, at once serious. "Maybe we should just knock him senseless up front and have done with it!"

Demitri stared at him curiously, still not able to read Mac's humor. Then his dark beard shook with a new rattle of mirth. Mac smiled also, destroying his look of gravity, then slowly he walked away muttering, "The damn Ruski thinks I'm joking."

Niloc held up the quartet on a small rise overlooking a clearing through which they'd just fled. If at all possible, he wanted to lay eyes on their pursuer or pursuers, and see exactly what they faced. The Paliece knew little about the People, his clan living farther away from the lowlands than Jehkal's. He did know their skeel could easily outrun the reptilian Thalk that the People rode. At least in the short run. But a Thalk could lope at a steady and fast pace all day long. If it came to battle of stamina, the People would win.

He and the humans had been chased for miles by the Aranu. Niloc alone had been chased by them for turns on end after the destruction of his clan, so they knew of that hunt and what to expect. This would be different. They needed either to elude the pursuit quickly, or do battle. What he saw in the next few moments would determine which. The four of them sat upon three skeel, Cam and Rebecca rode together. Den'al sat his own, and Niloc rode Shorn, the steed he'd raised from the time the colt had dropped from his mother to the cold uncaring ground. If the other two skeel had names, he didn't know them.

A skeel was a superior mount. Intelligent and aggressive. Seven feet at the shoulder, sporting tusks and hard nailed toes. Omnivorous, they could survive almost anywhere, and they were the pride and primary stock of the clans. A true and lethal weapon, but in a fight, not even close to a match with a Thalk. No! That took several warriors working in concert, and even then the odds were long. Thalk raided the clan herds, but thankfully, that was rare. How the People tamed such a beast was a mystery.

The People themselves were larger and stronger that any clan male and their scaled skin fairly shed the stroke of a blade. But Niloc felt they had an edge now, one proven so very effective since he'd met the humans. He called it a 'stick thrower' because there was no other clan word. The humans called it a bow, and the stick it cast, an arrow. A weapon that was unknown to clan or Aranu. Unknown to the People, and possibly to any race on this planet. It was a weapon that Niloc, Cam and Rebecca wielded with satisfactory and deadly precision. One that just may make a difference in the times to come.

The forest beyond the clearing was thinner, but only slightly, and Niloc caught movement in the thickness deep in the trees. A slitheringly smooth and sinuous movement, odd for an animal as big as a Thalk, and thankfully there was only one. *The advanced scout?* He considered, *The one which sounded the horn?* Others surely followed, but the wind was in their faces hiding their scent from both rider and mount. Niloc seized upon the opportunity. "Alt-sul, woman of the Drakil, we must attack!"

If he saw her bristle at being called someone's *woman,* he ignored it, and to her credit she readily agreed. They had debated this possibility for the last two hours while they attempted to elude the enemy, and the plan didn't need much discussion.

"From here, Niloc?" Her voice did not shake, though her eyes sparkled with fear.

"No! We dismount and move to the edge of the clearing. Shoot once with the stick thrower, then flee."

This was the plan they had set. To attack on foot with swords would be suicide. Even if they killed the warrior, the Thalk may continue the fight. It was hoped they could kill the warrior at distance and that without a rider the beast would turn in confusion. The problem with the bow was that, though they had practiced from a mounted position, it was very hard to hit a target and Rebecca and Cam both needed to shoot. Den'al, who had no bow, was best used from the saddle. Without further discussion, the three swiftly dismounted, nocked their arrows and moved down hill, leaving Den'al behind acting as their lone reinforcement and a charging distraction for when they retreated.

From the edge of the tree line they waited. Watching the indistinct form, oddly camouflaged in its golden color. It rode back and forth, searching for a trail that Niloc had used every craft he knew to hide. Dappled sunlight threw dull green shadows, further obscuring the scene.

For Cam, this moment was therapeutic; desperately needing to lash out at something, and that something marched slowly closer. Mentally, he walked through his shot. Three fingers on the string. Draw back firmly till the index finger and thumb cradled his jaw and the string kissed his lips. Short distance so aim low as the arrow will rise. Sight on the heart then relax the hand to release. Don't drop the bow arm until the arrow strikes. Practiced a thousand times and used efficiently to kill both food and Aranu. Now he would use it to lash back at the ones who kept them from Mac and the others. All this as he waited. Sweat trickled from every crease he owned and ran in a small rivulet down his back, the chill fall air bringing little relief to his adrenalin rush. Then, all discomfort was ignored as their target entered the killing field.

Rebecca tried desperately to ignore the complete alien-ness of the vision in front of her. She'd seen the warriors of the People, but only from a distance. To see it now, mounted on a lizard as big as a rhino, massively muscled and looking so much like a bipedal horny toad, almost unhinged her. Only the presence of Niloc on one side and Cam on the other kept her from bolting. Just at that moment, when her fear was at its worst, the wind brought a milky musky smell wafting over her.

Snake! her mind screamed. That was her last coherent thought as just as suddenly, the reptile spotted them. Eyes wide, it growled a command and the Thalk lunged forward, the warrior's spear leveled directly at her chest. Fear drove her next actions. Like a single warrior, the three drew their bows and rose. But the target moved so quickly there was no way to shoot the rider; the bulk of the mount completely blocked any hope of hitting him and Rebecca knew she was about to die.

As Niloc rose he saw their peril. He drew anyway and prepared to meet the charge, heart pounding and breath held in a great gasp. He aimed for the center mass of the charging animal, hoping beyond hope to do killing damage. Fingers tense, he was ready to release, when from the corner of his eye there was a flash of movement then a tan streak. With a snarl sounding like ripping cardboard, Saber launched himself at the Thalk, hitting the animal in the neck and burying tusks and claws into the leathery flesh. With a roar of pain that deafened them, the beast stopped and reared, nearly unseating his rider. Madly the Thalk turned and shook, reaching forward with a hind leg to strip away the offending ball of fur. That was all the opening they needed. With the target only twenty feet away, the shot was easy. Three strings hummed and three arrows flew, each shaft straight and true.

Swaying wildly in his seat, the warrior of the People, advanced scout and cousin to Shumak, never saw the arrows. One entered his side and two slammed into his chest. He felt little pain, just a sense of wonderment as the ground reached up to slap him in the face. As his eyes dimmed, he had a moment to roll over and stare stupidly at the feathered sticks protruding from his body. Death followed quickly.

Rebecca collapsed to her knees as reality rushed back. Saber disengaged and threw himself to the side, continuing his snarl to further distract and enraged the lizard. With a new bellow, the Thalk charged him. Deftly, Saber dodged, staying just in front and leading the beast away. Moments later both disappeared into the brush, the crashing and roars of pain and rage fading with distance. It was replaced a moment later by the sound of a new horn ringing in the distance.

"More come!" Den'al stated the obvious, his voice startling the others into motion.

"Quickly! To your skeel!" Niloc didn't wait to see if the humans heard or obeyed. He rushed to the body, braced with his foot, and quickly pulled the shafts. Only one came free with the arrowhead still attached, but he was unwilling to leave evidence of the weapon behind. He didn't know Shumak already had one in his possession, or that the Wilderness Commander was still perplexed at its use.

Hands red with gore, he ran back to Shorn and leapt into the saddle. Niloc kicked his animal into a run and the three mounts rumbled off through the trees. He grinned a moment later when Saber appeared beside them, ghosting their steps, apparently unharmed by his encounter with the Thalk. A smile because the Drakil, even in his absence, still watched over them. His smile faded only slightly as the sound of pursuit rose up from the valley behind.

Chapter 4

From their position, Mac and his small group could see very little of the city. Whether the city itself was known as Rayattl, or if it were only the area around it, Jehkal didn't know. The best interpretation of the word Mac could get was, 'Death Absolute', which meant that not only would you die; your very essence would be destroyed. Mac couldn't be sure if Jehkal meant the soul, or the ability to be reincarnated, or what! He couldn't clearly make out exactly what afterlife the clans believed in, even after his many philosophical talks with Niloc.

One thing was sure. Jehkal had fully believed he would die as soon as he crossed the line of skulls, and he could never have done so on his own. The fact he had not died had him very perplexed. To tell the truth, Mac wasn't sure Jehkal didn't think he really had died, and this was all just some sort of afterlife experience. To reassure him he still lived, Mac slapped him. The surprise on the clansman's face was classic. Torn between realizing it hurt, that his Drakil had just struck him, and his urge to draw his clav'l and slice off the offending hand, had his face arcing through all of those many emotions in succession. Mac half expected the warrior to pull his sword and attack, he simply didn't care. He turned his back on Jehkal and walked away, saying, "You're alive! Deal with it."

An hour later, Jehkal looked like he'd forgiven Mac. Mac still didn't care. What he needed was a sane Jehkal. Needed him to guide them as much as possible. He was the only local they had and Mac was determined to keep the superstitious bullshit to a minimum. But even so, Jehkal had no specific information on the

Rayattl. It seemed each of them was destined to be on a mission of discovery.

When asked how far the line of skulls went, Jehkal shrugged, “All the way.”

“Could the People guard ‘all the way’? Could they man the entire line? How far was that?” More shrugs. Jehkal either did not know or simply had no words to convey what Mac wanted. A half mile walk told the tale. The line of skulls was not that long after all. It didn’t need to be.

Using the same skills he’d learned in the military and the same skills each of them had honed on this primitive and very dangerous planet, Mac moved them forward. This was what the storied individuals in American military history called, *Indian country,* and they treated every bush as a potential hiding spot, every tree or rise in the ground a point of possible ambush. Something or someone in here kept even the Aranu away from the Rayattl. The question was; What?

They approached the city in a wide arc, pushing through thick undergrowth and a maze of blow down trees. Jehkal talked as if even animals that trespassed would die here. Nothing could be further from the truth. Alien birds abounded. Small animals scurried in the brush and ‘clipping squirrels’ were abundant, creating an incredible racket as they bounded away through the trees after sighting the group. These were the very same squirrels the humans had encountered upon being shipwrecked so long ago. The first animated alien life mankind had ever seen. So strange, with crab like claws, zero hair and a prehensile tail, and so commonplace he noticed them now only as an annoyance and possible threat to their safety. No way they could surprise anyone or thing with these natural sentinels around.

As he watched one bounce off through the trees, he paused. Mac was in the rear leading Baron, their only skeel and possibly their most important and precious possession. He stopped and peered at the city now looming over them, struck by a thought, *Melted!* That’s what he saw. Great spires which, instead of narrowing or squaring, grew larger as they gained height. Buildings that could never be built on earth. One building in the distance must be at least two hundred stories, growing from a small tapered bottom to a large disk at its top. Middle floor levels randomly flared out with little sense of symmetry or reason. At least until you stepped back and looked at it in the whole. Then it was clear. The builder of this great construct was not constrained such mundane laws as gravity. The creative impetus was beauty, not utility. Equal wonders could be seen throughout the fantastic city. Pyramids mixed with blocks and diamonds. Spheres interlocked with hexagons and octagons which flowed outward into spirals and the shapes of vast cornucopias. Mac had no words to describe it other than overwhelmingly alien. Too strange to be anything other than beautiful.

Color had dimmed with the ages, but the palette was rich, tending to blues and yellows. He tried his best to imagine this as a teaming metropolis and was left bereft. His mind simply couldn't conceive it. Damage was evident. Age told only part of the tale. War the other. Sometime in the deep and forgotten past a battle had been waged. Some buildings were whole and untouched; others blasted completely, yet with pinpoint precision. Still others exhibited the melted look which held his first impression. These buildings looked as if they sagged from old age, drooping and rippled. Mac could conceive of no weapon which would cause such damage or a mind that would want to create it. Could hardly conceive a world where a race this advanced could still be uncivilized enough to tear itself apart. It was a singularly humbling and frightening sight.

A whistle caught his attention driving away his thoughts. Demitri was waving from up the trail where the rise topped out. *Quit your damn day dreaming!* he chastised himself, then tied the horse to a tree and joined the Russian. Sue and Jehkal were there as well, lying on the edge of the rise and carefully staring over so as not to silhouette themselves to anything living below.

They needn't have bothered. Below was a scene that would have driven Dante to nightmares. They stared and stared, but only Sue spoke, and that was in a whisper, "Oh my God!"

Curiosity is the blessing of the intelligent, and a curse. Shumak knew better than to have the thoughts were currently racing through his head. As a wise man once told him, curiosity got the ground chukka eaten! And yet… Shumak was curious. He ran the battle over and over in his head. Even if Peri'il hadn't split their forces in a stupid move that got the imbecile killed. Even if the Hydral had not stumbled in to the fight, completely ignoring everything in its path, including killing blows (another curiosity that Shumak was mulling). Even if the ambush had gone exactly as planned, many things were not as they should be. *Why would the clan warriors and these new beings have come this deep in the territory of the People in the first place? Why were the Aranu so doggedly chasing them? Why? And why again!* Shumak had no answers. He had no prisoners to interrogate. No real clues. He had only one thing. The malady from which he currently suffered. Curiosity. And of course, being a logical being, there was only one true cure. The thought of it almost petrified him with fear. But the more he sat and contemplated, the more he was convinced. Though it cost him his Command, and possibly his life, to find his answers Shumak must follow his enemies. With a sigh he concluded, *I must brave the Rayattl.*

It was the belief of his people that to merely cross the line would result in a hideous death, and worse than death! When skulls were added it was with great ceremony and care, and it was counted a mark of bravery and honor to volunteer for the duty. The shaman talked from their dreams of the thousand possible deaths, each one more terrible than the one before. Only one thing was universally agreed upon; at least one of the thousand possibilities was assured. The People feared nothing and no one! But they feared the Rayattl! Feared the type of death that lasted forever. Yet the clan warrior and his oh-so-curious companions not only crossed without dying, the cursed place seemed to be their destination. Were their shaman more powerful than his own? Were they protected in some way? *Perhaps these Others are that powerful?* Shumak thought not. Else they would have stood and fought and not fled into the haunted place. *No.* The more he studied, the more he convinced himself. *They are not more than me. If they can cross, so can I!*

The Wilderness Commander rose from the tanned hide which softened his resting spot under a tree. His mind was settled. He let his eyes drift and set himself for a vision quest, the smoke induced journey of the Shaman. Only his journey would not be a journey of the mind, but physical. Shumak looked upon the world as one who dared confront death should. He paused and saw the beauty. Let it wash him clean. The mountains in the far distance, gray and misty, a place he'd never traveled. He witnessed a building storm as it pushed its way out from the birthing place of such things. Saw the Forbidden City, and the line of skulls that were to be his trial. Allowed his eyes to drift over the field and his command, his pride. The warrior flexed his arms which rippled with muscle, stretching golden skin that shimmered, slightly iridescent, in the sun. Shumak took a deep breath and held it, savoring its taste. He exhaled at last and called for his Thalk.

Shumak did not ask for volunteers to accompany him. Would not shame one of his own by having them quail at the last moment. He could order them to go. It was well within his right at Commander to kill them should they refuse. He would not. Shumak mounted and ordered his troops to remain. He would leave them guarding the Rayattl until he returned, or, should he not, until relieved. None questioned as he turned down hill and made spear straight toward the line. None knew his mind, and none made to stop him, but all watched. Some in confusion, some in wonder. Others in fear.

As he approached the line his eyes were drawn to a particular skull. One that still held skin and hair but no eyes, for the carrion birds were too efficient to miss that delicacy. This was the head of an Aranu, one killed yesterday by Shumak's own hand. This one he would watch until… He cleared his mind as the grinning face mocked him. In that moment he actually considered that Aranu Warrior his equal. Asked questions he never would have considered before. *What was he like? What was it like to be Aranu? Would someone mourn his loss? Did young await his return?* The face marched closer and Shumak's skin began to prickle. A few more strides of the Thalk and he would be there. He locked his living eyes with the empty sockets; bore his sight into the hollow black orbits. A lizard didn't sweat, even a warm blooded one, but Shumak's mouth hung open and he forcibly controlled the cooling gulps. It would not do to have is warriors see him, gasping for air, and pitching from his saddle in fear. A vision of that unhappy event raced across his inner vision and he chuckled to see it. In that moment, he crossed the line.

In that same instant he lost contact with the Aranu which had led him. It was two more strides before he realized he had now gone where even the holiest feared to tread. Two more before he let out a breath he didn't know he'd held, and two more before he finally believed. Believed he would not die. In those six strides he disappeared into the trees, from the sight of his command and into legend.

Mac continued to stare in horror and disbelief. Before them the city waited, and, like the prow of a ship, it thrust forward from the center of a valley ending with a single building, looking much like a bloated behemoth washed up on a beach. Accurate in image because the rest of the city lay immersed in a great lake which faded to a gray shore many miles distant. The vision an odd mix of silvery water reflecting both the skyscrapers and the storm laden clouds building above. Gentle waves washed down long avenues, and stains and aquatic plants gave evidence of rising and lowering water levels. Other buildings, or the wreckage of them, were visible in the shallows or as outlines of broken walls littering the shore.

But the destruction and evidence of war was not the horror that held him, that horror lay much nearer. The beach extended up from the water a hundred yards ending almost at their feet. Bleached white and rough, and beyond comprehension. For the beach entire, as far as they could see as well as the hill they stood on, was made completely of bones! Old bones crumbling to dust. Newer bones looking only months old. Full skeletons and partial, and most horrifying of all, the incredible number that were humanoid!

Sue whispered, "My God! What could possibly kill on this scale?!"

"War for one!" Mac echoed hollowly. He was absolutely sure that was the answer. But not the whole answer. There were too many *new* bones, though it was hard to tell age. The ones that looked old were polished or petrified, the newer still yellow and glistening. None they saw were crumbling to dust.

"But what else? We need to back up and re-think this before we find out!" He didn't have to add, *the hard way.*

Demitri began to pull back, but Jehkal was rooted to the spot. Never had he seen or imagined such a sight. The shear amount of water alone shocked him to his core. He could never have believed so much existed had he not been here to witness it himself. But the vast graveyard was more than he could possibly fathom; fully believed he saw an illusion. And while he lay there stupefied, he saw something else. A human word tumbled from his mouth, "L..look!" That, and a gasp from Sue, brought the two men back around.

A hundred yards offshore down one of the larger city avenues, the surface of the water began to riffle. Something large was moving slowly toward shore and it held Sue and Jehkal fascinated. But it was like a cold bucket of water to Mac. "Bows!" he yelled.

Three were pulled and arrows nocked. Jehkal rose unsteadily, but drew his clav'l and stood the line beside them. Mac knew '*discretion being the better part of*' when it slapped him in the face, yet they needed to know what was out there; threat or not. He believed they could outfight or outrun anything that came out of the water, and prayed he was right!

Whatever it was that approached, was seen as a dark bulk, indistinct and distorted by the waters refraction. Involuntarily, they took a step back. Thirty yards from shore the beast broke the surface, lunging forward into the shallows, its mass pushed forward by a last thrust, effectively beaching the animal. With all that the humans had encountered on this planet; the squirrels, the Hydral, the Aranu and the People, nothing prepared them for the hideously ugly creature that undulated itself up the beach. It was clear Jehkal had never encountered such a sight either, for he stood dumbstruck. As large as a Cadillac, it was a finned slug that poured itself onto the strand. It sat for a moment, then began an inchworm like lunging, moving forward in a ground eating crawl. A huge rubber lipped mouth dominated the front of a body with no real head. Other than the orifice, there was no real clarity to the beast, an animal with bulk rather than shape. Cold orbs, as pale as death, stood on stalks above the lips. These rotated and bore into them, watching but dismissing them as the beast rolled to a spot forty yards away. Then it stopped. Morbid fascination! That's the only thing that could have held them in place given the visceral revulsion they felt.

The beast paused a moment, one eye watching them the other swiveling to cover the rest of the beach. Then it began to rumble deep in the body, producing a sound like wet rocks squeezed and rolling inside a bag. The animal began to convulse, a tremor starting from its middle and rolling forward, rippling in waves, a grotesque parody of those washing the beach behind it. Slowly the noise and the waves built until the huge lips snapped open, revealing a gaping purple maw writhing with thousands of villi like organs. In a single great convulsion, the entire body arched in an inverted U and a mass of mucus and other material ejected from the opening, plopping wetly on the ground. The heap of gelatinous liquid and the exhalation from the maw equally contributed to a stench that had them choking and gagging. Mac fell back covering burning eyes, gasping and trying desperately not to vomit. Demitri had no such success and he could hear him retching behind him, a sound that nearly caused Max the same reflex. He gulped, trying unsuccessfully to find clean air.

"Mac! It's moving." Sue's voice was strained, but clear. She'd received less of a dose than the two men. Luckily the breeze changed its wayward course, and for a moment they had relief. He pulled his weapon back in front looking through tearing eyes. To their further amazement, the back of the beast extended and deformed, morphing into an appendage that curved into a hook. With reverse undulation, the creature spiked the ground, levering itself backwards into the water. In moments it was gone, only a small oily ring on the waters surface to indicate it had ever been.

"My Drakil! What was that?" Jehkal sounded desperate for a dose of reality. Someone to tell him that what he saw didn't truly exist. A dream that had visited him while fully awake.

Mac couldn't help him. "I have no idea, Jehkal." He honestly didn't. With as much confidence as he could muster, he said, "But I'm going down there and find out what it left!" He rubbed his eyes to clear the stinging and residual tears. "Jehkal and Sue, cover us."

Mac didn't think either of them wanted to go anywhere near that pile and he could see by their faces he'd never been more right. He looked at the big Russian, "You up to this?"

Demitri looked terrible. Of them all, he either got the heaviest dose or had the weakest stomach. Mac thought he would lose it again, but the big man steeled himself and nodded, "Just get me upwind of it!"

"Amen brother! I ain't going anywhere near that reek again if I can help it!"

As green as he looked, it was remarkable that the Russian actually smiled and waved him forward. With great caution they wound down the strand, keeping an eye on the water and the pile at the same time. Mac cringed as he walked on the crumbling bones and tried to ignore them and what they were. Together, almost shoulder to shoulder, they came close to the mess. Mac couldn't see what it was exactly, but he was pretty sure. He picked up the femur of some unfortunate and poked gently at the heap. With a soft pop, the mucus cover burst, splitting wide and spilling forth its contents; the perfectly bleached skeleton of a deer-like creature, and a less well preserved something that looked…fishy.

"Uhh shit!" Both of them backed up quickly. Evidently being down wind wasn't far enough as a new and fresher wave of stench caught them. Tears streaming, the men stumbled back up the ridge.

"As I figured," Mac's voice was scratchy. "Now we know where all the bones come from! That was one of the clean up crew." A deep and grateful breath of fresh air, then, "It looks like anything that falls into the lake ends up here."

Demitri held Sue. She was getting tough, but there were limits. Then again, Demitri may have needed a shoulder as well. Proving the theory didn't stop the shudder.

"Mac, what kind of world is this?" Sue wanted to be anywhere but here and Mac had no answers to any such questions.

Instead, he made a suggestion. "Let's back off a ways and make camp." He wanted to be near the city and poke around a bit. Somehow they had to find a way out of the Rayattl. After dark, possibly they could sneak past the line of skulls and past a sleeping guard. One thing was certain; they weren't going to swim out!

For now, the best plan was to be ready to fight or flee, and they weren't prepared for either. Yet it seemed there would be no time for either for as they turned, a scream of challenge from Barron announced a new threat. Behind them and below, a warrior of the People was slowly moving through the trees, searching for the source of the skeel's cry.

Mac yelled out an order, "Spread out! Find cover and look for more of them."

At the sound of his voice the warrior stopped, even from a distance the reptilian eyes bore into him, yet not in challenge. It held up a golden fist in salute, and yelled words. To his surprise, even Mac could understand what was said.

In broken Clan speech, the lizard yelled, "Wishhh talks! Nooo fightss!" A shock ran through each of them, and you could have knocked Mac over with the feather of an alien bird.

Across a gulf far wider than a mere hundred yards, the uneasy standoff continued. Mac watched the lizard man who sat his mount as calmly as if he ruled the world. As far as the humans were concerned, possibly he did. Five minutes passed and no other threat ensued, no other warriors appeared. Mac didn't know how they could be hiding, they were so damn big. But…

Without taking his eyes from the lizard or roaming the forest near and far, he yelled to Jehkal and asked his opinion. Mac made it clear early in their relationship, not more than a week ago, that whenever the hotheaded clansman *advised* him, it must be with total honesty and with no information withheld. The penalty for failing this mandate was exile.

"My Drakil!" Jehkal's voice was grave. "The People do not talk. They kill or capture and the clans avoid them."

As far as Mac could tell the clans feared nothing, so this statement was telling. The clans avoided because they lost in those encounters. Jehkal was also telling him that to trust a lizard would be to cut off your hand. Mac didn't completely trust Jehkal, but knew the young man was loyal in his way. Not trusting a big two legged weapon wielding talking lizard, went without saying.

"Demitri? Sue?"

Sue answered first, but Mac already knew what she'd say. "Talk to him from here Mac." Her fear was becoming palpable and contagious, but at least she held her weapon steady.

The Russian's deep voice sounded from behind. "He has us trapped! We must deal with him one way or another. Killing him won't be easy, so I say talk while we plan."

This followed logic and Mac's own thoughts, but try as he might he was having trouble setting aside his xenophobia. Of all things, he hated snakes the most, and this one, until very recently, was actively trying to kill them.

"Jehkal! Tell him to dismount and that you and I will meet him halfway."

"My Drakil! Please…"

"Jehkal, are you questioning me?" Mac's voice was stern and the warrior reacted like Mac had slapped him, but his displeasure and fear was still evident. It was a strained voice that shouted the answer.

"The Drakil tells you to lay aside your weapons and approach halfway! It is there we will talk!"

In Mac's experience with the clansmen, the mount was the same as a weapon, but before Mac could correct Jehkal, the lizard stepped of its animal.

For Shumak, this was the second major step in his amazing journey. To relinquish any advantage was an anathema. To meet an enemy without a weapon? Sheerest of folly. Yet he did so, and at the command of a lowly clansman as well. But to grow beyond what he was, he must seek and understand this mystery, and the dead could tell him little. In his mind he risked little, as he fully believed himself to be the battle equal of any ten warriors not of the People, even without weapons. No! Shumak accepted that his course would now be steered by another. *For now!*

Feeling oddly barren, the Wilderness Commander stepped from the cover of the forest and into the small clearing. His Thalk bawled its displeasure behind him, and the lesser beast of the clans continued its own incessant clamoring. Shumak ignored it. Something new held his attention. It was the something he'd come to see. One of the 'Others' was walking down the slope toward him. Perhaps his curiosity could now be satisfied.

Mac and a very reluctant Jehkal cautiously covered the fifty yards. Mac, his skin crawling as the alien eyes raked and appraised him, evaluated the monster they approached. Not as tall as he first figured. Demitri and Niloc were taller and Mac would have to look up, but only slightly. He headed for a spot that would keep him on higher ground and make the reptile look up. It paused in its approach, though he noticed how it walked in a loose hipped way, with movements sinuous and exacting, not jerking and sudden as its earthly cousins. Direct as well! It walked straight forward, regardless of the waist high brush patches it could easily have walked around. In a fight it would come straight at you. There would be no feinting or trickery, just brutal, overwhelming power. Mac made note of it, already planning strategies to fight this lizard man.

His impression was exactly the same as Rebecca's so many miles away; head like a hornytoad. Eye sockets protected by prominent orbits and topped with actual horns which swept backward. The body was hugely muscled, yet with the dichotomy of long slender almost feminine fingers. *Solid!* Mac had no wish to ever tangle one on one with one of these. He found himself wishing he was grasping a shotgun. This thing would take a terrible amount of damage and they were fortunate their bows were so effective. But up close and personal? *Shit!*

Fifteen feet apart they halted with Jehkal slightly in front, a waft of broken brush and the odd musky smell of the beast rolling over them. Mac spoke loudly in English, slapping fist to chest, "I am Lt. Colonel Mac Crowe, Commander of the Space Shuttle Atlantis, United States of America!" He could have said Mickey Mouse or, "I'm Batman," for even Jehkal heard it as just so much noise, but he wanted this meeting to start off with the reptile off balance, and he as the initiator. Plus the volume of his own voice gave him a certain amount of comfort, false though it was, and served to calm a heart that was hammering his chest. Then, in Clan he spoke, "Announce us!"

Jehkal drew himself up to his full height, trying to look as intimidating as possible, and failing. His posturing was lost on the lizard which had already dismissed the clansman in its mind and was staring intently at Mac.

The clansman persevered, "I am Jehkal, warrior of Clan Paliece!" He waited a moment for his declaration to have some affect on the mountain in front of him. He was disappointed.

"Behold, the Drakil!" Jehkal swept his arm dramatically at Mac. "One who comes from beyond the stars!"

Mac cursed internally for not giving the clansman some guidance. The last thing he wanted was this beast thinking they were crazy. Yet the lizard didn't blink at the statement, and Mac thought perhaps it didn't understand the words. Then it spoke, the mouth held slightly open. Very little facial movement tracked the sound which at first was simply hisses and clicks. The thing stood there looking like a big golden scaled ventriloquist without a dummy. Mac assumed the lizard was doing to him what he'd just done a moment before, and despite himself he smiled. Then,

"Be Ssshumak! Leder. Warriorss." Shumak spoke, working the words and concepts as best he could, his knowledge of the clan language coming from contact with the slaves the People had captured. But only the young of the clans. The older ones, such as the pitiful puffed-up one in front of him now, made poor slaves. Preferring death to slavery, as would Shumak. An actual point in their favor he conceded, but never out loud. His grasp of the language, further complicated by the incomplete knowledge of clan young long separated from home and family, his racial disgust at his inferiors, and the fact his vocal structure was never made to create such illicit sounds, made communication difficult at best. More than once he considered being done with it and simply killing them. Instead, he said, "Wishhh learns!"

Mac's command of the clan language was less than stellar as well, despite speaking it for months. Shumak's was barely passable, and Jehkal was less than willing to promote the process. But Mac was determined to learn as much as possible. This was an opportunity not to be passed up. A very dangerous opportunity, but….

Letting the obvious question pass, he asked one of his own, starting out the parley by putting the lizard on the defense. "Why did the People attack us? We meant no harm!" There was heat in his voice, more than he intended.

Shumak heard the words of this Drakil, then those of the clan warrior. Both were similar, but the one, much like he himself, had no skill with that language. Shumak knew now that indeed they were different. Separate. One question answered. Perhaps he could hold this other in higher regard. Perhaps the clansman was subordinate to this other. He considered this new one. He held command. That was certain. Had already shown himself to be as was Shumak, wanting to control all things. He considered the question posed. "Tressspasss. Bringss ugly onessss to landsss! Caussse killingsss! Why?"

By ugly, Mac assumed Aranu. *Talk about calling the kettle*! "We brought nothing," Mac slashed his hand in firm negation. "The ugly ones pushed us into your land. We did not know you."

Shumak flushed in anger and it broke through in his voice, "Clansss knowss usss!"

Mac had to be careful now, and, as was his new habit, mentally cursed Jehkal. It was he who neglected to tell Mac about the People. Not that it would have mattered. The Aranu pushed them, and to have stood and fought would have meant death. He would need to tread carefully. "I!" he pounded his chest. "I did not know you!"

"Thisss…" Shumak waved his hand at Jehkal without looking at him, choosing to ignore Mac's statement as well, "Tellsss you frm starsss!"

Mac felt a moment of panic. This was a turning point and he was about to answer the question when Shumak continued, saving him.

"What starsss?" Shumak had no translation for the word.

Jehkal began to point, but Mac stopped him by waving his own hand about in a general way. "Far away, where the *People* are unknown!"

Shumak stood statue still considering this. Although the shaman told him the People were the center of the world, and that all others were of lesser stock, and the world was not much bigger than the valley of life; knew these beliefs to be false. Many of these beliefs he knew to be so, simply from being on wilderness duty. The mountains in the distance were real! The world was wide, and the lands he could see from his border were larger than the lands he could see within.

Mac watched the play of muscles tensing under the golden skin, and as the lizard paused in thought, he pushed, "Will you let us leave?" Again he waved his hand around, gesturing out behind Shumak, then changed the question to a demand. "The People will let us go back to our lands!"

Shumak shook his head in what Mac could see was no, and he prepared himself for the inevitable, ready to roll away and draw a weapon, every sense on high alert and his breath beginning to quicken. But then, "Mussst learnss. Firssst!"

That statement saved them a fight, because Mac could see no point in continuing if they had no way out. Diplomacy won over force, for now. He tried another approach. "We did not want to come to your lands. We want only to leave, in peace."

"Heere noow! Musst lern."

Mac sighed in frustration. This damn beast held most of the cards, and all they had in trade was the information he was asking for. So it was barter and make the best deal possible. *Just what do I tell him? What are his triggers? What gets us out of here and which of my words cause a blood bath?* He suppressed a shudder.

"What do you want to know? I will consider your words, and if they are worthy… I will answer. But after! You 'will' let us go!"

Shumak did not know the word "worthy," but decided it was not meant as a slander or challenge because the being said he would "answer" in the same comment. It was the "let us go" question that made him pause. He hadn't considered this. In his mind, they were already dead. Even if he ordered it, he was not sure his company would let them out. Superstition would dictate that. Should he show up with these in tow, his men would think him mad, a ghost. Or worse, possessed. They would kill them, or capture and behead them lest their voices corrupt. Only Shumak could go back, and go back alone he must. Even then he could still die. Had considered his death the risk and price of his malady. The price of knowledge sought. His one and only assured way back across the line was to bring with him four heads tied to the saddle of his Thalk. Yet that was a thought for later. Now? He fell back on what he knew best; command!

"Knowledgess! Isss Pricce." In the mind of Shumak of the People, this was not a lie. He would let them go. To their gods. He was rapidly tiring of their evasion. "Howww? Howw crosss?"

Mac tried to read the eyes and was left with a cold feeling in the pit of his stomach. He didn't believe the lizard would let them go. It had no compelling reason. Not unless Mac could intimidate him. *Perhaps its time to pull out the 'Awe' card,* he thought, *but with caution.* Not the version a clansmen would try. Mac's version! He looked at Jehkal and told the warrior to go back and join the others.

Jehkal's eyes went wide, "My Drakil…"

Mac cut the air with his hand. "Now!" Jehkal cast Shumak an *I'll kill you if you harm him* look, then stalked noisily up the hill.

"Why disssmiss? No trussst?"

"I dismissed him because I could! I need no bodyguard." Shumak would now know he dealt with an equal. In Mac's mind, superior. And that Mac didn't fear him. A bold faced lie he hoped he could carry off! He placed an unconcerned look on his face as he continued his last train of thought, "I asked to be let go, but it matters not. We are powerful." He stared hard at the lizard, "We broke the line of the Rayattl! We will leave when we have finished!"

An audacious bluff certainly, but Mac needed information from Shumak as well. Information that could show them a path to freedom. Besides, Mac had no intention of letting this lizard man walk away and get back to his troops.

Shumak hesitated. He couldn't deny their power. They had crossed. Had they broken the power of the Rayattl? Had their act allowed him to cross as well? Unknown. He looked carefully at this one called Mac. A being that looked similar to a clansman, yet so very different. *Why would one of such power allow himself to look as low as a slave? Was even his image a ruse? Did he spout untruths?* Shumak called Mac's bluff and made a demand, "Shoow powerss!"

Mac knew a challenge was coming. This one was far too intelligent to be snowed by simple words and vaguely remembered actions that occurred a full day ago. Mac was prepared. While they talked, he snuck his hand inside a pocket, grabbing one of their last matches. Using his best theatrics, he rolled his eyes up till only the whites showed. Slowly and softly he chanted, then pulled forth the hand striking the match as he did so.

Shumak did something he had never done in his life. He took a step back from an enemy! This creature produced fire from the very air, and as he watched, Mac bent down gathering dry leaves and small sticks, applying the flame as he did so, creating fire where none had been only a moment before.

Mac breathed an internal sigh of relief as the match held its flame through the process. Then he sat and gestured to Shumak to do the same, acting as if producing fire were of no consequence, the least of his powers. Cautiously, and without ever taking his eyes from that hair covered alien face, Shumak folded his legs in a completely inhuman way, and sat.

Mac contemplated the face before him a long moment while listening to the soft crackle of fire and allowing a curl of blue smoke to wash the smell of the beast from him. “We are travelers from far away,” he began, pointing over Shumak’s shoulder. To the lizard’s credit, he did not look. “We search for knowledge. For the old ones. The ones who built this place.”

This time Shumak did look, yet not where Mac pointed, but over the human’s shoulder at the city skyline beyond. His own people had their legends. Legends that told of these old ones. How could they not living so close to the forbidden place? It was believed his people built the city and that, for sins unknown, they were cast out. It was said a time would come when the People would reclaim what was lost. Regain the world!

Shumak knew of the clan legend as well. One could not hold slaves and not hear their piteous prayers and uncouth beliefs. The clans also awaited a return, but the correlation of the two beliefs was lost on him.

“Why? Why olds onsss?”

Mac had a sudden inspiration. Perhaps there was a way to play upon superstition and unwritten histories. His stare hardened. “There will come a time Shumak of the People,” he began. “A time when knowledge…when learning will be more important than anything else we do. A time when struggle will be set aside. That time is near.”

Shumak listened. Shumak thought. Indeed, a change had already occurred. Shumak was talking as an equal with one he should rightly kill. One he was sworn to capture or eliminate. Yet this one talked of bigger things. Things beyond anything the Wilderness Commander had ever considered. In the world of the People, strength was power. One advanced through brute force or the more subtle game of finesse and subterfuge. In that moment Shumak became greedy. How far could he go with force and finesse if he added knowledge?

Mac saw it spark in Shumak’s eyes and in his posture. Saw through the alien-ness to the motivations boiling underneath. So he pushed, “Would you seek knowledge Shumak?” He left the bait dangling then looked away and added more sticks to the fire as if Shumak's decision was of absolutely no consequence.

Shumak of the People smiled, certainly intelligent enough to know when he was being played. Yet in this case, he was being led exactly where his heart yearned to go. Recognized also in that moment, that the being across the fire was no ordinary individual. For the first time in his life, Shumak wondered what it would be like to truly follow. To follow because it was his choice! Not because of duty, intimidation, or fear. Before him was no Peri'ackt. Certainly no Peri'il.

"I...," he pointed to his chest and tried his best to make this speech understandable, adrenalin coursing through him as if in the midst of battle. "I would learn!" The words more clear than any other time during this incredible conversation. Out loud he said he would commit to learn, but with defiance directed only at himself he said, *later I decide what is best.*

Mac heard the words and tried to read the sincerity. Decided then and there he would never turn his back on the lizard man. But also decided it was time to take another leap. Just as he had with Niloc. Just as he had with Saber, and as he had with Jehkal and his brothers. "Shumak of the People," he stated the name as carefully as he could and looked gravely, wondering if the lizard could read his emotion. "Would you join me? Would you become a seeker of knowledge for the benefit of your People?" Then the hook, "Would you follow my command?"

Shumak was silent, taken aback. When he'd set his feet upon this path, never had he envisioned this. All of his rash actions. All of his ignoring orders, flaunting the People's traditions and beliefs. Of outright heresy! None of it had come close to preparing him for this moment. Was this the true price of curiosity? Of knowledge? The loss of self? Could he really allow one not of the People to command him? His answer was attenuated by one simple physical law. Self will. He told himself he could follow this path as long as it suited him. As long as it served. He told himself he could always change his mind, and in that moment his fate was sealed. Sealed to Mac. He croaked, "SShumak learnsss."

Mac didn't react. Simply stared. Then the words that almost strangled him. "SShumak would follow."

Mac suppressed the urge to rise up and shout his bloodless victory and the possibilities it held. They had just gathered a new and very important ally. Inside he was screaming with relief, and a hundred other emotions rushed through him. Not the least of which was how to even begin to trust this man, and how he would possibly explain it to the others. On his face he forced calm and serenity, while rising and extending his hand in the human way. "Welcome Shumak of the People."

The lizard man slowly climbed to his feet, seemingly in a daze and looking curiously at the hand. *Was this a sign of pact? A sign of peace? Agreement? Subjugation?* Possibly it was all that and more. Without a ritual cut to mingle blood? Tentatively, he reached out and grasped the strange hand. Warm and smooth. Slender, yet with a strength that surprised him.

A simple act that perhaps proved a universal truth. People were people no matter what they looked like. *Now the hard part*, he thought, *selling it to the others.*

Chapter 5

Bleary eyed and stupid tired was exactly the state Rebecca found herself in. Swaying drunkenly on the back of her mount, not even dodging the smaller branches as they reared up out of the darkness. Didn't really feel them strike or scrape across her arms and face. The only thing holding her in place was Cam, and he was possibly in even a worse state than she.

A full day and a half they'd fled the relentless lizards, and it was only an hour ago they were able to finally shake the pursuit. A combination of rough country, the cunning of the clansmen, and of course, Saber! God thank Mac for sending Saber, for in her heart she knew he had. The cat was their rearguard and had repeatedly stung the People, aggravating their Thalk by springing from cover and raking their flanks, leaving behind bloody furrows and angry screaming beasts.

Seven of the warriors had tracked them throughout the day and into the night. Many times they heard Saber's snarl and the bellow of the Thalk. Then the horns of the People would sound and the seven would circle, hoping to trap and kill the cat. Each attack costing them time, and giving Rebecca and her group just that much more distance. That much more of a lead in which to erase tracks and lay false trails. At one point they became desperate enough to contemplate another ambush, but even in their depleted mental state decided rightly. That course of action was too rash and too dangerous. Battle would be joined only as a last resort, and now that unhappy ending could be avoided.

Saber was back, ghosting through the underbrush. A sure sign danger was far away. Danger and Mac. Their mad flight put them further and further from the Rayattl. Going back *now* was not an option. Now they needed rest! And most desperately, they needed food.

The skeel were stumbling, living their own vision of misery. Rebecca looked up as a cold rain began to fall, further adding to their woes. Yet still they didn't stop. Niloc wanted as to put as many hours as possible between them and their pursuers. To stop now meant they would simply collapse, and that couldn't happen until they were safe. At least as safe as a dense forest, a cold rain, and darkness could make it. Distance was the key, and he would push until the skeel were stumbling on their last legs. Rebecca rocked and swayed, her thoughts drifting to memories of earth, her wretchedness dragging on and on.

"Halt!" Dawn was a hint of color on the horizon and Niloc's order was low in volume, yet resounding in need. With that word, they did not so much stop, but ceased to move. Heads down, the skeel simply quit in mid stride, one going to its knees, almost throwing Den'al from its back. In the sudden absence of clopping hooves and creaking leather, a horn sounded in the far distance. Tensing they waited, fearing the worst. Another horn sounded even further away, then nothing but the rain dripping from leaves and the gentle panting of their mounts.

Niloc nodded in the darkness, "We stop here!"

Rebecca felt hands draw her from the saddle and lay her gently on furs that had been laid on the ground. Distantly she felt the difference. A dual thumb grip on one side, a human hand on the other. Heard the distant murmur of voices. She even felt Sabers fur, not realizing the animal lay beside her, lending the warmth of his body. She felt and she heard as if in a dream, then oblivion. Her last sensation was a single drop of cold rain that struck her forehead then ran down the side of her face. She followed its track with her minds eye until it warmed to the same temperature as the rest of the salty moisture coating her body. As the sensation disappeared so did her grip on reality, followed immediately by a deep and dreamless sleep.

Chalgu warriors, six hundred strong, marched out of the darkness, following the signs and trails laid by their advanced scouts. Little did they need the signs. Stench flowing from the target pointed out its direction from any point a quarter days march down wind. Even darkness was a relative term. The clear sky painted a vast panorama, illuminating the landscape with an ethereal beauty. A splendor that was lost on the warriors. This planet was far nearer the galactic core than the home of the humans, or even the original home of the Chalgu! On earth, the Milky Way was a light mist of stars spilled across the ecliptic, framed and eclipsed by the larger and nearer points of fire. On a night of full moon, most of the stars of the galaxy faded to invisibility. Here, the core of the galaxy was not only visible, the billions of tightly packed stars brought twilight even to the witching hour. An incredible visual slice from a cathedral only God could conceive! The planet's moons lent little additional illumination, simply brighter disks moving across the star field, and it was a rare night when cloud cover was thick enough to make it actually dark.

Prominent shadows followed the army which did little to keep silent or otherwise cover its movement. It had no need, for the object of tonight's exercise had gone to ground. Or more accurately, underground. The Chalgu army had marched over mountain chains braving cold and heat. Through valleys of desert, or forest and prairie. Marched and fought, and purged the land of intelligent life, all in a desperate search for the cause of their missing god. A nation in motion, searching for one individual. Perhaps he existed up ahead. Perhaps within the vast forest a few days away. As with the beauty of the panorama overhead, their surroundings mattered little to these warriors. Their lot was to fight and die in the service of the great cause. Here and now, or months away. This village or another. They would battle, their success foreseen! Not the exact when and where, only that it would happen. To not succeed was a thought none contemplated. To fail meant more than death. It meant damnation. So said the holy men. So said the signs written in the stars and on the face of storm clouds. So said the True Leader.

Four separate arms of the Chalgu army pushed outward from the Chalgu lands. Four separate campaigns, each meeting little resistance. Suffering more from the elements and the rigors of the march than any living foe. Then, this very morning, an advanced finger of fifty paid the price for such ease. Complacency cost the company commander his life. It also cost the army fifty seasoned warriors to an ambush executed by the very beasts they now moved to attack. It was the first actual defeat the Chalgu war machine had experienced since leaving their valleys so many turns ago. A defeat that sat heavily upon them and one that would not stand. The shaggy beasts executed their stratagem to perfection, rising up out of the low brush and grass to fall upon the fifty in a black swarm. The Chalgu had no experience with the Aranu, in fact had no idea what they were named. They knew them now! The hide covered vermin proved deadly, spearing and hacking the Chalgu with a vengeance, then retreating to their underground haven before the main army could close. A bitter defeat that gave the individual soldiers their first real reason to hate.

A very dangerous opponent indeed. But one that had trapped themselves in their own filthy holes, and one enemy the six hundred were bent on more than just destroying. After the battle, Acolytes of the True Leader would still test the brains, but no sharing of the body would occur. That honor would be withheld the shaggy beasts. As desperate as the army was for flesh, none would partake of this foe. For the true sign of distain. The true sign of hate was to leave the flesh to rot!

Mograth, headman of warren Kilkeep, knew doom when he saw it. Knew he'd reacted too late to save the young. Too late to save his harem, and too late to save himself. Not in his memory, or the memory of his fathers, had the Aranu encountered an enemy so numerous or so alienly hideous. If the reports from his returning warriors were to be believed, these beings were a sight to freeze the blood. His warriors prevailed in the ambush, but many died, and many returned with stories from a nightmare. He could see something in the eyes of those around him, something he never thought to see. Never thought possible in an Aranu warrior. Fear!

Now this. No adversary had ever survived to approach their caves. The only enemy who ever came here were either dead or soon too be. Aranu kept no prisoners. Kept no slaves. They kept only meat.

Praying to any gods was useless, for they had none. The Aranu, of all the races of this world, held belief only in themselves.

Belief that only they belonged here. That when they died they were reincarnated, over and over again, forever. So his impending death meant little, other than as a quicker avenue back to this world.

Yet the Chalgu would not embrace their new life quietly. All would fight, for the measure of your new life depended primarily on the number of Others one sent ahead. Mograth's only concession was to send one of his own to warn the other warrens. Individual death may mean little, but the Aranu had to survive as a race if he and his progeny were to be reincarnated.

These thoughts were interrupted by one of the sentries. The message, delivered in their clicking-whistle language, was simple. "My Chief! They are here."

Six hundred warriors stood and faced the dawn. The cold of fall penetrated deep as the dew froze where it formed, fingers growing numb holding spear or sword. Damp clothing grew stiff. They stood in mute communal misery as the ever increasing light revealed their goal. The Aranu warren was a series of interconnected caves that entered a shear cliff of bronze sandstone which stood over twenty warriors high. A cliff face which looked carved by the stroke of an ax. Each entrance was narrow and stained by the smoke of a thousand years of fires, and even now the entrances belched a foul miasma of charred meat. It seemed this foe would die with a full stomach. Individual entrances pierced the cliff at varying heights, accessed by paths carved from the living stone and worn with age. At the bottom of the cliff, beneath each cave mouth, lay a midden, and from this rose a stench that was thick enough to choke. No enemy was seen. No army rushed forth and if the scouts had not said they were there, none would have believed. Without further fanfare, the order was sounded. Twelve-hundred feet stomped as one, and six hundred spears struck six hundred shields creating a rumble that echoed off the cliff face. Then, in a rush, the six hundred attacked.

Mograth heard screams of anger, pain and rage. He heard the clang of metal on metal and duller meatier sounds as they echoed through the caves. Stood with eyes closed, listening as the battle approached. He'd chosen his own killing ground, his own dying ground. Mograth would be the last! Deep in the heart of the hill, the very place he was hatched, surrounded by the eggs of those who would not be born. Those who were destined to skip a generation before once again emerging. Almost stygian darkness would meet his enemy for he had no desire to look upon them. It was his secret fear that he would blanch at the last moment, hesitate in his strike from the fear of their form. *Yes!* he thought. *Here I end where last I began.* Mograth pulled back the hides that covered him. Cast off the many layers of fur, the warm air stinging the many open and oozing sores which covered his body, a price the Aranu paid for living in the ground. He would meet them as he came in to the world, naked but for a spear and sword.

A flicker of movement caught his eye, or perhaps it was a disturbance of the air. With all his might, Mograth thrust out his spear. He was rewarded with sudden resistance as the metal head rammed home, completely transfixing the body before him. The scream was long and satisfying, as was the rush of hot blood that pumped forth to coat his hands and thighs. Another flicker and he let go the spear throwing himself sideways, ducking the stroke of a sword and the thrust of a spear, both felt but not seen. Mograth rolled to the side, crushing a leathery egg, spilling the half formed youngling across the stone floor. He heard his opponent slip in the albumen and slashed with his own sword, again meeting the resistance of flesh, though he could tell it was not a killing blow.

A new scream erupted, this time in rage, clicking through a mouth never made to form words that Mograth could understand. He swung for the sound, putting his full weight into the blow while throwing his body forward, kicking out viciously and blindly, then felt his sword arm go numb as he missed his target and shattered the blade on the nursery wall. Off balance, he skidded as his own feet slipped in the ichors quickly spreading under him. He fell heavily, a woosh of air spilling past his lips. It was all the opening his opponent needed.

Mograth lay there transfixed, knowing what came next yet not prepared for the incredible pain of it. He felt the sword enter his chest, pushing through ribs and heart, only to continue its plunge through his spine and out, clanging on the stone underneath him. Mograth heard heavy breathing pounding on his tympanic membrane. Heard a primordial wail, not realizing it was his own. He writhed once more as the sword was ripped viscously down and out, opening him from sternum to crotch. Had there been light, Mograth would have been appalled to see his insides slung across the floor, a spray of dark blood painting the wall. Instead, he reached an arm upward toward his new life, not knowing it was hacked from his body, the life force within him dimming. So died Mograth, Headman of the Aranu warren of Kilkeep. So died all who dwelt there, and so died one hundred and three of the six hundred.

Rebecca's eyes startled open, stunned from a dreamless sleep to full wakefulness by a two thumbed hand pressed over her mouth. Her scream dying stillborn on her lips when she saw Niloc hovering above, holding finger to lip in a signal to stay quiet. The seriousness on his face took her from startled to frightened in a moment.

He bent down and whispered, "My apologies for awakening you so, Alt-sul." Silvery eyes bore into hers, reinforcing his caution. "Danger is near. You must come."

Once he was sure she understood, he removed the hand and backed away. Dim light filtering through low cloud cover assailed her eyes, and she notice how cold the day had turned. She also saw that the needles of the trees around the clearing held a dusting of snow and from under the warmth of her furs, she shivered. Ignoring the stiffness of limbs that protested, and the fact she desperately needed to relieve herself, Rebecca rose and grabbed and strung her bow, all under the appreciative stare of the alien. It was then she noticed Cam and Den'al were missing, yet all the skeel were tied up and muzzled back in the trees. Her question died on her lips.

"Come!" Niloc turned and moved gracefully and silently away while Rebecca cursed inside. Her first step was on a stick which snapped loudly. Niloc pretended not to hear, but slowed and shortened his steps so she could follow exactly in his foot prints. She did so, concentrating hard, knowing they needed to be quiet, but wanting the alien to be proud of her achievement as well, wondering why she needed that particular confirmation. She had no answer.

They traveled thus for about two hundred yards, the ground slowly rising and the trees becoming thicker. Concentrating on being silent, she didn't at first notice the sound growing in the distance. Nothing loud, merely a growing base cacophony. She stopped and stared ahead, seeing the ridge they were climbing top out, the forms of Cam and Den'al lying prone and almost invisible in their camouflage of animal hides nestled carefully under the brush.

Niloc paused and motioned her to crouch as he did, then crawled forward. Puzzled and filled with mixed emotions, not the least of which was fear, she moved up and settled in beside Cam. He looked over, his face crusted with mud and hidden deep in whiskers, looking rough and tired. He smiled and mouthed, "Morning!" then pointed down into the thick forest below. It was from there the sounds arouse. She stared hard and for a moment could see nothing. A low fog clung to the tree tops and a waft of snow gently fell in the distance. A scene of serene beauty with nothing at all threatening. Until she saw a flicker of movement.

Her eyes went wide and she gripped the haft of her bow in a bloodless fist. There! First she saw one, then another, her eyes boring into a small opening. Then, to her growing horror, she saw them by the score. *Aranu,* her brain screamed the hated name and instinctively she began to pull back, ready to run. Would have had Cam not whispered in her ear.

"Been like this for the last half hour! I've counted over two hundred." He looked calm and unworried, which served to reassure her so she un-tensed a bit.

"See! Look there."

She looked where he pointed seeing the movement of bodies, then her mouth rounded in a surprised 'O'. *Children?*

"Looks like whole families!"

Niloc threw a stone in their direction to get their attention and when he had it, silenced them with a look. Cam stared back balefully, their friendship not yet healed, but the point was taken. To have the Aranu discover them would spell disaster. Rebecca went back to observing the migration, the scientist in her telling her that's what they witnessed. She saw warriors and families. Singles and small groups. Many carrying bundles and all obscured in fur covered hides, most chanting in low voices as they moved, which accounted for the odd sounds. Scouts shambled along as outriders, and all in all it showed a certain military air.

For fifteen or twenty minutes they watched before it was over and the Aranu passed down the valley out of sight and hearing. Only then did they move, and only then did Rebecca wonder where Saber had gotten to. That question was answered a moment later as the cat appeared beside her, pacing them back to the camp. Only Den'al remained behind to watch their rear.

"What did we just see?" Cam directed the question at Niloc who shook his head.

"I know not."

The human wouldn't accept that as an answer. "What do you mean you don't know? This is your damn planet."

Niloc held his temper knowing his friend was on edge, not wanting steel to be drawn again. "Peace my battle brother. I have no knowledge of this." He spoke calmly, but Cam was ready to jump back in his face.

Rebecca pulled on his arm. "Calm down, Cam. It won't help any of us if you can't take control of yourself!" She half expected the pilot to turn on her as well.

Instead he looked back at Niloc. "Then guess!" His voice was tight, but not angry.

Niloc sat down and gathered his coat around him, a sure sign he would now provide them a lecture. Philosophical and exhaustive, yet with little substance. Cam sighed and sat as well, but Rebecca remained standing, thinking there may still be need to jump between them. Fortunately, Niloc talked to Cam as if their differences never occurred.

"Cam. Protector of the Drakil! I wish it were otherwise, but what I say is true. We of the clans know little of the Aranu. Beyond that they are our blood enemy, we have never needed to. Battles are not often, and to my knowledge, no one of the clans has any memory of where they dwell or how they live."

Cam and Rebecca tried their best to follow the speech. It was difficult to understand many of the words, but slowly they pieced together Niloc's thoughts. Much of it was expression, for Niloc was also remembering a clan lost to the very beasts they'd just seen. It was painful being the last and only survivor.

"What is true," he continued. "Is that any who tried to find their villages failed to return. The clans fight them only when we have to. Never have I heard of what we just witnessed, but perhaps they too move to winter pastures."

Niloc fell silent then watched as the humans discussed him. *How*, he wondered? *How to teach them something of which they have no basis? No knowledge. They are too new to this.*

"I think he means this is totally alien to him." Rebecca and Cam put together what they heard from the Sar-too with what they themselves had observed. Rebecca continued her thoughts, "From what we know of the clans, most of them migrate from winter to summer grounds following their herds. I can't imagine either the clans or the Aranu would have survived long if they were in a constant fight over territory."

Cam nodded, "You're right, Rebecca. Even Jehkal told us they never found an Aranu village. Had ever seen any young!" He mused only a moment, "So why now? Are we that far from the clans. I don't know about you, but what I saw back there didn't look normal or planned. It looked panicked"

"I don't know what to think, Cam. But there is a pattern here."

He looked up at her curiously, "How so?"

She was warming to her subject now that the evidence was falling into place for her. Theories began to solidify in her scientifically trained mind. "Think about it, Cam. Since we met Niloc and heard his story, his whole world has changed. Same with Jehkal. The Aranu are much more aggressive than ever before. They are displaying tactics they never did in the past! In fact, Niloc describes these events as totally unprecedented in their history."

God in heaven! Cam hated it when she did this. Absolutely detested it when she started talking in her 'Professor' voice. Though she made him feel like a shiny new college freshman, he held his exasperation in check. Just barely. "Ok teach. I'll bite. What's the grand theory?"

She looked down her nose in a most patronizing way. "Sarcasm doesn't become you, Captain! Now, use your head. What happened about the time these events happened to Niloc? What shook their world?"

Cam held his breath for a moment, then, "We did!"

"Exactly! We arrived. But why did that change them? What's the rest of it?"

Cam hesitated. He was sure he knew the answer but had no desire to confess a possible ignorance.

Rebecca wasn't fazed, didn't require his answer. "We can't think of this in twenty-first century terms. Oh bloody hell, Cam! We can't even think of this in human terms. These," she waved her hand at Niloc. "These clansmen and the Aranu are incredibly superstitious. Think of the ancient riddle they attach to Mac. They lost their moon, Cam!"

She threw out the last statement as if it proved everything, and in a sense, it did. That event was a catalyst for incredible change. She had no idea if the Aranu or the People worshipped the celestial bodies, but she'd lay even odds they did. Just the fact it disappeared would shake their culture to its foundations. *Bloody Hell!* she thought, even the planet felt it. The storm that buried the Atlantis was a direct affect of the moon/ship suddenly disappearing. At least that was the theory they all accepted because Niloc told them the weather was worse than before. When they'd discussed it over their many campfires, the only real question they had was why the impact hadn't been far greater. The sudden loss of Earths' moon would have spelled worldwide shifts in weather, tectonic plate shifts and possibly even orbital wobble. In essence, global disaster, and possibly extinction. Why that hadn't happened here was a debate they continued to hash over and over. But applied to the indigenous peoples, the event, however muted, explained much.

Niloc tired of listening to the noise they called English, understanding more than the humans would have believed, but right now the effort was too much. He interrupted them, speaking in the clan tongue, "I do not have knowledge of this!" He pointed to the valley, indicating the exodus they'd just witnessed. "But these things… these Aranu, were pursued."

A look of hope came into Cam's eyes and he blurted out, "Pursued! By your people?"

The look of pain that crossed Niloc's eyes went a long way towards mending the gulf between the two friends. Cam immediately regretted his words, feeling deeply for Niloc and the murder of his whole clan by the Aranu. He reached out a hand, "I'm sorry, Niloc. I meant by the clans. I didn't mean…"

Niloc halted Cam's apology, "You are not to be blamed for the loss of my people." He spoke softly and placed a hand over his heart. "But I thank you for remembering." He cast his eyes down for a moment, then looked up at the woman of the Drakil. "No! I think not the clans!"

"Why, Niloc? Why not the clans?" She asked.

Snow began to fall again as he spoke. The soft flakes a contrast to the violent world they found themselves in. "Many reasons," He said. "But mostly, a clan is too few to have moved them. And one does not move the clans together."

The humans knew this statement held a full book's worth of meaning. The clans were few and scattered, coming together on only rare occasions to trade their goods. From Niloc's description, it was very like the Rendezvous of mountain men of the old American West. At any other time when they met, the clans were just as likely to fight. No individual in their history had ever brought them together in common cause. The humans felt this was due most likely due to limited resources and high competition. Niloc knew it went far deeper. Knew in his heart that only one could ever unite them. And that one was lost in the Rayattl.

It was left to Cam to ask the obvious, "If not you... Then who?"

The answer came sooner than expected, though not from Niloc. A whistle from Den'al pulled their attention back to the ridge. He was waving for them to hurry and join him. As one, they covered the ground, coming back to the edge that looked over the valley.

"Look!" Den'al pointed down at the trees. In moments, a lone clan warrior could be seen picking his way, seemingly following the path of the Aranu.

"Look, Niloc! I told you so!" Cam believed the warrior was part of a bigger group pushing the Aranu. One that could help them rescue Mac.

Niloc knew better, but held his tongue. He was proved right a moment later when the weary and wounded warrior pushed through the trees, looked up at them his brows rising in surprise, then he promptly fell from his skeel.

Den'al gave out a grunt then rushed down the hill, for the stricken warrior was a warrior of Clan Paliece, his clan. Cam followed, but Rebecca and Niloc held back. Niloc because he knew his presence may distress the wounded clansmen even more than seeing a human for the first time. Distrust and outright animosity were most common when Paliece and Sar-Too met. Only the Drakil, and the common cause of survival, bonded Niloc to the two Paliece they currently had with them. This new one would not know that.

Rebecca held back for her own reasons. She justified as needing someone to be on alert. Watching for more Aranu. In reality, she was scared shitless! The enemy was just here, more numerous than she could imagine. Now a wounded man! She was brave. Had proved it time and time again. Knew it in her heart. But even that had its limits. So here she stood. Waiting.

Den'al recognized the warrior as soon as he got close, but the man's skeel stood over him and would not allow them to approach, eyes rolling with the unknown scent of a human.

"Rahkal!" Den'al called the man's name and moved cautiously closer.

The skeel sniffed once and found Den'al familiar. The faithful animal backed up and he rushed the final ten feet and skidded to a halt, kneeling beside his clan brother. "Rahkal!" he called again.

The wounded man groaned once, then his eyes popped open. "Den'al! Is it you?" He moaned again and tried to sit up though Den'al held him.

"We thought you dead." Rahkal wheezed.

"No! Not dead, though I mourn the loss of my true brother." He said it softly and full of emotion, and even through his own pain it was Rahkal who reached out to comfort Den'al.

"Then I also mourn a brother!" His next comment was stilled by a low growl of warning from his skeel.

Cam froze in place. He knew way too much about these temperamental beasts to take any risks with one he didn't know and one that didn't know him. For Rahkal, it was even more a shock. He backed up, crabbing across the ground while trying to reach his clav'l.

"Hold!" Den'al jumped in front of the human while still facing Rahkal. "Hold, Rahkal! He is a friend!"

Rahkal stopped, but still stared, not knowing what to think.

"Hold, Rahkal. He is more than friend. He is a brother in all but his race! Battle tested at my side." He turned to Cam and motioned him forward.

"Battle brother Cam! Know my Clan Brother, Rahkal. Son to Rakass, and true brother of Jehkal!" At the mention of his brother Rahkal cast about, searching, for he knew Jehkal to have led Den'al's party.

Den'al stilled him. "He is not here, Rahkal. But he lives." His statement held more conviction than he truly felt. Of all of them, he was the most skeptical of the Saber/Mac connection.

Cam seized the moment and moved forward, speaking the traditional clan greeting. "I see you Rahkal, and it is good! But you are bleeding. May I help?"

Den'al looked in horror at the puddle of red where Rahkal had first lain, then to the smear of blood down the saddle and flank of the skeel. "How are you injured?" he gasped, but didn't wait for an answer. "We must get you to Rebecca and Niloc!"

If Rahkal wondered about who or what Cam was, he hid it well. He didn't even flinch at the mention of two names he didn't know, though one was clearly of another clan. Instead, "I am spear struck! I know not how badly."

"Quickly, Cam! Help me carry him up the hill!"

Cam reached down and helped pull Rahkal to his feet then put a shoulder under his arm. They were of a height, though Cam would have outweighed him by twenty pounds. If Cam was struck by anything it was the change in Den'al. Withdrawn since the death of Sartil, he was now animated and loquacious. Cam heard more words from him in the last three minutes than in all the days he'd known him.

Rahkal gritted his teeth as they bounced him up the hill, his skeel following obediently behind. Amazing how quickly they accepted the humans. Amazing how quickly Rahkal had, though perhaps it was simply the fact he was in pain and losing blood. Yet when they reached the top and Rahkal saw Rebecca, true shock hit him. The warrior stiffened in their hands and dug in his heels, his eyes flying wide.

"What…?" was all he got out.

Cam should have expected the reaction. All of the clansmen were affected the same way, especially with Niloc's and his exceedingly high appreciation of the women. He groaned internally, *I sure as hell don't relish meeting a clan woman if the men are so friggin dumbstruck with the humans. Rebecca and Sue are ok, but…!* His was the jealousy of an unattached male with zero prospects and he was building an exceedingly dim opinion of the female side of the clans. *What the hell are they?* he thought. *Large, smelly and bearded?*

Rebecca didn't wait for introductions. Seeing the dripping blood she took charge. In English, "Cam! Get him over beneath that tree!" She pointed to the bedding where she had so recently awakened. Then in Clan, "Niloc we need medicine!" She used the generic term. Niloc knew what roots to find. Knew what leaves to pick. He left without a word.

Rahkal was alert but fading fast. Blood loss was becoming a real problem and his extremities were icy cold. He lay back and let them remove his clothes, studying the strange and exotically beautiful female. The even stranger male. Face covered in hair! Certainly not of any clan. Certainly not Aranu or any entity he'd ever conceived. As they ministered, he felt himself drift. He could hear their voices. Felt their hands. Watched the gentle snow as it caught in her hair giving her an even more angelic aura. These visions held his thoughts as he slowly succumbed to an exhausted sleep. The last thing he registered was a Greater Kraagen as it walked slowly up behind the female, but surely that was a dream. He sighed once more and passed out.

Chapter 6

Mac awoke to a cold morning filled with falling snow and a vision he could barely conceive even though it was brought about by his own hand. They were camped beside a small glade under a natural awning made of the limbs of living trees. The snow fell beyond in gentle curtain, coating the grass and the outer edges of the trees. Despite the strange form of the plant life, snow was snow. The white contrasting with yellows, light greens, and browns. Low cloud cover lent dimness to the picture and an insulation that made it seem almost warm, though he could see his breath with each exhale.

He gazed shifted to the fire. Light blue smoke rose in a single, spire only to be shredded by leaf and limb. Above in the sky beyond, it would be invisible, and with no wind, impossible to smell. Not that it mattered. They were inside the Rayattl and no one would be coming for them anyway. He looked again at the fire, watching the flames dance while amending his last thought. One had come.

It was here the vision became something more than incredible! Two individuals sat with their backs to him, talking softly. A third sat across, staring at the others with guarded eyes, and a fourth lay sleeping covered completely in a heap of furs. It was the three at the fire that captured the imagination. Three men! Three covered in fur coats and leather pants. All males and all so incredibly different. Jehkal sat at the far side, eying the new comer with undisguised hatred and no little fear. He was the toughest to convince and had the most reason not to be, for his enemy now sat amongst them.

Demitri sat next to Shumak talking and listening as best he could. The lizard man was the most incongruous of the three, sitting there with his golden scales and dark horns. Squatting more than sitting and looking far bigger than the Russian.

Mac laughed, *A damn lizard sitting there, warming his hands while talking to a Russian Astronaut who looks like a Neanderthal. Stubborn two thumbed alien on the other side shooting daggers. All I need now is Saber and a troll or a gnome! Damn, I need a camera.* He shook his head in amusement, *No one at homes' ever going to believe this.*

His thoughts drifted to yesterday. There was a near revolt when he walked back and told the others Shumak would be joining them. It was the closest Jehkal had ever come to yelling at Mac, and he couldn't blame him. The clans and the People had a bloody history and it came close to becoming so again. Sue practically freaked and she did yell at him, saying they should just, "Shoot him and be done with it!" To his credit, Shumak sat calmly in the clearing by the fire Mac had made. He sat there for more than an hour as Mac made his case. Only his power as Drakil swayed the young clansmen, and just barely at that. Only logic swayed Demitri. Only Demitri swayed Sue. Mac convinced the big man that if they fought Shumak, one or more of them may die!

On the positive side, Shumak could bring them so much new knowledge and some serious additional strength. Mac thought the lizards presence may even help bring understanding and peace of a sort to the clans and the People. Peace meant safety for all of them and a possible refuge from the Aranu.

Aranu, Mac thought. He'd changed his mind about their original strategy. He wanted nothing to do with any of the aliens, at least until the humans could define and dictate the terms. But avoiding all contact with the aborigines was proving impossible, and if they couldn't avoid them, he wanted to turn the eventual meeting to their advantage. It was Shumak who made it possible. After all, it was he who made the first move. The first contact. Mac still didn't know why, but call it intuition. Or perhaps premonition. Whatever the case, he'd ride that horse as far as he could.

Speaking of horses, Mac could see Baron in the distance. He was not hobbled or tied, but keeping as much distance as possible from the Thalk yet still be near his masters. Instinct and nature made them enemies, and the two shall never mix. It had taken a major part of yesterday evening to soothe the skeel and get him to quit screaming whenever the big lizard so much as twitched. An uneasy peace now reigned, for both had been fed.

In this, Shumak had proven most useful. They were starving and had found little forage so far. Then Shumak shows up with a veritable cornucopia of food in his saddlebags. None of them would touch the meat, Mac had visions of fillet of sun dried Aranu! But the rest was a little slice of ambrosia. Nuts and a dried fruit, even a very passable bread. Yes, Mac would have let him join a hell of lot sooner if he knew Shumak carried food!

For a moment Mac wondered what Niloc would think. Was there a passage in his prophecy about lizards? Maybe this would convince him Mac wasn't the Drakil. Probably just the opposite. But whatever he thought would be moot. Mac rose and moved to the fire. Jehkal cast him a warning glance which he ignored and sat down opposite Shumak, calling a greeting in English and Clan. Today he would try and learn some lizard lingo. Then he laughed to himself. That would be about like talking to Saber. He sobered immediately, he could talk to Saber, and from a distance.

His mental state must have been perfect, because just the thought of the cat was all it took. A 3D image of Saber appeared in his subconscious. It spun slowly as if he were seeing an animated model floating like an avatar on a computer screen. He circled the animal from back to front until he was looking Saber in an eye. Quickly that eye expanded, and he fell toward it. Like a computer game, as soon as he touched the eye, he was inside and looking out. A sense of vertigo spun his head, and without the clarity of the real world to stabilize him, to the horror those around him, he pitched over backward. Shumak, who was utterly unprepared, sat stunned, thinking his new found teacher had just died. Demitri was beside him in a second and Sue gasped, "Not again!" Mac knew none of it.

He drifted out-of-body, his face seeming only inches from the ground. Saber was moving quickly and the low brush flashed by, Mac actually flinching, thinking it would hit him. *Saber,* he called in his mind, *Saber, stop!* The cat did so, but not from any command Mac gave. An opening ahead showed a snowy field. Wherever it was, the snow had fallen heavier than here in the Rayattl. Mac started to call again when suddenly feet appeared in his vision. Feet and legs, walking slowly and covered in unmistakable fur. *Aranu!*

Saber peered out casting slowly left and right showing Mac several lines of the beasts, small and large. He was seeing the migration as Rebecca had seen it, though from only a cat's nose away. Saber had rushed ahead to make sure the threat was moving away and he was on that scouting mission when his master called. Mac could not know that, all he saw was a grouped and very numerous enemy.

Saber! Saber, where is Rebecca? The cat closed his eyes and held them shut a moment. For Mac it was like someone turned off the light in a room with no windows and he felt the connection slipping, but somehow willed it back in place. There was a flash and brightness returned, resolving into a snowy scene devoid of Aranu.

He implored the cat again, *Saber! Take me to Niloc. Take me to Rebecca!* But Saber was either not listening or chose to ignore his plea, instead continuing his scout. Mac changed it to an order.

Saber, he said sharply! *Take me to Rebecca.* The effect was immediate. The vision swung and blurred as the cat moved.

Saber was streaking through the forest and Mac had to close his eyes lest vertigo claim him again. It was like watching a high-speed chase on TV with your nose only two inches from the screen. What he didn't know was that his real eyes had never opened since the communication began. Closing his eyes was a mental act only.

Every few moments he would crack a lid and peer out, waiting for Saber to stop. He had no idea how long this went on, but knew this was the longest time he'd spent under the influence of the connection.

After a while the mad rush slowed and Mac opened his eyes as the cat ghosted along until finally he could see shapes up ahead. Familiar shapes which his brain translated into, *skeel!* Then further on he saw Rebecca. Relief flooded him to the point that he almost dropped out again. Then he saw she was bent over a body lying prone on the ground and his heart leapt once more. Even more of a shock when he realized the body was a stranger. *A clansmen! Dead? No!* The body moved.

No one was aware of the cat who sat quietly behind them while they attended the wounded man, and Mac had not the skill to make Saber go further. Frustration had him about to try a different tactic when something extraordinary happened. For Mac it was as if the world suddenly shifted on its axis. His vision blurred then spun and suddenly he was looking down on the tableau from a direction at least a hundred and eighty degrees opposite of Saber. Rebecca knelt over the fallen warrior while Niloc, Cam and Den'al formed a half circle around them. Saber sat behind, but was now looking up at him. Mac was so startled did fade partially out, then, by shear will, pulled the vision back in place.

What the hell is this? How? These questions were screaming in his head when the world swirled and shifted again. He was back inside Saber, looking up into the limbs of a large tree which over hung the clearing. *What am I seeing?* Nothing. Then a flicker of movement described an outline that was suddenly clear and Mac saw another cat sitting in the crook of a tree, looking down at him.

I was there! Mac felt it then. Felt the difference between Saber and the other. Knew somehow that he couldn't connect with that other cat except through Saber, but with Saber, it was very possible. Knew also the foreign cat's intent held no threat. Only curiosity. He didn't know how he knew! But he knew.

Perhaps the feelings and knowledge came from Saber because his emotion went far beyond what Mac was prepared for. She was a large mature female, and Mac could sense the animal attraction on a level far more powerful than any similar human emotion. Actually felt the pulse of testosterone in his body, and the musky taste of estrogen on the wind! Felt it so strongly it made him giddy.

Rebecca! he commanded. Nothing. *Saber!* he growled, *Rebecca!*

Reluctantly, the vision fell from tree to ground as Saber got up and walked slowly to over and brushed her leg. She jumped sideways at the contact, startled. He could see her anger then watched it fade as she realized Mac was there. Two hands cradled Saber's muzzle as she stared into his eyes and mouthed, "We are OK!"

That was enough. Mac felt great fatigue come on him suddenly. In a blink the connection terminated leaving him blinking and staring up into the face of Demitri, the pulse of Saber and the new cat's emotions ringing in his head. Shumak stood just behind with a look that was probably priceless. If only one could interpret the facial expressions of a horny toad.

"Help me up!" he croaked.

Four sets of eyes stared at him. Three in concern and one in utter disbelief. This was a profound moment for Shumak. Never had he witnessed someone so close to his gods. The Shaman of his own people were as children compared to this one.

Mac steadied himself then looked at the lizard. "My apologies, Shumak!" He caught himself and switched from English. "My apologies, Shumak. I should have warned you of this!" Of what? How to explain. But Demitri had already made the attempt while he was under and Shumak gave an answer Mac didn't expect.

"Oness ssshould nt assk frgivenessss, communing higher powersss! Honored to beee witnesssss." The lizard reached a tentative hand over where Mac thought his heart should be. It look like something a superstitious person would do to ward evil. Perhaps he was honored and perhaps he was just bewildered, frightened by another event so far outside his experience. "Toldss sssee frm eyeessss othrss. Ssssee eventssss frm dissstanccce?"

Mac's ears still heard the hissing and s'ing surrounding in his words, but his mind began putting the sentences together. Had to in order to compensate for his poor clan, Shumak's worse clan, and his snaky method of speech. The statement was asked as a question and Mac did his best to explain, seeing this as another object lesson. No opportunity should ever be wasted to overawe the natives!

Mac closed and rubbed gritty eyes feeling every inch of his weary body. "Yes, Shumak. What you were told is true. I have the ability to see distant events… through the eyes of an animal that the clans call a Greater Kraagen."

Shumak's eyes boggled wide at this and he shook his head in disbelief. Evidently Demitri had neglected that small piece of information. "Kraagn? Noo!" He assumed a sudden stance of defiance and potential violence, causing the others to step back, hands moving towards weapons. Mac waved them off with a cautioning motion. Clearly this would be one of the 'big' tests with the lizard. Mac intended to either seal, or definitively end, their relationship here and now.

"Kraagenss knwn to Peopless! Notss tameed!"

Mac puffed himself up and stared angrily at Shumak. "Do you say I lie!" His statement was forceful and backed with confidence. The simple fact that Mac was challenging a being with natural attributes which far exceeded his own, and Mac being weaponless decided the issue. Shumak was twice his mass with armored skin, claws, horns and a mouth sporting teeth that could tear his arm off. Yet it was Shumak who blinked.

Mac pushed on, "The Kraagen is bonded to me!" Mac slapped his hands together, weaving the fingers and showing them interconnected. "I command him. I see through him!"

Shumak stood and stared, having never learned the skills to back away from any position. To continue his defiance would mean battle. Yet to believe meant…? In that fateful moment lived hung in the balance. Shumak was saved from making a decision by Mac himself, who decided now was the time to reveal just how alien he really was.

"I command, Shumak of the People. I command the Kraagen because I am from the stars!" He pointed heavenward dramatically. "I and those like me are not from this world." He said the last softly, then pointed at one of the moons seen dimly in the morning sky. "We come from there."

Saber felt the female cat in several ways. First and foremost was through the connection to his master. Saber had been aware the other was near for some time, but because there was no threat, ignored it. Had she come close prior to the connection, there most likely would have been a fight. Now, Saber had *seen* her intent, not just felt it. Seen it in his mind with a bridge that now existed between them. A bridge which was completed and secured when he, Saber, handed his master off to the other. An action the cat had taken without conscious thought, the underlying order from Mac allowing enough latitude for Saber to give his master the best and clearest view possible. The command starting a function, much like custom software preprogrammed into his genes long ago, establishing a conduit that allowed the cats to become intimately aware of one another. As much memory as an animal could have, they now shared. They also shared a new bond. One formed by the simple fact that Mac had passed between them. They now shared Mac!

Saber's other feeling was emotion. Strong emotion! More than the allure of finding one of his own. More than male to female. More than simple sexual attraction. The link to Mac created a bond that paired them completely, in being and in service. From this moment forward they would hunt as one. They would fight as one, and be as one.

Without being aware of it, Mac had just added another to his growing cadre of strange followers. With a low growl the female leapt out of the tree and onto the ground right in front of some very startled bipeds. Saber returned the growl, dropped his eyes from Rebecca and sped off into the brush with the female in hot pursuit. In moments the scream of a hunting pair of Greater Kraagen sounded in the distance, chilling them all.

Chapter 7

Mac tried hard to ignore the bones that crunched, broke, or rolled under his feet. Crunched, broke or rolled depending on age, and too many of them rolled, much like the skull of one unfortunate whom would look very much like a young clansmen should it still be carpeted in skin and hair. A guess on Mac's part, given his limited ability to do forensic re-creation on the fly as they edged down the beach toward the alien building. He'd cringed as he dislodged it from a fairly fresh pile, his foot snagging a rib bone and sending the small hillock clattering on ahead on them. Cringed mostly from the racket it made.

Evidently Shumak had no such qualms. His huge feet stomped the bones to dust, causing even more wincing by the others who picked their paths with greater discretion and caution. Shumak would never be stealthy, but his massive presence was reassuring; if you could get past the rancid carrion breath that brushed Mac's neck every time he slowed. Shumak would inevitably push up next to him and cast a questioning look which Mac would ignore then push on.

A building loomed in the near distance and Mac would recall with relish the first moment he'd seen the Wilderness Commander of the People, so confident and arrogant, reduced to speechless awe and fear when first he'd spied it whole. The People never violated the Rayattl! Clearly Shumak had never seen the city, the lake, or its horrendous secret. The big lizard just stood there, staring and mumbling in his own tongue. Whether it was the city itself or the shear level of carnage that struck him, Mac could not know, and Shumak quickly hid his emotions, waving them forward as if it were they not he which stood frozen upon the verge. He'd turned away and re-tied his Thalk to a tree, perhaps the move was a veiled excuse to master emotions Shumak may not have known he possessed. Now, as they approached the building, Mac felt the reptilian eyes glued to his back and he wondered if the alien even saw where they went.

Shumak did have his eyes glued to Mac's back, and indeed, he did so lest madness overcome him. His first vision of the village of the dead nearly unhinged him. All of the superstition. All of the warnings of the Shaman. All the tales told round countless fires, never painted even a portion of the truth. Could have never come close to what he now witnessed. Nay! What he now approached! Only the unbelievable bravery of the lesser beings around him allowed Shumak to set foot upon this vast playground of the gods. Allowed him to advance upon a dwelling place of the damned! He had no fear of the dead. Cared little for those he'd killed; clan, Aranu or his own. But to cross this river of dead to reach the house of a god? He dared not close his eyes lest his spirit be plucked screaming from his flesh, chained and flayed, then driven to join those who toiled endlessly in the demon filled constructions ahead. This is the only possible explanation his tortured brain could offer. That this being, this Mac, wielded a great power which held the demons at bay was his only anchor; and in all truth, Shumak was disgusted with himself. Loathing of his fear and loathing of a situation that was self caused! Loathing of his reliance on the strange being in front of him. Would it end in the sacrifice of his life? He feared not. He feared the sacrifice would be far greater. Feared it would be servitude! To a demon, or to Mac? Perhaps one and the same. These thoughts occupied his entire consciousness, and so stepping into the shadow of the thing he feared most, bothered him not at all.

Mac approached the building cautiously, scrutinizing every shadow, every crack, nook and cranny. Anything which could possibly hide or present a threat. Dim light threw a shadow, and the broken overcast threatened to dump more snow. None of the whiteness had stuck so far, but the air was cool and the bones slippery with a rime of almost frozen wetness. With his bow gripped tightly in one hand, nocked and ready, Mac was ready to shoot, drop the bow and draw a knife, or run like hell, depending on the need. The others spread out in an arc behind him, all except Shumak who remained stapled to his back. Yet as they approached no threat emerged and Mac spent more time on details.

Seven stories extended up from the bone beach, though it was obvious the building was much taller and buried deep. How deep none could tell, the murkiness of the lake giving no hint. The late fall sun suddenly pierced the cloudy gloom and the building cast a long morning shadow back across the water, while gentle waves lapped the edges of the dull walls pushed along by a cold breeze. Twenty yards away from the structure, the rest of the vast city was swallowed behind until only it and the beach remained in view. Several openings gaped toward them high up the wall, and a series of balconies or walkways extended across the face and around the sides, though several showed damage; whether from age or war, Mac couldn't tell.

It was their intention to explore at least this one building before trying to escape. Over the last months the humans had passed, or were forced to pass on several other opportunities to discover what the ancients of this planet were all about. Even though there were dangers, both known and not, now was the time. But Mac was close to despairing. How do you explore something that you have no ability to get in to? They had no rope to speak of, and the only way in was twenty feet off the ground up a slick wall with no handholds. He raised a fist in silent signal, stopping the others. By agreement they wouldn't speak unless absolutely necessary, wanting to make as little noise as possible. Let sleeping dogs lay! Or in this case, hideous bone bleaching blubber monsters. No one wanted to see, let alone face one of those again!

Mac moved forward alone, drawing close to the structure till he was facing a wall fifty yards wide which loomed over him like the edge of a glacier. One corner fell into the lake and the other pointed down the beach, that side only about ten feet up on dry land. He studied the surface of the wall. Mac didn't know what to expect this close. Brick? Cement? Metal? What he saw was different from any material he'd ever seen. Totally smooth, and, if he had to guess, made of ceramic or silicon. He reached out, thinking perhaps a more tactile approach was in order. A single finger brushed against the material. Cold! Far colder than it should be he thought. *A conductor?* Gently he placed a palm, feeling more of the smooth cool material. He moved his hand further up, rubbing the smoothness.

"My god, Mac! Watch out!" He jumped back at Sue's scream. Probably more startled by the noise than a perceived threat because he saw nothing.

"What is it?" But he'd backed up far enough he could see for himself, and he stood there mute, as astounded as the rest.

Deep under ground something stirred. Long had it been since the touch of a sentient being caressed its programming into action. An alien touch; and one not included in the archives, but little did that matter, for this building was programmed to accept all. On earth it would be called a hotel. Here it was known as a Universe Residence, or had been! Long ago. Before the turmoil of galactic politics ripped this planet and its civilization apart. But the technology in this building did not know of war. It was programmed only to serve, and as a testament to its creators, it still worked, and waited. Still functional despite more than two thousand years underwater. Functional, yet with damage it didn't realize it contained. It's programming just slightly scrambled. Its data banks missing critical date references. To the computer it could have been the day after the day the bombs fell, it mattered not. The touch of the being sent shivers of data racing down its spars, deep into its bowels and, almost with a groan, the building responded.

As Mac watched, the building seemed to quiver and straighten itself. Distantly a rumble was felt, briefly stirring the water with small vibrating ripples. It ceased and an eerie silence fell, only to be broken by the others behind him as they moved, though he heard them only distantly. Wide-eyed he watched the wall, hand gripping his weapon ever more tightly. Another small tremor and he pulled back even further, ready to swiftly retreat back up the shingle. The only thing that held him was fascination, and the only thing that held the others was Mac. At least for now.

A quick assessment of its facilities showed no illumination in or out of the building, and no entry/egress point at the level of the touch. The computer didn't question why the being asking for entry was fifteen stories up; it simply commanded his nano-robots to serve. A billion or so of the objects rushed from their standing positions in the very fabric of the wall, directly to the spot where residual heat still burned on the skin of the building. Once arrived, they collectively executed the command from the Master Concierge below.

On the wall, a point began to glow a deep pulsing gold. Mac swore it was the exact place he'd touched. The glow brightened and began to swirl, a small vortex of light rippling under the surface of the wall, which quickly expanded outward to define a circle six feet in diameter.

"Mac?" Demitri's voice was tight.

Mac took another step back and risked a look over his shoulder. Sue and the Russian stood side by side, her head barely up to his shoulder. Shumak stood just behind having retreated even further, looking ready to bolt. Only Jehkal stood steady, but it was not from lack of fear, he was frozen to the spot knowing death was a mere heartbeat away.

"Everyone down!" Mac waved with his hands then dropped, flattening himself on his belly. He ignored the hollow sockets staring at him from a nearby skull, hearing the clatter of the others as they followed suit. Somehow, he felt running was not an option. Then, as a magician's sleight of hand, the glow expanded inward becoming a single spinning gold disc which circled a black point in the center, pulsing like a rapidly blinking eye. Each moment a new pulse and a brighter color until the entire circle was bright almost painful white. No sound just the spinning disc, and Mac was ready to leap up and run for it. He heard a groan from someone behind then a soft pop to the front as the light went out. Mac blinked twice thinking to clear his vision, but the sight didn't change. Where before there was a blank wall, a doorway now loomed. A six foot perfect circle, opening into a dark interior. On he was not at all sure he now wanted to explore.

"Mac! Let's back up." Sue's voice cracked and quivered.

"Ok! I agree." Mac, still on the ground, cautiously turned away from the hole to face the others. Shumak he saw merely squatted, where the others were flat on their bellies.

"All of you! Move back to the ridge. I'll wait here and cover!" His voice was a harsh whisper, but he felt like it rolled across the water announcing their presence.

Demitri shook his head violently, "No, Mac. Together!"

Then from Sue, "Shit! Look!"

Mac spun looking for a threat, but there was none. At least none apparent, yet something had changed. Where darkness was all to be seen beyond the doorway, a soft inviting glow now illuminated a corridor extending back into the building. A corridor and nothing else. *Now what?*

Jehkal was just about spent. Never in his wildest dreams could he have imagined the turns his life would take after having met the Drakil. His entire world lay shattered. Gone was the life he knew. A life of hardness and strife! A life which held little but hunting for survival and preparation for battle. Of jockeying for position within the clan. The same never changing routine, year after year. A life he'd so desperately longed to change. Now, he would gratefully shovel dung from the midden heaps as long as it was anywhere but here. Never had his dreams held such terrors as those found here in the Rayattl.

Those that were real unhinged him. Those that were imagined had him cowering like a squirrel in a bush! Only his great pride held him in place even as nothing more happened. This was possibly worse. The waiting. The anticipation of a death he knew was coming, but not knowing in what manner it would arrive. Only one other time in his life had such terror held him in her icy clutches. Left alone in the darkness as a child. Alone in a skin hut. Sitting in the very center and cloaked in a fur wrapped tight like a shield, his large bright eyes almost glowing in the dark as he tried desperately to stare in every direction at once.

It was the deepest part of a dark cold night. A night when a storm raged, and nearly starved night hunters prowled. He heard their screams outside and imagined them stalking. Pacing round and round, just on the other side of the thin hides of his shelter. Circling. Sniffing. Scratching! They knew he was there. Tasted his fear. In his mind he now relived it all again. The waiting. The imagining. No fire held back the blackness inside the hut, the wind whipping the walls and snapping the skins. Was it there! His head spun to the sound, looking to a corner that was even blacker than the rest. No! There, to the front! Was it there? Panic clutched his chest like a fist, tightening around his heart and threatening to slow it to a stop even though it was pounding hard enough to burst. No blinking! Eyes wide as another noise rose over the storm. There! He spun again and fell sideways, tangled in the furs wrapped so tight he couldn't move. Terror now truly took hold! There, in front where his face was closest to the hut wall. It was there his entire world concentrated and his eyes bored. From there his death would come. Flashes began behind his eyes from a brain starved of oxygen. Young Jehkal was holding his breath! His mind saw just how it would end. The claws slowly punching through the hide covering. The flashes of lightening glinting off glossy black points that extended longer than his young fingers. Claws, razor sharp that cut slowly downward exposing the storm and the animal from his nightmares! Suddenly there was a muzzle, gaping wide and full of venom dripping fangs bursting through the rip, snapping within a hands breadth of his face. He feels the heat and rush of rancid breath, reeking of death! Jehkal can't move, wrapped in furs and frozen in mind numbing terror! The muzzle lunges again and finally he screams! The primordial sound building from his soul, welling in an instant, and breaking forth past his clenched teeth when a hand grabs and yanks his ankle! In his memory, the sound of his shriek drowned out all else. Here in front of the building it was merely a whimper!

"Jehkal," Sue whispered. "Jehkal! What's wrong? We have to move back."

Jehkal remembered back to that time; when terror was so great a terror it made him soil himself. A time of humiliation which the other young of the clan never ceased to taunt! A single event that so changed him. Molded him and made him the brash young leader he was now. That he, at least, thought himself to be. But now? He struggled mightily to master himself. He saw a hole where before there had been a bright light, and before that a blank wall. Saw the Drakil prostrate in front of it. Attacked? Wounded? Jehkal heard the sound, but not the words of the human Sue. Didn't pause to think. In that moment he knew he had to overcome his demons, or die! And knew there was only one way. Bursting forth with a clan war cry, he thrust himself to his feet and charged!

From his position on the ground Mac heard the yell. He rolled over only to see Jehkal come charging forward, sword in hand.

"No, Jehkal! Wait!"

It was all he had time for before the clansmen was past. He swept out an arm and missed in his attempt to trip the man, then he rose and chased after. Jehkal bellowed once more then plunged through the door and into the corridor beyond. Mac followed him through, cursing and thinking only to protect the rear not realizing the others were right behind. In moments Jehkal fetched up against a wall in a cross corridor, stopping and panting and looking wild-eyed. He turned as he heard Mac coming, thrusting out his sword in defense. Only then did rational thought retake its hold. Recognition dawned in his mind and he sat heavily, sliding down the wall then looking up at his Drakil. He mumbled, "The demon's house is yours."

Mac pulled up short. First because of the weapon pointed at him and second because he realized they were now *inside* the alien building.

"Damn it, Jehkal!" He began in English, then stopped as a clatter announced the arrival of the others. Looking back he saw Demitri followed by Sue, a bewildered Shumak bringing up the rear. He swore again, "Damn it! Who the hell's out side?" But mostly, he swore at himself for chasing the foolish young clansmen into the building, effectively leading them all… To what? They were inside and nothing bad had happened, yet. Big emphasis on the 'yet.'

"Demitri!' he hissed. "Back to the door and be ready to get out or back us up." He made his decisions as quickly as he could, trying to salvage something from this fiasco. Switching to Clan, "Jehkal!" Mac didn't mean to be so stern with the obviously terrified man, but was having trouble controlling his urge to bend down and slap some sense into him. "Guard this hall!" he snapped.

Jehkal hung his head, but nodded affirmatively. Satisfied, Mac motioned for Sue and Shumak to follow him deeper into the building. They were here, time to explore.

Demitri was torn between his orders and Sue. Surely Mac didn't intend to lead her deeper into the dangers that were certain to be lurking within this place? He saw her hesitate, not wanting to be separated either.

"Mac?" he questioned.

Mac knew the argument even before it was uttered and held up a hand to still it. "You're the only one, Demitri!" He spoke in English so Jehkal and Shumak wouldn't understand. "Do you want the lizard guarding our only retreat? Or..." Mac flashed his eyes over his shoulder at Jehkal.

Demitri's jaws clenched as he implored, "But Sue..." He trailed off knowing the answer. Mac was right. Leaving Sue to guard was not an option and he certainly didn't trust Shumak. He was still of the opinion they should kill the lizard man and have done with it.

"I need her, Demitri."

The big man gave her a swift fierce kiss. "Watch yourself!" He said it to her, but his eyes were only for Mac, saying, *I hold you responsible for her safety!*

As if Mac would have it any other way. He switched to Clan. "We are going to explore this place, Shumak. Will you help, or must I leave you here?"

Shumak visibly straightened, his tongue hissing from between his teeth in distaste. Evidently his balls had been restored. Perhaps it was being off the beach. Perhaps it was being in the building that, while incredible, was so mundane in appointments his brain could now handle it. Perhaps it was the pending action. These were Mac's thoughts, but only Shumak knew it was all those reasons and many more. He'd fully expected the howling demons of some lesser god to be ravening the skin from their bones about now. His imagination led him to a vision of a glowing red hell, complete with every horrible thing that could possibly happen to a lizard, none of which now seemed imminent. He was content that he would live. At least for a while longer. "Ssshumakk sploore."

"Good!" Mac said. "Demitri, we won't go far! Yell if you see something." He said the same to Jehkal who seemed quite content to stay put and guard that little portion of floor he'd just conquered. Mac hoped he'd snap out of his funk if their collective fat fell in the fire!

"I go first, then Sue, and then you follow! At doors we stop and open them or look inside." At this point he had to described the term 'door' and 'corridor' to Shumak, basically pointing to the opening that let them in, and to the hall in which they stood. Then he described a proper recon. This was easier because Shumak was military through and through. Even if he'd never been in a building before, and with his inner turmoil currently under control, he was ready, even eager to, 'sploore!'

The hallway they were in held no distinguishing features other than being round with a raised flatness that served as the floor. No doors, no air vents, and no lights. At least no lighting Mac was familiar with, for the entire structure simply glowed! Every surface held the same luminescence, a pleasant fluorescence which surrounded them and cast no shadows. Mac wondered if lizard eyes saw it the same as human, the same color and same muted pleasantness. Wondered why he thought such a though right now, and why he even cared.

The corridor Jehkal sat in was perpendicular to the entry hallway, as Mac now designated it; though this one was larger by proportion, Mac being unable to touch the ceiling without jumping. He stepped into it looking both ways and was mildly surprised. The outside of the building was rectangular where this round corridor curved gently away and out of sight. *Why?* he mused. Again, no doors or anything other than the glow. *Which way?* It didn't really matter, so on a whim he chose right, and with a knife now clenched in his fist he began edging along, keeping his left hand on the wall. Not knowing why, but wanting an anchor.

Sue and Shumak followed, she also sporting a knife and Shumak his own blade, bared and ready. Mac looked back at them and smiled. *Indiana Jones ain't got nothin on us!*

RD-483, the buildings Concierge, was slightly confused. It *saw* the beings creeping along the hall, weapons extended, though they were not familiar weapons. No Pulsers and no Radian blades. These were not the ceremonial weapons which it was accustomed to. Most irregular! Each client of this or any Universal Residence carried a personal weapon, but as a mark of rank or status. Never were they brandished. If they were, the security programs would take over, the watchers would respond and that would be that. Yet now, no security program responded. In fact, as he consulted his checklist, most of the Concierges' co-systems were off-line or irresponsive. If it had been designed to tut-tut and purse its lips in disapproval, it would have. The Concierge had enough intelligence to feel disgust at such sloppiness as poor programming.

What to do? As it observed the procession of the visitors, the hand of one passed over the locking mech. of room LX-298. A room assigned to one - he quickly looked up the particulars – Rass-thath-Circon, High Counsel of the IMC (Interstellar Mining Conglomerate) hailing from Tri-Nebulon. Member of the Collective and one of the many Trade Ambassadors here to negotiate the new tariffs that were in the media and causing such a fuss. Another opportunity for a tut-tut as the Concierge reviewed the records. The Ambassador was severely overdue with his payment! An electronic note to accounting to contact the room and inquire was instantly composed and sent. The concierge couldn't know the long dead Ambassador would never pay. Didn't know the illustrious ambassador lay dead with a hole burned neatly through his skull; only knew the good Ambassador's mummified remains still lay on the bed inside the room. And a Universal Residence never violated the sanctity of a room! Would never spy, and so would never know of the Ambassadors demise. All of this in the nanosecond when Mac's hand brushed the lock and passed. He moved on and the Concierge was content that this intruder represented no menace to the Ambassador.

Looking further down the row of rooms, the Concierge attempted to determine the destination of these persons it now considered a threat to its guests. Very upset with itself that it had allowed them into the building without even inquiring whether they were registered, or had an appointment with someone who was. Another software coding issue. This simply would not do! Yet the Concierge was a toothless tiger. It could only wait and watch. But then, it considered, perhaps even a toothless tiger still has its gums!

Mac edged along feeling more and more ill at ease with every step. *What the hell kind of building is this? No windows. No doors or other halls. Just more and more of the same drab nothing.* Even more strange was the construction itself. The hall didn't continue its single curve. It S'ed along, sweeping in a back and forth and arcing in a very unconventional manner, the end never in sight. Disconcerting. They could only see a few yards ahead at any one time. Even more disturbing, Mac felt they'd traveled far further than physically possible inside the structure. He guessed they could have circled the building perimeter at least twice, though he chalked that up to the nerves and slow pace. Still, he'd had about enough of all this nothing. He was just about to call a halt when he spied something in the distance.

Convinced now of the ill intent of these intruders, the Concierge was determined to protect his clients at all costs. Normally there were no room numbers displayed on doors or walls, and a color probe would guide a registered guest, flashing along the corridor until the proper door was in proximity. Then the door would open, but only at the touch of the guest whose complete bio-signature was on file in the master data banks. Anonymity and seclusion were a must! A residences' clientele were the who's who of the galaxy and it wouldn't do for one to be unduly disturbed.

The concierge took a moment to more closely scrutinize these intruders. Three separate races were represented. Two were known, but the other was an interesting puzzle. On the surface the new ones seemed to be of the Collective Master Race, but as he analyzed them further he saw many many differences. None of the scans he could perform gave any definitive clues, though he referenced and crossed checked all known species. These were new. Not totally unusual. Since the galactic trade pacts had been officially sanctioned by the government, these Collective Representatives were coming in droves. So this new species could possibly be a newly arrived emissary to the council. If so, why would they not know the protocols? And why would their companions not instruct them? The other two races were most certainly members of the Collective. Unforgivable. The Concierge would lodge a strong, yet diplomatic, complaint with the Planetary Collective Embassy as well as his own Central Government. He cued up the missive and left it to automatically transmit just as soon as the communications outside the building were repaired. Then it sent another electronic command to maintenance. He paused a millisecond to wonder at the lack of response, made another note to reprimand that system, then placed his considerable attention back on the intruders.

Yes! The Collective should certainly know better. One of the Collective Masters simply sat there in corridor M-182 and did nothing. Obviously, he was one of the few of their lower caste, brought to the planet by their more august emissaries as servants. Obvious because it didn't have one of those disgusting animal body guards with it, nor the even more disturbing nano-robots coursing through its body. With typical efficiency, the concierge collected its bio and placed it in his hot-file, to be used as a major piece of evidence in his complaint.

Now… the other! It was participating as well, and this one was a Scillian! Not a Collective Master, but certainly a Collective member. In fact, the entire third level, twelve levels below this, was completely re-designed just to handle the peculiar needs of this even more peculiar race. Though the Concierge made no judgments on such things. Yet the bio on this one didn't match any in that entourage either. Another bit for the file!

The concierge soldiered on in it's strictly 'by the book' follow the protocol fussy way! A machine that would have been right at home in any Earthbound five star hotel. Though there was one big difference. Instead of a living breathing human, this entity was a mechanical computer system that in essence, was the building.

In the milliseconds it had been considering, circumstances in the corridor had changed. The intruders had stopped, and to its horror the Concierge saw why. A door to a residence had been left open!

Mac put his back to the wall and slid sideways toward an object that, while laying on the floor, seemed also to be growing out of the wall. This he quickly saw was an optical illusion caused by 360° lighting and a wall that curved away, hiding what it really was. Moving closer the object became clear. *A foot?* A child or adolescent if he was to judge the diminutive size. That it was dead was obvious, though all he could see of the leg was calf to toe. A shoe of some silky metallic material covered the foot, having shrunk around it outlining every bone. There was the impression that the shoe would change its size to fit whatever foot was put in it, and in this case, a foot that was desiccated and shrunken. The ankle and calf, exposed completely, showed the same signs of great age, and it lay pinched in an entrance they would never have known existed had the body part not blocked it. So seamless was the working of the aperture he couldn't tell wall from door. Only this poor dead soul gave him a clue, and he wondered just how many of these openings they'd already passed, and more importantly, what they contained? He stared down at the foot then looked wildly about, thinking doors could pop open from anywhere spilling enemies among them.

Mac's curiosity was great and he wished his desire was to push through and see whatever lay beyond, yet he restrained himself. Needing to warn the others first, he retreated without so much as peeking. The body would lay blocking the door for another few minutes as it so obviously had for the last who new how many hundreds of years.

He moved back to Sue and Shumak and quickly explained his finding. Sue started eyeing the walls with fear and suspicion. It took several tries to explain it to the lizard, Mac finally telling him a door could open anywhere, just like the one that let them in. That got his attention. Shumak didn't know which way to watch; head swiveling to see all directions at once. Even the ceiling, which Mac found particularly amusing until he thought about it. Then he himself started eyeing the floors as well.

This is bullshit, he thought. Then out loud, "Don't panic! Sue, if they…or it, wanted us, they'd already have us. Calm down, ok." He trailed off, holding her eyes with his.

She calmed, having decided it was time to get over her fears. She'd signed up for the space program with all its inherent danger and was not a shrinking violet. She'd been through some of the worst this planet had to offer, and survived! She decided then and there she was over it! Not the fear; that would always be there. She was over letting it be a beast that could control her. "I'm ok, Mac!"

And meant it. He could tell by the clarity in her eyes and the controlled calm in her face. *Good girl!* He saw the change as he'd seen it in others. In young men after the first bitter taste of war. They changed. Still scared, but the fear was controlled. It was then that they became dangerous! From now on Mac wouldn't be bothered at all to have her guarding his back, and it was she who said exactly what he wanted to hear.

"Let's go check it out!"

With even more caution, the three creped back to the door. Sue and Shumak had eyes only for the leg, but Mac needed them to keep watch. In other words, looking everywhere else! He sorted it out quickly, and then prepared himself for something new.

RD-483 was beside itself! What to do? What to do? It clicked a few million switches as it fretted. These intruders were about to enter the room of a registered guest, uninvited and with weapons drawn! Quickly it checked the register. The occupant was a local. By this it meant planetary local, one of their own. In this case, the august Madam ALgoo-tilith of the Arangu Imperium. The Concierge didn't evaluate the list. Wouldn't have known that two millennia ago the persons on this floor, and in several similar Universal Residences, in cities on this planet and others, attempted in vain to avert galactic war. Their deaths only the first in billions! Didn't know the august person in question lay mummified in the doorway, preserved by the perfect environment inside the residence. Her body position preventing RD-483 from completing its appointed duty. In this case, closing her door! The concierge sent another frantic message to security. Disappointment was the only answer it would ever receive.

Mac turned the corner to look into the room and gasped, a sound audible enough that Sue rushed to him only to stare down in revulsion as well. The vision that held them was not only horrific, but the most complete dichotomy he could ever have claimed to have seen. Here lay a woman, though that was only a guess, based on the dress it was in. A shimmering silver wrap which looked like it just came off the rack. Like a sack, it contained the blackened and shriveled remains. Shrunken skin encased the body, just as it had the foot. There was nothing left more than a mummified, although well dressed skeleton which stared up at them. What hair the skull originally sported had fallen out sometime in the distant past. It lay in a neat corona around her head eerily complimenting some kind of jewelry encircling the neck and wrists. These details they registered though it was the other details that shook them.

Hers was a narrow face, her jaws gaping wide in the rictus of death exposing long yellowed fangs. The arms, jointed much higher than a human, ended in a three fingered hand tipped in dark claws. Though these, rather than weapons, were neatly trimmed and painted. The humans stood there shocked, and as much as they wished to deny it, the evidence was overwhelming. Here lay an Aranu female, seemingly civilized and dressed to do the town. Mac just couldn't wrap his mind around this. It was like putting lipstick on a psychotic orangutan! It just didn't fit. Still, here it was.

"My god, Mac!" Sue's voice was a mixture of awe and disbelief. "Did the Aranu build this place?"

"I sure as hell don't know, Sue. But one thing's for sure…" She looked at him with a query on her face. "They lived here at least!"

It was Sue who bent down and touched the beast. "I can't believe it. A whole city of these things walking around. I can't picture Times Square with a half million Aranu toasting the New Year!"

"Me either. But obviously the ones we've encountered and this one are a bit different."

"Slaves?" This would fit in well with her theory of an uprising or civil war that was responsible for destroying the planet.

"I don't think so. Dressed too good."

"Hooker?"

This really brought his eyes up. Nothing could be quite so repulsive as that thought. "God I hope not!" As tense as it was, he had to give her credit because she laughed.

Over his shoulder, Shumak looked down and began mumbling in his own hissing tongue. Mac ignored him, stepping over the body and into the room proper. He'd just got a glimpse of the space inside; bed and several other pieces of furniture, a door leading to another space and what looked like luggage scattered about as if the room had been rifled. It was all he saw as the lights went out!

RD-483, the toothless tiger, did the only thing it could think of to protect its charges. It had no ability to harm. No ability to chase or otherwise hamper these beings. It did the only thing it could see as practical. He took their light! An inconvenience to his other guests to be certain, and he prepared for the numerous complaints, detailing a part of his greater self to comp. whatever needed to be comped in order to keep the peace. The rest of the artificial intelligence simply watched.

Sue screamed, and Mac felt a moment of panic. He yelled at her though she was only a few feet away, "Sue!" *Are we attacked?*

The blackness was complete. He could see nothing but the afterimages behind his eyes. He held out the knife wondering what the hell to do and worried he'd injure one of his friends in the blackness.

"Sue! Stop." But her first scream had already faded into hyper breathing. "Shumak?"

"Am heerrss," came a disembodied voice to his left, shaky, but controlled.

"Sue, are you ok?"

She took a deep breath, "Yes! Just startled, Mac. I'm sorry." He heard the voices coming as ethereal sounds from the darkness.

"Freeze and listen." He whispered the command, wanting the silence to determine if any living thing moved toward them, his mind traveling down paths better not taken. All he heard was their breathing, amplified by the dead silence and Mac imagined the mummified corpse now standing behind him, reaching for his neck with its well manicured claws. Action was the best cure.

"Sue, move back into the hall with Shumak. I'm going to have to feel my way out of here."

He heard her stumble into the lizard then a gasp and another stumble as she pulled back. Mac smiled thinking the lizard was the last thing she wanted to run into in the dark. *Well,* he thought, thinking of his own fears a moment before, *maybe not.* But he had a hunch that any real threat from inside this place was long dead. Still! He stepped forward, arm stretched out seeking the door, cringing as he felt the bones of the Aranu woman crumble to dust under his foot. Her collapsing ribs sounding like pistol shots in the small space. He stepped again crushing a leg then stepped through the door and into the hall, clearing the door by feel. When he was clear he heard Demitri's bellows sounding in the distance.

"Shumak! Back the way we came. Follow the voice." He said it fast, hoping the lizard would understand.

Shumak did. Like the rest of them, he wanted not one more minute in this foul place. "Fllowsss Sshuummak!" he rumbled once, then put a hand on the wall and walked carefully away.

It would be real interesting if Demitri and Shumak met in the dark. Mac couldn't let that happen. "Sue?" He questioned the dark. She answered at his feet, having knelt there after exiting the room to present the smallest target possible.

"I'm ok!" She reached up and somehow found his hand, which he gripped and hauled her to her feet.

"Yell to Demitri. It's the only thing that'll keep him back! I don't want him thinking Shumak's the boogey man!" He almost regretted saying that because he felt her stiffen.

"Don't worry, Sue!" he said to assure her. "If something was in here with us we'd already be dead!"

"But the lights?"

"I don't know, Sue! But I think it's a malfunction of some sort." He squeezed her hand. "I don't know why, or how, but something still works after all these years. For now we just need to get back to daylight. Besides. I promised Demitri I'd not let anything happed to you, and by-god I don't want to face him if you even get a little bruise. So watch yourself!"

He said it with far more confidence than he felt, but it seemed to satisfy her. Hand in hand they followed the lizard, shouting for Demitri all the way.

RD-483 was completely and smugly satisfied with itself. The intruders were retreating and other than touching lock after lock, seemed to now be effectively harmless. His messages of apology to Madam ALgoo-tilith went unanswered and it assumed she was otherwise occupied, so with nothing else to do the Concierge waited and watched.

By feel and by sound they made it back to the entry hall where Jehkal remained on guard. Demitri had threatened him with his life if he moved and the normally brash young man stood wide-eyed as they loomed up out of the darkness. Demitri met them at the half way mark, reaching Sue by feel then grabbing her and retreating quickly back the way they came. None of them wanted to be in here any longer than necessary, though Mac was already planning a new expedition with torches. At the junction the light from the outside was a bright disk they could hardly look at, so bright as to be painful. Yet a promise of escape they boiled toward.

Jehkal was the first out, spilling from the hole and stumbling to the side. His sides heaving so great his relief and joy at breathing real, un-demonized air! Demitri and Sue next, then Shumak, with Mac bringing up the rear in a headfirst plunge. From outside it looked like the building vomited bodies.

Mac gasped as he exited the cold breeze a shocking contrast to the warm stale air inside. Collapsing, he sat in the bones beside the door, breathing deeply of the shear wonderful cleanliness. Raising his face to the clouds his brow was kissed by a flake of snow.

Today would be another blustery day and in that moment of idle he wondered how long till real winter set in and just how bad that winter would be. He ignored the world around him until a frightened gasp, from whom he didn't know, snapped his head around.

Then, "Mac, move!" Demitri pointed wildly at the doorway. As Mac fell away its edges began to glow in the same manner as before when it opened. In moments the entire opening was covered with swirling lights and Mac knew the door was about to be slammed in their faces. His plan of future exploration seemed doomed to die with the sealing entrance. Quickly he grabbed a femur from the piles around him and thrust it into the center of the light hoping to block it open. With first contact he felt resistance, then a growing vibration running up the bone causing dust to fall from it in a cloud. Not knowing what was coming. Mac let go and backed away. Instead of dropping the bone stuck in the light, the half left outside all that was visible, looking as if it were stuck in bright flowing mud. With a final bright flash the lights went out, and the bone, sheared in half, fell to the ground. Mac sat staring, suddenly weak, remembering his first impulse which was to stick his leg in to block the door.

"Holy shit!" he mumbled. The wall where the door once stood was as blank as it had been before Mac touched it not more than an hour before. Gone was the opening, and gone was his hope to do anymore exploring.

For a few minutes no one spoke. None sure what to expect next. They'd been invited in then kicked out! Why, and by whom rattled their minds. When it became obvious nothing else was going to happen, Demitri asked a question, "Was it worth it?" He asked it in anger, thoroughly pissed at Mac for endangering them.

Mac hesitated a moment. *For a friggin hotel!* Then he smiled, "Yes, Demitri! I think it was." Then he saw the blood running down the big mans face, running from under his hat. "You're bleeding by the way! You need a doctor?"

Sue gasped in concern, but Demitri waved her off. There was real heat in his voice now. "I am serious, Mac! We should not do this again." By which he meant, "Don't you dare put my woman in needless danger!"

Mac wearied of this argument. They'd had it so many times. "I know how you feel, Demitri," he sighed. "But you know as well as I do we can't pass up opportunities like this. What if I ask you? What if there *was* something in here we could use? Something critical to our survival? Something that would save the women if we had it?" Unfair to play on the man's emotions, but he said it anyway. "A weapon… or medicine? We've discussed this."

Demitri shook his head, "No, Mac! You discussed it! You wanted this." The Russian rose to his feet. "We just want to survive! This could have killed us."

Shumak didn't know what to think at that moment, watching the obvious disagreement. If he were commanding this group, the big human would already be dead. No one dared brace a superior in the world of the People. Again he was torn. He'd survived the demon cave and at some point realized this Mac was not omniscient. Was not some shaman with powers far greater than his own. What he was, was a fearless leader! A motivator. And something else. Something still hidden from Shumak, but something he was willing to follow to discover, at least for now.

Mac knew when and how to pick his battles. This wasn't it. Demitri wasn't challenging him, he was simply and deeply upset about an action he felt terribly unnecessary. Mac didn't point out that last night they'd agreed this was a very necessary action. They were trapped in the Rayattl, and in some far fetched scenario, this building may have offered a way out. Now? They were still trapped.

"Need I point out we are still in danger? Calm down, Demitri. We need to keep our heads. Especially in front of the natives." He talked calmly and smoothly as if this were just another discussion. Shumak and Jehkal saw the tension, but he wanted them to see it as insignificant. Demitri knew it as well and slowly his anger dissipated. He was about to make further, more considered comments when a clatter of bones sounded from up the beach.

"Weapons!" Mac yelled and as one they turned to face the threat. Fear was like an adrenalin bomb bursting in their systems, followed just as suddenly with relief. Somehow Shumaks's Thalk had slipped its tie and was coming to them. Where they had snuck down, the big animal came without caution, crushing and scattering bones and creating an incredible din. Mac smiled; at least one of them would have a ride up out of here.

The beast was fifty yards away and about twenty from the shore when there sounded a hiss and a splash of water like a whale breaching somewhere very near. What caused it the group couldn't see because it was somewhere behind them, beyond the building and out of their line of sight. With a roar, the Thalk challenged, turning head on rushing towards the water. It hadn't taken more than three steps when a rotting stench wafted over them, causing Mac to gag. A smell that was far different from the blubber beast they'd encountered the day before. Here was the reek of muck and decay, and a million deaths. The Thalk took another step and reared, flailing the air with its front feet. Its challenge was loud, yet the answer was deafening.

The unseen creature emitted a high ear piercing shriek, loud enough that Mac dropped his bow needing both hands to cover and protect his eardrums. In the same instant there was a hiss like the passing of an arrow, and the Thalk screamed in pain. Mac watched in shock as an articulated tentacle lashed past the side of the building, cutting the air. A full foot wide and ending in a barbed claw, the arm aimed unerringly, burying itself deep in the Thalk's chest. This was a mere echo of the hideous scream they heard a moment before. The lizard thrashed and bit to no avail as the arm took its life, slowly dragging the struggling beast to the edge of the water in a scatter of blood and bleached bones. The next scream was Shumak's. He burst forth in a war cry and charged.

"No!" Mac yelled, body tackling Shumak's legs and dumping the surprised lizard onto his face, nearly breaking Mac's ribs in the process.

"No, Shumak!" he managed to wheeze out. "You can do nothing."

Demitri lent his weight holding Shumak down and also yelling no. Perhaps it was the suddenness of their action and the shocking strength they displayed. Shumak would never have guessed these small beings possessed such physical power. Perhaps it was because his breath had left him entirely, escaped through his mouth from the impact of a skull to his diaphragm. Or perhaps it was the fact his Thalk had given up its fight, struggling weakly now as it was drug away, floating away in a growing pool of red water. Whatever the reason, the fight was gone. It probably saved his life.

"Come back, Shumak." Mac whispered in his ear. "We need to remain calm till it's gone."

He nodded at Demitri who crawled off the lizard and back to the shelter of the wall. Another high piercing screech sounded across the water. This time it was bearable, the beast further away and no longer facing them. Unknown to Mac, the Thalk had saved them from the real threat of the Rayattl. If the beast had discovered them none would have survived the hundred arms of the keeper.

They waited in silence for a half hour, not daring to move or make any noise, watching intently with eyes barely blinking. The clouds thickened and snow began to fall in earnest as they abandoned the shelter of the building and carefully crept back up the beach. Even Shumak became stealthy. As they moved, they watched the water and the city, never taking their eyes from the threat until they were again cloaked in the shelter of the forest. A welcome relief as it was far from the shore, putting the lake, and the city, out of their sight. But far from comforting, for now they felt truly and completely trapped.

A weary and beaten group made it back to the camp, finding a wandering Baron along the way. He'd ripped his own tether, probably in fear of the scream of the water beast. But he seemed no worse for ware and was happy to see them, even Shumak, though the reptilian ignored him. Shumak was subdued and withdrawn, the entire experience being far too much. They were all in shock. Sue and Demitri set down, mechanically starting a fire. Jehkal wandered into the brush, Mac hoped to find food.

Mac tended Baron, retying him and brushing the coat with sun dried grass, yet he was with the skeel only a few moments when Jehkal yelled frantically from the ridge overlooking the line of skulls. *What now,* he thought. It was a shell shocked group that responded, grabbing their weapons, rushing uphill to the clansman.

As they approached Mac was surprised to see Jehkal standing in the open, staring down. *What the hell is he thinking, exposing himself like that?* Mac's thought was stillborn, as were his words of reprimand. When he crested the top and looked out onto the field beyond the skulls, it was Shumak who groaned when he saw what lay below. The view horrified them, but him most of all, for in the killing field another battle had been fought. Shumak's entire command lay scattered and slain, each warrior surrounded by the lifeless corpses of their enemy. Each a small oasis's of death. Two of the reptilian warriors here, one there. A few dead Thalk, and many many of the enemy. The Aranu!

Chapter 8

Quiet lay over the forest. A quiet that was welcome to Niloc given the events of the day. So much had happened. Aranu! The strange behavior of Saber and his new mate. The wounded clansman. Too much, and yet much to consider. Sitting silently, he sat the watch in a cold camp. None dared risk the comforting heat of fire. Den'al was wrapped in fur and fast asleep next to his clan brother. Rahkal was in a deeper sleep. One induced by the leaf of the sacred Cerinil plant. Sacred because of its power. Power to sooth and assist in healing, and exceedingly rare. Niloc considered it a small miracle when he'd stumbled across it in his search for medicines for the wounded man. With the Cerinil he would sleep till morning no matter what. Rebecca and Cam lay together, though wrapped separately, each seeking the warmth of body and comfort of their own kind. In truth, now was the loneliest time the last of the Sar-Too had ever felt in his life.

Tomorrow would bring decisions. The news brought by Rahkal guaranteed that! Even through his delirium he'd spun a tale which seemed unbelievable. According to Rahkal, a new and formidable enemy was invading the clan lands. An enemy fierce enough to push even the Aranu from their hidden dwellings, making them flee in desperation. Such an exodus was what they witnessed today. A flight which pointed like one of the humans arrows, strait to the Rayattl, and the heart of the Drakil.

In was not known if the Aranu feared the haunted places as did the clans, and so obviously did the People. What did, '*Lost to darkness he returns'* really mean? Niloc's interpretation of the words may be imprecise. A fact which he continued to discover time and time again. One of his constant doubts was how, *how to be sure the foretelling was accurate? How many voices, and how many turns of the planet had given it change?* Staring upward, he watched the stars as they drifted through cracks in the clouds. *What was up there? What other worlds? What other people? What wonders?* He sat and he thought of these things, and many others. Finally, the echoes in his mind settled and he simply sat, wrapped in the warmth of his cloak and staring out into the thundering silence that was the night.

Rebecca awoke once again to the feeling of eyes staring at her back. A cold dawn was breaking grey in the east, the light filtered and smothered by misty clouds which promised moisture before the mid of day, whether it be rain or snow the only mystery. She blinked a few times clearing the grit from her eyes, then shivered as the small movement made a crack in her covers and sent a draft of cold rushing down her neck. Exactly the place she felt the eyes boring into her. Slowly she rolled over, meeting the clear cool stare of Rahkal. Rolling to a setting position still holding her blanket, she spoke in Clan, "Good morning, Rahkal. I am glad to see you are better."

It was a pale face that watched her. Clearly the young man was feeling the affects of his wound. He was lucky, the spear having skidded off his ribs laying open a long furrow of skin, but doing no real internal harm, even though it bled profusely and a couple of those same ribs were cracked. It was blood loss that nearly did him in. A few stitches and Niloc's miracle drug had done wonders. Her words seemed to break his spell and he looked hurriedly aside, greatly embarrassed. "I am better. My thanks to you lady. For Den'al has told me you are responsible for my recovery."

He was having trouble with his words and she was not sure he was that much better. She was about to correct the notion that it was her alone that had helped him, but his next words were a direct question. He took a deep breath to gather his courage, "My lady, what are you? An apparition? A dream?" his voice trailed off.

Surely he had spoken with Den'al or Niloc! Cam even. None of the others were about, but she was sure they would not be far. "I'm not sure how to answer your question, Rahkal. I am flesh and blood, just like you."

Rahkal shook his head and held up his two thumbed hand as evidence. "No! Not like me." There was no heat in his voice. Only wonder, a little fear, and, if she read it right, hope.

"Den'al tells a tale that shows greatness has weaved its web around you. You and the Drakil!"

So she thought. We've gone there already. 'Simple' won't work, so she tried the truth. "I am no dream, Rahkal. I... and Mac," she decided not to use the title Niloc had bestowed. "And Cam! We are humans."

He tried the English word, "Huumanns."

She nodded. "Yes. Humans. And though we are different," she held up her own hand. "We are much the same."

He thought about that statement a moment. "Den'al tells me you do not come from here." He patted the ground beside him. "He says you come from there!" He pointed up and made the statement as if it were an absolute truth, and the hardest thing he'd ever been made to believe as well. Den'al would not lie! Perhaps a Sar-Too would, but not a Paliece. His face shed emotion. He would not let her tell him Den'al was wrong, but knowing beyond all reason she would.

She smiled at his dilemma. "Den'al is wise in this, Rahkal."

Her declaration was simple and she didn't elaborate. It was this that settled it for him. He would ask the *how* later. For now he'd used up all his courage, and he sat back against a tree to continue his observations of this fantasy woman whom he believed had healed him.

Rebecca didn't have to suffer his stares long as breaking branches announced the arrival of Cam. She grinned as he tried to sneak up behind, though she knew it was him. None of the clansmen would have made a sound until they were within an arms length.

"Good morning, Cam." She didn't turn as she said it.

"Shit." Cam's soft curse preceded him into the camp. "I don't know how these damn hillbillies do it. I try, Rebecca! I truly do. Around them I feel like a bull in a you know where." He didn't wait for a response. "Did you eat? There's some of that dried meat what's his name brought." He switched to Clan, "Hey Rahkal! Glad to see you up. Are you going to live?"

Human humor had little effect on the wounded man. Rahkal frowned, "I do not know if I will live. It is not up to me."

His face was the epitome of seriousness, making Cam laugh which caused the young man's face to darken in anger.

Cam sobered immediately, waving his hands in a dismissing gesture. "I meant no harm, Rahkal! It is my way."

If Rahkal was convinced he didn't show it, yet he did look away. If it were his brother Jehkal sitting here the outcome may have been different.

Cam switched to English. "Damn touchy these locals. By the way, Rebecca. Quiet night. No Aranu, and no People. In fact it was silent and still. Not even wind."

"Why didn't you wake me for a watch?"

He shrugged off her comment. "No need. Den'al, Niloc and I handled it."

She was about to cut him off at the knees, both for antagonizing Rahkal and not including her in the watch. It seemed all the males babied her since the loss of Mac and the others, but she bit back her reply. She knew she'd lost it after the battle and after that when they were forced to flee. She'd been a lost soul in the last few days. The fear and anger and anguish had almost been too much. But she, much like Sue, was made of far better material than that, and now was the time to prove it. She was the lynch pin. Cam and Niloc revolved around her. They'd kill each other without her. *No excuses,* she told herself. It was up to her to mould them and drive them. "Where are the others?"

"Foraging! I expect them back in not too long. We agreed not to go far." He gave her a knowing look, "Just in case."

Just in case an enemy showed up? Just in case the bloody chick freaked out? *Yes,* she thought. *I deserve it.*

Beyond Cam and over the shoulder of Rahkal she could see Niloc making his way back, arms full of plants and tubers. Beyond him, Den'al. One pitifully small animal dangled from his belt and other roots were gripped in his hands. *At least we won't starve.* She thought of her English heritage and what the world thought of British Cuisine. Blandest of the bland. *My god what I'd give for a Shepard's Pie!* Just the idea of another meal of ROOT made her want to puke. And with no fire they couldn't even roast it!

She didn't wait till Niloc was completely in camp. If she were going to live like this it wouldn't be without Mac. She knew the risks. Heard all the arguments. Somehow they would just have to get them out of the Rayattl. She announced loud in the clan language, "I have decided. We go back!"

The only answer was the far off howl of the beast known as a Greater Kraagen which seemed to echo in agreement.

Hatchik-al, warrior of Clan Grouw-sul, had yet to earn his third name. Had yet to join with a certain maiden of the clan in order to claim that privilege. Watching the clearing next to the stream, he knew he never would. His death marched there and he shuddered. Not so much at his impending death, that was a part of life, and though he was greatly attached to his young life, he was honored to give it that others might live.

No! It was the mechanism of that death which caused the warrior of only twelve winters to shudder. Below, creeping through the trees, was an enemy his mind had trouble accepting. Hatchik had prepared for battle since the day he could first hold a stick and call it a sword. Hatchik had killed an Aranu, and received a wound in a long ago skirmish when the enemy attacked the Grouw-sul's scattered huts. A slight wound to be sure, but one that showed very well to the young girls, for it marked his cheek! A wound he was proud of, and hopefully, an experience which might just be enough to see him through to his death. *Might*, because below marched a nightmare enemy none had ever told him of. The elders and experienced warriors could not, for none had ever heard of nor seen this enemy. Now he, and the seven other youths with him, had the privilege to be the first to face them.

Hatchik was the chosen leader of the rear guard and it was he who would execute the planned diversion. It was he and his command that would die so the clan could escape. The other warriors, the real warriors of the clan were a-field, continuing the hunt for winter stocks, and Hatchik and his seven were all that stood between the enemy and the elders. The enemy and the women and children. He didn't recognize himself a member of that latter group anymore. No, he was now a warrior true! He puffed out his chest, determined to be the bravest of the brave, and gave the command. The command to attack.

As one, the Chalgu Company swung with military precision at the first cry from the clansmen on the hill. Altil himself, True Leader of the Chalgu and his routine were just behind, and it would be very bad indeed if they were ambushed. A shame that had been visited upon other advance companies. A sounded whistle and a shouted command was all it took. As if a single warrior, the one hundred swung about and presented arms. The attack was a true surprise and it showed on the faces of the Chalgu as eight children, mounted on juvenile skeel, rushed madly into their waiting arms.

Hatchik screamed with the rest, letting his voice vent, sounding girlish and shrill to the Chalgu, but brave and vicious to the boys. It also lent another purpose. Their voices together told them their comrades were still with them. Had not quailed at the last. It was their voices that spurred them on. The clatter of hooves and the bawl of the skeel added to the clamor, and Hatchik could almost believe that the very noise itself would carry the day! He was disabused of that thought as his mount cleared the trees. There before him, only seven long strides away, waited the enemy. More than he could count stood arrayed and all of them seemed to be pointing spears at the center of his small chest.

In that moment he almost lost faith, though it wouldn't have mattered if he did. His skeel was hemmed in tightly by those of his companions to either side, and the animal had the blood of the hunt in its head. The charge would go forward no matter what young Hatchik did. Seeing the whole was too much, so the frightened young man selected a single target and concentrated solely upon it. For if he were to die, so would at least one of his dreadful enemies.

Around him the world became a blur, the noise fading until his world consisted only of himself and the lone warrior in front of him. A warrior from a race he could not name. A warrior he found he didn't hate. Seeing it clearly now, the feelings that consumed him were loathing and fear. Bloated and white the warrior stood; covered in little but a belt containing a dagger and some other small unknown items. What covering it wore was cast aside and it fought nearly naked. Four arms ended in pale hands, a spear clutched in two and a sword in another, the fourth waving a small shield emblazoned with a multi-legged insect. The creature stood on two legs that ended with oversized feet sporting three toes and a great dew claw halfway up the calf. A ridged head swiveled about on an overlong neck appearing bulbous and adorned with small black eyes, two slits of a nose and a bloodless fleshy lipped mouth held tightly closed. No hair, fur, or feather marred the skin which fairly glowed in its whiteness. A whiteness spoiled only by great blue veins pulsing and tendons roping underneath. Its body followed the head in its shape, being bulbous and paunched below the ribs. As tall as a tall clansman, with bands of muscle now rippling in anticipation of ripping the life from one young warrior.

All of this Hatchik saw in the next three strides. A vision emblazoned upon his brain for the rest of his short life! With two strides left, Hatchik sawed back on his reigns causing the skeel to skid and rear high, flailing its deadly nails in the face of the enemy. Distantly, he heard the screams of his companions and the crash as skeel burst upon the line, yet he only had eyes for his opponent!

The white warrior flinched but held its ground as the hooves lashed out catching and splintering the small shield as well as the arm underneath. But the soldier had already committed its spear, thrusting forward burying the head and two feet of wooden shaft in the chest of the skeel. Hatchik felt the impact and the woof of air involuntarily expelled from his mount. Mortally wounded, the animal fell forward on top of the enemy warrior. In a fit of rage and pain the skeel stamped the life from its killer, mashing its head in a splatter of blood and brain.

Hatchik had no time to revel in his victory. He slashed to his left blocking a spear then pulled his body wildly back, a sword just missing his chest, the violent movement of his body upsetting the balance of the beast that was quickly failing under him. Almost in slow motion the skeel stumbled over on its side, spilling its rider at the feet of the enemy. With a roll, Hatchik tumbled over his shoulder and then to his feet slashing wildly with his clav'l; the pride of his life and a gift handed directly from the fist of his sire. Back and forth he swiped, then stopped as silence fell about the field. Hatchik stood within a circle of steel and white flesh. Eyes-wide he turned around, staring at the warriors who topped him by two heads. He saw no mercy in them. Saw none of his command. Only he himself! One small and very frightened boy. Silently he steeled himself, gripped his sword even tighter, and lunged!

Altil, True Leader of the Chalgu, heard the terrible screams of the small warrior and smiled as he pushed forward, trailed by those of his entourage around him. He smiled for the scream meant there would be bodies to test. Those with him knew the scream meant fresh meat, and at this stage in the invasion, both items were equally important to the army. Important to all but Altil, who looked only for The One and cared not at all whether the army had fresh sustenance.

Hatchik cowered in terror and pain. His battle did not end in the death he'd anticipated, and he knew his situation now was far worse. His wounds pained him. Seven touches of the spear! Seven wounds ranging from a small scratch on his hand, to a vicious cut which severed the tendons behind his right knee. Seven badges of courage which he had earned fighting the enemy in the circle. Slashing left and right to the guttural liquid jeers of his foe. Knowing they played with him as he screamed in frustration, until finally, exhausted, he fell to his knees and held his arms wide, begging them to end it. Yet they did not. Instead, they kicked the sword from his hand then stood back, standing and staring in eerie silence. Waiting. For what he didn't know.

He endured their alien stares in his own stoic silence, gritting his teeth at the pain. There would be no tears, even for one so young. Such was the metal of Clan Grouw-sul. Moments later, his resolve was tested again as the circle parted and one by one his friends were drug forward and thrown at his feet. It was then he nearly lost it. Here were his childhood friends; some looking as if they slept, and some with hideous gaping wounds. All dead. Terror and pain forever frozen upon their faces. Last to be thrown down was small Silchik-al, one winter younger than Hatchik, his head nearly severed. This was too much. Hatchik closed his eyes and silently wept.

It was thus that Altil found his living victim. Hatchik heard a change, a murmur from the circle and a shuffling of feet. In a moment of prescience he knew his death had come and his eyes snapped open. As hideous as his captor were, a figure stepped into the circle which far exceeded them in all forms. This one reeked of death. Still robed, the beast was covered in dried and rancid blood, as if he bathed in it daily and never washed. Even the fur on his robes was matted and crusted with blood as well as other material that bore no more thought. Where the warriors were fit and strong in their alien way, this one was obese and ancient, giving the impression he flowed forward in a blob rather than walking, and even Hatchik could see the mad gleam in his eyes. A gleam that nearly loosed the young man's bowels.

Hatchik smelled a fire burning, newly started with more green wood than dry. He heard the murmur of many more warriors beyond the circle, and soon found a pattern in the noise. These in their multitude were chanting in a ritual cadence, and that chant was building in intensity. Watching in morbid fascination, the old one grasped the arm of Silchik and drew him close, cradling the body gently, reverently. Then, with a flick of a knife almost quicker that he could see, the head came free, the blade finishing the imprecise work of the short battle earlier. Eyes-wide, Hatchik moaned in horror as his friends headless body was dragged away through the crowd to the fire beyond, a trail of blood like a crimson furrow along the ground. Then the old one grabbed Silchik's head by his hair and plopped him upright in the dirt. Hatchik was never more thankful than that moment when his friend's eyes were turned away; for before they seemed to implore Hatchik, even in death.

Hatchik knew of nothing that could possibly be worse than this. *What could the old beast be doing*, screamed his terrified brain? He began to rock back and forth, caught up in the rhythm of the chant now echoing loudly around him. His eyes so wide he could not blink. His heart hammered faster than ever it had in his young life, sweat running from his body as freely as the blood down his calf. So wide his eyes the warriors around him could see the reflection of the ax as it descended, splitting the head of young Silchik, and splintering the mind of Hatchik who didn't even flinch as his friend's blood splattered his face! Six more of the grizzly rituals did he witness, seeing none of them, for his soul had already fled. When his turn came the gathered warriors were cheated of any sport, because the one known as Hatchik was merely a vessel holding a barely beating heart and a brain that would tell Altil nothing.

So ended Hatchik and the seven! None were there to see their bravery. None to see their sacrifice. But many would mourn, and the clan would remember young Hatchik and how he saved the clan that morning. For the only thing that stopped the army of the Chalgu was a testing, and the testing of one still living was a long process indeed.

Chapter 9

Mac watched Shumak from across the fire. It was evening of the same day they'd found his entire command slaughtered by the Aranu. Shumak had taken one look at the devastation, groaned in anguish, then turned and walked away. They found him back at camp, sitting on a rock silently polishing his sword with a dry rag. He'd stayed in that position the rest of the afternoon, snow lightly dusting his back as he sat deep in thought. Mac approached him several times, but got not so much as a grunt in response. Jehkal built up the fire while Sue and Demitri prepared a meal. Snow fell and melted, making life generally more miserable and sucking out the last of their motivation.

Their escape lay open, but none of them wished to venture out into the hands of the Aranu! The forbidden zone behind the line of skulls was a sanctuary; an illusion certainly, but refuge none the less. So here they sat as darkness fell, each holding their own council. Each waiting for the morning to reassess. A new day that would hopefully provide new possibilities. Thus it remained until Shumak broke the silence.

Shumak, Captain of a wilderness command was no more. Now he was Shumak the traitor. Shumak the abandoner. Shumak of the People, without a people! Yet these were not at the top of the thoughts he'd turned in his head throughout the day. First was the demon's home, which in his mind they'd barely escaped. So much for the power of the human, yet Shumak admired the bravery and command of the beings. Then the devastating loss of his mount! A Thalk which had been his since he'd tamed it in personal battle, beating it into submission and thence service. An event which defined the transition from hatchling to warrior. Humans would call it a right of passage. Yet for the People it was the right to life, for if you failed the Thalk would feed upon your corpse.

Even as a young lizard a Thalk was supremely dangerous, killing many a would-be master.

His command lying dead in the field was almost more than Shumak's mind could handle! This was the final betrayal of his kind. Though in truth, Shumak was only sad for himself. He mourned the loss of those who once called him captain, but only as it applied to him and his status. Followers could be replaced. He always saw them as nothing more than a well formed and wielded tool. But now the tool was ill-used and because of that singular event, he could never go home! Never attain higher rank, mates, and a village that would call him Chieftain. His loss, all due to his curiosity. All because of this curse that afflicted him. The thirst for knowledge! He may attain it, but never could he explain why he was away when his command died, not even to himself.

This was what Shumak mulled. This was his conundrum. No longer did he believe in the other world power of the one called Mac. He knew these new beings held more knowledge, but certainly they held no more power than even he. Yet the seeking of knowledge was what had brought him to this place in time, and with his way home severed, he had decisions to make.

Mac was sitting beyond the fire watching, always watching. Shumak had ignored him earlier when the human tried to question him. Did he not know what Shumak had done? Shumak did not understand them, so how could they possibly understand him? *Enough,* he told himself. He had considered his choices and now he must take a path. One led back to his people and Peri'ackt his chieftain, and certain death! One dictated he become rogue, alone and bereft. A target for all. An extended miserable existence with no promise but an eventual and unpleasant death at the end of it.

His final path followed the one which had landed him in this miserable predicament in the first place. Curiosity and the continued seeking of knowledge! Perhaps someday he'd be able to use that knowledge. Use it to regain favor and rejoin his people. This is what he now sought. A bargaining chip in the game of thrones. Knowledge for life and position in the hierarchy of the People. This path; the one logic dictated he take, was actually the hardest. To do so he must follow through on his promise. He must follow the human! Before it was just words he'd spoken with no real intent. Before there was always a way out. Now, however, the certainty of the decision made him hesitate. Shumak was used to being in command. Used to being obeyed. Feared! That would not happen now. If he attempted to exert control, someone would die! A fact that bothered him only because the end result of that action would be one of the paths he'd just rejected, or the permanency of death! Little did he know what an incredible journey his feet were now set upon.

Shumak rose from his spot at the fire as four sets of eyes locked on him. He ignored all but one. Mac saw a change as he'd watched the lizard man across the fire during the last hour. Saw the internal struggle. But he was unprepared for the suddenness and change in the lizard. Shumak went from still and silent, and staring into the flames, to standing and advancing on Mac in the blink of an eye. In his first two steps he had his sword out! In the next it was reversed and pointed at Mac, hilt first! Too fast for anyone to react with anything other than surprise. Had Shumak wanted to kill him, it would have been quick and unpreventable. Mac heard the gasp from Sue, the curse from Demitri and a growl from Jehkal. He knew that, were Saber anywhere near, Shumak would be nursing a throat that no longer worked. Shumak halted only a sword length from Mac and waited.

Mac pushed to his feet. The others were already standing with weapons drawn so he cautioned them with a look. They stood on a razor edge! One false move and... He didn't want to contemplate the, and... With more conviction than he felt, Mac grasped the hilt. Shumak tightened his grip on the sharp blade, squeezing until blood ran down the steel and dripped from his fingers. No pain registered on his face and his stare was as steady and rigid as the steel that pierced his flesh!

"Shuumksss bld isss Macsss!" *Bld?* Mac didn't know if 'bld' meant blood or blade, but whatever it was, Shumak was pledging it to him and him alone. *Just what the holy hell am I supposed to do now?* Something was expected, but for the life of him Mac didn't know what. Shumak didn't release his end and if Mac dropped the hilt it would pull the sword lose, making an even more terrible wound and possibly ruining his hand. Was this a ritual of blood for blood? Was Mac expected to cut himself in a similar fashion?

Shumak understood his confusion. How could one not of the People ever understand the People? Perhaps this was the only time in history when one such as he pledged to any other.

"Take!" Was his simple request, the word far more clear than at any other time when Shumak spoke.

Mac did the only logical thing he could, he pulled the sword. With a 'shik' sound that made him wince, the blade came free, the last six inches smeared in red. Shumak stepped back, his eyes never leaving Mac's. This was his way. He had to do it fast before his mind could change. It was all or nothing, much the way he lived his life. Shumak was now fully committed. He slapped his bloody fist in salute, red running down his arm and splattering his chest as he spoke the most powerful word he knew, "Drakil!"

Mac slept away a restless night. Tossing and turning until dim grayness and cold made even that impossible. A second day of low clouds and on-and-off snow was in the offing, the Indian Summer he'd so hoped for was not to be. Just how cold would it get here in the lowlands? And exactly how low were they? None of his reluctant army could tell him. Shumak already felt it was *cold!* and Jehkal simply said it would be colder than this. Neither had a reference. Mac asked about snow and accumulations. Jehkal said to his waist, then said probably only in the summer pastures. Shumak grunted and indicated some seasons were worse than others and the shaman had yet to enlighten him on how to tell! His attempt at sarcasm?

This morning, the change in the lizard was subtle, but his demeanor shifted to the sullen side, and after the events of the prior night Mac could understand why. The act of fully pledging to Mac was an act Shumak needed time to deal with, even though it had been voluntary. Voluntary, but incredible and very powerful! Only someone undoubtedly committed and absolutely serious could have done it! Mac would never forget the feeling of pulling that sword free. The memory of the sound still caused a shudder. That act alone finally convinced the other humans of Shumak's sincerity. Even Jehkal looked upon the scaly beast with a new attitude, but perhaps more importantly, the clansman looked at Mac with renewed respect. For the young clansman, anyone who could tame one of the People was a force to be reckoned with! Or at least to be allied with. But Mac knew the action had been forced upon Shumak. Forced by another action that his own free will had drawn him to! Even so, Mac still shook his head in wonder, no longer worrying about turning his back on the lizard man, a move that caused his skin to crawl just a day before. Now? Now Mac would need to discover how to bring the big creature out of his funk. Perhaps that would solve its self. In time!

"Do you wish us to bury them, Shumak?" Mac asked the question, then spent the next few minutes explaining. Even Sue and Demitri tried to get through.

"Honor them." Was Demitri's attempt. "Show them they were important to you."

Sue was more matter of fact. She said, "Keep the birds from eating them for gods' sake!"

Shumak stared at them as if they'd stood in the sun too long while holding their breath. For him, those that had died were insignificant when they lived. Dead was dead. You only used them as an example, and now that the Rayattl was merely dangerous, not haunted, they had even less value. He told them such. "Noo ned cutsss head's! No sspiritsss!"

Which the humans interpreted as, 'the souls have fled and the People did not find the need to bury anyone.' How about burning? Mac had asked, not because he wanted to bury, or burn, or do anything at all with the dead reptiles, and he had even less inclination to go near the Aranu! But he wanted to begin to understand how this walking patch of boot leather ticked. The answer, when it finally dawned on Mac what it truly meant, was startling. Shumak really didn't care! Another fact Mac would keep in the back of his mind for his future dealings with the Wilderness Commander. For now, Shumak was pledged to him, but Shumak was first and always for Shumak!

Mac abandoned the attempt in favor of the new discussion which raged about what to do next. At least between the humans. Shumak watched and listened, Jehkal simply waited on the decision. They were of so little help they finally gave up on clan speak and went back to exclusive English.

"I say we go after the others! And quick. Can't you find them, Mac? You know. With Saber?"

She wanted him to sit down here and now and use Saber as some kind of four-legged mobile GPS! "I don't know if I can, Sue." No lie, he didn't. Yet he had some ideas if he could establish a link to the cat. "If I can get Saber to look at some landmark. Something large like a mountain. Then we have a chance."

"Chance?"

Mac was sorry he used that particular word, but this wasn't the time to ignore facts. "Look, Sue! I want to find the others as much as you do." *More so probably.* "But hell! They could have gone in any direction. I can't exactly ask Saber. If you haven't noticed, he don't talk much!"

Mac regretted his sarcasm. Especially in such a heavy tone, but, as with most of their discussions, this one had gone round and round and he was done. Besides, he didn't even know if Saber was around anymore, much less available and responding to him. The female cat could have made sure of that. He'd explained to them what happened with his last *connection!* Told them of the new cat and its' hold on Saber. Who knew what had transpired since?

"I'm sorry, Sue." He looked at both of them because Demitri took his sarcasm as hard as she did though. Where she was hurt, he was mad, the anger a dangerous glint his eyes. "I didn't mean it like it sounded," he continued. "But I'm tired of talking about it. You both make a lot of sense. We will go after them. But not today!" They knew they weren't ready as much as he did, and as much as they desired to be gone. "Tomorrow will be soon enough." He saw the argument boiling up.

"Listen!" He stopped her before she could argue. "We aren't prepared. No food for starters! Let's take today and gather some. We stay away from the skull line in case the Aranu are about." Just the mention of the name got Jehkal and Shumak's attention. "No need to remind everyone to keep away from the beach. Tomorrow, after I'm rested, I'll try Saber. Then we scout and leave! But we go slow and careful. I want a clear shot at getting back here if we have to! At least the Rayattl gives us some protection."

"Yes, Mac!" Demitri grabbed the idea. "Perhaps we can make it a base. Send out one or two of us at a time." The Russian was grasping a line of logic he agreed with because he meant to protect Sue at all costs. By one or two of them he meant anyone but her, but Mac wasn't about to split them up again. He didn't have to voice his intentions. Sue made it very clear, even to Demitri.

She stuck up her chin and set her jaw, "We all go! I'm not going to be left behind. What if..." she stopped at his gentle hand on her cheek. He'd already crumbled.

"Yes, love. You are right. All together." It was the first time Mac had heard the endearment spoken out loud between them and it sealed and effectively finished the discussion.

Mac spent the next hour explaining to his alien friends, then all of them went and did what all locals do. They foraged!

Late in the night Mac wondered if they'd waited too long! The wind howled as a storm lashed the small camp. The fire was banked, but throwing meager warmth toward his lean-to, and he huddled under two furs wearing all the clothes he owned. It wasn't just that he was cold, he was miserable. Rising quickly, he threw a few more sticks on the fire then retreated back to his bed and watched as pellets of corn snow flew past. He risked a glance at the lean-to containing Sue and Demitri, feeling a moment's jealousy at their shared warmth, quickly burying his thoughts as to how Rebecca might be keeping warm. Mac spent the next three miserable hours of his watch feeding the fire and waiting for the dawn.

"Mac!" The voice startled him. *Damn! I was awake a minute ago.* He swore he was. This life was taking its toll.

"What is it, Demitri?"

"Its morning."

Mac avoided the obligatory, 'No shit!' as Demitri was just stating the obvious to get the conversation going. Instead, "Am I supposed to be impressed by your stunning insight?" Mac rolled over as he said it, giving the Russian a wry smile to let him know he was joking. At this point, any and all were taking even the small stuff wrong.

"No, my friend! You are supposed to wake up and lead us." Demitri also had a sparkle this morning. "What is it you Americans say? Sunshine?"

"No, Demitri. It's, 'good morning sunshine!' But that's assuming you want me on your bad side." He eyed the roasted tuber in the man's hand with feigned interest. "But I'll forgive you if you hand over the potato and back away! That way no one gets hurt."

"Well, my American friend! It is good you have your humor back. You may need it on this most auspicious day!"

Demitri made good on Mac's demand. He handed over the tuber; which Mac would shortly make believe was a burrito, and stepped away, revealing a bright cold morning. The storm had passed, leaving only some drifted snow of no consequence and temperatures well below the day before. But the sun promised warmth, beaming down from a cloudless sky. Demitri was right. It would be a good day to start. Though the sun was already two hours above the dead city, they'd let him sleep. *Damn!* he thought. Then decided against making an issue of it. They were right, he'd needed it.

Rebecca said move and they did. Rahkal's wound, while leaving him weak, was cleaned and bound and he was as good as he was going to get without days of rest. Rebecca offered to wait a day or two for him to gain his strength, but she wasn't insistent. A fact that bothered her conscience because she knew she would've been more firm were it one of the humans who was injured. Or Niloc! Fortunately, Rahkal made it easy for her. His brother was in danger and he would crawl if need be. This, and the new enemy he reported, pushed them all on.

Backtracking, they followed the same route they'd taken the day before while fleeing the People, passing the dead lizard man with barely a glance. Its body frozen and half covered in the skim of new snow. Cautiously yet quickly, they pushed back down the trail. Niloc, Cam and Den'al scouted ahead, finding no enemy but much evidence of the Aranu exodus. This was a major point of concern. They certainly didn't want to catch them.

Throughout the day she saw Saber ghosting between the trees or sitting hidden in brush watching their progress, greatly relieved. She, like Mac, feared the cat may have abandoned them. Of the new cat she saw no sign, though they heard the growling and coughing of two cats, so knew it kept pace with them as well. She had no idea why the new one had attached itself to them, but as long as Saber stuck she'd be grateful. She would feel hat much safer, more watched over, and much closer to Mac.

She passed the day watching Rahkal, calling rests when needed. Other than that it was a routine of watch about and huddle in her furs against the cold snowy day. They halted at dusk, made a cold camp and waited for the dawn. Like Mac's, it was a long night indeed, though unlike Mac, the dawn found her once again on the move.

It was Mac's intention to spend a quiet hour preparing for the attempt. He wanted this to be a *quality* connection. Needing to *see* something that would tell him where the others were. Wanted, as much as anything else, to prove to himself that he could do it. He never got the chance.

Jehkal was busy loading their meager supplies into the carry bags on Baron's saddle. Shumak sat against the bole of a tree, staring at Mac with those unfathomable eyes, waiting. Sue was nowhere to be seen, probably in the bushes doing what nature demanded. He saw the sun shining off the glossy hide of the skeel, and the soft dance of the ribbons woven in Jehkal's hair. All of these things he saw with crystal clarity. Then, with a single thought of the Kraagen, his vision shifted.

"Mac!" Demitri yelled, as his friend pitched forward.

Mac didn't hear the yell nor feel the impact as his knees struck the ground. This was the most powerful connection he'd ever felt and it was confusing and overwhelming. Two entities vied for his attention. Two separate visions looking down on the same familiar spot. One far stronger than the other with a feeling that was uniquely Saber. But the other asked for his attention as well, unmistakably the female cat. From a height, and with blurred double vision, he saw the line of skulls and the field of dead in front of it! The shock was ice water poured down his back, severing the connection as effectively as scissors cutting a string.

Groaning, he felt hands roll him over till he was staring up into the Russian's eyes, thinking to himself, *I've got to stop doing this!*

"Mac! Shit, Mac, are you there?" Perhaps it was the Russian using one of Mac's favorite epitaphs. Perhaps it was the vision he'd just witnessed. Perhaps both, but Mac smiled disarmingly up at him.

"They're here!" If there was any doubt about who 'they' were, his statement was echoed and confirmed by the sound of a Greater Kraagen screaming in the distance.

Rebecca and her small troop pulled up at the sound of Saber's cry. It wasn't a cry of warning or the howl of the hunt! This was different and caused them to pause, then Den'al, who was furthest forward, came charging back on his steed causing a jet of fear. She gripped her weapon and waited grimly for him to arrive.

"The Rayattl!" He was out of breath as he reigned in, but his statement held all their hopes and her pulse raced even faster. They were near the last place they'd seen Mac.

"The Rayattl lies just over the hill!" His look said there was something more, then he blurted out, "There are many dead."

Her heart dropped to her feet and the young clansmen was shocked at the sudden change. Quickly he placed his hand over his chest, palm out. A clan sign of apology. "My apologies, Alt-sul!" He shortened the Drakil-Alt-sul to infer a more personal address. "Only the dead of the Aranu and of the People lay scattered upon the field."

If he thought this would obviate her fears, he was gravely mistaken. "My god. Mac?" she murmured. Then, "You said, dead! What else, Den'al? How many of the People are there?" She was trying to keep her hopes alive.

A confused look built upon his face. She'd spoken rapidly and he did not fully understand. It was Niloc, newly arrived from scouting the right, who clarified the question.

Den'al's eyebrows rose in understanding. "My Alt-sul! Only the dead remain in the field. I have not seen any who still live." Again, this attempt comfort fell far short of the mark! She cast a pleading look at Niloc, then Cam who had also joined them.

"We will find the Drakil, Alt-sul! He is safe. I feel it is so!" Niloc tried, but saw she was too far into her nightmares.

She stepped around him and headed for the nearest skeel. It was Cam who grabbed her. "Wait Rebecca!"

"No!" It was a voice of determination.

She pulled her arm away, but he grabbed her again spinning her back to face him. “You do him no good if you just barge out there! What if the enemy isn’t all dead?” He shook her arm, “What then?”

She looked him directly in the eye and never had he seen her more determined. More in control. He was taken aback. “I’m not blundering anywhere! I’m going scouting.” Her gaze raked the others. “Well?” she let it hang for only a moment. “Are you coming… or do I have to find them on my own?” With that she turned her back and they had to scramble or be left behind.

Less than five minutes had gone by. Mac was still explaining to them what he’d seen when Saber burst through the trees, startling them all, especially Baron who screamed in fear and defiance. Shumak, who until this very moment never believed a word about the connection with the Kraagen, was shocked to inaction! The lizard man stared, eyes bulging as the big cat barreled into the still sitting Mac, bowling him over backwards and smothering him in alien cat licks and playful bites. A scene which continued right up until Saber caught wind of Shumak!

Saber stiffened and woofed, head down and tail whipping as he eyed the big lizard. Mac, his leg still caught between Sabers, recognized the danger and yelled, “Hold, Saber! Friend!” Grabbing the cat by the neck fur he pulled him over, a move he couldn’t have accomplished unless the cat allowed it.

“Friend!” He said it again, holding on to the cat while pulling himself from under.

“Shumak.” He addressed the warrior without taking his eyes from the cat. “Move slowly forward and extend your hand!” It was said softly but with command, both to the lizard and the cat.

Sue, looking on from the side, saw the expression of doubt, fear, and wonder on the lizard’s face. At least that’s what she thought she saw. Should things go badly, she had her money on Saber.

Saber continued to glare and growl at the alien, but waited on the command of his master. Shumak, despite his carefully controlled dread, drew near and held out his fist. Saber sniffed and sniffed as Mac made soothing cooing noises, but it was the smell and the connection that closed the deal. Saber saw the scent of his master upon the beast. His mark! He recognized the other scent, Shumak's own as experienced through the connection, and finally, he smelled the creature's intent. No harm, anger or threat was directed at Mac. Had there been, no amount of persuasion could have kept him from Shumak's throat.

After another quick sniff, a cat's eye stare and woof to intimidate, he turned away, completely ignoring Shumak and planting his full attention back on his master.

They didn't see the other cat, but Mac felt her presence, out there, somewhere. Perhaps the Rayattl was intimidating, or maybe it was simply the humans, clansmen and Shumak that kept her back. One thing though was sure, where Saber was, Rebecca and the others would shortly follow. Hopefully with extreme caution. Despite his excitement, he would proceed with the same.

Saber lay purring at his feet and Mac felt better than he had in days. Soon they'd all be together. He believed it! Fortunately, they were packed and mostly ready to go. Mac had already explained to Shumak what to expect when they finally found the others. Who the group comprised and as much as he could about each one. The bigger problem would be explaining Shumak to them. Mac asked him to hang back when they met to avoid any unpleasantness. Shumak understood. He didn't mind a good fight, but right now he preferred it not be with his new allies.

Mac told them the order of march. They would skirt the edge of the Rayattl to where the line of skulls met the edge of the forest south of the field of battle. From there they would cut across the line and escape into the forest, then circle wide looking for their friends. And while Saber may have been a little confused when Mac said, *scout,* he did as he was told, circling around the point where he knew Rebecca to be instead of cutting straight to her. But the master ordered and he obeyed. Saber was not worried. He and his new mate were the only ones completely sure no enemy was near!

Mac was out on point. He was a hundred yards in front of the others and sneaking carefully around a pile of brush when the scream of a skeel sounded behind him. Baron had scented something, and his call was answered immediately by identical calls to the front and from more than one skeel. Mac's heart jumped and excitement threatened to whelm him. Moving quicker and without caution, he fairly stomped through the brush until a flash of movement brought him up short. He waited and watched a moment more until a familiar figure loomed out of the brush off to his right, a mere ten yards away, on foot and scouting just like Mac.

Mac smiled and couldn't resist, "Lost, Mr. Mitchell?" He said it softly so just he and his friend would hear, but Cam nearly jumped out of his skin.

"Mac!" Cam yelled, running the last ten steps and grabbing him up in a huge bear hug. Then he stepped back as if seeing his friend for the first time. "My god, Mac! Its great to see you. We feared the worst."

Mac smiled as simultaneously they asked, "Where are the others?" Neither needed to answer as a snapping of sticks from several directions announced multiple arrivals.

First in was Jehkal, who gave Cam a solemn salute, saying, "I see you Cam, and it is good!" The traditional clan greeting.

Cam smiled at the man, telling him they had a surprise for him, but didn't elaborate. Then Demitri, leading Sue on Baron, burst upon them. There were many more hugs and slapped backs till Cam was surrounded and the questions flew. A welcome scream from another skeel halted the party and Niloc came in on Shorn, the normally stoic warrior grinning from ear to ear. He stepped down and rushed Mac, stopping short and grabbing Mac's hand in a completely human gesture he'd learned from them. As he shook it he said, "My, Drakil. It is very good to have you in my eyes again!"

Mac returned the gesture and the sentiment, but the initial excitement was beginning to wane and his concern was growing. *Rebecca?* Niloc turned away to greet Demitri and the others and Mac was beside himself. *Where…?*

The words were barely out of his mouth when, "Mac!" It was a screech of joy, and suddenly, Rebecca, leading the clansmen from his vision, came rushing through the trees.

"Mac!" she cried again, tears streaming down her face.

His joy equaled hers. She pulled dropped the reins and stumbling into him. It was his turn to be surprised. Reaching out, intent on giving her a hug in greeting, his eyes flew wide as she planted a fierce kiss right on the money! A kiss, after his moment of surprise, he returned full force, his arms snaking around her feeling the warmth and welcome shape against him. It felt like it would go on forever, but was over way too soon. She pulled back, "Oh, Mac! I thought…"

He stopped her with a finger to the lips. "It's ok now. We're all together again."

Looking into his eyes, she was poised to say something more, but whatever she was about to tell him would remain unsaid. Their moment of intimacy was interrupted by a yell of joy from Jehkal, "Rahkal!"

The Paliece rushed to the clansman he now recognized as his brother, and who was swaying in the saddle, his eyes rolling in fatigue and pain. "Rahkal!" Jehkal reached his brother's side, reaching up to help the man from his saddle and down to the ground, then further as the injured clansman lay back against a tree with a sigh. "My brother, you are here! How?"

"Jehkal. I see you my brother." His voice was pained.

Concern suddenly held the older clansman. "You are hurt!"

Rahkal just nodded his lips tight, but his grip was strong. "I am spear struck. Aranu! But the Alt-sul and the Sar-Too have tended me. Let me rest and I will be fine."

Jehkal looked up at the others now gathered around, looking for confirmation. Rebecca knelt and placed a hand on Rahkal's forehead checking for a fever that wasn't there.

"He's going to be fine, Jehkal! Truly. He just needs rest."

Jehkal looked from her to Niloc and back. "My thanks to you both!" He rose and gave his first ever hug to the human female, then his first ever salute to a Sar-Too! "He is the last of my family and very close to my heart. I am indebted."

Niloc accepted the salute with a surprised nod, but Rebecca brushed it off. "In the human world… in my world, Jehkal and Rahkal are now my family." She rested her hand on his arm and he nodded his thanks, accepting her words. With another nod of gratefulness he returned to his brother.

Sue couldn't stand it anymore. It was her turn to hug Rebecca, then Demitri's turn, followed by a new round of questions and happy answers. Mac waited, answered a few then raised his voice, “Everyone wait!” He had to say it twice till they calmed.

Mac would meet Rahkal later and get the full story, but there was still one left for them to meet. “We have someone else with us!”

At least that was what he meant to say, but the chance was gone as Shumak boldly walked into the small clearing, causing immediate pandemonium!

“Oh my god…”

Several enraged screams of the skeel!

“What the….”

“Enemy!” This last was shouted by Niloc as he pulled forth his clav’l and rushed. Cam, stunned, but only an instant behind, pulled his own weapon, and Rebecca looked desperately to her skeel where her bow lay uselessly across the pommel.

Mac bellowed louder than ever before in his life, “Hold!” He grabbed Niloc’s arm as the warrior rushed past. The Sar-too, surprised by the move and the shout, was spun around eyes wide. Mac yelled again in Clan, “Friend!”

Demitri rushed to place himself between the potential combatants, hands up and waving. At least Shumak had the good sense not to enflame things pulling his own weapon. He stood there in all his considerable reptilian glory, his great arms folded across his chest. Everyone froze and stared, even Rahkal, whose eyes popped back open at the first shout.

Mac ran in front of Demitri and waved for their attention pulling their eyes to him and off of Shumak. “I’m sorry!” he shouted. “I didn’t expect us to meet like this.”

He walked over to Shumak and placed his hand up on the lizard’s shoulder. “Shumak is a friend! He has chosen to join us.”

Shumak grinned evilly, secretly relishing the havoc he’d caused. Casting his gaze at each of the new ones in turn, he said in Clan, “Drakiiilll. Sssumakk. Frnds!”

You could have carved the silence with Niloc’s clav’l, right up until the trembling Sar-Too breathed out a line from the ancient words of legend,

“The serpent at his feet!”

Chapter 10

If Shumak was losing sleep over what Peri'ackt, Chieftain of all the reptilian People; at least those inhabiting this small part of this particular continent, thought of him, he needn't have bothered. Peri'ackt had far bigger problems than worrying about one wayward Captain, and the loss of an offspring he'd held in minute esteem anyway. Had the times been normal, Shumak and his entire command would have paid a high price for allowing Peri'il to die. Such was the price of failure, even for the loss of a seventh son. Truth be told, the only reason Peri'il had been anywhere near Shumak and the border was because Peri'ackt had grown disgusted with the outright ignorance and stupidity of his youngest. Peri'ackt had driven him from his house at the point of his sword, telling him to go find a place and be useful, or die trying! Peri'ackt laughed at his own prescience. It seemed Peri'il had taken the advice to heart.

Yes! Had the times been normal... But now, a crisis as never before seen in the land of the People consumed him in total. His lands were invaded! The northern border settlements were gone, some destroyed utterly and some with their entire population, warriors, females and young, fleeing for their lives. Now the word that three of his other sons were missing.

Fuming, he slammed a great scaled fist down onto a table which shattered under the assault. The People didn't flee anyone or anything! Their lands and borders had been secure and inviolate for as long as any had memory, and it was not complacency that caused this to be so. No! The warriors of the People ensured it. Yet now the very existence of the People was at risk, and by a threat from a completely unknown foe seemingly bent on nothing less than genocide! That is why Peri'ackt found himself many miles from his home, in a tent in the middle of a war camp on the eve of battle. This is where word of the death of his seventh son had found him, and the fate of his people would most likely be decided.

Word of this new enemy arrived some several turns of the sun past in the form of a female and her wounded hatchling. The enemy and the devastation she described had been unbelievable, and un-believed. Easily dismissed as the ramblings of one too long without food and distressed at the imminent death of her young. Not believed until a warrior from a border enclave arrived on a dying Thalk babbling the same incredible tale.

Peri'ackt had sent forth the Spear of War! A call to arms for all warriors of the People. A call to meet here in this valley, to face the enemy to win, or, to die! Four hundred answered his call and more arrived by the hour. An impressive array of the might of the People! Yet Peri'ackt had one thing he'd never before felt. Doubts. His scouts described an enemy far in excess of his own, and while he believed any one of his worth five of the clans or ten Aranu, he recognized this as foolish bravado. Never had the People fought in such a group as he now had assembled. His was an army of dispersed warriors, used to protect a vast territory where enemies were weak. Now they faced an unknown enemy with unknown capabilities? One which already demonstrated its ability to rout his warriors. Yes, he had doubts indeed!

There was a grunted question outside the tent followed by a quick and low exchange. A moment later, his second son pushed through the flap and saluted.

"My Chief. A warrior has arrived with dire news. I think you should hear him!" Peri'ackt merely nodded, wondering what other dire news he would hear. A moment later a young warrior in the livery of the one of the Border Commands entered and prostrated before him. Dirty, exhausted and seemingly wounded on every extremity. The Chieftain looked down and was startled to see the warrior held the broken spear of an Aranu!

"Speak!" he commanded.

It was a weak voice that answered, though from fatigue or fear Peri'ackt could not tell. "My Chief! We were beset by Aranu. I alone survive."

Peri'ackt cared little about the warriors' condition. He bellowed in rage, bent down and pulled the warrior to his feet, then from them, lifting the terrified lizard up to look him in the face.

"Is this how you were taught to report!" Spittle sprayed between them. "We! I! By the gods," he growled. "I should break your neck here and now." A threat that was only a moment from fruition as the young warrior's eyes bulged from a purpling face, Peri'ackt's fist closing around his throat. "Who are you? What command, and how many damned Aranu? And where, by the One Holy Serpent, were you?" He shook the warrior till the Aranu spear clattered to the floor.

Peri'ackt calmed himself, then said in a steady and deadly voice, "Your life will be forfeit should you utter one more vague fact." He released his grip, and to his credit, the wounded lizard fell to his feet and no further.

He cast his eyes down, "My Chieftain!" The voice quivered, but held. "I am Umak, First Sept of Wilderness Command South. We were beset by an army of Aranu as we guarded the Rayattl! Two suns have passed since the battle. I alone survived."

Peri'ackt thought for a moment. *An Aranu army as well as the pale beasts from the north. In league? Guarding the Rayattl? Why and why?* The Rayattl was where Peri'il met his end. A battle had been fought with Aranu some clansmen and what that sycophant, Liss'atl, second to the incompetent Captain Shumak, had described as 'Others!' A new race in league with the clans and now trapped in the Rayattl. Or was.

He controlled himself. "Did the Aranu army follow you north?" Peri'ackt had left little in way of defense behind them and now was no time to split his force. The People's fate was truly in the balance.

"No, my Chieftain. They and their females and young continued south."

Peri'ackt almost burst a vein he'd gone so purple in his rage. Very nearly he came across the few feet separating him from the warrior. Had he done so, he would have strangled the miserable excuse for a lizard with his own tongue!

The warrior knew his mistake at once. He'd neglected to tell of the females and young. No army marched thus. He was about to offer an explanation when a fist struck him in the back of the head, flinging him back to the floor. A fist delivered not by Peri'ackt, but by his son, and a fist that saved his live. At least for the moment.

From his new position on the ground he quickly explained how they were surprised by the Aranu. The terrible and brave fight against hopeless odds! Clearly embellishing in an attempt to save his skin. A skin Peri'ackt intended to have dried and hung from a banner by morning!

The Chieftain's voice was dripping sarcasm. "I would have thought that even an incompetent such as this Captain Shumak," he turned his back and spoke to the four winds. "Would not have been capable of having his command surprised by an army of women and children!"

The warrior's eyes darted about the room in sudden desperation. "My Chieftain!" he quavered. "The Captain... The Captain was not with us."

Peri'ackt turned back, his voice deadly calm, "Not with you?"

"No," he stuttered. "Captain Shumak had already gone into the Rayattl."

Peri'ackt truly did grow purple as he strangled back his scream of killing rage. Shumak now was now in the very forefront of the Chieftain's mind! *Into the Rayattl?* It was inconceivable! *Impossible!* He said aloud, though still to himself, "No one can go into the Rayattl. Not and live!" *Was the man insane?*

The wounded warrior interpreted the ensuing silence as a question. "I saw them enter and live my Chief!"

Peri'ackt turned and looked down at the man. "Them?"

He nodded, "The clansmen and the Others! I saw them enter and saw them alive even a day later." He stammered, thinking more information was a way out. "I saw Captain Shumak cross the line on his mount. He told us to remain on guard then rode in. I did not see him after and know not of his fate."

Peri'ackt tried to be as calm as possible. "These Others. Did they include Aranu?" He had no idea what to believe at this point. Perhaps stress and blood loss had addled this one.

"No! No Aranu were with them." He answered then saw the anger build again in Peri'ackt. He quickly amended, "My Chief!"

"After the battle, did any Aranu cross the skulls?" The question was sharp, and one hand smacked the other palm making the warrior flinch. Peri'ackt needed to know if he faced the combined forces of Aranu, Clan and these Others as well as the white ones! He never got the answer as screams and horns sounded in the night!

Peri'ackt and his son burst through the tent flap, spilling into the night where the sound of battle seemed to be all around. The clang of metal on metal and cries of pain or victory competing equally for their attention. The Chief of the People could see torches waving wildly in the dark and the glow of tents being consumed by flame. Figures danced in the dark. Duels being fought by twos or in small groups. Each dancing wildly in the oldest dance of all. The dance of death! A quick look was all he needed to know the battle was already lost.

What are these new enemies that they spring from nowhere and fight like demons in the night? This thought passed quickly through his mind as his Thalk was brought to him, screaming and almost berserk in its war rage. How Peri'ackt longed to let loose this beast of war. To stomp and slash his enemy into submission, death or slavery. Oh how he longed for it! But Peri'ackt knew that now was not a time to stand and fight. Now was a time to save what could be saved, then run like the very dragons of legend were on their heels!

He bellowed to his son, "Sound retreat! Save us from this mess!" Peri'ackt used a fist to smack the head of his mount and turned it south despite its' protestations. He heard the call of the horn. Heard the answers in the dark. Far fewer than he'd hoped. Heard it all as he pushed south and away from the disaster.

Peri'ackt would live to fight another day. So would three hundred and three of his warriors. Including one lowly First Sept of Wilderness Command South named Umak, who followed the Chieftain despite the threat to his life. A wise decision! Three hundred and four escaped the field. Almost a hundred remained behind. They required testing!

It was a singularly surreal moment after Niloc spouted his words, “The serpent at his feet!” Indeed. Surreal and silent, then a moment later pandemonium, at least on a verbal scale. Shock wore off and questions flew. “How?” “Why?” “When?” and ten more Mac couldn’t make out between the English and Clan words, and several people answering at once. Shumak simply stood there, not moving and not saying a thing. For that, Mac was eternally grateful. One wrong move…

It was a roar from Saber in the distance with the answering call from his mate more than anything that stopped all conversation dead. Wild looks were cast at the forest then settled on Mac, for he was keeper of the cats! He would know of any danger the cats knew about. And, strangely enough, he did, and not because of his link. He understood the calls on a level he couldn’t explain. The pair was hunting. But for food, not the enemy. Still, it was a wake-up call. They were vulnerable and outside the dubious safety of the Rayattl!

They moved further up the hill into the deeper heavier cover. Mac smiled as he watched the others. None of them would allow Shumak out of their sight if it could at all be helped. All except Jehkal. He rode behind Rahkal holding him in place. Jehkal only had eyes for the safety of his younger brother.

No one wanted to meet any more Aranu, and none of them, most particularly the reptilian Captain, wanted to be anywhere near a confrontation with the People. As best they could, they covered or erased their trail and buried themselves in a deep copse being careful to scout two decent escape routes and arrange as much of a defensible position as possible. Then they settled in to reunite and reassess.

Afternoon deepened into night as storm clouds again built in the east. No fire greeted the dark, only the shared body heat from a group far more diverse than this planet had seen gathered in two millennia. Five humans, three descendants of the Collective Master Race, and one outcast Scillian who had no idea his ancestors had been brought to this planet by Niloc’s, only to be stranded by a war none could remember. And, as such things go, some shared more warmth than others.

"Oh, Mac! I thought we'd never see each other again." Rebecca shuddered slightly, emotion and the cold night grabbing her in equal measure.

"I know," he whispered. "But it's ok. We're all together now." He stroked her coat and the shoulder underneath gazing at her face, pale in the soft glow of the galactic light streaming down from above. They lay together in the semi-dark. Body to body and yet not, fur and clothing separating skin from skin. Proximity to the others prevented anything more despite Mac's overwhelming desire. Kisses they shared, some to the amusement of those around them, some in private. More would come later. For now, just to hold her and know she was safe was enough, and he did just that. He held her for the next two hours as they shared their experiences while the group was separated. Most of it a rehash of the afternoon. He promised her safety. He promised that she and he, and the rest, would never be separated again. Promised it with his heart, though he realized his ability to make it reality was limited at best. They were as leaves in the storm flying madly at the whim of the winds.

The news of the flight of the Aranu and this new unknown enemy changed everything. To be alone in the wilderness was not an option they could exercise any longer. Tomorrow they would make for the winter grounds of one of the clans. Mac hadn't told anyone yet, but that was the decision. He watched Rebecca as she softly snored, listening to the murmur of voices in the dark. A buzz from several and none he could identify with certainty. Niloc sat the watch and that left few possibilities. No one was talking with Shumak. He put the sounds from his thoughts, having one more goal before he slept. Mac cleared his mind then formed the image of a certain alien cat. Softly he called and waited.

Saber was as still as the rocks he hid between. Not a ripple of muscle, a twitch of the tail, or blink of an eye to alert the prey he could smell approaching on the trail below. Even the cold night breeze was taken instinctively into his favor. It rolled across his fur never lifting a strand. Somewhere in the darkness the female stalked the same animal, pushing it to an ambush it could never escape. He held his eyes closed lest their glow warn their quarry, using only smell and sound as his tools. It was this tableau into which Mac inserted himself.

Saber felt his master's presence, and that his master was in no danger and under no stress. With no orders, he carried on with the hunt. Mac immersed himself in the experience. He saw nothing and for a moment wasn't sure the connection even happened. Then Saber cracked his eyes, just the tiniest slit, and the world beyond left Mac no doubt. He quit concentrating and simply went with the flow, no longer wondering or forcing, just letting the sensation of the link fill him. There was no panic and no sense of urgency as in the other connections. Mac thought Saber was half asleep, though he sensed something more. Anticipation. He also sensed the other cat. A force tugging at Saber and tugging gently on Mac, begging their attention.

With a single thought, just like switching a channel, Mac was with her. Unlike Saber, her eyes were open wide as she stalked, and Mac was struck by the difference in her mind! Saber's was ordered and familiar and one in which Mac stood out prominently. This one was more primal and he was buffeted by emotions. Paramount at the moment was hunger and thrill! Mac watched a moment as she pushed through the low brush. He couldn't see the quarry, but the hunt was on. He switched back, intrigued to be in the thoughts of the female, but at this point, far more comfortable in the mind of Saber. He was there only an instant when the serenity was broken.

Mac felt the change a moment before Saber's eyes popped opened. The cat bunched his muscles then leapt forward in two bounds, the second a long leap. With the world twirling, Mac/Saber sank his teeth deep in the neck of an animal much larger than himself, feeling the rush of hot liquid burst in his throat. He knew the wound was mortal. But mortal was not dead! The animal bucked dislodging the cat, a move that once again disoriented Mac. It was sudden and unexpected, his vision changed with a bump from the front shoulder to a view over the back. Mac was rewarded with an incredible and terrifying sight. Tearing down the trail was the female! Eyes narrowed with terrible intent. Each bound slamming her paws into the ground. Claws extended, chewing the dirt and throwing it skyward behind her, her fur rippling with from the dense muscle underneath. Mouth open in a wide snarl and fully extended saber teeth. Mac saw the last vision a prey animal would ever have when these great hunters attacked! It petrified him.

The view shifted again when the female struck, tumbling all three of them. Another lunge and it was over and the animal lay dead at their feet. Soon their feeding would begin. A sight Mac truly had no wish to see let alone participate in. Saber paused just a moment and Mac gave him a mental stroke or two, then he dropped the connection, almost unaware he'd done so. He left the cat with a parting command, "Bring her to me at first light."

Mac settled back under his blanket then reached for a bladder of water and drank deeply. For some reason he needed to rinse the taste of musky fur and coppery blood from his mouth. Moments later he'd fallen into a deep exhausted sleep.

Niloc sat in the dark watching, listening and contemplating. His watch would extend late into the night and this was the best time to dwell on the things that required special and deep thought. To the one above he cast his message of thankfulness, grateful that the Drakil was once again within his protection. He shuddered to think of how it had occurred. And how, should his original plan to take the Alt-sul to the clans have won out, even over her objections, the event may never have occurred at all. It was a near thing and without the Aranu migration that spurred them to action, the Drakil may have been lost forever!

Such was the capricious nature of God. He sighed, still in shock at having so much of the prophesy now laid bare before him. Inside the Rayattl the Drakil was truly lost! The visions described by the Drakil and the others proved beyond doubt that in the Rayattl, the next world was very near, the shadow world in which only vision walkers could tread, and return! Death was less than a step away in such places, and not only had the Drakil returned, he had done so while protecting all those with him as well. And bringing the other! A serpent! *The serpent at his feet!* Niloc repeated this phrase over and over in his mind as he looked across the dark, his eye locked on the hulking form of the beast. *Beast? Not so.* Now it was a friend. At least to the Drakil.

He considered longer. There were many confusions here. The Drakil himself had told Niloc time and time again to abandon his, "Superstitious Beliefs." Told him of a world where such things did not exist. The Drakil had convincing arguments. He spoke of the Rayattl in terms that held no hint of the afterlife. To Mac, the Rayattl was more akin to the world the Drakil had lost than anything malevolent or supernatural. Niloc almost believed him! Which of course was part of his current conundrum. How could he not believe what the Drakil said? His voice should be law! But the Drakil denied the ancient telling existed. Or, Niloc amended, denied that it had anything to do with him or those in his van, Niloc included.

Yet the clans lived for those ancient words! They told of an end to their suffering, their privation. An end to the constant fighting amongst themselves, an end even to fighting the Aranu. It would herald the great beginning. Niloc settled back and sighed again. *No,* he decided. In this the Drakil was mistaken. But only because God had placed him here, but not yet fully revealed his propose, not even to the Drakil!

As he saw it, the Drakil could not be faulted. This was simply another part of the great plan. Niloc must ensure Mac's survival until that time came. Then the one above would clear the mind of the Drakil and reveal to him his destiny.

Niloc consoled himself with the facts as he believed them. The pillar of fire and the lost moon. These were the first signs. The unsettled weather and the Aranu, who attacked in far greater numbers and with far more cunning and destruction than ever before. The Greater Kraagen that no one could tame. The fact that Mac had crossed into a world where none before was able. Not only did he survive and return, he brought forth with him, the Serpent! It all fit! Mac was the Drakil and Niloc would be his guide until it this path as fully traveled.

His thoughts turned to the new enemy. The one spoken of by Jehkal's brother. A new and most powerful enemy. Niloc looked out on the night and felt the wind which brought the sting of frozen moisture, a promise of the weathers change. It was much like the unknown power sweeping down on his people. He looked to over to Mac for reassurance and hope, then far to the east where the new storm was rising!

Mac had the last watch. A dog watch of less than two hours that would end just as the sunrise began the new day. He was a reluctant man indeed as he left the warmth of his bed, packing the furs tightly around the sleeping form lying next to him. With a smoky breath of cold air, he made his way toward the bushes to answer the call slogging through a half inch of new snow. Partway to the trees he sidestepped a form that was huddled on the ground and rolled in the fetal position. Shumak lay there, covered only in his Captain's uniform; leathers with the fur still attached, but turned to the inside and covering his arms and lower legs not at all. Where skin was exposed it was covered in un-melted snow and for a moment Mac panicked. Where he came from a lizard was cold blooded, but… He stopped and looked a little closer. Shumak's breath was shallow but firm, obviously in a deep sleep. He'd have to ask Rebecca. She was their biologist, maybe she would be able to tell. Perhaps Shumak's race was the ultimate in dinosaur evolution. Perhaps, if an asteroid hadn't changed earth's environment and killed off the dinos as some believed, the earth would have a few billion Shumaks' rather than Macs'! Whatever the answer, if he was warm blooded, his skin must be incredibly thick to insulate against the cold and not allow enough heat loss to melt the snow. He rose and shook his head. Yet another bit of this place he didn't really understand.

Two hours later, he'd put thoughts of intelligent dinosaurs behind him and the snow had thankfully trickled to a stop. Only a few flakes still fell, though the sky was overcast and low and the world smelled as new as any Mac had ever experienced. It was cold and fresh and Mac felt nothing bad could happen today. The alien sky may be green and the *world* a few hundred or thousand light years away, and he may be surrounded by aliens he could have never imagined a year ago, but the snow was still white and friends and comrades were still dear, no matter what their race. They were all together again and he felt damn near immortal, though he stepped back from such thoughts. They could be fatal. It mattered little; he had nothing but good feelings to start this day.

Late the night before as they finished a meager meal, he'd warned the others of his order to Saber. He read their skepticism, but also saw it was far less than before. They were on the verge of true belief and Saber, showing up with his mate at the appointed hour, could very well seal the deal. As the sky brightened he smiled. Mac had no doubts the cats would show. He felt them!

Spectacular! Mac heard the camp stir behind him but he only had eyes for the sunrise. Their camp was high on a hill overlooking the fantastic city in the east. The clouds hung low, but in the distance they parted, giving Mac a crystalline view all the way to the mountain range in the far distance. The sky grew brilliant as the sun burned through a misty sky with silver and gold streamers, soft flakes falling between. Almost he could imagine this was a fairytale world where nothing existed that wasn't beauty and harmony. The feeling complete when Rebecca moved silently up and slipped her hand in his. She sat there quietly, enjoying the glory as much as he. They watched days birth until the rim of the sun cracked above the horizon announcing the day.

"Incredible, Mac! That was just incredible."

He glanced at her, the morning light shining in her eyes. "It really is quite a place." He paused. "A real Eden! I just wish it had a few less serpents." He glanced back at Shumak who was sitting up and stretching. "No pun intended."

Her face clouded, not humored at all. "He scares me, Mac. Scares the bloody hell out of me."

Mac nodded, knowing just how she felt. He had the very same feelings not too long ago. But Shumak had every opportunity to be one of the bad guys.

"I understand, Rebecca. And I think we should watch him. But…" He would like her to see it his way. The same way Demitri and Sue did.

"He made a choice, Rebecca. He abandoned his people." She made to react and he put a hand up, stilling her. "But he did it for the right reasons. He wanted to learn. Needed to learn. He took a chance on something frightening for the greater good. Shumak desired knowledge to help his people. Rebecca, he thought beyond his superstitions and primal fears."

"Does that make him right? Or good?"

Mac had to concede her point. "No! The more I learn from him the more I know he's far from good. But I think he's honorable. In his way. I watched his reaction when we saw his dead company. He abandoned them for knowledge, but he fully expected to return. He thought he was the one in danger, and crossing that line took far more courage than I would've had were the situation reversed." Mac was still trying to convince himself of why Shumak had made his decision, and what Shumak really wanted. But he still believed. Otherwise he would never have let the lizard anywhere near the women.

"Anyway. He can't go back, so he's stuck with us. And us with him. At least for now." She looked like she wanted to argue that point as well, but a sudden movement in the brush stopped them both.

Right on time! Mac thought. A brown flash, then a large brown body emerged from the undergrowth knocking white crystals from the limbs in a small cascade, his paws leaving large blue shaded cups in the snow. Head high and proud, he headed straight for Mac. Saber looked neither left nor right as he strode up, and to their delight, held a bloody haunch from the animal he and his friend killed last night. The cat stopped a foot away and gently lay his offering at his master's feet. Mac smiled at Saber and scratched his ears, and in typical cat fashion, Saber pushed his head sideways to make sure his fingers hit the best spots. Mac heard Cam come up behind them.

"You know, Mac. I'm not a fan of your typical lazy assed tabby cats!" An understatement. Cam probably originated the, 'Can't find your cat? Look under my tires!' bumper sticker.

"But," he continued, eyeing the meat. "That has got to be the most useful animal I've ever encountered." He stepped forward to retrieve the haunch, then quickly back as Saber gave a menacing growl, laying back his ears in warning. "On second thought…"

Saber brought the food for Mac and it was for him to claim. His message clear, 'Step away from the meat and no one gets hurt!' Mac was a little shocked, but he laughed it off. Saber was his and it seemed, very territorial. Even Rebecca pulled away.

"It's ok, Cam." Mac reached down and grabbed the bloody hoof, picking it up, surprised at the weight. Forty plus at a guess and Saber carried it in his jaws as if it weighed nothing. Forty pounds of meat would go a long way for the group and he'd put up with a few catty temperaments to get it. Saber ignored them as Mac handed the meat behind him. Cam took it gingerly, watching Saber with a wary eye. The cat yawned once and rolled over, stretching out for a good belly scratch. It was then they saw another brown flash in the bushes.

"Look! There's the other one." Sue's call caused the female to pause.

Mac called softly and she edged nearer. He only had eyes for the female as the rest of the world dimmed around him. The others stood in a semicircle behind, and he could feel their fear and awe. All except Rahkal, who lay watching from his blankets, wide-eyed and wondering how he could possibly escape if things went wrong. Each person held a weapon, but knew better than to draw. Saber was already eyeing them. Mac couldn't blame them though. He told them she was Saber's mate, and that she was now connected to Mac in much the same way as Saber. But he'd never met her other than through the connection, and he had no idea how she'd react. He warned them to be calm and not over react. They tried to take it serious. At least the clansmen did, but probably the only one who believed both cats would show up at the appointed time was Mac!

True to his earlier thought, Mac really had completely and utterly convinced every individual in the group that the connection was no farce. Each of them now believed it, and each with a mixture of emotion. It was a truth and a reality. Mac could not only telepathically communicate with these beasts but call or command them and they would obey. The actual level of that control and command was still a question, and trust was an unknown. But the connection? It was real. Saber they could pass off, he was after all, a pet. But when the female came out of the bushes on her belly and crawled up to Mac, even Shumak stood in awe.

Once again Shumak had to reconsider his supposition on the real level of Mac's power. Perhaps he truly was the Drakil these clansmen claimed him to be. Shumak was certain Mac was mortal. As mortal as Shumak himself! Yet he was something more as well.

She came forward until she was beside Saber and held long enough for Mac to look her in the eyes. Sleek and two shades darker than Saber and half again as big. Saber was impressive. She was magnificent. Eight feet not counting the tail. She stopped and looked up, giving Mac a reluctant purr and dropping her ears in submission. Yet she was still wild. He reached out a hand. Barely had it moved toward her when she spun and fled back into the forest, the echo displeasured screech sounding loud. Saber didn't move. He lay there and purred as if all was well in the world.

"Well... That's going to take some time." Rebecca's voice was respectful and a little awed. "Thank God they're on our side!" She was back at Mac's side and the comment was her acceptance. There were times her fear of Saber had been overwhelming. Now, she, like the rest, accepted the inevitable. Mac was their leader and Mac commanded the cats.

That same morning though many days away, Altil sat by a fire staring into its dancing glowing depths. Studying the patterns and discerning messages revealed only to him. A column of blue smoke curled from the blaze, flowing up and passing through the vent in the very center of the tents crown, only to be shredded to nothing as it exited. Outside his tent, the winds blew, and snow followed along in a blizzard of flakes which would coat a man in fluffy white before he'd walked a full twenty paces. Of course the Chalgu were no men! His warriors braved the storm as best they could, sheltered within their own small tents of skin. Skin of those they'd conquered, and some of these tents were new, blood and hair still fresh. The storm raged and the temperature dropped, the tempest having done what none of their enemies had been able to do. Altil and the heaviest arm of his army had been stopped by the fall storm.

Yet he was content. Today the True Leader would accept this small defeat. Staring at his fire he would divine the unknowable. He would search out the paths traveled by the rest of his command, the eastern and the two western arms, and he would stare into the embers until The One he sought became clear in his mind. Absently, Altil reached and drew a bloated finger through the clotted pudding which lay filled a chalice of bone next to him.

The bone was the skull cap of young Hatchik, and the pudding a fermented mixture of the Clansmen's blood and marrow dug from the cracked femurs of each of his friends' right legs. Altil's fat white finger stood in sharp contrast to the deep crimson blackness which clung to skin and nail as if the blood still held life. It did not drip as it passed from bowl to mouth where a thick blue tongue pushed its way past bulbous and bloodless lips to encircle the finger like a caress, lovingly removing the paste and drawing it in like some obscene living straw.

Altil felt the rush as the mixture was rolled about his mouth, absorbed directly into his bloodstream through millions of villi carpeting a maw that was related in structure to the slug beast which cleansed the bones in the lake. An animal introduced by the Chalgu from their home planet, and given in gift to the planetary leaders just prior to the war. The fermented blood reacted quickly with his body chemistry, providing a rush to his brain that caused his eyes to bulge even further. The narcotic inducing a clarity that was uniquely Chalgu.

First Altil would seek the progress of his army. He stared unblinking into the shimmering heat, the waves of it flowing across the white coals like the ripple of clear water over rocks in a stream. Watched the subtle play of the flames as they danced along the wood, only to flutter and go out near the edge, always a new flame to follow. The deep black cracks in the embers were a map of the world, each telling a story as it changed and was consumed. From living wood to ash he watched, the very life of the tree passing with the smoke and the remains telling a story only his mind could unravel.

The Chalgu army was built as were the Chalgu. Four arms reaching wide to envelope the target, the two in the center being heavier in number to reflect the body of the beast. Altil was the head. All four arms marched at his will and all four would continue until The One was found, or until Altil called them off or perished. The embers spoke, and to the west he saw his army had crossed a huge barrier of mountains, cutting into a deep river valley pushing the cave dwellers before them. This army swung wide and would break into many fingers grasping or blocking the enemy, herding them toward the center. Thus to Altil. In the east, and almost ten marches of the sun apart, a similar story unfolded. Two arms were there and one remained high on the plain swinging out in an arc. The nearer arm pushed many of the race like young Hatchik before them. Small battles were fought and many of the fingers stretched far. Some of them many days ahead of the main arm, each with a purpose. To scout or to terrify, to sow havoc and drive the prey. Resistance was met and dispatched or bypassed and left for the stronger follow-on forces, and not every foe they encountered was sentient. An entire finger had been destroyed and devoured by a mind-beast. A nuisance, but…

Altil had no worry his quarry might escape. It was as plain as the ash in front of his face. For not only did Altil see the present, the fire revealed the future. Not the when or the how, just his certainty that the goal would be achieved. The god would return. Again, the object of his desire, as always, appeared in the center of the fire. Just as he'd first seen it so many turns ago. A time when the grass in the high valleys sprouted anew through the aged snows of winter. Then as now, in the center of the blaze stood an ember more resilient than the rest. One which refused to be consumed. This was the one they sought. The Chalgu would reach and pull and circle, and somewhere within his net The One would find himself caught. Today? Perhaps not. But in one of the tomorrows that lay open before him he saw it.

One division of Altil's army probed deeper than the rest, a fist of one hundred which struck like a spear down the great river valley. A fist that spread wide its four fingers, each with twenty five warriors. The fingers branching and following different trails, each many miles apart and each with varying degrees of success. One had been wiped out to the man by a large force of the People. One mauled a similar number of Aranu, and one had met no resistance at all. This group brought dishonor upon itself, having no choice but to secure its food from the beasts of the land as no enemy could be found to provide.

The fourth and last group battled its way through a series of rearguard actions placed by another troop of the lizard people. Twenty five soldiers started the march, and fourteen had been left on the trail behind them, proof that no war is easy. It was this group that unknowingly lay in the path of The One!

"Well?" Mac's question was in English thus to the humans. They sat in their lean-tos' which captured the heat of the fire and blocked the breeze, making it almost comfortable. The fire a luxury they risked only because the snow and the wind would effectively disperse the smoke, and because they needed to spend a day discussing the past few days and their future. Specifically, "Just what the hell they were going to do now!" Those were Cam's words, but they summed up the situation which Mac had spent the better part of the morning chewing over with his various comrades in arms.

Everyone but Shumak who had no opposing opinion, agreeing that finding a clan to spend the winter with was now their best option, his own people not even being considered. The only real discussion left was how, where, and with whom? Of course, Jehkal and the brothers wanted it to be the Paliece. They guaranteed the Drakil and his company would be most welcome. He was, after all, the Drakil! However Mac thought the idea of putting Jehkal's loyalty to the test in front of his own people may not be their wisest choice, a thought seconded by Niloc who cautioned Mac privately and quite firmly. In his experience the Paliece were not to be trusted.

It seemed the Paliece tended to be instigators. Should bad blood be found between two clans, the Paliece probably had a hand in it. Always playing for advantage, though, he told him, a lack of honor was not the issue. They valued loyalty almost to an extreme, but that loyalty rarely extended beyond the edge of a Paliece village.

Mac accepted Niloc's opinion, although with a grain of salt. The humans had yet to figure out clan society, its rules and mores, its ingrained prejudices and age-old conflicts. Probably they never would.

Of course Niloc had no clan to take them to. The Sar-Too were gone! Wiped out by the Aranu last spring just before Mac and Cam had rescued Niloc. But Niloc did offer an alternative to the Paliece. He knew a valley where two clans wintered. This in itself was a testament to their temperament, spending the cold months as a big extended family, intermarrying, trading and crafting for the good of both. Jehkal even agreed, although reluctantly, that the Valley of the Moon where the Cal'dil and the Briss'y met at first snow, was a good second choice. However, there was a drawback. Distance. The march would take them as much as a week or ten days, and for certain they would have to re-cross the river, then backtrack.

Both Jehkal and Niloc felt the best route to either destination was back up the escarpment, though neither was certain where the Valley of the Moon was exactly. Rahkal was more sure, thinking he could get them there by striking through the forest. But he ultimately agreed with his brother about going back up on top. A move which could take a number of days off the trip, but a move Mac had no desire to take. He looked to the sky then the forest, watching big flakes swirl in eddies of wind as they were pushed around the trunks of the trees. The horizon was down to near zero, he couldn't see a hundred yards, let alone to the far mountains. He had zero yearning to be caught in the high country with weather that could kill them just as dead as an Aranu spear! His vote was the longer route, hence the questions he posed to the humans. Paliece or the Valley of the Moon? Should they travel along the river where they may/probably would run into their various enemies, verses the more uncertain dangers of weather, which they had no chance to evade? Thus his question, "Well?"

"I'm all for the Valley of the Moon!" Cam, as outspoken as ever was first into the breach. "I like Jehkal and all, but I don't know if I can handle a whole damn clan of him."

"I don't know," Sue said. "We aren't even sure these other clans are going to be there. What if the Aranu or these new ones got there first?"

"Hell, Sue!" Cam wasn't keen on other ideas clouding his opinions. "The same thing could be true of the Paliece. We just have to go with the safest of poor choices. I think it's the Valley of the Moon."

Demitri's voice was sharp, "We do not know if the Valley is safer!"

"I know that, Demitri." Cam moderated his tone a bit. At least he had some good sense. "But you've been around Jehkal. I think we need to keep him away from any more of his *brothers* until we have a few more allies. I think he's loyal, but…" He didn't have to add, "Why tempt him."

None of them thought Jehkal above using the Drakil to press any advantage he could get, after all, he wanted to be Chief. They remembered the brashness and belligerence he displayed when they first encountered him, and how he'd lorded it over Den'al and his brother. Though it seemed like an eternity ago, it was less than two weeks.

The discussion had been going on for an hour with Rebecca yet to weigh in. She had to be careful not to be seen as just parroting what Mac wanted, but she think Niloc and his counsel were sound. The Valley of the Moon was her choice, and she wanted the less direct route with all its potential risks vs. the absolute peril of the high plains.

She said as much, now that the decision had to be made. “I’ve heard it all and said little,” she began. “But I’m for avoiding Jehkal’s clan as well… unless it’s absolutely necessary.” She stared at the fire as she spoke. Her hair spilling out from under a fur cap leaving her looking every bit the true wilderness adventurer. Mac found her painfully gorgeous. “Both lie in the same general direction, so if the Valley is a problem we simply move on to plan two.”

The opinions were well and good and it was important they talk this out, but they were talking as if this was a summer vacation they were planning. Mac knew they were acutely aware of the dangers in just getting to Plan One, opting for Plan Two meant they were in deep shit. Still, overall he felt pretty good about their situation. Now they had more weapons at their disposal. Shumak and the new cat were incredible assets. The group had long range scouts and shock troops with the cats, muscle with Shumak and the skeel. Light cavalry, and long range weapons with their bows. All in all, a formidable group. Though he cautioned himself, they were formidable as long as the odds were not too steep. And there was the fear that was always in the back of his mind. Every engagement left injured and dead on both sides. In this case, that meant friends.

So much for the assets, now he counted off their liabilities. At least the major ones. They must protect the women and of course Rahkal. He was able to travel but still very weak. They only had five skeel so mobility was a problem. They were limited to the speed of a walk. Food supplies were almost non-existent and none of them, even the clansmen who knew *approximately* where they were, knew the country. Top that off with an enemy they knew nothing about nor where they might be. And this new enemy was pushing their main threat, the Aranu, all over the map. What before was a dangerous world, was now very dangerous indeed.

The new enemy was a major unknown. One problem was that Rahkal had not actually seen them so the details were sketchy at best. Mac wondered if they might actually be a fever induced figment. They might be, but they sure as hell couldn't count on it. He tried not to dwell on those details. Really, all they could do was move with great caution, avoid contact with any enemy they found, and, should that prove impossible, terminate whoever they were with extreme prejudice! He chuckled, *just like the bad ole days back on earth.* Except these weren't the Special Forces troops he'd been with then, and the enemy was without doubt, far more dangerous than any drug lord or trumped up dictator's troops. When he thought about that, it scared him senseless! He didn't let on though. Like the situation or not, he was their leader.

"Ok!" He said it loud and this time in Clan, wanting everyone to hear. "We've talked about it enough. Tomorrow we head for the Valley of the Moon."

Jehkal looked stricken for a moment, but his stoic clan demeanor fell back over his face like a mask. Den'al merely nodded and Shumak stared at him as if he didn't understand at all, which was probably accurate. Mac would have a side talk with him.

Niloc nodded in assent and Demitri looked like he might buck the decision, then he looked at Sue. She nodded her agreement and that was enough. Rebecca and Cam were a non-issue and Rahkal was sound asleep and in no position to complain anyway.

Mac looked around one more time. "As soon as the snow lifts a little we'll forage. Rest until then. Me? I'm going to see if Saber and his new friend can't kill us something edible."

The group looked better now. More concentrated, and even though the decision was not unanimous, it was still a plan. They were together and determined to find a place that was safe. Somewhere out of the way to sit out the winter. For now, that was enough.

Chapter 11

It was a night for contemplation. Tomorrow things would change, most certainly they already had. But tomorrow they would go with purpose. The group had now become more like a clan than a group of disparate wanderers, and a stranger tribe Niloc could not have imagined. Simply to see what the Drakil had drawn to his banner was a privilege. But Niloc was the first and could claim great honor! He was the clansman without a clan; now of the clan. The ultimate clan of all, the Clan of the Drakil! The only banner which could claim the Greater Kraagen as its patron beast, and under which all others would fly.

Next added were the Paliece. Not the entire clan, just its representatives. This was the way the rest would come, in time. Bonded in blood, bonded by battle.

Add to this the serpent! Shumak had come to the banner of his own free will. Niloc wondered if other serpents would follow. Would Shumak be a token, or the ambassador of his people? To hear his story one must assume 'token.' One given selfishly and without regard to history or ancestors. Niloc watched him across the fire, his back to the meager heat. The serpent looked out on the night and only to his own future, and whatever he thought, he kept his own council. But who could know what was to be. The serpent was part of what was to come. For good or for evil he was here. It was foreseen.

Shumak watched the night much in thought, just as the clansman behind him. Shumak could feel his eyes and sensed questions but no malice. Which of course, surprised him. Situation reversed, the People would never accept one like him. And he was sure the clansmen, on their own, would never have either. It was The One, the Drakil which made it possible. Shumak did not play down his own part in this. Never a modest person, he gave himself his due. It was after all, his curiosity, his break of tradition and the abandonment of all his people held as faith, which brought him here. But…!

It was The One, he conceded. Even those around the Drakil, those of his own tribe saw Shumak differently. If it were up to them, Shumak would be driven out. They would have killed him. He laughed to himself, *they would have tried!*

He stared at the myriad stars peeking through the broken clouds, his mind turning to the Drakil whom he saw as something more and something less than he seemed. The Drakil was not magical, certainly not all powerful. That had been proven in many ways, and Shumak was amused by the blind worship he saw in the weak minds of the clansmen. But the Drakil was different, far more so even than his being something called 'human'. The Drakil was a flame! The other humans held no such spark. It was the Drakil, and he alone, that held them together. He was the only thing that kept Shumak here.

Mac's command of the night stalker was the truest shock. The animal was feared, even by the People. A killer! Yet they came to the Drakil as if tame, and, if it could be believed, and it was hard for him to doubt, the beasts talked to him! Shumak searched his memory for any tale, or lore, or teaching of the wise, which could explain it. Finding none. Nothing other than the superstitions of the clans, and surely he could put no stock it that. Now they said that he, Shumak, was included in their beliefs. That this moment was preordained by their legend, that Shumak was further proof the ancient words held truth. He laughed again, *how convenient for them.* As if their words could explain Shumak and his actions. It was his opinion that if a thing or an event was uncomfortable or unexplainable, the clansmen would just add it to their mantra, mould the words to make it fit. In his belief, they were simple and unworthy. They even made poor slaves.

He sighed, looking around the camp through his slitted eyes. Silently he wished the wounded one would die. Were they of the People, he would be left behind in the morning. Not out of spite or malice. Because he was no longer efficient and would slow them down. *They were weak.* Shumak told himself these things as he pondered.

He was a product of a harsh environment and strict military upbringing. Yet had he the time to do a self analysis, he would realize his previously ordered mind was now wandering from thought to thought, almost aimlessly. Subconsciously he did catch himself and brought his thoughts back to the original contemplation, the Drakil and the stars!

This was the strangest tale of all. Shumak saw the reaction of the Drakil when it was mentioned, his shifting eyes, as if the subject was taboo or not to be shared. The one called Niloc believed the fantastic story to be true, that was certain. He had mentioned it once, and it was discussed in quiet while they were in the Rayattl among the humans. Shumak shivered at the mere thought of that loathsome place, the true low point of his life. Never before had he felt such fear and he swore never to again. He was frustrated yet again as his mind strayed from its path.

Shumak once more looked skyward, catching the fiery points in the sky. It was the belief of the People that each point of light was indeed a separate world. Each a new place to do battle after this one was finished. The warriors of the People fought their way from death to glorious death until, by martial prowess, they earned their way to paradise. Yet Shumak realized this belief was a true matter of faith. He really knew nothing for certain; he could remember no prior life.

But how? he thought. What if indeed the Drakil did come from one of those points of light, a point Shumak was not yet ready to concede, *how?* How had they traveled? As leaves on the wind? By the chariot of a god? By magical passage? How? Shumak suspected the answer was much simpler. The Drakil was from much closer than those fiery points. His eyes drifted to the distant mountains. Shumak determined that there was only one way he could ever be sure; he would watch and study this fascinating creature until he discovered the Drakil's true reality.

Jehkal was greatly disappointed and not a little frustrated. He lay next to his brother, watching each breath with great concern. Rahkal had laughed at him earlier, accusing him of being an old woman! "I promise I will not die until you return!" he said. This prompted by the Drakil who had ordered Jehkal to accompany Cam on a foraging trip. He had refused, which brought anger to

The One. Jehkal was a stubborn man and he understood this to be one of his less favorable traits, yet it was one he could not change. It took the good natured chiding of his brother to move him, and he was angry with himself because of his conflicting loyalties, part to his brother, part to his clan, and now a bigger part to the Drakil.

It was this conflict that caused his current discontent. Jehkal wished to take his wounded brother home. Also, he wished to bring the Drakil to his people. Yet neither outcome was to be. When the sun rose they would travel a different path. One which would virtually insure that his position and his power would be severely limited.

Tomorrow they would seek the Valley of The Moon and the clans that met there. It would be these that would have the honor of First Banner of the Drakil. An honor he felt belonged to the Paliece. An honor he longed to bring to his people. One which would seal his place. His position in history. Only briefly did he wonder that it bothered him so. Such things were difficult for one like Jehkal. One who often sought his reflection in still water. And the image that looked back always carried the mantle of a Chieftain. In the Drakil he saw an avenue to the leadership he so craved.

Even so, through all his shortcomings, Jehkal was loyal. Thus his current conundrum. Loyalty to the Drakil and all that was held sacred by clan society, versus his inherent distrust of any other clan and his undying loyalty to his own. He settled back with a sigh. It was said by the old ones that sometimes things took care of themselves, and a young warrior should have faith and a strong arm to see him through. Indeed, it was a long, long way to the Valley and anything could happen. Jehkal would be loyal, but… He would not let an opportunity pass him by should one present itself. *Yes!* Advantage and opportunity. To him, this was the mark of a leader.

Human and Clan, Aranu and Chalgu, or the People. These were not the only players which would weigh on the mind of The One; or the Drakil, or Mac, depending on whose eyes saw him. Another player was set to appear.

Far off, beyond the Sea of Tears and beyond the great mountain range which held its eastern boarder, a cold front was bending south, pushed by the curve of the jet stream. The disruption from the loss of one of the planets moons was still being felt as the planet searched for equilibrium. Even a moon as small as Vi-t-ry, due to its close orbit, would have an impact. One of the first large storms to occur had buried the Atlantis! Other massive storms plagued distant parts of the central continent, and others had devastated islands, both costal and out to sea. Cold waters in the northern ocean and warm air pushed north from barren deserts a thousand miles away provided the moisture; the jet stream provided the engine. And though the broken clouds of the night held the promise of a decent days travel ahead, Mother Nature had other plans.

Cold, clear and crunchy snow! That was the darkness of predawn which greeted the group. They shared meager food and sounded general, though good natured grumbling as they mustered out of their makeshift beds. The darkness was broken by the snorting of the skeel, and their louder trumpeting when Shumak passed near. The noise muting the rustle of feet over the frosty ground and the hiss of melting snow thrown on the fire to quench the last embers. A steamy pile of skeel droppings mixed with their musky damp fur, lent an underlying perfume to the plethora of other scents. Unwashed bodies wrapped in unwashed clothing being the primary, but if you stepped away, even for a moment, the world around came alive. A wonder for all the senses.

This is what Mac experienced as he wandered to the edge of the clearing. His intention to call Saber. The crisp cleanliness of a late fall dawn, rife with the ozone-y scent of fresh snow and the even crisper aroma of frost covered foliage. He listened to the night sounds. Slowly dying away with the darkness as the sun pushed its rays into the eastern sky. New sounds rose to greet the morning. Birds for the most part, unseen, but not unnoticed. Mac shivered, but it was a good shiver. One you felt with a new day dawning, and the feeling that all things were possible. He stared out at the growing light, seeing high wispy clouds which grew pink, then red rimed in bright silver, presaging the sun. The sky itself growing from black to a deeper green. A green that would be noticeable only as a light emerald in the full light of day.

Mac paused and drank in the spectacle. Then, as he watched, his good mood slowly bled away. Over the mountains there appeared a pencil thin line of dark clouds. Clouds not seen only a few minutes before. A thought passed behind his eyes, a saying from his younger days. *Red sky at morning, sailor take warning! Now why would I think that?*

The clouds, so many miles away, caught more of his attention and brought more and more concern. It was the distant mournful howl of Saber which snapped him back. *That's a howl of concern. Saber feels it too?*

"Niloc! Jehkal! Shumak!" he yelled towards the camp, no longer worrying about the enemy. Saber would have warned him of that long before now anyway. In a moment everyone had joined him, not just those he'd called.

Demitri came up on one side. "What is it, Mac? What the hell are you being so loud about?" Even if Mac suddenly wasn't, the Russian was more than worried about unfriendly neighbors. "Did you see something?"

Mac looked to Rebecca then the others, surprised to see Rahkal standing there, curiosity on his face. Pointing out at the sunrise he asked them, "What do you see?"

Cam snorted in disgust. "Shit, Mac... Tell me you didn't call us out here to look at *another* friggin sunrise!"

"I said, look!" Mac's voice was sharp and look they did, right where he pointed. To a horizon which seemed to be boiling, the dark clouds rolling upon themselves. He spoke in Clan, "Have you ever seen a storm build like that?"

"My, Drakil!" Jehkal was first to answer. "We of the Paliece know the ways of the wind. I have not seen its like." His finger pointed toward the distance and Mac thought it trembled.

"Perhaps it will not come this way." Niloc's voice was soft and contemplative. "Drakil, we may need to find shelter and put off our travel."

Shumak merely grunted. He would do what ever the Drakil wanted, but he would not let these clansmen have the only say. "Ssshuumak sseess bfr! Timmss of lossst moonssses. Stoormsss bads asss thss onss. Manys diesss."

Demitri stepped closer. "Look at that." He whispered his statement; in awe or so not to frighten the women, Mac wasn't sure. But Mac had already seen it and the others could not miss it. The front edge of the storm clouds crested the mountain chain. *No!* he thought. *They dwarfed it.*

"We go! Now!" He said it loud and clear.

"Where?" A question he had no answer for. But he had an idea of where not to be and that was here.

"Up the valley and away from the low country. We need to find a really thick part of the forest or an overhang like we found when we first came off the escarpment. Fast!"

A big problem because that overhang, and any like it, were across the river next to the cliff. Many miles distant. No way could they cross the river now. Not with that mother bearing down on them.

"Or a cave! I figure…" he looked back at the storm. "I figure we have maybe three hours. That means we search for half that time, then settle for something. Then we build shelters and gather as much fire wood as we can. No time for anymore foraging. Unless you stumble across something..."

His words were cut because Saber bounded into the clearing. His female friend was unseen though Man knew she was close. The cat stalked right up to Mac, flipped his ears back and snarled at Shumak just to make sure he knew his place, then settled to his haunches and looked, waiting for a command.

Mac had an idea. He pointed to each of them in turn and said their names, then at the skeel. Finally he pointed at Saber and gave a mental command. *Find shelter!* The cat's ears came up and he looked over at Shumak as if asking, *you sure you want him too?*

Mac hit him again, *Shelter! Now!*

Saber growled once more low in his throat, then, with a blindingly quick move, spun and sped away, his claws throwing snow crystals into the air. They sparkled in the cold light as they drifted back to earth. The only evidence of his passing.

Mac didn't bother with their questioning looks. If Saber found something he would tell them. For now, "Let's go. We separate into three groups."

Rebecca grabbed his hand. "No, Mac! Not again."

Cam backed her up. "Absolutely not! We can't get split up. Not again."

Mac smiled. That's the last thing they were going to do. Ever again. "Calm down and let me finish. We split up, but only out to shouting distance. We have to cover as much ground as we can."

There was more grumbling, but it was quick lived. Ready or not, nature was going to have its way, and they had little idea what to expect and less time to prepare. Mac's good thoughts from earlier were gone. Though he was eternally grateful for far horizons, and his habit of watching the sunrise. Sleeping in could get you killed!

Just in the shadow of those distant mountains, the far eastern arm of the Chalgu war machine faced the same storm, though with far less warning. The army lay in the mountain shadows, and the plains beyond were bright, bathed in the new day sun. Like Mac, this army was just breaking camp, and the rumbling they heard far up in the mountains was the first inkling they had of trouble.

Three full fists paused in whatever task they were about, looking toward the foothills which extended into the dark mountains above. They too were anticipating a clear day in which to make a long march. One that would take them all the way to the great escarpment seen as a smudge in the distance, and a goal they were two days behind in achieving. The growing rumble, at first ignored, now commanded more attention as the storm, still twenty miles distant, began to compete with the rising sun. Flashes could be seen outlining the very tops of the peaks. Far off lightening becoming almost constant all along a front which measured in mountain chains, not miles. As they stared in confusion, the first towering black headed clouds became visible, lined in sliver from the sun now masked behind. The army, to a man, knew they were in trouble. Here, where the foothills had just begun their rise from the plains, there was nothing that remotely resembled shelter. Low brush to which they'd tied their tents was the tallest feature on an otherwise featureless landscape.

A trumpet sounded and the army turned. Abandoning anything not already on their backs, they faced toward the oncoming storm and rushed forward in a race to the death. In a few short strides, the first fingers of icy wind began to buffet them.

Those who were fast might just make the hills and find some crevice, cave, or sheltered corner in which to hide. The slow would have few options, and less chance. As they ran they realized this was an enemy that would take them to the afterlife with far more ease than any earthbound foe. It was a race. And the prize was quite simply, life!

Most of the migrating creatures of the plains had already followed their age old paths to the lower valleys. Those few who remained, the herd animals and the hunters that sustained themselves on their flesh, now fled as one. Streams of beasts flowing in living rivers raced before the storm. The rumble of hooves and their bawling screams soon drown by the winds that chased them. Terrified animals with a single mind, escape. Ravines and large rocks, brush and holes, obstacles normally avoided. Now they were plowed through without thought. Leaving in their wake the trampled broken bodies of their slower heard mates. On they ran until they could run no longer, exhaustion bringing them to a numbed halt. Tongues hanging from parted lips, eyes rolling and sides heaving, they simply gave up and hung their heads to wait.

In fury the storm descended the mountain slopes, braking over the Chalgu like a tsunami, shattering them. Those few who made it to the tree line were greeted with hurricane gusts that toppled those same trees upon them. Debris of every description was kicked up, driven as if by a sentient mind and driven hard enough to pierce the flesh. Whole trees were uprooted and thrown down until it seemed the ground quaked and rolled with the blows. Their situation desperate, and to make it worse, in what seemed the blink of an eye the temperature plummeted. Yet this was just the prelude. The full weight of the storm was still to come.

The clouds had boiled for hours as they swept down the continent. Each minute ice crystal was sucked upward from the bottom of the billowing towers, gathering more and more molecules of water as they rose. Pulled to unbelievable heights until they stalled, then gravity and downdrafts caught and hurtled them earthward. As they neared the bottom of the super cell, the great convection caught them again, halted their fall and pulled them back into the maelstrom. Some few escaped and fell to earth, but most continued the cycle, growing larger and larger until finally even the strength of the storm could no longer hold them. This was the weapon that shredded Altil's eastern arm. With a roar that overcame the wind and thunder they came. Hailstone as large as baseballs, falling at a hundred miles an hour, killed outright or shattered bones and pulverized internal organs. In moments more than half the army was down, piteous cries of pain and terror lost in the howling maelstrom.

Those un-injured dove to the ground and pulled their dead or wounded brothers over them in a morbid attempt at shelter. But the storm was unrelenting. As if wielding clutching fingers, the wind pulled at the bodies flipping them away, exposing the living and dealing new destruction. For six full minutes the hail and wind pounded the Chalgu before passing away out over the plain. Few of the warriors crawled away unscathed and they were too shocked and weary to deal with their wounded. But this was only the first wave of death. A moment of eerie silence fell, barely enough time to take a breath, then the fallen warriors were pelted by a blinding wall of sleet that soaked them in an instant. The half frozen moisture driven by a new wave of winds washing down from the heights. With this final blow the temperature plummeted, and snow filled the air so thick it became hard to draw breath. Not that it mattered. There were few lungs left to draw the air. Mercifully, those few lasted only a few minutes longer.

Mac paced along the uneven ground in half a trance, one hand hooked in a tie rope looped around the horn on Baron's saddle; the other clutching his coat to keep it closed. Over his back was slung his bow and fifteen arrows in a hide quiver. He prayed the only thing he'd need to use it on was dinner. So far, none was to be found. Thankfully, no enemy either. Rebecca rode the skeel and through silted eyes he could see Shumak, striding in his thick limbed way off to the right.

Of all the things that had happened to Shumak, the walking was the worst. Born to the saddle and used to commanding mounted troops, he was positively grumpy when they started any trek. He even grumped as he walked to the latrine! This same attitude afflicted the clansmen as well. Their skeel were status symbols as much as transport and none of them had need to walk much more than a mile in their previous lives, let alone for miles and miles on end.

They did not move in silence now. They stomped and crashed about, yelling from time to time to locate each other over the growing wind. Around them the trees creaked, clacked and groaned, and what few leaves remained on branch or stem fluttered wildly. Mac figured fallen leaves would have become a swirling nightmare had the light snow not held them down.

"Yo!" Off to the left. That would be Jehkal, walking beside his brother's mount, calling out in the approved signal. *Yo,* to signal where you were and anything else to indicate you've found a spot, and found or not, Mac was about to call a halt. His mind partially adrift to search for Saber, and partially following the black menace growing behind them.

Unknown to the troop, the hail had spent itself out on the plains, saving them from that misery, but the wind was the result of a pressure wave pushed out in advance of the towering line of clouds. As the storm approached, what it lacked in artillery, it would more than make up for with wind, moisture, and killing cold.

Another "Yo" to his right and he looked over his shoulder, startled at how fast the storm was moving. His estimate of three hours was easily cut in half, and they'd only been searching for fifteen minutes. A strong gust slapped his back, almost toppling him and pelting his body with ice crystals. Mac felt a moment of panic. This storm was a killer! He could feel it and they were woefully unprepared and nearly out of time. The call to halt was on his lips when his vision suddenly shifted!

Rebecca felt the tension on her saddle as Mac went from walking to dragged baggage. "Mac!" she yelled, pulling her animal to a halt.

Only ingrained training got the skeel to stop. Baron was acutely aware of the storm and wanted nothing more than to run. She sawed him to a standstill and leapt down to where Mac was on his knees, rope still gripped in a hand, eyes rolled up and unseeing.

Saber was insistent. His master had given an order and he'd fulfilled it. Ranging a mile ahead, he and his mate found the promised haven in a boxed canyon that terminated in a cave which was large and deep. Its' only occupants were nocturnal flyers and several ursine creatures already in the stuporus confines of hibernation. One other beast, larger than Saber, was happy to escape with its life. It fled into the forest as soon as the two cats provided a challenge inside its den!

Mac/Saber saw a major landmark at the mouth of the canyon. An outcropping of stone that rose like a spire above the canopy of trees. Easy to see if you were near, easy to miss in a storm. His vision shifted and his world reeled as the image was handed off to the female. She stood outside the cave, her gaze going from the entrance to the spire and back, giving Mac the perspective he needed once they were near. A vine covered rock wall obscured the view of the cave mouth, concealing it so effectively they could walk right past never knowing it was there. Part of his brain, that part not intent on survival, was fascinated. The incredible detail of the vision and the unbelievable intelligence of the animals defied explanation. He made mental notes then gave another simple order to the cats before he broke the connection.

Two things happened at once. Mac's eyes rolled back down and he coughed and sat up, looking around at the faces staring at him in worry and disbelief. The echo of a cat's howl echoing faintly but insistently on the wind. Mac looked to his most staunch supporter, at least as far as Saber was concerned, and said, "Sabers' found a cave!"

Niloc's eyebrows arched up. It seemed even he was still a partial skeptic. In the back of his mind Mac held to the thought, *they'll see soon enough! How many times must I lay their doubts to rest?* In the next moment the second thing happened, and he wondered if he'd get the chance to answer that question as the storm broke over them with a vengeance.

By fortune, they'd stopped in a thickly overgrown copse and that saved them in those first few moments. The wind, already howling, gusted to hurricane force. All around they heard the scream of tortured wood as tree after tree ripped from the ground or were twisted and whipped beyond their limits until they splintered. Mac felt it with the first gust! A temperature that was already approaching freezing, plummeted and with it came wind driven ice crystals that slashed at them, cutting into any exposed flesh. There were no words possible. The skeel screamed and stomped and pulled away, Rahkal's mount flipping him off then crashing off into the forest quickly disappearing in the near whiteout conditions. So loud was the wind that Rahkal's cry of pain was swallowed, his mouth moving as if in mime.

Mac rolled to his belly and pulled his coat around him, covering his head with hands that now bore the brunt of the speeding ice. In seconds they were numb and he no longer felt the sting of a hundred tiny cuts. A thump he never heard rumbled through the ground as a hundred year old tree crashed down beside them, scattering its broken branches in every direction like shrapnel, mercifully missing everyone.

A nightmare could never have created such a storm as the wave of bitter cold drove snow and anything loose as fast as missiles. If it went on much longer they would die of exposure, but it would be suicide to rise and flee. Mac huddled miserably in his small cocoon as the snow piled up around him, drifting against anything which would hold it. Pushing his head up just far enough to look out from under his cover of fur, he was rewarded with a virtual whiteout, seeing nothing beyond three feet. His hands were blue and his body was quickly loosing what little heat it contained. Shivering uncontrollably, he could stand no more. Despair fell upon him in that moment and Mac, the one they looked to for strength, the one they called Drakil, almost gave up. Then the first wave of the storm passed.

An eerie almost silence greeted them as the wave passed up the canyon, the wind dying to a few miles an hour. They could hear the front as it flowed away. Mac quickly pushed himself off the ground. "Everyone up! Anyone hurt?" he yelled out, even though his greatest desire was to collapse. *Don't let them wallow in their pains. Give them purpose and don't let them think too much about dying!* Sage words remembered from a Master Sergeant after a particularly nasty fire fight. Advice as pertinent now as it was twenty years ago and several hundred light years away.

It was a changed world he looked upon as the mounds of snow covering his friends began to move. Trees were down everywhere and at least a foot of snow had fallen, most of it piled in drifts. Shorn stood over Niloc, shivering in fear and cold and bleeding from a number of superficial lacerations. One of the wounds in his quivering flank still held the sliver of wood driven there by the wind. Baron stood beyond them behind the big tree Mac had felt fall, his saddle stripped from his back laying tangled about his legs. Mac panicked!

"Rebecca!" he yelled. A moan and the mound of snow nearest him cracked, and like a new hatchling, she pulled herself from the enclosing shell. He rushed to her and helped her up. "My god, Rebecca! Are you ok?"

She looked weary, cold, and scared, but she shook her head, her red locks frozen stiff where they peeked from under the fur cap. "I'm fine, Mac."

She saw his look. "Really! I'm fine. What about the others?"

One by one they emerged into the dimly lit forest. Demitri and Sue together in a huddle. Shumak emerged like a lizard god and grabbed a great handful of snow, hurling it skyward as if that gesture alone could still the clouds which boiled above.

Cam startled Mac with a hand to the shoulder, Den'al right behind. "Everyone accounted for. But Rahkal took a bad fall and re-opened his wound. His skeels' gone too."

Rebecca gasped and pushed past them, rushing to where Jehkal knelt over his brother, her feet compacting the snow with a rubbing sound as the stepped through it. Mac and Cam on her heals.

Rahkal grinned up at them, smiling through his pain. Perhaps just happy to be alive. It was a shocking scene around him with crimson splashes and a bright red puddle staining the virgin snow. Rebecca quickly pulled back his coat and cursed. Most of the stitches had popped and blood flowed freely.

"Damn! I have to re-stitch it. Get my pack from Baron."

She looked up because Mac hadn't moved. "No time, Rebecca! We have to go. And now!"

"But..!"

He looked at her and shook his head, "No! Pack it with cloth and tie it off. We'll fix it in the cave."

Her eyes flashed and her anger slashed him with more force than the wind driven ice a moment before. "What cave? He could bleed to death before we find some damn cave. We need to make camp. Here! Now! Before anything else happens."

The others watched the exchange. Expectant. It was in English, but the anger transcended the language barrier. Mac paused only a moment. He could take the consoling or conciliatory approach, but he looked to the sky and saw they had no time. The clouds promised more of the same, or possibly worse, and the wind was already beginning to rebuild. Mac didn't take the time to explain. He did what commanders do, despite the personal cost! He commanded.

"Bind it like I said and be ready to move in five minutes!" He turned away so she would have no chance to argue, but heard the muttered "bastard" anyway. *So be it,* he thought.

"Everyone up. Lets go!" He called back to Jehkal, "Put your brother on Baron as soon as she's done!" Mac didn't hear a response, just assumed the man would do as he was told.

The other two skeel were gone, and like the old times, they were left with Shorn and Baron as their only mounts.

"We have to go. Now!" He snapped again.

"Where?"

"Which way?"

"Let's build a shelter here and start a fire!"

Mac had no time for questions or arguments. "No!" He yelled it now with all his anger behind it. "Listen to me! We will not stay here. I know none of you believe me, but Saber has found us shelter. We go. Now! If we stay here we die."

As if to punctuate the statement, the wind gusted through the trees, rebuilding its strength and carrying more snow to throw at them.

It was Cam who grabbed the reins that dangled to the ground, grabbed the saddle from under Baron and drug the beast over to Rahkal. As he passed Mac he spoke under his breath. "I hope to hell you know what you're doing."

Mac sighed and shook his head. *I do too!*

In short order they were done. Rahkal was bandaged, mounted and tied in. Rebecca, pointedly ignoring Mac, stood by them taking up position beside the wounded man. Niloc led Shorn and the rest waited on Mac. The question obvious in their eyes. What now? Or where now? And how far? Mac closed his eyes and prayed, then pressed them even tighter and called, *Saber?*

Saber stood and stretched, pulling himself from under the pile of blow down trees where he sheltered. The worst of the storm passed and silently he backtracked toward his master. He was perhaps three hundred yards away when the call came. The big cat laid back his head and screamed!

Mac tried to contain his grin as his eyes popped open. Self-satisfying as it was, he simply pointed toward the cry. Even as faint as it was in the wind they could recognize Saber. "Let's go!"

Mac pushed through the underbrush, breaking a trail. His feet were soaked and the cold was really beginning to sink in, but Rahkal had the worst of it. He could only sit in his saddle and huddle against the body of the skeel, every bounce causing him to grit his teeth in pain. The others trudged along. Some in misery, some in disgust, some in both.

Mac looked about the snow covered scape. Nothing moved but the trees swaying and the brush whipping. No birds or small animals. They knew! They new what was coming and had already gone to ground. Or died! Mac took this as a sign and pushed on even faster. So intent on his trail that he jumped and yelped when Saber rose up out of the brush only a few feet away. He recovered quickly, smiled, and grabbed the big cat around the neck scrubbing his head with a hand.

"Good boy, Saber. Good boy!" The cat purred and reveled in the attention and would have lain down and rolled over for a belly scratch, but Mac stood, pointed and commanded, "Go!"

Saber, sprang up and ran out twenty feet until he was almost invisible in the growing storm, then looked back to make sure his master followed. Mac mouthed a, "Holy shit!" Saber was taking them ninety degrees from where Mac had been leading them. If Saber hadn't shown up, they'd have strayed off, searching in futility until they simply couldn't go on. With new determination he set the pace. Mac kept the cat in his vision and looked back every few steps to make sure he could see Cam who was next in line. For a few minutes he could see the others, then the storm grew in intensity obscuring them to the point he could only have faith.

Around them the world became white! Mac squinted against the color, not bright, but swirling to the point of making him dizzy. The wind was a physical assault as it pushed and pulled and beat against him, the cold making every move a hundred times harder than it should. Freezing wind stole the breath as he pushed on, Cam's hand in his. He'd stopped a moment ago and reached out to his friend to make a human chain and prayed the others had done the same as speech was impossible! The wind was now constant and, though not a fraction of the first wave, it stripped the words as they left the mouth.

His world became internal. His thoughts beginning to drift. *I told them so! If we'd stayed we'd be dead! I told them so. Where's Saber? Oh, yes. By that tree looking back. Is Cam still with me? I don't know. Can't feel my hand. How far? I hope Rebecca's ok. What's that noise?*

Without realizing it, Mac had stepped into the lea of a rock-outcropping where the storm was partially blocked. What he heard was the lessoning of the wind and the sound of thunder in the distance. A sound that had been growing unheard over the raging wind. He was pushing two feet of loose snow with every step in his self appointed task of breaking trail, and he stumbled and fell as he trod suddenly on barren ground, his breath coming in great gasps. He felt a tug as Cam tried to pull him back to his feet and looking up he saw the tail of a cat as it disappeared into the rocks.

That shouldn't be possible. An exhausted mind tried to figure it out, but the vision just kept going on. Now he saw a face peer out of the stone. He started when Saber pulled back disappearing again, feeling the cat's insistence mentally pushing him. *Just a few more feet. A few more feet,* echoed behind his eyes. With what felt like superhuman effort, he pulled himself up and stumbled forward, almost going back to his knees. Almost! Then Cam was there, grabbing him and half carrying him around a corner into darkness and sudden silence.

Cam pulled him further in and sat him against a wall before rushing back to the entrance. The cave was freezing, but it felt swelteringly hot after braving the gale outside. Niloc was just outside, a surprised look on his face when Cam suddenly appeared. He would have walked right past because, while the entrance was large, it was around a blind turn. Shorn balked only a moment then allowed himself to be led into the darkness, more afraid to be outside than the unknown ahead. Den'al, hand in hand with Demitri who mostly carried Sue, were next. Shumak pushing in right behind. Left outside was Baron with Rahkal slumped over his shoulder, Jehkal on one side and Rebecca on the other, their frozen hands looped in frozen ropes, heads down and unseeing.

Cam rushed back into the storm and grabbed Rebecca. Taking her weight, he'd just unwrapped her hand when a bolt of lightening lit the landscape, the strike obliterating a tree only a few yards away. Baron screamed and reared, tearing the other rope from Jehkal's grip. The animal bucked in wide eyed terror as the tree burst briefly into flame. It shuddered then toppled into the snow steaming and hissing right beside the frightened beast. Rahkal, tied to the saddled, could do nothing except hold on. With a final rear and terrified scream Baron pulled away. He turned then stampeded off, bearing the helpless Rahkal into the storm; the wail of despair from Jehkal falling dead on the wind behind him.

Shumak was watching from the mouth of the cave. He flinched as the thunderclap and blinding light slapped the small boxed canyon. The unseen sides funneling and concentrating the noise, the concussion knocking snow from branches and the sound thumping and echoing in his chest. Perhaps nature sounded a challenge! Perhaps it was heroic. Shumak did not think. He saw the skeel bolt and run. He bellowed a war cry at the uncaring clouds and rushed out into the storm, chasing the fleeing skeel. The lizard man was enveloped in white and disappeared before anyone could act to stop him.

Mac heard the shout and the cry. He was just recovering his wits, his breathing slowed as his body compensated to the new surroundings thinking it now might live. He stumbled to his feet and pushed past Niloc into the blinding white beyond. He didn't know about Rahkal or Shumak, only saw Rebecca and Cam. And Jehkal kneeling in the snow, struggling as he tried to pull away from them, desperate to plunge into the storm where he would surely die! Mac yelled but they couldn't hear him. It didn't matter. Cam was easily stronger than the clansman, especially now. He struck with a fist, clubbing Jehkal on the chin. Then the earthman picked up the limp body and carried him inside. Rebecca was on his heals, falling into Mac as she entered the cave, crying and spent. All of them, to a man, or woman, collapsed, too staggered, shocked and weary to speak. Except for Jehkal who lay partially stunned by the blow, muttering over and over, "Rahkal... Rahkal..."

Mac looked around the gloom. Only ten minutes had passed since they made it inside, and where they should have been thankful for their survival, they only mourned. Niloc stood by the entrance watching the storm. Rebecca sat beside him and the rest were dimly seen, though they were only a few feet away. Exhausted and disheartened, Mac probably more so than any but Jehkal. He'd saved them, but the cost was great. Setting that thought aside for a moment he concentrated on the cave, his brain needing something to focus on as it came out of shock.

Mac had no idea how big the place was or what may be in it. Shorn was convinced they were not alone, stamping his feet and rumbling in his throat to warn the darkness. Saber was there, back in that same darkness. Mac could feel him! And her. Both cats huddled together, each cleaning the others pelt while ignoring the rest of the world. Mac couldn't see them, not that it mattered, they were there. He could smell them. And he could smell other creatures. The musky urine smell of wild animals was thick. He wondered if they hid back in corners waiting to pounce, or trembling in fear! The latter he thought. If Saber and his friend were in here, it was certainly fear. And if Saber was unconcerned, so was Mac.

Fire! Mac's adrenaline heat was fading fast and he recognized the deep bone chill that would shortly have him and the others quivering with more than cold. His mind was back and firmly in control, practicality overcoming his grief. Getting to his knees he searched around the floor. Maybe there was a nest or something! Some wood?

"What?" Rebecca's voice sounded wearily behind him. "What, Mac?"

"Fire," he croaked. "We need a fire."

He heard the shuffle around him as the others recognized his words and soon everyone but Jehkal was searching. Some small dry pieces were found and gathered to the center. But much more was needed, much more before they started it with this their only dry kindling. Mac gave no order. They knew. Den'al, Niloc, and Cam silently volunteered. They would go out and brave the storm to find fuel. Cam was just heaving himself to his feet when outside they heard a bellow!

As beat as he was, Mac was the first to the entrance, stumbling outside where the wind and cold gripped him again causing his eyes to stream tears in the sudden brightness. He didn't care. There, at the cave mouth, one hand on the rock wall and one hand wrapped in the reins of a skeel, stood Shumak. Baron stood shaking behind him, Rahkal still tied to his back, his blood staining the side of the beast but his chest still moving. Miraculously, both still alive. Eager hands pulled Rahkal from the saddle carrying him inside where Jehkal cried unashamedly to see his brother. Cam pried the reins from Shumak's frozen fist and led the frightened animal into the welcoming dark as well, but not before looking into the eye of the serpent and nodding his head in great respect.

Demitri and Den'al helped the exhausted warrior. Shumak was spent. He'd done the impossible, fought the storm and chased down a panicked animal five times his size. And returned, having rescued Rahkal! Why? Of course this was a question even Shumak couldn't answer. These beings around him were important to Mac, and Mac was important to Shumak. Perhaps that was the reason? And perhaps the reason was much deeper.

Chapter 12

The storm was a freak of nature, yet also a product of nature and as such, nature had a way of dealing with it. The very forces that stirred it into existence now worked to kill it. A monster half a continent long, but as thin as a snake; only thirty miles thick at its widest the super charged energy could not last. The further it progressed the weaker it became until it was merely and bad snow storm as it passed over Altil and his tent. A low pressure system from the great desert was sucked southward and it slammed into the front which had weakened considerably. The warm air pushed up over the cold and broke its back. But even then it caused catastrophic damage in many isolated areas. Water spouts and tornados ripped across the landscape and thunderstorms raged as wild as mini-hurricanes. For Mac and crew the worst had passed even as they found shelter, though they could hardly tell as it continued to rage outside. An hour later it became more apparent. The snow turning to sleet then rain, the warm water washing the snow away in rushing torrents.

Snug in their shelter, they watched as the drifts became rivulets and the rivulets rushing streams almost as treacherous as the cold and snow earlier in the day. An amazing turn in the weather. A typical fall morning which had turned into hell and by mid afternoon was back to nothing more than a very wet late fall day. The biggest question and concern now was just how long the torrent would last and what might come next?

A fire burned hot to feed their spirits and fresh meat slow roasted over the coals to feed their bodies. Saber had once again provided beyond their hopes. The cave had been occupied after all. Mac felt a moment's guilt at having to slit the throats of lethargic beasts which had sheltered here, seemingly in safety for their long winter slumber. Guilt notwithstanding, they sure smelled good as they cooked. Three of the carcasses lay spread over fires filling the cave with a smoky delicious aroma. Enough meat to feed them for a week or more.

Mac stood alone in the back of the cave at the edge of the light. Night was falling and Saber and his friend had fled into the evening to do what cats do. Certainly they weren't hungry. They'd stopped outside to gulp down the viscera of the dead animals before running off. Mac could feel them, envying their ability to run free. A freedom he desperately wished for. To be on his own, without responsibilities and without the lives of these people he held in his hands. That's how he saw it. They were a fragile group held together by him and him alone. Yes, they were all capable and some, Shumak and the clansmen, could survive without him. But they could not survive together! Not without him as the catalyst.

He sighed as he watched the dual fires. Funny in a way. Shumak was now accepted as one of them. He sat talking quietly with Jehkal and Den'al, the wounded Rahkal sleeping peacefully beside them. In the clan way, Jehkal exclaimed long and proudly of his new *brother!* Detailing Shumak's exploits in an almost poetic manner, surely to forever live in the lore of the Paliece. Shumak seemed amused to be an honorary clansmen and Mac was more than mildly surprised at how gracefully he took it. But the lizard stopped short of allowing Jehkal to gift him. His pride would simply not allow the tying of one of Jehkal's hair ribbons around his wrist. "No!" he had stated flatly. That had been a tense moment. Jehkal would have taken great offence had the refusal been complete. Shumak had the sense to understand this and even better sense to not refuse completely. The ribbon was now tied on in the lizards pack, and to him it was probably akin to a scalp! Mac smiled at the double meaning. *Yes!* They would not be fast friends, but they could be cordial adversaries.

The other circle of fire contained his human friends and Niloc. Another group brought even closer by the trials of survival. Yes, most certainly the group had come together. With one exception and that was Mac himself! The events of the day changed everything. He was now the odd man out. The Drakil. The Commander. The keeper of the cats!

It was a subtle change with some, namely Cam, Demitri and Sue. With them came more deference, and a lot more looks out of the corner of the eye. It was more obvious with the Paliece. They practically fell over themselves if he approached. Even Shumak looked at him in wonder, more so in the presence of the cats. Only Niloc was unchanged. After all Mac was the Drakil!

His sigh was heavier as he watched Rebecca. With her it became… complicated! She apologized of course. Not because she was wrong, but because she hadn't truly believed and the proof made Mac so much more. So much different! In her eyes he'd been her partner, her potential lover and mate. *Now?* he thought. He had no idea. He'd rebuked her. Commanded her and ordered her, and despite her best judgment, she'd obeyed. Yes she'd apologized, but the apology was as cold as the wind outside, or the backside of the moon. Only time would tell if it truly healed all wounds. His heart ached but he would leave it be and perhaps time would.

Mac let them debate! Late the next morning, with clear sky all around and nothing but dripping plants, a cold breeze and thoroughly washed gullies to show the storm had ever been, brought a sense of complacency. They sat outside in the sun and relaxed, discussing a favorite subject. What to do next? Follow through with the original plan, or stay here. He let them talk, only half listening. Laughing to himself he said, *in a bit I'll bequeath upon them my pronouncement.*

Looking down the canyon he decided his first assessment of the storm fell short. There was more to show of its destructive force. Much more! From where he stood he could see out over the forest and several miles toward the great escarpment. Up there the snow still held. Like icing on a cake it covered the rocks. Looking closer, he shook his head wondering at the great force of nature they'd barely survived. Awesome really. He shouldn't be able to see the escarpment, nor the mountains beyond. Huge trees, freshly uprooted lay like ten pins, completely flat as if one great gust had thrown them aside. Their roots, with earth still clinging to them, thrust like dirty fingers toward the sky. Looking further and saw even more devastation. Whole swaths of forest lay in tumbled heaps. *How did we survive that? How could anything?* Yet even as he watched he saw alien birds soaring in the distance and one of the ugly squirrels leaping from limb to limb. How indeed!

A small silence impinged upon his musing. The debate had run its course, at least this portion of it. The talk had fallen to small muttering. Expectant. He let them stew in it a while. He knew what he wanted to do. Knew what they needed to do. Mac had no desire to sit here stewing in this damn cave for the winter. He went through a few of the arguments. Plus side. Out of the weather, defensible with little risk, at least little that he could foresee. Down side? Food! Was there any about? Water was a half mile away. The snow could get so deep in the canyon they might not be able to get out. And it was a cave! Not a huge cave. They'd be at each others throats outside a month. *How the hell long is winter around here anyway?* The aliens told him different stories. It seemed everything depended. Depended on the length of the winter fur on the back of a skeel. Depended on how deep you had to dig to pull a Parth from its den. Whether a shaman's bones creaked in the fall or ached in the spring. Depended on the color of the third moon. A moon that no longer existed! *Hell, it probably depended on how many lice you could pick off Shumak's ass!* That last visual caused him to sputter out a laugh he couldn't quite hold in, covering it with a hand as he looked at them. He hadn't been listening so had no idea the group consensus. No matter. *I'm the all powerful OZ for god's sake!* Sputtering again he coughed and looked at Rebecca. Their nurse and doctor.

His answer was a question to her. "Can Rahkal ride tomorrow?"

Watching their eyes he saw some relieve, some disappointment and Rebecca's flashing anger. His mirth died. She didn't answer right away, judging his seriousness and forming her response. Her tone was bitter and it cut him! "It would be better in a week."

The others looked away, uncomfortable. Was this the way it was to be? A constant struggle between them? He kept his tone even, "That wasn't the question, Rebecca. Can he ride tomorrow?"

She looked ready to lash out. The last refuge for her pain was Rahkal! He at least, was in her control. He was the one who needed her. "It may not kill him."

Mac just stared at her, ignoring the others. She shifted her eyes and after a moment said, "It will hurt him, certainly… but he can ride."

"Thank you!" he said as gently as he could. "Tomorrow we go."

He looked at the others. They already knew the risks and the drill. Two skeel. One to carry supplies and one to carry Rahkal. Each of them would carry their weapons and personal items, mostly along the lines of extra cloths. The meat would be smoked by then and water was not a problem, there was plenty along the way. They would be fine. If only the weather cooperated. If only it wasn't too far. If only they could find the damn place. He sighed, but only to himself, *If only!*

One thing they would surely do was mark their trail back here to the cave. Should anything happen, should they be separated and lost, they would meet back here. That simple fact. Having a haven to run too made the trip less daunting, and in reality, they each knew they couldn't wait. Not a week. If the decision was to go, they had to go before real winter set in. These were the same factors and feelings they'd faced only two days ago the night before the storm. So much was the same. Then he looked at Rebecca and realized so much was different.

A few miles away, in a cave very similar to Mac's, a dozen Chalgu huddled around their own small fire. Tomorrow, eleven would emerge and continue their mission. Today they would sit and eat and watch their comrade die. He was struck by the stem of a tree as the wind blew it past. Three inches of wood stood out from his crimson stained pale white belly. Four inches more lay inside, and, as was the nature of such wounds, it was a long and painful death. Not that this was the reason his brothers waited. Each had sustained various injuries themselves, one sporting two broken arms. They, like Mac, would lick their wounds for a day. Tomorrow they would emerge from their dark hole like puss from a festered wound to continue Altil's mission.

The Valley of the Moon was in many ways the ideal wintering ground. A stream wound its way down the center of the valley from where it welled up from a spring at the base of the escarpment. Clear, cold, and clean year round. The valley itself was a mile and a half deep, cutting into the shear wall as if it were laid open with an ax. Grassy meadows provided grass, and forest provided cover, wood and wildlife. The mouth narrowed to a quarter mile, widening as it cut back into a boxed canyon. Jumbles of rock fallen from the shear walls spread in a huge fan, providing ample cover for defense. Should that become necessary and the defenders have enough warriors. Perfect for wintering because hunting and fishing could be had in plenty just outside the mouth. It was these very details that made it ideal for life. And a death trap!

Should the entrance be invested by a foe, the only way out was a narrow trail that switch-backed up the cliff. Those lucky enough to escape would find themselves upon the Sea of Tears and discover the true reason for its name. It was miles to the next cut that allowed escape from the heights. In winter it may as well be ten thousand. Sweeping winds and sub-zero temperatures. Snow drifts covering cracks and ravines that could swallow a man whole pushed those fleeing even farther out on the Sea, until a mile became ten. Further west the lands leveled, and this is where the traditional clan lands bled from summer to winter pasture. It was from the west the Chalgu pushed. The west and the north, and now even the south. The Cal'dil and the Briss'y clans were already there. This was their home. Their tradition. It was also the place of destiny. Where, unknown to them, worlds would collide. Even now other clans and many of Shumak's people were fleeing before the enemy, unwittingly headed towards that single point. The Aranu crisscrossed the land as well, though always herded that direction. Even now The One, the Drakil and his group did the same, oblivious to what they faced.

A cry from the right stopped them cold in their tracks. Mac went to a knee and stared in that direction, trying to see under tree limbs which blocked his view. He was not tense. The call was part of their agreed upon signals, and the cooing cluck of the tree squirrel only said, "Stop! I've found something." Pausing, he paused listened for more. Though they'd been on the trail for two hours, the day was new and smelled of damp fresh split wood. The sky was brilliantly clear having been washed by the storm, and cold enough that he drew his coat a little closer about him, leaving him wishing he had sun glasses as he squinted into the morning.

He sat and waited, easing the glare on his eyes by hiding them behind his lids. *Careful!* he admonished. *Don't fall asleep.* A real possibility given his fatigue. Snapping twigs off to his right announced someone's approach, though he didn't open his eyes. Instead he concentrated, trying to identify the person by his other senses. Senses more highly attuned than at any other point in his life. A small smile started at the edge of his mouth, though it would remain unseen by his stalker given the week's old growth of beard.

The fact that the person advancing had not called out told him much. Shumak, though he could move silently, could not still the wheezing hiss of his breath. Niloc would never be rude enough to sneak and the other clansmen wouldn't dare it. That left the humans. He considered as colors swirled and danced from the sun that beat upon his eyelids. *Demitri? No!* This one was too quiet. *Sue? No!* She would be Demitri's heals, the two of them making even more noise. *Rebecca?* This though brought a certain amount of pain. She was avoiding him and would have hissed or thrown a rock by this point. His 'barely' smile became a grin, "What have you found, Cam?"

"Damn! Was I that obvious?"

Mac eyes popped open, surprised at how close his friend had gotten. "Next time…" He wrinkled his nose. "Get upwind."

Cam gave him a hurt look and his own sheepish grin. "At least my roses smell better than yours."

"Maybe so, Cam. But my roses are my own and I rarely smell them anymore."

"Yeah? Well, we should all be so lucky." He gave Mac a pointed look to make sure he caught the double meaning. Which he did, but let further banter pass.

"So what have you found? Gold? A case of beer perhaps?"

"No. Not that good." He sobered a bit. "We found Rahkal's skeel."

Mac eyes widened. This was great news. They desperately needed another mount. The loss of two of the beasts in the storm was a terrible blow. Then he noticed Cam wasn't acting very happy.

"No, Mac. It's dead. Looks like it ran straight into a tree and crushed its skull. Rahkal's going to be real upset, but at least we have his weapons and his packs."

Rahkal would be very upset. As with all clansmen, he'd been very attached to an animal he'd raised from the moment it dropped from its mother. Tragic, and a terrible loss to him personally, even more so to the group. But the supplies were a boon.

Mac reached out a hand, "Help me up and let's get everyone together. We'll rest here for a few."

The others were spread out within hailing distance, moving in military order and they'd all be paused, waiting the signal to move. Mac reached to grasp the offered hand, looking up at Cam who blocked the sun, adding an almost angelic corona around his head making his features impossible to discern. Mac stared at him, stumbling slightly, then more so. Shocked as his friend's body slowly began to change.

He stared at the reaching hand as five very human fingers thickened and paled. Stared even harder at his friend's body, watching it extend and widen, his neck becoming longer, his skull growing ridges. Mac's breath caught. Against the broader body, two more arms rose into the bright sky, a long spear grasped in each three clawed fist. He saw this as a hideous outline that rippled and flowed and was uncertain, as if an image overlaid reality. Then the vision before him suddenly turned as if hearing something calling in the distance. The face became visible, fully exposed to the sun. A face that was flat and pale white with prominent fleshy lips that protruded like those of a carp. This was all Mac saw, so shocked by the terrible visage he broke the connection, drawing a great gulp of air into lungs that had been too long deprived. Coughing, he looked up at Cam who was once again Cam, not a beast that looked like it had died and lay immersed for twenty years.

Cam looked down in grave concern, cursing this connection that took his friend seemingly at will. "Mac! Mac!" he called twice. "Breathe, Mac, what is it?"

Mac coughed again and shook his head. "Enemy!" he croaked, then sat up. "Make the signal, Cam! The enemy is near."

Cam's eyes widened, but he nodded, putting off his questions. He turned and trilled out a call that meant "Danger" and "Rally." Calling it again until he heard the same call float back from several directions, the sign that all had heard. Hopefully, any enemy about would think it only the trilling of a family of ground birds that had been separated and were searching for the covey.

Turning back to Mac who was now on his feet he asked, "What, Mac? Aranu?" He'd never seen this look on Mac's face before. He looked haunted.

"Not the Aranu, Cam. I don't know what the hell they are, but they got four friggin arms!"

Whatever else he was going to say was drown by the arrival of Niloc leading Shorn with Sue clinging to his back, Demitri striding next to them, a look of concern visible even under his dark beard. Despite the noise of them crashing through the forest, they maintained their discipline and didn't shout out questions. Mac merely waved them into a pseudo defensive position. He had no idea where the enemy was nor how many, he only knew they were near enough to be a concern to Saber.

Mac cursed himself. *I've got to get on top of this son of a bitch before I get us all killed!* Beating himself up about his lack of control over the connection, and with no firm information there was only one way to get it. Set everyone up to watch and defend, then try again. Saber was out there waiting, Mac could feel it.

His thoughts drifted only a moment, but long enough for the others to arrive. Last to arrive was Jehkal leading his brother on the back of Baron, Rebecca following closely one hand on a stirrup. Just as his eyes met hers she stumbled over a small blow down. His heart lurched though he remained seated and shifted his eyes to Rahkal, who proudly gripped his clav'l newly retrieved from his dead mount. Everyone now had a weapon in hand except for him, a situation he would rectify shortly feeling the comfort of the bow slung over his shoulder.

"It seems the enemy that Rahkal said is attacking the clans has found us." He said it without preamble and he watched the play of emotion, ranging from fear to grim determination. To their credit, not one asked him how he knew. They knew how.

Cam was first with questions, "How many Mac? And where?"

He steeled himself, the vision he saw still caused his heart to race. "I saw only one…" he paused. "I hope to hell there aren't many more than that."

He spent the next few moments describing the beast in his vision and watched as their fear grew, though he tried not to oversell it. He didn't want them unmanned before even sighting the enemy. But he couldn't let them off easy and just hope they never encountered the pale beasts. He knew his sighting them in the flesh without the benefit of first *seeing* them through Saber would have left him frozen in shock, and a moment's hesitation meant certain death.

"Four arms?" Sue's was incredulous; her fear was giving way to disbelief. "Maybe Saber was mistaken." She said it hoping for a reprieve from what was to come. Hoping that saying the words may change the facts.

Mac shook his head, "There is no mistake! What I described is exactly what Saber saw." He held up his hand. "No more talk!" The last statement an order. "Perimeter watch now! Den'al and Jehkal…" He pointed to positions thirty yards apart, then physically pushed Cam and Demitri into another defendable position behind a group of blow downs where he felt their bows would be the most effective.

"Niloc! Mount up and be ready." He wanted the mounted warrior and Shumak as his mobile relief. Sue and Rebecca would guard Rahkal as well as Barron and their rear. Mac couldn't pull the wounded man off his mount and replace him with one of the others. Even though it might be the best strategic move, Mac wouldn't leave him behind and that's exactly what would happen if they were forced to run.

He looked about. Everyone in place and watching. Waiting. *Good! Now back to reconnaissance.* This time on his terms. Sitting down he closed his eyes, concentrating on grounding his mind by holding firm to the earth. He dug his hand into the cold soil feeling a tingle as the sensation traveled up his arm. This would be his anchor. He called, *Saber!*

The response was immediate, and different. For the first time his awareness was in two places at once. He still felt the cold dirt and still heard the soft sounds in the clearing where his body sat. This felt *right!* If need be he thought he could actually speak to those around him and still be connected. Even more profound, he felt with certainty that this was how the connection was meant to be.

Saber, scout! His simple command was backed up by his mind sending a flood of additional instructions. *How many enemies? Where? How are they arrayed? Are they aware of us or you?* So many questions that Saber was momentarily overcome. Mac calmed himself. *Let the cat do what the cat can!* he admonished himself, yet he felt infused with power. For once he really understood the connection. Understood the possibilities. Knew he owned it!

While he waited for Saber to move to a new position he reached out to the female. Just as Saber, she answered immediately though the mind he met was less ordered, more wild. He smiled as she put up a token fight. He pushed harder and just as suddenly she submitted. She was his.

She was moving, crawling through the undergrowth and he could see little beyond her nose. Mentally he switched to Saber experiencing a moment's disorientation as the thick foliage suddenly vanished. Saber was looking down into a small meadow from a perch on the limb of a tree. There in the center of the clearing stood one of the white warriors. Mac's breath caught again. They were bigger than he first thought, as big as Niloc. It was a frightening sight. Nothing on this planet, not even Shumak or the Aranu, screamed 'alien' as much as this one did. He watched awhile and saw only one.

Mac held Saber motionless as he studied the beast. Four arms, each looking uncomfortably proficient with the weapons it carried. Draped in a fur, the rest of the body was indistinguishable, but the head and face were very clear. The skin shimmered as if bathed in sweat or mucus. The flat face sported two large black disk-like eyes. Eyes that didn't seem to move in its head. Mac watched as the enemy; he called it that now, swiveled from side to side surveying its surroundings. *An advantage for us? Maybe they don't have good peripheral vision.* He looking with a scientist's eye trying to make educated assumptions and wishing Rebecca could see as well. Her training would be invaluable. It was fairly easy to make guesses when you knew the beast was a ways off. And he was certain he wouldn't trust his precious hide to uneducated assumptions should he have to go *mano-y-mano* with one.

Mac made the attempt to be clinical. Assess without emotion. That became impossible when the beast looked up and opened its mouth. Whether or not it saw Saber Mac couldn't tell. What he felt was the deep primordial hatred Saber held for this being. It was palpable and pulsing through their link. This was the first time Mac had ever *felt* any emotion from the cat.

They looked down and Mac continued his observation. No jaw to speak of, the fleshy lips simply yawned in an 'O' like some great sphincter irising open to expel a hideous breath. He had a clear view down the gaping maw and felt his gorge rise. Saber pushed back on Mac showing his own displeasure. The cat wanted to attack and only Mac's firm command held him in place. It was morbid fascination that held Mac. The mouth yawned wider and wider until Mac could have placed his arm inside with ease. Then it ceased its movement as did the beast. It seemed frozen as it stared skyward, but Mac still saw movement. Inside the mouth thousands of villi writhed and waved, seeming to pulse back and forth like the tentacles of a sea anemone in time with the surf. With a speed that was shocking, a blue tongue he had not at first seen lashed forth, swinging too and fro as it tested the air. This was the only explanation for the alien behavior he could come up with.

Saber's discontent was becoming more and more palpable, yet still Mac held him. The white beast suddenly became animated, waving its arms. Mac waited, he knew what to expect. As if they'd popped from the earth, more of the warriors appeared. They came from the bushes and from around large rocks until the small clearing held eleven, each identical to the next as if stamped by a cookie cutter from the same pale dough.

Was this it? He hoped to God it was. On a whim, he switched to the female and was rewarded by the same clearing at a lower angle and far to the right. Now he was looking up, lending the warrior a towering presence. Mac gave her a simple command and she looked to the trees. It was difficult and hard to focus, but finally he spied Saber still sitting up in his tree, wonderfully camouflaged. Mac pulled away and back to himself, leaving them with a simple command. They needed to know how far away the enemy was so he told the cats, *Come!*

Opening his eyes the brightness momentarily blinded him. The visions were in his mind not his eyes and it took a moment for the pupils to adjust to a sun so low on the horizon. Taking that moment he let the sun bath his face. It was one of those mornings when the radiation heated your skin while everything in shadow was uncomfortably cool. Especially if you were kneeling motionless as Mac had for the last few minutes. Even colder after the vision he'd just witnessed and it felt wonderful just to be alive. From his peripheral vision he watched the others as they alternated looks, watching the brush and watching him. They were very attentive and certainly on edge, more so when Saber suddenly appeared, ghosting right between Den'al and Jehkal, both giving a yelp of surprise. This brought Mac rushing to his feet.

Too soon! he thought. *Saber's here too soon. The enemy is close!* That thought became a conscious thought just as a horn pounded notes on the breeze.

Sil-casus, Oot of the Fist; roughly equivalent to a Corporal, was in command of the last ten warriors of this third finger of the Fist. A position which he'd never thought to occupy, but one he was determined to fulfill to the fullest extent of his abilities, and thus, complete the orders of the True Leader. It was he who recognized the storm for the killer it was, and it was he who found a way to survive. Though in truth, the cave had fairly opened in front of him and he almost fell in. In his pragmatic way he felt this fortuitous event simply sealed his mandate to lead. If one such as he could know pride he would be beaming it to the world because the other warriors now held him in highest regard. Yet such was the discipline of the Chalgu that if he'd walked on instead of falling into the cave the others would have followed, even to certain death. He did not, they had survived and he was now king. At least of these ten left with him.

The Chalgu emerged from the ground hungry and determined to quench that need. His greatest current fear was that they would need to resort to Re-dan. (Eat 'not' of the enemy) A sinful act while on campaign. Sinful in the eyes of the True Leader and a disgrace that would haunt his new position. Sinful, though necessary if they were to continue the Great Mission. The last of their provisions had been consumed as they huddled awaiting the end of the storm, the last of their provisions being the meatier pieces of an unfortunate Aranu female killed several days before.

Yesterday, as they emerged from the ground, no enemy presented itself. Their hunger that day went unabated, and though terrible, they still had not gone Re-dan, for Sil-casus had a feeling. An intuition. Some sense that told him the enemy, and sustenance, was very near.

Then, this very morning, the dawn winds brought him confirmation. He'd raised his head to the sky, opened his mouth and let the breeze tell its story. The nose slits on a Chalgu were little more than ornamentation. What air passed through them served only as an anti-siphon to the larger orifice below. Chalgu were creatures of taste. The millions of molecules wafting by on the breeze told Sil-casus many things. It told him winter neared and that a new yet smaller storm would strike in a day. It told him of trees and bushes moving toward their dormant winter state and the death of the grasses. The breeze gave him the position of numerous small creatures which mistakenly thought their silence could hide them. He tasted the insects that crawled in the dead leaves and detritus beneath his feet. But mostly he tasted the enemy!

His eyes glowed, knowing battle and death were near. Sil-casus knew no fear. It was not a trait the Chalgu possessed in great abundance. No, there was no fear, but there was confusion. He'd fought the Aranu, though he didn't know them by that name. He tasted none here. A good thing as he'd developed a serious dislike of their filthy, stringy, puss ridden flesh. He'd fought the clans and tasted the flesh of the People, having partaken of one at the last gathering. Both species he tasted on the wind and that in itself was curious and confusing. Had they joined forces? Did they now fight together? Something to note in his report. But there was something more.

He tasted the cats and dismissed them. A pair of scavengers hanging about to feed upon the carrion and offal of war. They were of no consequence. He tasted the skeel! These fought alongside the warriors of the clans and were to be respected. Of these he would be wary. He counted as he tasted each individual, knowing now exactly how many he faced. Knew one was wounded, tasting the crusting blood and the tinge of decay. This was one less to fight, it would die easily.

Sil-casus assessed his knowledge of the different races and how they fought. How formidable they were individually or in groups. He catalogued and planed. All of this in the few breaths that passed through him. Yet it was these same breaths that caught in his throat. Something new was in the air. It was this taste that caused him to shiver in excitement. A taste he'd never experienced! A taste unique and overflowing with life and intelligence, and something more. His heart flipped and raced because the Ooot of the Fist knew he'd found The One! Sil-casus raised his snout to the sky, drew a deep draught of air then sounded the call to war!

Mac had little time to plan. The enemy was moving closer with every passing moment and every instinct told him they must stand and fight. They could not flee in this tangled mess with only two skeel, and running from these creatures would be short lived. Quickly he described the disposition of the enemy, noting only a few more details and the number they faced. They nodded with steel determination. If it was to be a fight they would stand. Satisfied with what he saw he nodded then quickly set the order of battle as more horns sounded on the wind.

Despite his joy and the certitude of having found the one, Sil-casus was still Oot of the Fist now raised to Commander of this small force. They didn't charge pell-mell, they advanced. Ordered and in discipline as befitted the Chalgu. Two in front as scouts and two out wide as flankers, he himself carrying the center of the line. Only briefly did he consider sending one of his fighters back to the host to report the finding, rejecting the idea. Altil would connect with him soon enough anyway. The True Leader mentally calling every two turns of the sun in his search for how fared his far flung army. Sil-casus had only one more warrior than the enemy, and though he had no doubt of the outcome, it never hurt to command a superior force. Besides, it would now be his glory to deliver the head of The One to the True Leader. He wanted no advanced warning making its way to Altil just to have some upstart Oot-alta, who'd never tasted real combat, could steal his prize and claim the never ending rewards promised to the taker of The One! No. This was his time. He sounded the advance. As one, his Fist moved toward destiny.

A hundred yards away Mac could hear the crashing of heavy feet as the white warriors pushed and hacked their way through the thick foliage. He'd moved his own fighters to the back of the clearing ensuring a clear field of fire and room for his heavies to maneuver. They were using it all. Bows, Calvary, heavy foot and shock troops, every trick he could think of as they prepared to give battle with no quarter. None of the enemy could escape to bring back more.

A gasp of fear to his right as Rebecca spotted movement. Staring hard he was rewarded with his first *real* look at what they faced. Only forty yards away and pushing under the limbs of a low evergreen came the first corpse white beast with four arms.

Sil-casus saw his far right scout stop, then motion. He was close to the enemy. Hand signals allowed Sil-casus to adjust his line then he hooted the order to move forward. Noise was not an issue. The enemy knew they were there and had chosen to stand and fight. *Too bad for them,* he thought. His only concern was the heavy undergrowth and blow downs which hampered the beauty of his straight line, no real problem though it did deal a small blow to his pride. Had he been a more seasoned Commander, he would have worried less about this small detail and more about what lay ahead. What he lacked in seasoning he made up for in confidence.

In moments they would be in spear range of the unseen enemy and no other race could best the Chalgu one-on-one. His pride and training and recent experience would allow no other thought and his dual hearts beat faster in anticipation. Soon his eyes would behold what the army sought! His scout held position and waited as the line closed and came even. Then, with a final push between two trees, Sil-casus stepped out and into the clearing to see exactly the enemy he faced, and the true mien of The One.

Mac watched the first warrior, obviously a scout, stop and motion behind him with one of his arms. The lower right he noted, which released its spear to make the signal. He growled an order to 'hold' when both Shumak and Jehkal moved forward to engage. Mac wanted the whole short dozen in sight if possible. They needed maximum shock in their first attack. Right now, the only shock was on the faces of his friends, and rightly so. His own mind was having trouble accepting the physiology of the creature. The head and face were enough to cause nightmares, but the lower torso, with its extra arms screamed alien! And wrong! He caught himself wondering how a joint like that could possibly work. Yet the beast was undeniable. It stood there in the flesh.

Even more flesh than in his vision. The beast had cast off its clothing making the sight that much more repugnant in its nakedness. It made the skin crawl even though he knew what to expect. The others were deeply shocked as well. Ready to lash out in fear or break and run. Either event would prove their undoing.

"Steady now!" he said. "It's just a target. Aim for the center. Put an arrow or sword in it and it will die just like the Aranu." He kept his voice calm yet loud enough to break their panic.

"Remember the plan. Wait for the rest." He talked in simple clipped sentences to hold their attention and it seemed to work. Fortunately they didn't have long to wait. Like puss extruded from the skin, eight more emerged from the trees, advancing in a line. Even though he knew there should be two more, he could wait no longer.

Mac shouted, "Now!"

Sil-casus heard the shouts and noise of a language he did not know, though he recognized the sounds as words, instinctively knowing what they meant. Orders! He braced himself for the first real test of his own command, preparing to hoot an order to charge. By plan, they would race to within a two spear lengths, raise shields and hurl the weapons. The Chalgu would not wait for the spears to strike. They would rush as a single mass into the pitiful creatures beyond. In his Commanders eye, only the big lizard and the two mounted on their beasts where a real threat and as such they would be first targeted. Or would have, had his plan survived first contact.

His rational mind, the part not immersed in battle rage, paused in curious wonder at the weapons wielded by the some of the warriors he faced. Those like The One. He gave them this mark because the race was so much different than any he knew, though which one actually was The One, he could but guess. Though, if he must wager his life, the wager would be the on one who shouted orders. It was this beings weapon that Sil-casus watched, and on which the life he'd just wagered would be won or lost. A thin stick held in its middle by a puny fist, with an even smaller piece of wood held as a cross. If his mouth had been designed to laugh, Sil-casus would have let it roll in mirth.

Quickly he crossed the clearing, almost to the designated two spear lengths and prepared to throw his spear, arm muscles bunching, the feel of wood heavy and secure in his fist. His eyes furrowed in question as his target bent its weapon into a curve, then watched amazed as the stick suddenly snapped back straight.

He and his warriors were so close they saw only a flash of black as the bows released. A scream to his right pulled him to a stop, stunned to see three of his warriors writhing on the ground with small shafts of wood buried in their flesh and scarlet blood pumping from the wounds. Screaming a warning to the rest he called for shields, but it was already too late. In that fateful moment his line was broken, his order drown by the roar of the enemy.

Faster than he could believe another volley of shafts winged in. Sil-casus felt the wind as a shaft whizzed past his face as well as a heavy smack as another buried itself in his shield. The force of the blow knocking him back a full step. Another of his warriors was down, a fifth hobbling on a leg now hampered by the two feet of feathered wood protruding from his knee. He had little time to stew in his shock as the enemy released its' third wave.

"Niloc! Jehkal! Shumak!" Mac yelled the names, but there was no need. The three had started their charge as soon as the second flight of arrows were in the air, Shumak easily keeping pace with the skeel. Only four of the enemy warriors were on their feet and one of them wounded. Each picked a target as they bore into them. Though the Chalgu were shocked and confused, they were still warriors and it was four against three.

Niloc was on the far left and first to engage. His opponent crouched and extended a spear over its shield now held to front. Its free arm was swinging a sword over its head in a sweeping arc making a compact and deadly target the likes of which the Sar-too had never before faced. Attacking straight on would mean the death of Shorn, a spear to the belly the reward of the charge. At the last moment he swerved right; a move that surprised the Chalgu which anticipated a turn to left that would have brought the clansman's sword to bear. The Chalgu spun, falling off balance in an attempt to protect himself by ducking behind his shield. Niloc gambled. He leaned over, slamming his own shield into that of the enemy, snapping the beasts spear in half and nearly loosing his life in the bargain.

He'd dealt with the spear and shield, but this was like fighting two warriors in one. The Chalgu's sword swooped in and only their bodily impact knocking the Chalgu backward saved Niloc from a vicious cut to the neck. As it was he pulled back taking a long slice under the chin that burned like fire and lent deadly purpose to his next move. Instead of breaking contact, Niloc spun Shorn into the warrior pushing the weight of the skeel down upon the Chalgu. The white warrior hooted in pain as Shorn stepped on and crushed a foot. Niloc sawed his mount to a halt and swung over and down, his body half out of the saddle, the clav'l neatly cleaving the skull. Effectively and spectacularly ending the combat.

Shumak waded straight in on his opponent, ignoring the others weapons with complete disdain. A single two handed swing of his sword sliced through the spear and the top third of the shield, sending splintered wood flying in an arc. The Chalgu, staggered by the weight of the stroke and the stunning assault, stumbled back, thus saving himself from Shumak's decapitating stroke which came back in a figure eight far quicker than the white warrior could have believed. Shumak stepped forward, pressing his attack as the enemy gave ground, confident of ending this quickly. He was stunned at how easily the Drakil and his people had killed half of the white warriors. Dismayed was more like it, and he desperately wanted part of the kill, knowing this would be a battle to tell over the roasting haunch of a Parth!

Yet his opponent had other ideas. It stepped under Shumak's next thrust and smashed the splintered shield into his ribs. It was like hitting a stone wall. The Chalgu staggered back once again, but not before parrying Shumak's return stroke as they broke. The two separated and squared off, their entire world now only a few feet in diameter. Each had taken the measure of the other. Now the gods would have their sacrifice. With a great clang they came together once again, locking swords, the Chalgu punching with his shield.

Realizing it could not win a battle of shear strength, the Chalgu rushed forward in a desperate attempt to stop the reptile, grabbing Shumak with its free hands, grasping each forearm in an iron grip in a desperate gamble to still the lizard's sword. It would prove to be his final mistake. With his arms pinned Shumak pushed forward, using his massive body as a ram then thrusting with a knee, catching the Chalgu square in the stomach. The feeling was soft and giving to Shumak. It was a hammer to the Chalgu. The rock hard bone of the lizard's knee pressed upward finding little resistance until it met and splintered the lower ribs, lifting the Chalgu up off its feet. The hideous mouth went wide as it spewed forth a rush of rancid breath and acid spittle.

Eyes forced wide in pain and shock, the white warrior knew its end was near. It clung to Shumak with desperate strength, knowing that if it disengaged the lizards' sword would take his head. Another knee to the severely bruised chest collapsed the diaphragm and numbed its fingers. Shumak violently pushed the Chalgu away. It tried to flee and fell backwards smashing flat on its back, what could only be a grimace of pain and fear on its ghastly face. It didn't have long to wait. Shumak strode forward and planted one foot on the arm that still held a sword. With a mighty overhead swing of his own weapon he cleaved the head, blood and grey matter spraying up and out in a fount as the sword carved a fissure from crown to jaw; an unknown and justified pay back for the many that had fallen under the ceremonial ax of Altil, the True Leader.

It was Jehkal's privilege to face two opponents, though as he charged he swerved Baron so the enemy was lined up one behind the other preventing them the opportunity to engage in tandem. The move was clever and calculated, allowing the skeel to fight the way it was trained. Baron, eyes wide and mouth open, screamed out his rage between his tusks. Jehkal let him have his head and the skeel took full advantage, rearing into the air and lashing out with iron hard toes. The Chalgu tried the only thing it could to stem the attack. Bracing against its shield it thrust forward its spear. Yet the shaft was held in its center and thus was inches shorter than the legs of a skeel. The impact was nothing short of spectacular. Mac would later recall it as a cloud of splintered wood and a white sack, sans weapons, flying in a backwards somersault. The warrior hit a small tree, snapped it in two then fell boneless and unmoving across a bush.

Jehkal readied himself to attack the second. That warrior was hobbling away dragging a leg hampered by an arrow through the knee. Seeing his companion so easily dealt with had taken the fight out of him and he attempted a fighting retreat. Jehkal bent to cut him down, but Baron had other ideas. The battle rage was on the beast and he rushed the fallen warrior. The humans had never seen a skeel in true battle mode and the skeel demonstrated why they should be so feared. Baron reached down and grabbed one of the Chalgu's arms in his mouth, the tusks ripping into the flesh. Mac heard the snapping of bone from thirty paces. Baron pulled the warrior from its feet and shook it like a terrier worrying a rat, the body flopping about as if none of the joints retained their connections. Then, with a further scream, Baron dashed the body against the bole of a tree where it crumpled in to a very dead heap. Only then was the skeel satisfied and willing to heed his very frustrated rider.

Sil-casus was as brave as any Chalgu ever to walk in the light of this alien sun, but he'd just seen his entire command wiped out in a matter of moments. The flash of his second in command flying past dead before he hit the ground was enough to spur him into motion. Gratefully the great beast and its warrior went thundering past missing him completely. Sil-casus took that moment and the confusion of battle to exercise discretion and retreat in a very hasty manner. He'd suddenly developed a new and more practical tactic, it was his intention to gather his two flankers and flee. Flee the wrath of The One! Had his mind been as rational as it was only a few moments earlier, it would have reminded him the wrath of Altil may in fact be far greater, but death later is always preferable to death now. He spun and waded through the trees, not daring to hoot for fear of the attention it would bring, desperately hoping his retreat went unobserved. Unfortunately for him, it wasn't!

Mac saw the flash of white as the warrior fled. He also knew the count. Three more were left. He closed his eyes and called softly, *Saber!* The connection was immediate and Mac was there watching the final play.

Sil-casus left the sound of battle behind and ghosted his way through the brush, silent as only a Chalgu could be. Ahead, to his relief, knelt one of his warriors and he cautiously waved him back the way they'd come. Just as the warrior stood Sil-casus saw a blurred flash of brown and the warrior was bowled over, disappearing into the deep scrub. Sil-casus could see nothing of the attack, but he heard! Heard the snarl and scream of a hunting cat and a terrified hoot that was suddenly and permanently cut off. Sil-casus had no idea what enemy had just attacked, his brain unable to comprehend the true answer. Instead, he knew a fear and dread he never thought to feel.

Sil-casus had seen battle. He'd killed and been wounded. None of that caused much more than a passing flutter of trepidation to his twin hearts. As did all Chalgu, he gloried in the blood. Gloried in service to the True Leader! Yet the sight of that brown flash and the screams of hunter and quarry sent an image to his hind brain, evoking a primordial terror. A dread that loosened his bowels. Wild eyed he looked for escape. He turned to his right, legs weak and shaky, his body reluctant to follow his command. It knew what his educated brain did not. To the great cats, fleeing meant prey. Not that it mattered either way. Sil-casus took another halting step and truly froze, his mind numbed by shock. Only a short spear throw away, almost hidden in the long grass, two coldly intent eyes locked with his.

Mac watched the end of Sil-casus. Saber/Mac saw the female cat take the other warrior as Saber stalked this one. Mac saw the surprised look. The shock as it locked eyes with the cat, the defeat. Like so many beasts of prey, when they realize they are about to die they simply give up. That's what he saw in this warrior. Then there was only a blur of white flesh and red blood as Saber lunged.

Sil-casus barely felt the impact as the cat sideswiped him, knocking him off balance and spinning him to the ground. But Saber was merely maneuvering around the weapons held so impotently by the Chalgu. As he passed, the cat spun and bit him in the throat, pulling him to the ground and pinning him to the turf. Even then Sil-casus felt little pain, though his throat was pierced by four inch fangs and his life's blood gushed from his severed veins. The body covering him shifted and claws dug deep into his shoulders, his throat remaining in the mouth of the cat. Sil-casus stared up at the sky, curiously clear and bright, only a few branches marring his view of forever. He felt the cat tense once more and thought, *this is it. Now I die.* Then he screamed as the true pain seared his body.

Saber bunched his muscles and with a single backwards sweep with the claws of his hind feet, ripped open the belly of Sil-casus, spilling ropes of intestine about the frost browned grass. So ended Sil-casus, Oot of the Fist, Chalgu warrior of the Army of Altil the True Leader.

Only one Chalgu warrior remained and he ran faster than ever before in his life, two of his arms, broken in the storm, flopping and ignored at his sides. Through deep brush it fled, over a small stream and into the heavier forest where he hoped to elude any pursuit. He ran for his life knowing the steep price of failure. Time became a blur to the young Chalgu as oxygen starved muscles began to slow him down. His speed diminished as did his fear. He stopped a moment and listened. Silence. The Chalgu waited. Slowly it dawned on him that he'd won. His pursuers, if there were any, had been lost. Perhaps they did not search. Did not realize he was near and thought they'd killed all who attacked.

The Chalgu knew happiness. He would live to tell the True Leader of The One. Looking around the scape his mind began to clear, planning his next move. Shelter! He needed to hide until he was sure he was safe and then he could truly escape. His path away from the battle had been familiar and he found himself near the cave that sheltered them in the storm. His shelter!

The warrior moved into the welcoming darkness, allowing the cooler air to caress his naked skin. Soon the cold would make him regret leaving his cloths behind, but not now. He could retrieve them later and it was a simple joy to realize he was safe. He moved deeper into the darkness then closed his eyes and opened his mouth to taste the sweet air. Breathed deep and drew in a billion molecules of scent. The Chalgu froze at the first bitter taste of musk, realizing suddenly he was not alone in the cave.

Fear was a simple thing compared to the terror that engulfed and froze him in place. Then Saber growled deep in his chest and the horror became liquid as hot urine spilled down his thigh. It was the last sensation the Chalgu warrior would ever feel as Saber leapt unseen from the stygian black.

Chapter 13

Two days later they were far up the valley a few miles beyond where the small group had descended the escarpment in the dark while outracing a storm. The decent felt like it was so long ago though in reality it was less than three weeks. Yet so much had happened in that small span of time. They'd met Jehkal and gathered his group, battled Aranu and lost Sartil, Den'al's brother, to an Aranu spear. Then the incredible bank of fog in which they were separated from each other, Mac and Jehkal almost succumbing to the lethal stare of a Hydral. Participated in a battle between the People and the Aranu in which they themselves were the target. The group was split in that battle, Mac and his half, barely escaping into the Rayattl. Niloc and Rebecca back into the wilderness.

Attempted to explore a drown city and found just a hint of alien technology that was beyond belief; a small glimpse into an ancient past that was so very far in the future. Then, incredibly, they were reunited, adding Shumak of the People and Jehkal's brother, as well as a mate for Saber to the ever growing clan. Things had greatly improved, until the great storm nearly killed them and a new and deadly enemy found them. An enemy which seemed to be far more organized than either the Aranu or the People. Mac still counted the latter the enemy as well, even though one of their Wilderness Commanders now called him friend. Shumak certainly didn't speak for any of his race but himself.

The battle with the Chalgu showed how dangerous his little group was, able to deal death to every one of the hideous white warriors with minimal injuries to themselves. Niloc would sport a fine new scar under his chin and Baron would be nursing a fractured toe for some time to come. Mac prayed that every encounter would have an outcome weighed that heavily in their favor.

Thinking of the skeel caused Mac to look at Baron as he picked his way down the trail, Rahkal clinging to his back. The skeel limped but seemed ok as long as running wasn't in the equation. How long could that hold?

Saber and his mate had made quick work of the last of the white warriors as it tried to sneak away from the disaster that killed ten of his brothers. Mac came across the body the next day at the mouth of a cave deeper in the forest. Or at least what was left of it. The cats ranged far after that, searching for more. Any more Aranu. Any more People and any more of the strange new enemy. None seemed to be around.

That they were very lucky none denied! Superior weapons and surprise won the day, and only the fact the enemy numbered so few allowed them their victory. Once again their bows had been decisive, a weapon that so surprised their enemies it gave an incredible advantage. This would last only as long as the enemy did not of know it and their numbers when they attacked remained small. According to Rahkal, that may change. The rumor rushing through the clan said that there was an army out there! One that was pushing the clans from their traditional haunts. Rebecca and Niloc had seen a large group of Aranu, most probably displaced by the white horde, and these would be just as deadly as any if not avoided. So the order of the day was to seek safety in numbers, and that meant the clans. As quickly as they could travel they headed for the Valley of the Moon, and hopefully to sanctuary. Not knowing how far away that truly was, and with one big obstacle standing in their way. A river they'd crossed once before that almost killed them.

Peri'ackt, Chieftain of the reptilian People, had never known such a defeat. Nor were there tales of such in their long history. His warriors were the single most formidable force on the planet. At least that was his belief, and one-on-one he may have been right. Yet the enemy was clever, and more numerous than the blades of grass in the field over which he now looked. They'd won battles against the white foe, but lost more, and now to his dismay, his warriors were on the brink of exhausted collapse, and his

People, male, female and young, were in more than just danger, they were on the brink of annihilation. The enemy had surrounded their lands and squeezed them, pushing them ever eastward. Now, pushed up against the escarpment with no escape, they would have to stand. This is what Peri'ackt feared most. That event would spell the end. He could only hope that somehow some of the outlying settlements had escaped. That they would live to carry on his race, for there would be none from these that followed him.

He looked upon the remnants of his People. A camp was setup upon the meadow, fires flickering in the gathering dusk. What lay before him held all his remaining warriors and their families. It also held families of warriors that had already fed the Chalgu war machine. The names on that list would be long and may soon include himself. With the dawn they would run again, and a rear guard would attempt to hold back the tide. Even now he could hear the echoing hoots and eerie whistles of the Chalgu warriors as they settled into to their own camp. Calls that would continue throughout the night just to keep them unsettled.

Why? he asked himself once again. *Why did they not finish it?* He knew they could. The People were done, ready to collapse. If he were the enemy commander he would finish it now, tonight. Instead, they were being herded. They had been for two days. It was a puzzle his mind could not fathom. The push was renewed after the great storm had passed, and Peri'ackt racked his brain, trying to find some way to use this fault in the enemy's strategy to allow them escape.

The Chalgu Commander did have reason not to press Peri'ackt, to not finish what he so desperately wanted to finish. The People had proved far fiercer than he could have believed. Yet that was not the reason. His army and its many fists and fingers had attacked and battled the filthy Aranu. They had lost many warriors to the clans, and more to the People. Yet this was not the reason. The army battled hunger when no enemy was to be found. Had survived storms and heat and the privation of almost a full season on campaign, yet this was not the reason. The reason this curious and frustrating strategy was none other than the True Leader himself.

Word had come from Altil that The One was indeed inside their net! That 'word' had come in the form of a mind command given to each and every member of the host. Altil, by right of being the True Leader, had the ability to mind-speak with any individual directly or entire group of his choosing. Though in truth, it was painful for the object of that communication and the Commander's mind still echoed with Altil's last words.

Somehow Altil knew their target was within their reach. Was The One over that rise in the camp beyond? Could the Commander deliver the head to Altil? Perhaps he could. But he would not be allowed that glory for the True Leader had changed his mind. No longer was The One to be killed. If at all possible, that entity, whatever his race, was to be captured alive. Why? Altil had not said and the Commander would not ask. His life was far more dear to him than questioning a bad order. Especially an order from Altil who, it was said, was touched by god. He shuddered once more. "If at all possible" was the order, seemingly giving some leeway in the execution of the capture of their target. In reality it meant, should he fail, execution would be the best possible outcome for him and those under his command. Not for the first time did the Commander long for the comforting warmth of his nest so far away, and prayed he'd actually live to see it again. Nor would it be the last.

Soft flakes of snow fell gently though sparsely across the landscape. Low thick clouds lent a twilight tranquility to the early afternoon and with the air this calm, the flakes could be heard as they touched a leaf or hissed into the water flowing silently past the small patch of beach. Another day had passed under their feet as they first came upon, then skirted the river, watching for a myriad of dangers and the break in the escarpment face which would signal the Valley of the Moon. The river was in front of them and the rock face stood implacable in the distance, flat and shear with no break to be seen. And danger was close at hand: It was Tawnee that warned them.

The female cat that had attached herself to Saber and subsequently to Mac, though he was unsure which attachment was stronger, had to have a name. It was Sue that picked it, likening the name to the female's beautiful tan/brown coat. Even more important, after the naming, Mac found it easier to mentally switch between the two cats and could now call her directly. Using her name he could connect to her just as effectively as Saber, so it stuck, and it was her warning that drove them from the higher ground to the river. A warning that came suddenly as Mac, striding along beside Baron, suddenly stopped with the vision of a host of Aranu marching directly at them.

Tawnee shadowed the Aranu as Saber, screaming out defiance, attempted to push or lure them away. Meanwhile, Niloc and Shorn blazed a trail straight to the river and so far they had escaped the notice of the greasy hide covered enemy. Had they known it, they may have been surprised because these Aranu had no interest in them whatsoever. Pursued by the larger enemy, they were hell bent on escape. But such random events can have far reaching consequences. Some might even argue preordained. And the move to the river may prove to be a godsend. Or a trap!

At the river they found a ford of sorts solving their need to swim the wide expanse of cold water. None of them relished the thought of braving the deep waters like they had when the Aranu first chased them across so many weeks ago. That move came close to killing them and the water was even colder now, evidenced by the rime of ice along the shore and the random chunk ice floating by. Mac guessed two hundred yards to the other side. *How deep?* A big and unknown question, though they could see shallows riffling the water here and there almost like stepping stones. It was the darker slower water between that caused them pause, that and the sharp eyes of Cam.

"I swear it, Mac! Something's over there. I saw movement… around that big rock. Just to the right of those three trees that look like a 'W'." His whisper was harsh and he pointed as if Mac could tell one big rock and three trees from all hundreds of others.

He talks like I won't believe him! Mac sighed. The group seemed to think that if the *visions* didn't come from the cats, he wouldn't believe them. Narrow minded thinking like that could lead to disaster and Mac recognized fully that it was his fault. Part of it was his continued strained relationship with Rebecca, and part was his exploration through the cats. As a result, he'd turned inward toward Saber and Tawnee and away from his friends. A fault he would have to correct, and soon.

Since they were in heavy cover it took a good bit of describing, but finally Mac zeroed in on the area that Cam pointed at. More than a little difficult to see, given two hundred yards and equally thick cover on the other side. He was grateful for their own thick cover and the fact they hadn't simply blundered in and exposed themselves. Equally amazed at Cam's eyesight, thus just a bit skeptical. Not that he'd actually seen something, just that he could have. What could it be? An alien bird? Deer-like animal? It paid to be cautious, but the Aranu were still out there somewhere behind them. Maybe there was something or someone over there on the other side. If Mac were the commander of an army guarding the ford, he would have posted someone just where Cam said he saw the movement. An early warning and easy ambush or defense against anyone trying to cross.

Remaining silent he stared, not just at the spot Cam pointed to either. He allowed his hunters eye to look at every potential hiding place, concentrating not on the trees or rocks, but the spaces between. He looked under and through, staring at each spot for a count of ten while searching for a line that didn't go the right way, a shape that was not quite as it should be. Cam did the same, and so far, nothing more revealed its presence.

"I know it was there," Cam was insistent.

Mac whispered back, "I think you're right!" Only to be rewarded with one of those, "You're just saying that," looks. But Cam seemed satisfied that at least he'd made his point, and Mac was glad too, if only because this gave them an excuse to rest and more carefully plan their next move. With still several hours till dark, they were cold and beat and needed to recover before attempting anything. He was fairly certain the Aranu were headed away from them and it was time to eat, rest and plan.

Nothing appeared, so after a while Mac said, "I'm going back to the others." He glanced to where his friend lay concealed in the tall grass beside him. *Good cover*, he thought.

"Can you stick it out a bit more? I'll send someone to relieve you in a half hour or so."

The man shivered, mostly from the cold, but nodded. "You know where to find me."

Mac smiled, “No heroics now. If you see something don’t go try and kill it all by yourself!” The humor was lost on the normally ebullient young pilot. Mac sobered, “Seriously, Cam. You see something, hightail it back, ok.”

The Captain merely nodded. Mac snuck slowly backwards in a full military crawl. He was almost to Cam’s foot when the man finally responded. “Bring me a chicken leg will you?” Mac smiled a second time. Cam was still Cam.

A hundred yards back from the river and you wouldn’t know the ribbon of water even existed. The thick forest changed little right down to the bank, overgrown and thick. A testament that it had never known the axe and rarely fire. But here, where he found the others, an opening held all the necessities of home. Browse for the skeel and wood to make shelter and fire. Most of which were being utilized to great advantage. It was almost a routine now. When you stopped for any length of time, you first sought then set up defensive positions, posted sentries, then created shelter, in that order. It was a thing of beauty to watch how quickly the clansmen and Shumak could put a camp together, each in a different manner and each teaching the humans their tricks along the way.

More and more they were becoming a team, their differences; race, prejudice and old wounds being put behind them. It was something to see a lizard man, a two thumbed clansman and their mad Russian working side by side or back to back, exchanging banter like old campaigners. The only sour spots in the whole scene were the lack of a fire, meager food and Rebecca!

She sat under a lean-to tending Rahkal who truly no longer required or wanted her nursing. He was getting stronger and his wound had knitted nicely with no sign of infection. Even taking short walks as they traveled, claiming it was actually more comfortable than riding as the skeel were not the smoothest of animals and his wound didn’t allow him to roll properly with the jarring gait. No, Rahkal didn’t need all of her attention, but he was certainly receiving it. *My god that woman can hold a grudge*, he thought, longing to go over and patch things up. But he could not. Not yet. That would have to wait till after they were safe.

Quickly he explained the situation. As he saw it, something 'may' be waiting on the other side, but something surely was on this side! Saber and Tawnee shadowed the Aranu who were headed down the valley and that was good. However that only solved one problem. What if? Yet there really was no 'what if'. It was absolutely certain there were other groups, either Aranu or the white enemy out there, and he had no interest in meeting any of them. One way or another they needed to cross, and here lay a ford that would make that far easier and less dangerous. Unless it was guarded!

There was only one good way to find out what was over there. "I'm going to pull the cats back and send them across to scout the far bank. We'll sit here and...." He never got the sentence out as the crashing of breaking sticks sounded behind him. They had no time to do more than jump to the side when Cam burst into the clearing.

He stood up from where he'd dove for cover. "Holy shit, Cam! What the hell are you doing? Trying to get yourself killed!" Mac was pissed but Cam didn't care, he had news.

"I told you, Mac! I told you I saw someone over there." Mac froze, a cold spike of fear replacing the adrenalin rush from a moment before. Cam had said *something* before, now it was *someone.*

Shit! He was almost afraid to ask. "What are they, Cam? Aranu?" He was already running contingencies in his head. *How do we sneak around them? Cross in the dark. How about the freezing water? Send the cats to attack or distract them? Maybe we don't try to cross and just keep going. Did the enemy spot Cam? Do they know we're here and now have us surrounded?* His mind was rushing and it took a moment for Cam's words to sink in.

"Mac! Did you hear me? I saw a clansman!"

Niloc claimed his right as first advisor to the Drakil. It would be his honor to cross the river and meet the clansman, or clansmen who watched the ford. It would be he who would announce, as he called it, "The coming of the Drakil!"

Honor? Mac thought. Niloc would be lucky if they didn't try to kill him first and interrogate the corpse after. Yet these were his people and even Jehkal was surprisingly on his side. Should the encounter come down to a fight, it would be an honor bound affair following tradition and ritual. And it would be one clansman against another no matter how many opposed him. They would first meet and circle and posture. Insulting each other extensively and loudly before any blood could be spilled, and as far as either Niloc or Jehkal knew, no state of war existed between any of the clans likely to be near the Valley of the Moon and theirs. Certainly not with Niloc's! They were all dead except for him.

With a lack of information and less experience Mac could only agree, but he wondered if the white warriors may have changed the rules. Humans got trigger happy in times of stress. What about aliens? Still, they'd proceeded with caution. Whoever they were on the other side, they didn't have bows so Niloc should be safe at shouting distance, which is exactly where Mac wanted him. In the middle of the river shouting to the far bank. Niloc bristled at that, saying it would demean the Drakil to be announced so.

Mac's eyes sharpened. "Then don't tell them I'm here!" he snapped. Which shocked Niloc enough to relent.

"So be it, my Drakil." He hung his head and crossed fists, palms in and in front of his chest in acquiescence. So it proceeded, the rest of them remained hidden but close to the bank in case Niloc needed them; Jehkal mounted on Baron ready to charge. From there they watched as the last of the Sar-Too gently eased his mount into the water and headed toward the center of the river.

Eneri, warrior of Clan Cal'dil, had watched the ford for three days with nothing to show except eternal cold and endless boredom. So agreed the other three warriors with him. Two from his own clan and one Briss'y, all assigned to watch and ordered not to return until relieved. Another three turns of the sun until the warmth of their home fires would again warm their faces. As bored as they were, they were still alert as the world around them had become most dangerous indeed. The new enemy had yet to molest the Valley of the Moon, but they were all too aware of the threat. Several other clans, or their remnants, had fled to the valley seeking its safety. It was only a matter of time before the enemy followed.

Eneri knew the white warriors had been seen on the Sea of Tears above, though many days up river from the valley. It was said they also swarmed the far side of the river as well. And several bands of Aranu, never before seen in such numbers, or with their females and young, had passed this very spot. They had not attempted the crossing, simply looking across the water before disappearing into the forest from which they'd emerged. To which Eneri was truly grateful.

It was said the white ones were pushing them and certainly it looked as if that was true. Yes! They would come and Eneri would be ready. Ready to count the numbers and flee with the information and his life. Bored and on edge, he was totally unprepared when a clansman from a tribe thought long dead strode his mount into the river.

The warrior looked ethereal. Perhaps it was his carriage; regal and commanding despite obvious months on the trail. Perhaps it was a trick of the lightly falling snow, partially obscuring the form and lending mystery. Perhaps it was his size, much bigger than most, or perhaps it was the beatific glow on his face as if he knew great power or certainty in his life. Eneri was mesmerized as the skeel carefully negotiated the shoals, each step casting droplets of water about the glassy surface of the river. Each step foaming white as the foot plunged to the depths, and the face of the warrior never once shifting after locking eyes with Eneri. Not in challenge, in expectation.

The warrior halted exactly in the center of the river and continued his piercing stare. Waiting! Eneri had little choice. Custom demanded it. Reluctantly, he stepped from hiding raising his fist in salute. "Hail warrior!" he shouted down.

There was a pause as if the Sar-Too evaluated him. Then a deep sonorous voice rolled across the water. "Hail warrior of the Cal'dil! Be not concerned for I am Niloc, last of Clan Sar-Too… and I bring with me a gift to your clan. A great gift to all clans!" He paused only a moment, not giving Eneri a chance to ask the question that was obvious, therefore un-needed.

The voice continued, booming even louder, "Behold, I bring with me the promised one of legend. I, who wandered far, was rescued from certain death by him and those that follow his banner. I watched as the Greater Kraagen was bound to him, body and mind! I was there as the serpent pledged. I bear witness to all this, and I am first of the clans in his eyes. What say you warrior of the Cal'dil? Are you ready to be seen and received by the Drakil-at'sakaal ?"

Niloc's voice was deep and full and echoing back across the water and Mac was at once surprised, embarrassed, and pissed at the bold claims. The fool was again pronouncing him savior of the world. Mac would have strangled him with his own tongue had Niloc not been sitting a hundred yards away in the middle of a river.

Whatever Mac's reaction, Eneri was truly and deeply stunned and had no idea how to react. *Was this Sar-Too mad?* He'd seen this before. For some, great tragedy or great injury sometimes caused the wits to flee the body. Sometimes the wise ones returned from their god walks touched like this. Each was to be treated with respect and honor. They could not be harmed unless they threatened harm to others. Only then could they be killed and still the act risked one's soul. Yet here was one yelling absurdities at the top of his lungs when their enemies could be anywhere! Eneri felt well within his rights to strike the fellow down, and he was just about to order his warriors to do just that when movement on the far shore stopped him cold.

Much later Eneri would sit and tell his tale to the rapt attention of any who were near, accepting many a drink as well as food and other gifts as honor for being the first. His stature in the clan was greatly increased by his stories, by the simple fortune of being in that one special place at that one special time, and even his embellishments could not do the actual event justice. This is how he told it;

"That was the day I first saw him." He would begin in soft voice, drawing his listeners close. "That was the day of days, when the Drakil was revealed to me. I sat my watch waiting to see the hoard which was said to come and sweep us away. The white warriors coming to claim the heads of all the clans. I sat and watched." He used the singular, leaving out the other members of his small band of guards as a matter of convenience, because after all, it was he who first conversed with the Drakil.

"Through the mists I saw the Sar-Too come crossing the water, moving with purpose and without caution. I hailed him and bade him stop… for he was one thought dead and I knew not what he was about." The story seemed much better if he neglected the part about his silence and confusion. "The Sar-Too of course was no ordinary warrior. How could he be and survive the death of his clan? He was a holy man, and I recognized immediately he would bring great tidings." Eneri would pause, casting his eyes about the fire and those around it. There was always a fire. He insisted on it because it caused his eyes to spark with mysterious light.

"The Sar-too proclaimed loudly and I moved to still his words for the enemy was near, yet it was then the Sar-too told me of the Drakil!" The name always brought small gasps or raised brows, and some would reach to touch him. "I, of course, listened and waited, for this was no ordinary claim. No young warriors boast." He paused for effect, staring intently at those gathered before him. Then he continued, his voice building. "And I had not long to wait. As Sar-too sat still, the Drakil sent forth to me his first sign!"

This was true. Eneri waited and said nothing that day. Mostly because he was so surprised at the incredible claim. His surprise turning to shock, fear, and dread a moment later when behind Niloc on the far shore, Shumak rose up out of the grass. He strode calmly across the river, each step throwing gouts of water until he stopped and stood next to Shorn, staring at poor Eneri with his cold reptilian eyes. Mac was angry, but he'd bowed to the inevitable thinking the best play was to back Niloc, fool that he was, up to the hilt. So he sent Shumak.

At this point in his story, Eneri had no choicc but let his audience know of his surprise and no small fright. None would have believed otherwise as most had seen the hugely muscled golden reptilian warrior up-close, though he led them to believe he would stand his ground even if it meant defending the ford against a hundred of the People.

"Of course I would not let them pass." He said this off handed, as if it were of no importance. "I would not. The warrior spoke bold words, but one sign does not a fulfillment of legend make!" Eneri's superiority began to creep back into the tale. "And the Sar-Too and his friend stood in the water and waited on my pronouncement. I let them wait as I deliberated. Finally I broke my silence. "What other signs do you have?" I ask them."

Now his embellishments had to take a new turn, for on that day poor Eneri had stood mute, his mouth hanging open in dismay, his gullet clearly visible to Niloc and Shumak. The only thing that held the two warriors from moving forward was Mac's order, because before that happened they needed an answer to the one big question. How many warriors held the ford, and would they prove friendly or hostile?

Next, Mac sent forward Den'al and Jehkal, but only to the edge of the water. Neither were mounted and he would not have them shivering in the river like drown rats, or further dishonored because they were not mounted. Though if the cold was bothering Shumak you would never have known. He was a rock, standing as a statue and ignoring the skeel that rocked slowly back and forth beside him.

The Paliece were easily recognizable to Eneri. Their dress and the colored strings in their hair leaving no doubt. This alone may have convinced him. The Paliece and the Sar-Too were certainly no friends and it would be strange indeed for these and the reptile to be as one.

"I witnessed the next sign as the Sar-Too made his pronouncement. "Behold!" he said. "The Drakil begins to gather the clans to his banner.""

Eneri smiles to the crowd. "Only two? I yell in challenge and the Sar-Too's eyes darken as if to him I have spoken heresy." There are uneasy smiles around him. All now know of Niloc, advisor to the Drakil.

Niloc himself would remember that day differently and say that Eneri had finally stood up and shown himself, but his words, far from a challenge, had been low and strangled, barely audible and far from lucid. The Sar-too was greatly angered. Eneri had neither revealed his strength in troops nor invited them to come forward. And he had not challenged! Still he held though, Mac was not done.

A hush would fall over his audience as Eneri drew himself up to tower above and over them. He always spoke with them seated because of course, Enerii was not a tall man. "It was then I first saw him." He proclaimed.

That day, the rest of the party had stepped one by one out of the thicket to stand beside the Paliece. Four humans and Rahkal.

Only Mac held back, mounted on Baron and with his final surprise at hand. Eneri and the three with him almost fled at that point. They knew of the People and they knew of the strange white warriors, but the humans were something else entirely. Even at two hundred yards they were distinctive. But it was not that which caused them panic. It was the Drakil!

"I stood and saw him come. All around was still as if the world held its breath." His voice drew down to whisper, bringing his audience closer, then it boomed forth. "There was no shout. No beating of drums or the blare of horn. The trees and bushes parted, and he simply appeared as if by the very hand of god. I knew he was The One foretold, glorious and mounted a skeel larger than any other!" Completely false as Baron is slightly smaller than Shorn.

"The Drakil stabbed me with his eyes, even across that gulf. Then plunged his mount into the river and started toward me." Eneri's voice quivered now. "He reached the Sar-Too and paused, his eyes still locked on mine. Then…" Another pause to again draw the wide eyes around him. "Then…" he whispered, bending down. With a great flourish, Eneri reached behind him and motioned as he'd seen Mac do that day, then rose to his full height, threw his eyes above the crowd and shouted. "…he called… his beasts!"

As indeed Mac had. With a wave and mental command, the two Greater Kraagen raced from cover and plunged into the water. In great leaping strides they crossed the river, disappearing again into the brush just down stream of Eneri, leaving him to wonder if he'd actually seen them, or witnessed a vision.

Then the Drakil yelled to him, "Warrior of the Cal'dil! Will you let us cross?"

Of course those simple words would not do for Eneri's story and he tended to grow it larger and bolder with each telling. But on that day he'd motioned his small company up out of their hiding places. Only their shock at the tableau displayed before them kept them in place, and they rose wild eyed searching around frantically; looking desperately for the cats. Sure that they were near! The bellows of their skeel told them so. They were right. Saber and Tawnee had already confirmed the size of the party guarding the ford and Mac was determined to cross now, even if it meant the lives of the Cal'dil and Briss'y.

By now, Eneri was suitably impressed and thoroughly cowed. Not only did they cross, he and his warriors allowed their own skeel to be used as transport across the river. This impressed his audience almost as much as the part about the cats, the Drakil's Kraagen, because a warrior never gave up his mount. Yet it was done and that afternoon, safe and dry, the Drakil and his new friends shared hot food more plentiful than they could have dreamed of, prepared as only the Cal'dil knew how, and spread with care and dignity as if for a chieftain. Mac was grateful to their hosts and felt better than he had in many days. Though he sat back and tried to ignore their hidden looks or outright stares, he was consigned to the idea they held him in awe.

Chapter 14

Mac sat in a hide covered hut surrounded by three things he'd missed in the last few weeks. Warmth, food and security, though he had second thoughts about the latter. Unsure whether the esteem the clansmen held him in offered freedom and power or cloistered servitude as some kind of religious figurehead. Whenever he appeared outside, any clansmen within sight practically prostrated themselves in awe, or stumbled over themselves in their hurry to offer service. Quite annoying really. Mac finally asked that one young warrior to be assigned to them, to guide them and see to their needs. That same young man sat across from him now, wide eyed and nervous and unsure what exactly was expected of him in his new duty. By his look, he expected at any moment to be made a human sacrifice. *Clansman sacrifice*, Mac amended, chuckling. The sound eliciting looks from those around. He closed his eyes and ignored the boy, for that's what he was, being no more than twelve, leaving the introductions to Jehkal. Sitting back with a sigh he relaxed, letting his mind put the last two days into perspective.

The morning after the meeting at the ford, Eneri sent one of his warriors, accompanied by Niloc and Jehkal, hurrying back to the Valley of The Moon. They would carry the incredible news. Mac and the others, led by Eneri, would follow at a much slower pace. Necessary with many of them being on foot. As if in procession they followed the young Cal'dil, who led them like a peacock with its chest puffed out. And it was Eneri only. He'd left his last warrior, and one of those that had come with Niloc, to guard their backs and watch the ford, and to keep him far from Eneri's his glory.

If Mac was concerned about their welcome, it was somewhat alleviated the next morning. The long two day walk promised by his guide was cut short by a beaming Niloc who arrived leading what he called, a "Chieftain's Escort." He led a train of twenty warriors representing four separate clans with empty mounts for each of them. All except Shumak of course!

The train itself was extraordinary. Evidence the world was changing, the greater war causing the fiercely independent clans to amend their traditions. While the Cal'dil and Briss'y had long wintered together, other clans be never be allowed to do more than send a few warriors to conduct trade, and that only by negotiated terms favoring the two. The white warriors now made that separation not only undesirable, but impossible. Unless the Cal'dil and Briss'y intended to kill the steady stream of refugees showing up on their doorsteps, or turn them away to the mercy of the enemy!

The Valley of The Moon was a magnate and haven for those who fled their implacable foe. A haven because it seemed out of the way, untouched and hopefully hidden. Little did they know that it retained those qualities for one reason only. That being the fact it was almost the exact center of the great ring of Chalgu armies pressing and herding The One. Even now the refugees continued to stream toward the valley, each group with a different story of defeat or horror, and each followed closely by the Chalgu.

Such was the situation in the Valley of The Moon and the reason four clans represented the escort. Cal'dil in their tanned leather coats, stained in intricate patterns each distinct and oddly beautiful. Briss'y in their earth tone patchwork which Mac saw would be excellent camouflage in almost any terrain. Then there were warriors from Clan Zith'al, with bodies squat and muscular and faces brutally tattooed. A decoration that was actually the result of scaring inflicted by acid applied in swirling patterns. Chemically altered visages which were etched then dyed in fiercely bright colors. Mac couldn't imagine the pain involved. The last of the group, to the great delight of Den'al and Rahkal, were familiar warriors with colored strings dancing in their hair. Their clan had also made it to the valley.

It was this time of great change that made impossible a necessity, only this confluence of events could push the clans together in common cause and defense. According to Niloc, the people he'd spoken with knew this to be the end of their way of life. Possibly the end of all life. He described an entire people on the ragged edge of despair. There were remnants of many shattered clans in the Valley, each living huddled in small groups with no chieftains or wise ones to guide them. Some told that they'd been separated from the rest of their tribes. Others described butchery and battle with no quarter. Only seven remained of the once proud Grouw-sul. They knew it was so, having seen the destruction of their clan much the same as Niloc had witnessed the destruction of his own. And still the refugees trickled in, with more and more stories describing the same, deepening an ever growing sense of hopeless despair.

These were the very events that prepared such fertile ground. Ready to accept when Niloc and Jehkal bore the incredible news of the Drakil. One who would deliver them from their misery! Not just the finding of the Drakil-at'sakaal , but of his eminent arrival, their tale backed up and witnessed by the warrior Eneri sent with them. Word buzzed around the valley like wildfire as hope replaced desperation. The wise men quickly cast their stones, or birds' feet and sticks, or dried Parth testicles, or whatever it was they used to help them see the future. And being truly 'wise' men, they prudently fell in line with the mood of the people. Proclaimed loudly that the one coming was indeed the Drakil.

The Clan Chiefs had little choice and bowed to the will of the soothsayers. Though they were understandably reluctant to offer sanctuary and a place of honor to one who would claim power over their people, and worse, themselves. To not do so risked civil war. There were few chiefs and their warriors were close to being outnumbered by the refugees of broken clans. They accepted the inevitable. They would embrace the Drakil and the strange group he brought, however reluctantly. It was in their thoughts, and their private council, that this Drakil may have an unfortunate accident should he prove less than he seemed, or an inconvenience.

These possibilities were in Mac's thoughts as well when they met Niloc's party. He saw their desperation and the hope in their eyes, even behind the cover of looks that pretended to be uncaring and fierce. Mac saw clearly the position he was putting the Chieftains in. That they would use him to advantage or kill them all. Had war not been in the offing it may have been different, but not now. They would do exactly as Mac would do in their position, and that's why he'd pulled Niloc to the side that day and told him they weren't going!

"My Drakil!" Niloc gasped, incredulous. "You have to come." His mind screamed, *This is the culmination of the Prophesy. The entire reason for Mac's being. He must come. It is the only way to save us!*

"Listen to me, Niloc. Listen to yourself!" How could he make his friend understand? "They're desperate. This isn't what we came for. This is a trap… not a haven. We'll go somewhere else."

For the first time since Mac had known him, Niloc bristled in anger. Not that he'd never seen the warrior angry, he'd just never had that anger directed at him.

"There is no other place, Drakil!" His voice was deep and pointed. "This is what must be. The enemy is near. The end is near!" A hint of desperation fringed the anger. "Only you can do what must be done. Only you can save us."

Mac laughed in his face. "Look at me, Niloc! Look at us." He swept a hand toward Cam and the others. "I know what you think and I can't explain why this legend seems to point at me. But I tell you this is wrong. I'm not what they hope I am. I'm not what you think I am. If we go there we will just be another group of refugees stuck in a trap."

Niloc looked stunned. "My Drakil, no! It is not as you say. The Kraagen! The lizard man!"

Mac held up his hand, trying a different track. "It doesn't matter. If I go to the valley they will expect me to save them. That means they won't try to save themselves. I can't save them, Niloc… and I won't have their blood on my hands!"

Niloc was desperate. Never in his life had he felt so helpless. Not even when he faced certain death on the lonely plains at the hands of the Aranu. That was acceptable. how a warrior should die. This was different. He'd brought the Drakil this far. Here to the brink of his destiny. He must not fail. Yet to insist? Or worse, to physically make him go? What then would be the consequence?

Mac saw it in his eyes. The internal struggle, the battle between friendship and duty and Mac would forever wonder which would have won. But in the next moment the sound of hooves thumping from a running skeel rumbled from the direction of the ford. All to soon a desperate warrior burst upon them, reigning to a stop with a gasp.

"There are Aranu at the ford!" he exclaimed, and with those simple words Mac's fate was sealed. The way out was blocked.

Four hours later they were at the entrance to the valley. Mac would never forget his first view of the haven, cresting a hill just at the edge of dusk and true dark. They were up on the slopes having pushed to the higher country to avoid the meandering river and possibly hostile eyes on the far bank. As they cleared the tree line he looked down into the cut and saw a sight that caught his breath. Several hundred campfires flickered brightly up and down the valley, making it look like a small city camped in the trees. Closer to hand were torches held high by a hundred or more fists, their owners standing in silence. Waiting. Waiting to see Mac. To see The One. He who they would believe to be the Drakil-at'sakaal !

Things moved swiftly then. They were ushered through the crowd, still in near silence, and into the center of the makeshift village then admitted to a great lodge which held the clan leaders and war council. All along the procession the people stood and stared, not daring to believe and hoping nonetheless. Many reached out, almost, but not quite touching him, and he was struck by the sight. Women held children up to see, and warriors stood stoic and unafraid. Mac found it uplifting. Here was an entire race driven to war and the brink of ruin. Chased and harassed by an implacable enemy, some seeing horrors they could never have dreamed. He'd expected them to look ragged and unkempt. They were completely the opposite. Each clan was distinctive and prideful in their presentation down to the smallest individual. This was not a beaten group. This was a people whose hope had been restored and the reason was surely not lost on him. It was Mac who was embarrassed, though he held it behind his own mask of stone. His was the ragged and disheveled group, truly looking like what they were. Desperate ship wreaked survivors, begging food and shelter, and safety. It was he that was filthy and tired, and, dare he think it; afraid.

They'd crossed through a dark forest interspersed with cooking fires, each carefully tended outside huts or tents, or lean-tos. Individuals leaning in to witness the strange and wondrous procession as they passed, yet only until their eyes fell upon Shumak. It was then they turned aside in shock and fear, hands clasped in symbols of warding. Though these were quickly replaced with silent stares, for who were they to judge. Here strode the Drakil! And though he did not look as any could have guessed, he, in their minds, had certainly arrived. Here with his warriors though few they be. Here with a sign from the legend, the serpent. Some wondered about the Greater Kraagen. They'd been told of them, but none had laid eyes upon them. Other than Eneri. And none would for now. Mac held the cats outside the valley. Partly for the safety of the people and partly because he wanted eyes where no others could see. And most importantly, because they may have need to escape.

They continued their trek in silence until the great lodge loomed out of the darkness. An actual wood building, topped with a steep pitched thatch roof, surrounded by flaming torches on tall poles and a much larger crowd. It was then he looked over his shoulder, seeing the multitude behind. It seemed everyone they passed had gathered and followed in their wake. Here they and their escort reigned to a halt surrounded by folk of every description, though held back by a ring of warriors that by look represented every clan. Each holding a clav'l, blades bared and clasped in a two thumb fist and held point up against the chest, the long blade throwing their faces into dancing shadow behind their formal salute.

Four men pushed through the ring. Each more lavishly dressed than any others in the throng, and each looking powerful in both arm and spirit. All four striding forward until they were ten paces from Mac. As one they swept swords from sheath and repeated the salute given by the honor guard. Drums pounded suddenly, flaying the silence in a great roll of thunder that startled his mount and sent a thrill down his spine. To his credit, and all of those with him, there was no over reaction to sudden moves. Not one weapon was pulled, not even Shumak's, though the reptilian warrior was hard pressed to keep his calm. The first test was passed.

One of the four took another step forward and the silence returned. He looked up and pierced them with a look. Mac saw mixed emotions pass through the man, though he couldn't pinpoint any single one. Awe? Distrust? Fear? Treachery? He would keep a careful watch on this one.

"Drakil?!" The man looked around as if questioning which one of the disheveled alien travelers could be a legend revealed. Mac simply sat and stared. He would not allow this one to put him off his guard by rising to obvious baiting. Did Mac detect a sigh? Perhaps another test passed.

The warrior locked eyes with Mac. "Drakil-at'sakaal . I am Solonar, son of Alonar, Chieftain of the far walkers and the clan known as Briss'y. I welcome you to the Valley of the Moon, the traditional lands of my people. I welcome you on behalf of all the clans represented here, and all those missing." He paused a moment as if the next sentence was difficult for him to speak. Yet he was duty bound.

"Drakil, what is ours is yours. Ask and we will give you all." His voice trailed off as his eyes were cast down. Never, in all the history of the clans, had the traditional greeting held so much meaning. For Chief Solonar, the greeting may be the end of all that he held dear.

Mac held his tongue and the eyes of the other chiefs as he considered an appropriate response. These were proud men. And were backed against a wall. Who could really know what the enemy intended? Whether it would really find them. Yet their people had just been given a gift that they themselves could not deliver; hope! Niloc and Jehkal were very convincing, and the message had not been delivered to these four exclusively. Had it been, Mac was sure this welcome would have been far different, and the swords, rather than being unsheathed in salute, may have been buried in his back. Men of power gave up that power only with great reluctance, or great struggle. *A honeyed tongue may be best,* Mac thought. As well as something to set these men at ease.

He stepped down from his mount, a move followed by everyone in his party till only the escort remained in the saddle. *Better to deal with them eye to eye,* he thought, though Mac stood taller than Solonar by at least a head. He stepped forward, followed by Niloc, Sue and Demitri, but Mac waved them back. He wanted as little intimidation as possible, and he didn't want Niloc meddling with his words.

If the Chief was at all intimidated by a strange visitor from another planet, and one proclaimed to be the center of a millennium old Prophesy, he certainly hid it well.

"Solonar, son of Alonar, Chief of all the Briss'y," he began formally. "My thanks for your kind words and warm welcome." He did not shout, but he projected his voice loud and firm so that as many of the gathered as possible could hear.

"My thanks also to the Cal'dil, and the Zith'al, and the Paliece." he said, recognizing each of the clan chiefs by their dress and station if not by name. "My thanks also to those I do not see." He said 'see' rather than give insult by lack of recognition. "I am known as Commander Macintosh Crow of the spaceship Atlantis from the planet earth!" he said, interspersing English with the clan language, making his title as long as possible and pointing to the sky as he explained, smiling to himself as many around him followed his hand to the stars, including Solonar.

"Long have we been away from our home, and long have we been on the trail chased by many enemies." Let this be the explanation for the way he looked. "And long have we searched for the safety of your valley. Your welcome gladdens the heart and we will repay you with knowledge… and in many other ways." Leave the promise open ended and not specific. "Chief of the Briss'y, if you will indulge me, I will introduce those of my own clan."

Solonar could not disallow it, though he was unsettled, afraid of what titles and powers the Drakil would bestow upon his own. Also unhappy that he had not taken that initiative himself, promoting the clans. He'd been worried he would give too much to the other chiefs, thus missed an opportunity. Solonar nodded, lips tight, hiding his gritted teeth.

Mac was trying to be as diplomatic as possible, though not knowing for certain the protocol expected, he was treading on dangerous ground. Nevertheless, if the clans were hell bent on attaching a title to him that extended some respect and protection, he wanted to insure the same pertained to all of them. The question was who first, and who last. Stepping back he stood beside Rebecca.

"Chief of the Briss'y, know Dr. Rebecca Carver. Trained as a healer with knowledge much different than that of the clans. We can learn much from each other." He did not say superior knowledge, and his choice of her first was calculated. As a female, she would be less of a threat to a male dominated society and her designation as a healer was something they would value greatly. It would be the first step to earning their keep in a very positive manner. And he was counting on her beauty that had so captivated the other clansmen, to unsettle his mind. Plus, his choice of her first was a peace offering between her and him, if only she would accept. To her credit, she held up her chin and looked the Chief in the eye, daring him to question her. He did not. Mac moved on using English only with the names.

"I would have you know my protectors. Captain Cam Mitchell, Specialist Sue Rael, and Dr. Demitri Karkov. Their weapons are fierce, as know many Aranu and white warriors. Though none we met still live" This caused a stir and a murmur of voices. Let the clans understand they had been blooded and were not afraid to kill. And they were to be feared.

"All came with me from the stars," Again the flourish of a hand toward the heavens. "And we stand together." A message that an insult or attack on one would be an attack on all.

"Chief Solonar of the Briss'y, I would have you know my brothers!" Mac would now bind himself to the clans by right of brotherhood. He moved to Niloc. Was that a look of dismay on his face, or could it be guarded approval.

"The last of the Sar-too you have met. One thought lost. Though we rescued him upon the Sea of Tears when his death was certain, cornered and surrounded by a Mord Cell!" There was a communal though subdued gasp behind him at the mention of the most elite of the Aranu warriors. "Together we honored Jamil, his dead clan brother and fought the Aranu side by side. He is first of the clans to us, and we accept his counsel." Now Niloc truly was dismayed. He'd thought his confrontation with the Drakil had terminated their relationship. Now his pride soared and his head held higher.

"See the warriors Den'al and Rahkal, warriors of the Paliece who have bathed in the blood of the white warriors as they defended me. Know also that each of us morn the true brother of Den'al. Sartil died in our service, and we honor his bravery and true duty." There were many mysteries and stories to tell and Mac would have all the clans clamoring to hear them. Indeed, as he paused he heard the murmurs begin again in the crowd.

"I see not Jehkal!" He said this louder than the rest of his speech. Mac had not seen the warrior since he and Niloc left for the Valley. Was he in trouble with his Chief? Where was he? Mac need not have worried. In typical Jehkal fashion, the young man took that moment to make his entrance, stepping around his Chief and walking forward. Jehkal would not miss an opportunity to advance his standing in the eyes of just about anyone. Mac was going to make sure that his standing was indeed memorable. He waved him to his side then moved to stand beside Shumak. The lizard had a very curious look on his face, understanding little of the fast flowing words, his hand never straying far from his weapons.

If any of them need fear for his life, it would be Shumak. The clans and the People had been undeclared enemies for centuries with many battles between them. Only the river and the escarpment limited their contact, but whenever the two races crossed paths it went badly for the clansmen. Many a warrior would never again answer the call of his Chief or the cry of his child due to the weapons of the People.

"Chief Solonar of the Briss'y. Chieftains, and people of all clans. Behold something impossible. I present to you Shumak, Wilderness Commander of the People, slayer of the mighty Hydral!" The murmurs became gasps that flowed like a wave.

"See you also, Jehkal, Captain of the Paliece and named protector of the one you would call Drakil!" Whether Jehkal could claim the title of Captain or not was beside the point. Mac had just promoted him. Jehkal now stood beside Shumak preening like a peacock. Mac placed one hand on each shoulder, one at his eye level and one much lower. The two together presenting the impossibility to which Mac had just alluded. "Warrior of the clans and warrior of the People… standing side by side for common good!" Mac proclaimed it loudly. "These two warriors who would be enemies… instead are friends. Shumak, who braved the killer storm to rescue a wounded clansman. Rahkal of the Paliece!" The rumbling in the crowd grew louder.

"Jehkal and Shumak who have stood side by side against the white ones. Shumak and Jehkal who followed the Drakil into the dreaded land. Hear me clansmen and know that both are brave and both are true… for both have crossed the line of skulls and beheld the mysteries of the Rayattl!"

There were shouts and cries now. Not of anger, but of wonder, for at this point none would question the Drakil. A point Mac would need to be very cognizant of. The sound did not die down, and Mac took that opportunity to scan the faces of his friends, all nine. *Well at least none are shooting me daggers!* The noise went on until Solonar feared he would loose all control. He signaled for the drums which quelled the noise and restored decorum.

Mac cleared his throat, "These are strange times people of the clans. And times of great change. These who share my counsel are my brothers, and in my eyes are the same as me." *So don't you dare touch them!* "You know us now, and we humbly accept your welcome and your hospitality."

Mac then crossed his arms with clasped fists in Clan salute, finishing a speech that was far longer and different than what he'd intended. Yet he'd made no claims, and in doing so, tried to put the Chiefs at ease. Only time would tell if he'd succeeded.

Each of the other chiefs now strode forward and proclaimed themselves and the more important members of their clans. Mac smiled because Chief Zukal of the Paliece now kept Jehkal always near him. Shumak was the flavor of the day. The fear was still there, but now, so was the game. Who would be the first to speak with him? Who would be the first to offer a friendly challenge, a test of arms? Who would be the bravest? There was a long line of reluctant hopefuls.

Later there was a feast and long speeches from many people. All welcoming the Drakil and professing he truly was The One. All believing he would save them. Mac put on a brave face, but inside he was seething. Wrestling with the big question that was ripping him apart, *How?*

This same question was still in his head the next morning as he sat in his hut quietly listening to the talk around him. It was just a buzz of voices and he used it as a distraction to allow his mind to wander. *We should have run!* It was almost a mantra that permeated his thoughts, refusing to leave. He was second guessing, thinking that he would rather have taken his chances with the Aranu. Maybe they could have. The Aranu had crossed the ford in numbers, but then they fled east, away from the valley. A move confirmed by the clan scouts and by the cats.

He sighed at the futility of it, now they were trapped. Both physically and morally. They could not just leave! Couldn't just disappear. As much as the Chieftain's may have wished it, their people would never allow it, and it may well tear their fragile alliance apart. Therefore, the human's freedom was compromised. They were not captives though they were certainly prisoners. Mac had sought safety. Instead they found more danger than he could have ever imagined. The white warriors were coming, and the humans were trapped in a boxed canyon, and in an obligation he neither wanted nor believed in. Yet he saw it in the people's eyes whenever they looked at him. The hope. Their belief.

Mac considered their limited options. They could try to escape or they could stay. He could deny and refuse the mantle of Drakil, or he could embrace it. Escape seemed near impossible now. A hundred sets of eyes watched their every move. They were truly and figuratively the center of the valley. An attempt to escape meant a fight, and one, even with stealth, they might not win. People would die. Friends would die. Could he live with that? Perhaps there was a way to get Demitri and the women out. But to where? A worse fate? Starvation, privation, or the Aranu? He had no idea what the white warriors did with their captives, but his mind physically recoiled thinking about the fate of anyone captured by the Aranu. A vision of the half eaten clanswoman found by Niloc and Cam the day after their decent from the Sea of Tears filled his head. Remembering how the Aranu had cut pieces off her living body and roasted them over a fire as she slowly died, staring at them in horror and agony. *No!* They would stay or go together, there was no other option. Unfortunately, right now the cards said stay.

So what of the second part of his quandary? The Drakil. Again he felt the paint drying way too slowly around the corner he'd been put in. Mac had come to the valley hoping somehow to become part of this group. To join the clans. That had proved to be impossible. Instead, they had joined him! Silently, he cursed Niloc for the ten billionth time. But again, he knew this was far bigger than the Sar-too. As much as he'd tried to deny it, as much as he'd tried to dissuade his friend, he'd never even shaken Niloc's belief. Now, in this situation, his denial would become exceedingly dangerous. These people believed he was their Drakil! Believed it as only those who face certain death, then are given sudden hope, can. It bordered on religious fanaticism. He was their future! And he'd never felt so helpless.

So, in spite of his misgivings, he would be this Drakil. He would do his part. And just maybe, somehow, they would live to see the spring. Maybe, just maybe, the white army would miss them and pass them by. The clans would have their little miracle, and Mac and his friends could go and find somewhere to live in peace. *And maybe Shumak will sprout wings and a little pink tutu!* That final image made him chuckle.

Niloc sat in the corner he'd claimed as his own and watched with great interest the internal struggle of the Drakil. He knew his friend never believed in what he truly was. Always did he deny his destiny. Yet he could no longer, as it was here. Niloc felt the truth of it with every fiber of his soul. This was the time. The time when the world would change and the Drakil would lead them from this current darkness and on to a better world. The clans were gathering under a storm cloud they could not escape by themselves. The signs were complete, and Niloc counted himself blessed to be here for the end, and the beginning. He prayed to be given the chance to live through the coming days and witness these great events. But no matter what happened, he would stand by this alien man. He would guide him, and if necessary, die for him and for his people.

Other eyes watched Mac as well. Rebecca sat in her own private misery as she too saw the play of emotions on his face. Emotions he always tried to hide but never quite could. At least not from her. He'd hurt her more deeply than she thought was possible, and what was worse, she knew it was mostly her fault. She had pushed and pushed in her fear and exhaustion. The separation when she thought him dead nearly unhinged her. Then to have him back, with the strong emotions between them, unspoken yet undeniable, building everyday. Maybe they'd built too much and with the pressures around them, she'd snapped when he crossed her. Ordered her! And he'd been right. She knew it and he knew it, yet it was a wedge and a wound that was glacially slow to heal. If only he would talk to her. A glance or a look that would tell her it was ok. Maybe he couldn't make that first effort and it would be up to her? And maybe her worst fear would be realized; that this business of the Drakil would take him from her permanently.

Cam watched them all! He watched his friend, not knowing how to help him in his dilemma, other than be his friend. And his protector. Mac said it to the chiefs. Cam felt the weight of the duty and responsibility Mac now shouldered. Wished he could heft part of the load on his own back, but this was Mac's deal.

He sat, fingering the newly sharpened edge of his clav'l. A sword given to him by Niloc way back in the spring. The clansman told him the protector of the Drakil required a clan sword, and Niloc had entrusted him with one owned by his fallen brother, Jamil. He accepted the weapon, the duty and all the training Niloc had given him, and he would carryout that duty. Even if it meant protecting Mac from Niloc and his damn legend!

Shifting his gaze he looked at Rebecca. Watching her watch Mac. Seeing the pain that was written upon her features, obvious to everyone except for Mac. Cam tried to talk to his friend. Told him to go to her. Apologize if need be. Whatever it took. But Mac said no, his own sadness evident.

"Not yet, Cam." he'd said. "It's too public and we need more time. I'll go to her when we're safe. I can't be her lover and her leader! It won't work. You saw what happened. Next time it could get us killed. She and I will just have to wait."

It hadn't happened yet. His eyes shifted back to Mac. *May not ever.* The Drakil was a beast none of them really knew yet, most of all the wayward Commander of a long wrecked space shuttle. So Cam would do what any good second did. He would watch the back of his commander and be ready.

Mac's thoughts continued to drift amid the dull babble around him, absently allowing his senses to wander. He heard without hearing. Smelled the scent of those individuals who sat near, and the fire, and the food. No single scent overpowering any other. His eyes drifted closed and he saw nothing but the dancing play of dim light across his lids. His tactile sense centered on fine granules of sand as they drifted through his fingers, falling in a gentle drift back to the dirt floor from whence they were pulled. No individual sensation more noteworthy than another, his mind wandering like smoke on a windless day. Drifting as if it had free will. It was therapeutic. He needed to put aside the Drakil. Put aside the responsibilities and cares that faced him and simply rest his weary brain.

It was into this drifting pseudo contented nothing that the familiar tingle of Saber's presence grew. Mac was not even aware of him at first. He was more of a lighted picture in a dark room seen from very far away. Yet as it drew slowly closer it captured his attention and pushed the muffled sounds and mixed smells to the fringe of his awareness, then beyond that until the vision was all that existed. Normally Mac would have recognized the 'feel' of the cat right away. Up till now he'd believed he had the connection mastered. But this was so different his subconscious simply assumed he'd drifted off to sleep and the dream landscape around him was the result.

From on high was his view, as if he at the brink of a great cliff looking down on the world, at least a beautifully small piece of it. The view was idyllic. Fluffy clouds filled a light green sky out to a horizon which held a darker line, promising yet another storm. Nearer to hand, the forest evergreens stood framing the hardwoods, which, mostly bare of leaf, stood as sentinels along a wide slow flowing river, the brush underneath both impenetrable and glorious in its fall mantle. It was post card perfect.

In the hut, Cam saw Mac's face relax then grow a slight smile as if his dreams were pleasant, and indeed Mac was smiling inside at the pleasure and peacefulness of the vision. Contented yet curious since the small stretch of river seemed slightly familiar. Concentrating harder he tried to study the details. The play of water over shallows in the center of the river. Rocks exposed here and there and a hollow under the brush on the far side. *I was there!* The realization came suddenly, rolling over him like thunder. Before him was the ford they crossed yesterday as seen from Eneri's side.

Cam saw the change as Mac's face grew taut and he motioned the others. They knew what was occurring behind those closed lids. However, their guide, the young clansman, had no idea what was happening, other than his new charges had gone suddenly quiet and were staring in concern at the Drakil. Some gripped weapons and some held their breath. Already uneasy with their strangeness and awed to be in the presence of a legend, the boy sat with eyes wide and fearful. Something was happening to the Drakil and he would witness it. He would then be expected to detail all that he saw to Solonar the Chief. He knew his duty, but he watched with growing dread, and it was all he could do not to run from the tent.

Mac's brain began to race as the vision began to fade. *Saber!* he called in his mind, then pulled his concentration and focus back to the cat. Saber never sent a vision unless... unless danger threatened. Saber's eyes suddenly narrowed, and like the zoom on a camera, the vision zeroed in to a point on the far shore. A move that was disorienting and vaguely nauseating to Mac and he would've closed his eyes if his mind had that ability. Instead, he saw movement! Something was there, right at the place where Mac and the others had so recently hid under the brush. Yet this shape was large. At first the movement was simply a shadow which moved differently from those cast by the vegetation. A patch of scaly skin that merged with the brush. Then a leg materialized as it was thrust through. It stood still only a moment before carrying the rest of the body into the open. Mac amended that. Bodies. There on the far bank, and mounted on its Thalk, sat a warrior of the People.

Saber's vision swung again, this time panning to movement below Saber's hiding spot where Mac could see two clansmen, the ones left to watch the ford, shifting nervously in their concealment like quail ready to flush. The vision swung back and the lone lizard warrior was joined by two more. Mac could see movement behind them then more of the People pushed through the undergrowth and on to the bank. He saw more in lines back in the trees. Warriors on Thalk and many on foot, females and young mixed in among them. This was no raiding party!

Mac's eyes popped open and he surged to his feet, pointing at the young clansmen whose eyes were wide as saucers.

"Take us to the chieftains." he told the boy. "We must hurry!" Then he rounded on Shumak, "Come with me now! Your people are at the ford"

It was like dropping a stone into a calm pond. The ripples spread outward until they reached a shore near and far. In this case, the shore was the furthest edges of the makeshift village within the valley. Mac started it as he burst out of his hut followed by all of his followers, each more grim of visage than the last. The lizard man matching stride for stride with the Drakil, their young escort running along side, unsure and frightened. As the wave moved outward the crowd and the noise that followed them grew. Even if one of the guards had not ran ahead to tell the chiefs, they would have been warned well in advance of his arrival nonetheless.

So it was that Solonar, Chief of the Briss'y as well as the other three chiefs, those of the Cal'dil, Zith'al and the Paliece, met him outside their headquarters They stood ready for him, though it was Solonar spoke. "My, Drakil! Is something amiss? Has someone offended you?"

His voice oozed with insincerity and Mac wondered if "someone offending" may have been ordered. He didn't hesitate however. "Chief Solonar! I see you and it is good." Mac began with the traditional greeting which caused the chief to flinch as he himself had neglected it.

"No one has offended, but I must have a word with you and the other Chieftains," Mac looked around at the growing crowd. "In private." If at all possible, he wanted to avoid a panic.

Solonar saw something in the Drakil's face. Perhaps something to exploit. Something to discredit this… this threat to his authority. Show everyone that the so-called Drakil was nothing. A coward even. For that is what he interpreted in the face before him. Fear. It was a mistake he didn't know enough not to make. Perhaps he should have considered that the face of a human could not be read the same as one of the clan.

"Surely, my Drakil, your words are for all." He waved a hand around. "Everyone should benefit from your wisdom." His voice was smooth and condescending and the words immediately threw Mac into a foul mood.

He looked the Chief directly in the eye, changing his approach. Now was not the time to play timid with these men. Now was the time to show strength and reveal some of the true power of the Drakil.

Putting steel in his voice and dropping the formal address he stepped forward, staring down at the shorter Briss'y. "Some words have more power than others," he turned to the other Chieftains, effectively dismissing Solonar.

"But perhaps the Chief of the Briss'y is right." He said this with venom as if the words were the furthest thing from the truth. His voice rose loud and clear to be heard by all. "It may be that these words should come from me rather than in a more diluted form." In other words, from Solonar. The meaning was not lost on the chief and he glowered, his eyes shooting fire.

Mac turned to the gathered clans and put a hand on the Shumak's shoulder saying, "For you who do not know him, this is Shumak of the People. You have seen that he follows the Drakil." He paused a moment, raking the crowd with his eyes. "Shumak has fought beside me in honor, and defended me without regard to the risk of his own life."

Mac saw the gathered warriors watching him with curious expressions. This was not what they expected. Something of portent certainly, but not praise of an old enemy. Yet still they hung on his every word. "Shumak braved the great storm and saved the life of Rahkal, brother of Jehkal, who is one of you."

This caused a stir. Many had heard rumor of such a tale though few truly believed. But undeniably, there behind the Chieftain of the Paliece stood both of the clansmen named, and both nodded that it was so.

"I tell you now that more of the People come this way. Many more!"

The stir became shouts of dismay. Many eyed him with suspicion and many looked around wildly as if lizards would spring up in their midst.

It was Zukal, Chieftain of the Paliece who stood forward. "My Drakil!" he said in a cautious voice. "I honor Shumak for his service too you and my clan children. But please, explain what you say. Did you bring more? Do they follow you?"

"No, Chief Zukal." He spoke calmly, but still loud enough that most could hear. "No… I did not bring them. But they come none the less. I think they are driven by the white enemy as were you, and I would welcome them as friends!"

More gasps and growing shouts. Mac felt his friends close around him and someone at his back, though no weapons were drawn. It was Zukal who called for calm. In truth it took some time and was a near thing to the panic he had tried to avoid. All the while a smug Solonar standing calmly with his arms crossed, satisfied the Drakil had just made a fatal mistake.

"If you did not bring them," Zukal asked. "How do we know they will come?"

Solonar was smiling now. Surely this *thing* who presumed to call himself the Drakil was now trapped in his lies, and when found out, the clan warriors would tear him apart. It was only left for Solonar to give the order.

Yet the Drakil had no intention of failing. "Chief Zukal," Mac replied firmly. "Even now they are crossing at the ford." The chieftain looked at him brows furrowed, clearly not believing. "I have seen them." He pointed to his head, letting them know that his knowledge was the product of a vision.

The clans were reasonably superstitious and recognized the special talents of their wise men, so the claim of a vision was not unheard of. Yet most wise men only achieved such visions after days of self-induced privation or with the assistance of certain sacred roots which were prepared in secret ceremonies. The practitioners were as likely to die as have a vision, and most wise men were old and withered before their time. And the visions of the wise were never specific, tending to give broad guidance on changes of weather or the direction of game to be hunted. Perhaps the sex of an unborn child or god's decisions on marriage or the need for battle. This was not what the Drakil claimed. His was a vision which could be proven as truth within a few hours. A vision, which on its own, would forever settle whether the being in front of them was truly the Drakil-at'sakaal .

The gathered clans drew back from him as Mac seized his next opportunity. He would not ask. Instead he would paint them into a corner similar to the one he'd found himself in earlier that day. They would accept him now or let them go. Or kill them. Mac looked at the chieftains. "We will go to the ford and meet them! And we will have peace!"

Solonar stepped back as if staggered, and Zukal's eyes widened. "Peace?" Zukal was incredulous. "They are invading our lands!"

Solonar stepped forward barreling his way in between them, casting Mac a look dark enough that Mac's hand strayed toward his knife. "You believe him!" Solonar practically yelled at Zukal who now looked very uncertain.

Here it was Mac thought. Solonar drew the line and it was Zukal who must choose whether to step over. He hesitated, further emboldening Solonar who started a verbally barrage, dropping all pretence of belief. "This… This thing," he pointed at Mac. "Is not the Drakil! I say he is an imposter!" Spittle flew from his lips as he spat his words and Mac heard the growing sound as those gathered, first startled, now began yelling and arguing loudly, the crowd swaying back and fourth on a razors edge. Niloc stepped forward realizing full well how far the mood had changed. Fear, uncertainty, and doubt began to rule, and soon it would be mob rule, ensuring bloodshed and ruin for all of them.

"Hold!" he shouted, but none heard. Jehkal stepped up to yell with him, as well as his brother and Den'al. Mac mentally cursed himself for a fool as he watched the near chaos. He'd misjudged Solonar and his misjudgment may cause people to die.

"Hold!" Niloc shouted again, though this time he pulled his clav'l, raised his shield and banged them together. Still no one headed and Mac feared the naked steel would precipitate violence. But these were the clans and Niloc knew them as no other.

"Hold!" he yelled again, and this time was joined by others who banged their shields as well. The sound was deafening so close to Mac. He held his composure, staring at Solonar as if not bothered in the least by the uproar. The others, Cam, Rebecca, Sue and Demitri, pushed even closer. If no one else was smart enough to know fear, they did. Even so they backed him up, armed only with a single clav'l wielded by Cam, and long knives held by the rest, their bows left sitting or leaning uselessly back in their hut. Shumak anchored their circle like a huge and golden marble statue. And, standing in the middle of them all was the small clan warrior charged with being their guide, trembling yet excited, watching the riot with great wonder. He would certainly have stories to tell his friends. *If only I live through the next few moments,* his unspoken thought. *If only the lizard doesn't step on me.*

Slowly the noise died as Mac's friends restored order, the attention of all now on Mac and Solonar. Mac continued to stare at the chief, his voice loud and his words said with purpose and meant not for him, but for all those gathered. "Believe what you will Solonar," Mac would give him no honor. "For I claim no title!"

Again the gathered warriors erupted, this time in dismay, and Niloc stood in shock at his words. It took some moments for the Sar-too to regain his wits, and for he and the others to again calm the crowd.

As quiet prevailed once more, Mac continued, "I claim no title." He held up his hands to forestall anymore interruption. "For that is something the clans must decide." He would put it on their shoulders. "But I ask you," he said sadly. "Would we now fight amongst ourselves? We do so at our peril. To do so will lay victory at the feet of the white ones?" Mac ignored the outcry at the mention of an enemy. He stepped to Shumak. "Things are not as they were, and our very existence hangs in the balance!" Mac once again placed a hand on his friends arm.

"Old hatreds must be put aside. And here is one who has been wise enough to see the future. Has Shumak not joined us of his own free will? Has he not proven a friend and battle brother?"

Jehkal took the hint and moved over to Shumak followed by his brother. They stood with the Drakil and the reptile warrior in a powerful show of solidarity, knowing it could cost them much. If the Drakil should lose this battle of words, the best they could hope for was to be cast out.

For Shumak it was even a more powerful moment. Never had he felt as he did now and he had no words to describe it. Fear? That emotion was certainly high on the list. Not of these warriors, though they could certainly kill him. No, the fear came from what he now believed the Drakil would ask him to do. *The Drakil will ask me to go back to those I abandoned!* Shumak would have trembled had his physiology allowed it. And more unbelievable to him he answered, *I will!*

"I care not if you believe in me," Mac Continued. "Or in my vision. But I go to meet the People! Follow me if you will." This time he said it as a challenge. A challenge to Solonar to stop him. A challenge to the clans to join him. This was a chance to avoid a battle with the lizards that would kill many of those around him. Mac didn't ask them to join him or else, but it was a challenge nonetheless.

Solonar found himself trapped. He saw clearly that the other chieftains were unsure yet leaning toward belief. Or at least acceptance, possibly avoidance. Also, he saw his own people were in awe of this being, and most clearly of all, that should this Drakil win, his own power and station would be cast aside. All this would come to pass if he did nothing. Could the others not see it? Were they blinded? Solonar was not, and he was not willing to 'go' with this imposter. He was not willing to see and make peace with the People! His mind rejected the idea that this pretend Drakil could know they were there at all, even though the first niggling of doubt began to invade his thoughts.

The 'what if' was too terrible to contemplate. What if the human had seen, or more likely, was somehow in possession of such knowledge through an agent unknown to the clansmen. Solonar shook his head. It did not matter. The outcome was the same. Loss! Power was everything to Solonar, and to give it up; give control of his warriors and his clan to this Drakil. *No!* His mind screamed it. He would not. Not and still live. Solonar accepted the stare of the Drakil and shot it back. Now was not a time to show fear, and the words he spoke were sharp and shocking to every living being who heard. "I reject your vision! I name you false!" he spat. "The truth shall be known. It shall be decided by right of arms. I, Solonar, son Alonar, Chieftain of all the Briss'y, challenge you to a Blood Fight!"

There was true pandemonium now. Niloc had gone white and many in the crowd came to blows. There was much yelling and shouting, for all the clansmen knew what the humans did not. This challenge was a challenge reserved for those who would fight for control of a clan. A chief must be strong and he must rule with iron, but in this world, all were strong, or soon dead. In most clans, the mantle of power was handed down from father to son and so this challenge was rare. But when it occurred, it was to the death, and to refuse it was also death.

Niloc stepped to the Drakil with great sadness in his soul. He let the others, including the chieftains, try and regain order. It was up to Niloc to explain this to Mac. Why had he not seen this? Why had he not prepared the Drakil? So many things Niloc had failed to tell him. So many things the Drakil had refused to hear, denying even now that he was The One!

As he stepped next to the Drakil he was surprised by what he saw. Not the fear he expected, but contemplation. The Drakil was deep in thought, though still he kept his eyes locked on Solonar. The ring of his friends was tight and Niloc had to push between Cam and Shumak to reach him.

"My Drakil…" he began, but Mac waved off his comment. He was absolutely clear about what had happened. This chief, no, this man in front of him feared for his way of life. This was a violent society and Mac had no illusions this confrontation could have been avoided. It was preordained the moment he'd stepped into the village yesterday evening. He kept a stone face, but cursed himself once again, knowing he knew far too little of these tribal traditions and had no time to learn. Breaking contact with Solonar, he turned to Niloc and saw his distress.

"My Drakil…"

He heard, but Mac only wanted the answer to only one question. He asked, "Do I have to kill him?"

Niloc hung his head missing Mac's confidence. "It is a fight for supremacy. One of you will die. If you refuse to fight him, you will die. The clans will not follow you and we… none of your banner will survive unless you kill him."

Thanks, Niloc! Mac thought. Nothing like the fate of hundreds being in your hands, not to mention your own fairly precious life! Mac's brain was working at a furious pace. He knew he could never match a clansman with a sword. He needed options. Niloc was looking at him as if he would refuse, and that made him smile. *As if!*

Mac took the clansman by the arm and turned him so the both faced Solonar. He whispered, "Niloc my friend, I won't refuse. I can take him." Mac looked at the chief who stood with a scowl, awaiting a reply. Solonar was a fireplug of a man. Shorter by a head but much more muscular, with arms as big as Mac's thighs. *Would that make him slower?* Mac couldn't count on it. *Would he be over confident?* Probably. But Solonar was in the prime of his life and a natural killer. He also had a lot to lose. Far more than his life, he was fighting for principal and for his clan. Solonar looked glorious in his patchwork boiled leathers, more than a cut above the average warriors' cloth. He wore a band of what looked like polished copper around his head to hold back his long black hair, and to show he was a true chieftain. Mac would certainly have his hands full.

Again he whispered quietly to Niloc, "As the one challenged," he asked. "Do I get my choice of weapons?"

Now Niloc did look distressed. "Yes my Drakil, but it must be personal combat." He was thinking Mac would pick his favorite weapon, the bow, but Mac had no intention of doing that. "Do I have a choice of time?"

Again the distress, "It must be before the sun reaches the far horizon, my Drakil."

Mac sighed. It was early morning and he looked up watching the play of clouds, thinking it was good to concentrate on something beautiful before you faced death. There was now a deafening silence around him.

Cam leaned in, "Let me take him, Mac! I'll gut the bastard."

Mac looked at his friend, trying to visualize the clean shaven captain who'd lifted off with him in the Atlantis so many months ago. No longer the happy go lucky pilot. Bearded, filthy, and dressed in furs and boiled leather. Any man can become a savage! Of all the things that had happened, this saddened Mac the most. “No, Cam. It’s me he challenged. Though if he kills me, you have my permission to cut him to ribbons!”

Mac was trying to make a joke, but he knew that if he died Cam and the others would die also. They looked like they wanted to say something as well. Rebecca’s face was white with fear. *For me?*

Solonar had waited long enough. He was emboldened by Mac’s silence and the obvious confusion the challenge had caused. As Solonar suspected, this one was a coward and a pretender. He opened his mouth to push the issue, and was thoroughly dismayed when Mac overrode him with his reply.

Mac’s voice boomed, “Your challenge saddens me, Solonar! For I will look upon your death as a great loss!” If Mac had slapped him Solonar would have looked less surprised, and the look on his face was most comical.

“I accept the ritual challenge. And I will gladly lead your clan when the sun sets tonight!”

Solonar was raging inside and he was visibly shaking. *This thing! It thought it could challenge him? Thought it could win!*

Mac won the first battle. The physiological one, and before Solonar could recover he hit him again. Mac drew himself up to his full height and looked down on the Briss’y. “You have asked for a Blood Fight and I shall certainly give it too you. And after we have our dance I will take your clan and go to meet the people!” Mac spoke with great confidence, further deflating the Clan Chief.

“As the one challenged, Solonar, it is my choice of weapon and my choice of time.” Silence greeted his statement, and small things captured Mac’s eye. The play of sunlight across the assembly and the small breeze which fluttered the fringe on a warrior’s coat. The gentle sway of individuals as they waited in anticipation, and the myriad smells of smoke, leather, grease and unwashed bodies. Mac considered only a moment, his choice following his training.

“Solonar of the Briss’y, I choose this!” Mac pulled his long knife and held it high for all to see.

Solonar smiled slightly. He knew the knife as well as the sword. This was good and his confidence raised a few notches.

"As for time?" Mac cast his gaze about, then up as if to gage the sun, then back to the Briss'y. If Solonar thought his opponent was a coward, that notion was squashed completely when Mac said, "I choose now!" His voice carried all across the crowd, echoing back from the wall of the chieftain's hut, and such was its power that once again Solonar looked shaken. The Chief of the Briss'y nodded once in agreement, then he turned away to prepare.

"Are you sure about this, Mac?" Cam was helping him stretch and loosen his muscles as his friends crowded around.

Mac didn't look at him. Didn't look at anything really. He was preparing mentally for the trial to come, clearing his thoughts. Not thinking at all about the man he would shortly try to kill. It was just a target. *Let the training and reflex take over! Thinking can get me killed.* If you think you die. He remembered his lessons and more, his real life experience. Mac was Special Forces trained, and he'd spent endless hours working with and against knives. He'd even studied with a Grandmaster in the art of Daga! The Pilipino method of fighting. He was far from a master, but he was not foreign to cuts and killing. A wise man once said, "If you approach a man who knows how to hold a knife, run away." Many times he'd practiced Palitan. If you chose to fight with blades, be they long or short, you must be willing to get cut, for almost no other form of fighting was as personal or frightening. You must set your mind and body to accept a wound in order to gain advantage. This was the essence of Palitan, the art of give and take! Mac wondered if Solonar was equal to the task.

"Mac! Are you listening to Cam?" This voice got his attention, for they were among the first words Rebecca had cast his way in a very long time. "Mac! Don't do this. We'll just leave. You don't have to…"

He shook his head at her, his voice more sharp than he wanted. Again he'd hurt her. "You heard them! If I refused they would kill me." He softened it when she cast her eyes down, saying, "They'd kill you."

She shook her head. "You don't know that for sure." But her voice held no conviction and Mac reached out and grasped her arm.

"I know it... And you know it. This is the only way."

She didn't respond and Mac sighed, turning away before seeing the tears flooding her eyes. A good thing, as that would have undoubtedly broken his concentration. He pulled his knife and tested its weight as she walked away.

The knife he held was not strictly a dagger and was larger than he'd have liked. But it was well weighted and centered with an edge honed to a razor, full on one side and a third of the way from the tip to hilt on the other. He flipped it around his palm, reversing the blade against his forearm then back out using his left hand as a distraction, sweeping through a few moves to warm up and calm his breathing. Then he was ready.

A ring of warriors was quickly prepared, all Briss'y and Mac's people as tradition demanded. Only kin to the fighters could contain them, all others fighting for a position to see over their shoulders. In the center Solonar waited as Mac stepped between Niloc and Demitri and onto a killing field of beaten down grass. Once inside the ring there was no more ritual, and no rules. Mac had barely taken two steps when the Briss'y Chieftain charged, and the screams and calls of his warriors became deafening. Solonar believed he could end this quickly by taking the pretender off guard and muscling him to the ground. His plan was to pin the slighter man then play to the crowd, showing off his superiority. Then, with a great sweeping slash, he would cut his throat. That or plunge his knife into the heart, where ever that might be.

His confidence was huge as he rushed forward, sweeping his blade in a move that had before won him many a contest. With and grunt heard over the shouting throng they clashed, and Solonar was hugely surprised when Mac not only met the charge, but caught and blocked the upward stab of his knife on his own blade. Chest to chest, Mac forced the other's knife out and up in an incredible display of strength, then he punched forward with a knee strike. Solonar saw the move and blocked with a leg, pushing Mac away with a forearm punch. Groaning, they disengaged, but not before a slash of fire ripped across Solonar's chest. Mac had drawn first blood with a strike that drew a shallow line of crimson six inches long, their break of contact the only thing keeping the

Briss'y from a wound that would have killed. Solonar was enraged staggering back in wide-eyed dismay!

Mac had enough experience to know that most knife fights were wars of attrition, many stopped by blood loss from numerous wounds rather than one major cut. This fight however, was not to end that way. Solonar was zero finesse and a hundred percent brute strength. What he hadn't counted on was Mac's superior quickness, his skill and stunning power. Mac was from a planet with gravity stronger than here. This, plus his training and excellent physical conditioning and months of survival on a planet where it seemed everything wanted to kill him, had him at peak fighting ability.

Solonar attacked again, and again Mac parried the stroke. punching with his left shoulder, his body blow throwing Solonar to the ground in a bone jarring heap, the dust billowing out from under him. Mac could have killed him then, but to do so may have been seen as somehow beneath him. That was confirmed a moment later. The warriors, stunned to silence by the events so far, called to Mac in voices of approval as Solonar slowly rose to his feet. He looked at Mac now with caution. And fear. His breath coming in gasps from lungs that just had the air brutally forced from them. Mac saw the change, though Solonar tried to hide it behind a mask of stone, but it was there. Defeat!

Solonar stood and waited. Twice he'd attacked and twice tasted the power of this man. Once he'd been cut and the second time he'd come a hairsbreadth of having that blade drawn across his throat, at least one cracked rib his reward. Twice shy, he circled cautiously, waiting in defense for Mac's attack. He had not long to wait. Daga is an art as well as a weapon system. Part of the art was feinting, miss-direction and matching move for move. Watching two trained warriors in battle was bewildering with the speed in which it was conducted. Blades blurring as the slashed and cut. Even more bewildering when it's coming at you and you have no defense. Bewildering and terrifying and Solonar knew, without doubt, he was about to die.

Mac moved with deceptive speed, sidestepping right, then suddenly left as Solonar's blade made to follow. His own blade traced a figure eight, punching forward and back like a viper giving his opponent no clear idea from where the blow would come, where to defend. In desperation, Solonar slashed out with his blade, missing, then pulling back in a frantic move to cover. Mac had to smile. The man almost made it.

Mac hammered Solonar's blade hand with his left. An open hand with the fingers curled back, the blow pushing the blade hand out and away, leaving Solonar wide open. With the full momentum of his body, Mac pushed inside the clansman's guard and buried his blade, point first to the hilt, right in the center of Solonar's throat. Hot blood gushed out over his hand as he drew the blade forth, followed by a sigh of air escaping the newly made mouth. Solonar's eyes were wide as his body went suddenly slack, his weapon falling from a now useless hand. Mac grabbed him before he fell and helped him gently to the ground where Solonar's eyes somehow found his.

"It did not have to be this way." Mac told him in a sad voice. "Go in peace." He pressed the dead man's eyelids closed, then placed Solonar's arms across his chest, bowing his head in a moment of silence for the man he'd just killed.

Mac rose to silence, looking about the circle finding every Briss'y warrior with his fists crossed against his chest in salute, most bewildered. His friends stood stunned. Disbelieving! Mac stood next to the fallen chieftain and took several deep breaths to calm his nerves, letting the adrenalin bleed from his system. He'd fought, the other died. It was wonderful to just close his eyes and realize how good it is to still be alive.

A commotion to his right brought him from his musing. He turned to face the other chieftains who pushed into the ring. Zukal looked down at the dead Solonar, undisguised shock on his face. Plainly he didn't believe Mac could best the Briss'y Chief. He knew for certain that, had the positions been reversed, he could not have prevailed. A fact and a fear that always plagued him whenever he and Solonar met. The same barely disguised fear and intimidation the Briss'y forced upon everyone. Still, Zukal could not be glad of his passing. What would happen now?

"My Drakil," he said, folding his fists and nodding his head in honor to an equal. "By right of the Blood Fight, you are now the lawful Chieftain of all the Briss'y."

Mac had to chuckle. *From his tone, Zukal must think I'm going to challenge him and take his clan next.* "Chief Zukal. I regret the death of Solonar, but he would not have it otherwise." He raised his voice to address all the leaders, letting his emotions carry him. "Does anyone else wish to challenge me? If so, now is the time!" He looked at each Chief, then at the warriors gathered around. None would directly meet his eye.

"Good!" he said firmly. "Because I have no more time for it! Niloc, bring me a skeel. "We leave immediately to meet the People!" He left no doubt that anyone could refuse.

Of course it was not that simple. Immediately turned into two hours as things were organized. Mac was shocked to learn that by killing a clan chief in ritual combat, earned him more than honor. He'd just inherited an entire clan. By right and recognized by all, he was now, Lt. Colonel James Macintosh Crowe, true and rightful chieftain of the Far Walkers. The clan known as Briss'y. Unprecedented in all the histories and for once, to Mac's great relief, not foretold in some ancient dusty misspoken legend. His new clan included fifty two warriors, twenty plus extended clan families including children, women and the elderly. He now owned personally, five skeel, an assortment of weapons, a chieftain's tent and most disturbing of all, a wife and two sons. Solonar's personal household. Mac had yet to meet the woman, and it would be some time till he did. The grieving widow, now his wife, would spend the next three days secluded in mandatory mourning. Nor would he meet the youngest son who was yet to come to manhood, whatever that meant. There seemed to be no set time for this ultimate right of passage. It appeared to be a deed driven event, and Mac had yet to figure out how such things were determined. He tried not to think about the wife, having no earthly idea what was expected in that arena. He had no idea how he would explain it to Rebecca either. And, from the looks of the other clan women, he shuddered to think just how 'handsome' his new wife might be. Even Cam hadn't found them remotely attractive, and he was not known to be especially picky.

Almost immediately after the killing of Solonar, each Briss'y warriors had filed past their fallen chief, then personally offered Mac a salute and the hilt of their sword. After a moment's confusion, which fortunately Niloc was there to clarify, he blessed the offered weapon with a touch of a hand. Each warrior held his eyes a moment, the cast them down in acknowledgement while giving a name and a sire. Mac despaired of remembering any after the first two, so complicated where the pronunciations. He did however, remember the last one.

"My Drakil, my Chief!" The young man spoke in a firm voice, not betraying emotions which lay in turmoil just beneath the surface. Mac studied him, seeing a handsome warrior in his prime, his long hair tied back with a leather cord knotted in blue stones revealing a face vaguely familiar. Not as tall as Mac, but it was no effort to look in his eyes.

Breaking the routine of the other warriors, he cast his eyes down then quickly back up, almost in challenge, saying, "I am known as Solonak, son of Solonar, the Chief of all the Briss'y. By right of combat, I am now your son."

Niloc hadn't warned him of the consequences of actually winning the Blood Fight until Solonar lay unmoving on the cold and dusty ground. Mac was all too aware of the consequences of losing. So this simple statement, delivered in such a mater of fact way, floored him. He took a deep breath to steady his voice. "Well met, Solonak." Mac gripped the young man's shoulder. "I grieve for your loss, for Solonar was a great leader." He had no idea whether the dead Solonar was a good leader or father or the most evil bastard on the entire planet, but these words were all he could think of.

Solonak waited for more as Mac hesitated, so it was the young clansman who reached out to assist. "My Chief. I know you to be..." He searched for words that would not be considered offensive. "...new to our ways. It will be my honor to guide you if you so wish it. It will also be my duty, and my honor, to fight at your side. I will be the shield at your back. It is my duty. I will never fail you." He paused, but only a moment. "My Drakil. You bring great honor to the Briss'y. You will be chief of all the clans and the Briss'y will be your shield and your sword. 'We' will never fail you."

Mac considered the warrior's words and their actual meaning. Solonak would not avenge his father, nor would there be anything to fear from the rest of the clan. Niloc would have to provide guidance to confirm the interpretation, and he would need a lot more than words before he trusted his tender back to any clansmen, let alone the Briss'y, and certainly not the son of the man he'd just killed. Yet he said the only words he really could and still remain diplomatic, "I will seek your wisdom, Solonak. And I will count on your sword and the strength of your arm."

This was not the complete acceptance Solonak sought, but the words seemed to satisfy the young man. He nodded, then bent to help several other warriors carry away from the presence of his father, the body of the former Chief of the Briss'y.

Chapter 15

Dusk was falling on Peri'ackt as he made his way through the encampment, and he feared the same could be said for his people. With no idea how many might have escaped the great net cast by the enemy, he feared these pitiful few were all that remained of his proud race. Why any of them remained alive was still a mystery. The white warriors harassed and pushed, but they had yet to force the overwhelming battle that would end it all. They most certainly had the army to do it, outnumbering his own warriors five or six to one, and their strategies were devilish, negating even the great weight and advantage of the Thalk. All Peri'ackt and his warriors could now do was retreat and hope! Hope a way out somehow offered itself to his beleaguered folk.

Now, to make a dire situation even more precarious, earlier today they'd crossed the river, moving directly into lands held by the clansmen. Indeed, several clan warriors were watching the ford, and they had escaped, fleeing before his advanced scouts. Would the People now be pinned between two armies? It is what he feared. Yet so far the white ones had not appeared at the rivers edge, and so far the clans had not challenged their right to live.

This thought had just cleared his mind when horns sounded from the woods far to his left, Sudden trepidation erupted icily in his gut. This was the direction in which the clansmen had fled.

"To me!" he yelled, rushing to the pens that held his Thalk, the horns continued blaring out their mournful and urgent warning, leaving no doubt an enemy approached. Quickly, Peri'ackt detailed as many warriors as he dared to hold the ford. Others he sent to prepare the females and young to flee or fight. The balance formed a battle line, then they waited, sitting atop restless mounts as the darkness continued to deepen under the trees.

Horns sounded in the distance and Mac halted his warriors, not wanting to stumble into the People and cause needless bloodshed. Saber and Tawnee had given him the layout of the encampment and general positions of the forward sentries so he was prepared for their discovery of his approach. By his order, the clansmen made no effort to conceal themselves or be quiet. Mac wanted the People to know they were coming. An order which caused Chief Zukal and the others who followed the Drakil no little anxiety. No one approaches an enemy and announces themselves so boldly in this manner, unless the command overpowering and undeniable force. No one in their right mind at least. It was foolish and deadly. Yet none of them challenged, even when he ordered the lighting of torches which would clearly show the enemy their disposition. Bunched and non-threatening, exactly as Mac wanted.

Perhaps even more perplexing to the clansmen, Mac allowed no scouts or skirmishers, telling them there really was no need. *Let them wonder*, he thought. But they were more than nervous, thinking they were about as vulnerable as a new borne, and offering their necks to the sword. They could not know that Mac had them covered. His cats were out and scouting, and even now he *saw* the muster and quick battle formation of the People. It was a fierce sight indeed.

"Chief Zukal?" Mac looked at the chief, judging him and finding him shaky, yet steel underneath. *Good.* "Will you go and meet the People with me?"

"As you wish, my Drakil." Zukal felt the skeel shift underneath him, praying the Drakil really knew what he was about. Legend foretold a time of great change. A man who would turn traditions upside down. Show them new ways and new ideas. Fervently and for the future of his people, he hoped this is what the ancient words truly meant. And, despite his professed yet weak belief, he prayed Mac really was the Drakil that was promised. If not, the next few minutes did not bare thinking about.

Niloc and Jehkal would also be part of the parley, as well as Sue and Demitri; Rebecca had refused to come, staying behind in the Valley of The Moon. Tending to the sick that needed her was the excuse, and Mac bit his lip and left her behind. Last of the delegation, yet the most important, was Shumak. Mac looked down at the warrior. He'd give a lot to know what was going on behind those snake-like eyes right now, but he could not. With more confidence than he felt, Mac signaled and the six moved forward. They only went about fifty yards until they were in the center of a clearing, well away from the protection of the rest of the warriors and hopefully, looking like the emissaries he wished them to be.

Indeed, much was going on behind Shumak's eyes, and Mac would never know what it cost him to take those few steps forward. Shumak had abandoned his command, essentially abandoning his people. Now the Drakil expected him to be the ambassador between those he'd left, and the enemy he'd joined. His sins had come back to haunt him. It was Shumak that supervised the disaster which claimed the life of the Chieftain's son. The least of these sins would forfeit his life. Shumak knew exactly what to expect, for he knew his People. This delegation was doomed and quietly he walked himself to the slaughter. *Walk!* he swore to himself. *I will die on foot like a tied Parth. My neck sliced and killed for the evening meal!* Never in any scenario he'd built in his mind could the great Shumak have envisioned such dishonor. Such disgrace! To crawl back to Peri'ackt. Only pride and friendship kept him from bolting, running as far from the confrontation to come as his un-mounted feet could carry him. But he'd been given a choice and a gift by Mac, and Shumak would even fight his own race for the honor of friendship if need be. He the loner captain. He who in the past bent every effort for the benefit of Shumak and Shumak alone. A visible shudder passed through him. Proud Shumak could make no sense of it as he hung his head and strode to his fate.

Something is not as it should be! This was the first thought Peri'ackt had when he saw how the enemy was arrayed in front of his warriors. *No! Not arrayed, they were grouped!* Here in the near dark was a scene that confused him. *Trap?* For some reason he could not explain, he felt that was not so. Perhaps it was unreasonable hope? His warriors could easily overwhelm this small group of clansmen. They were bunched and sitting their mounts as if they had no care in the world. Indeed, several were advancing, and if Peri'ackt's eyes did not deceive him, there was a warrior of the People walking among them. *Walking? A captive?* Peri'ackt thought not. It was inconceivable that any warrior of the People would allow that to happen. A warrior of the People would fight to the death rather than become a slave. No, there was more to this. Much more. These clansmen wished to talk. *Unprecedented!*

Had his situation not been so desperate, Peri'ackt would never have allowed it. With a single command his warriors would sweep them from the field, and he was sorely tempted to order just such an attack. Yet desperate times bred desperate decisions and he would not spend his warrior's lives needlessly.

"Issat'l!" he barked at his second.

"My Chief?"

"Gather an equal number of warriors," he ordered, pointing at Mac and his group. "We will go and speak with them."

"My Chief?" This time the question was incredulous!

"Issat'l," Peri'ackt's eyes were piercing, his scaled fingers caressing the hilt of his sword. "I do not repeat my orders."

Issat'l cast down his eyes. He backed his Thalk away as he said, "It shall be done my Chief." Moving with haste, he couldn't get out of his Chieftain's sight quickly enough.

Great trunks of trees sprouting heavy evergreen laden limbs cast a gloom of shadows across the darkness. It was back under these trees that Mac could see movement, quickly becoming shapes. Those shapes became the outline of reptile warriors mounted on their lizard steeds. The humans, with their earth born eyesight, made out the details and the count well in advance of the others. Mac could see many more warriors that sat well back in the shadows. Without doubt the People far outnumbered his own. Yet only six approached, an equal number to his and a good sign. Mac was committed to his course, but that didn't stop him from shuddering. This was another calculated risk that could take their lives.

Six pairs of eyes, glowing from the flickering light of torches hissing and sputtering behind him, detached from the gloom and strode forward. *At least they sent emissaries.* His biggest fear, one supported heavily by Shumak, was that the reptile leader would attack first and ask questions later. Mac understood the risk, and he was counting on the quickness and maneuverability of the skeel to save them should an ordered retreat be required. A contingency he'd planned for which was simplicity at its finest. If he yelled, they would scatter like quail and hope to hell none of them caught you. But now the emissaries of the People came forward, and Mac had the satisfaction of seeing the doubts of Zukal and the other clansmen quashed and his own fears eased. They believed him now! He'd been right and the People were willing to talk, and they'd witnessed his prescience as well. Earlier, two shaken clansmen who'd fled their watch at the ford had described the scene of the People's crossing almost exactly as had Mac many hours before.

Looking left and right he saw their fear and their awe. Both of him, and the approaching lizards. They were, to a man, and woman, tightly gripping their weapons. He could hardly blame them. His fist was numb from gripping his own. Yet to draw would invite disaster.

"Hold now!" he told them, forcing his hand away. "Everyone take your hands from your hilts, palms out. We come in peace. At all costs, remember that." A necessary repeat of instructions he'd given earlier and repeated often. *No mistakes now!* Taking a deep breath, he ordered, "Dismount!"

This he hadn't told them, knowing they would refuse if given time to think. Mac stepped down from his skeel and walked in front, then looked up at his party in challenge. Reluctantly, one by one they obeyed, though each kept a grip on their reins and a single step from the saddle. Prudent, and now completely necessary because the skeel were beginning to snort and balk at the approach and smell of the enemy. Mac handed his reins to Jehkal and told the rest wait, then he motioned to Shumak and Niloc. "Let's go meet the neighbors!" he said it in English so the humor was lost on his companions, though they may have interpreted his words as great wisdom for both nodded solemnly and followed. Though in truth, Shumak looked as if he were being led to a firing squad. His mouth slightly open showing a bit of black tongue, his breath coming in short pants. Mac took them fifteen long strides from the safety of their friends, and waited.

Peri'ackt walked his Thalk forward with purpose, snapping saplings and only moving around larger trees. These puny warriors would know his power. If they thought him weak because he'd accepted their audacity to call him to truce, he would disabuse them of that notion quickly. His musing was an attempt to build up his arguments and decide for himself how to deal with this curious turn of events. A brave front, yet in truth, he was as unsure as he'd ever been in his life. This was entirely new ground for the chieftain and his bravado was a necessary cover for his uncertainty.

As the two groups closed the clansmen dismounted and two of them, plus the warrior of the People, walked forward, essentially giving themselves to him. Peri'ackt frowned. Certainly this was not a trap then, but a warrior did not go on foot to an enemy! To do so was to act without honor. Peri'ackt bristled with anger and indignity. He stopped his advance to consider and calm his mind. Perhaps he did not go to meet an enemy, though that would be determined by him. Perhaps they thought to avoid conflict, rightly fearing the People. And perhaps it was something altogether different.

Mac saw the change when the lizard men stopped, and he feared all was lost. Shumak told him their only chance, and it was small, would be to meet his people as equals. That meant mounted. But Mac felt this was too close to a challenge. He wanted neutrality. Neither with a perceived advantage, and, more importantly, he wanted to make it absolutely clear they didn't want a fight. So it was on foot the he would meet them. Though now he conceded that may have been a serious miscalculation. The next few moments would tell, and likely whether he kept his head. Mac needed to keep the momentum in their favor, so he nudged Shumak. "Call to them. Tell them we don't want a fight. Tell them we welcome them and wish to talk of the common enemy."

Mac kept his eyes on the People and waited, yet Shumak did not respond. "Shumak?" He looked at his friend who stood like a rock next to him.

If a golden skinned and scaled creature could turn white, that picture described Shumak. He stood there frozen, for there before him was the one being in all the world he did not wish to see. There was his Chieftain. Chief of all the People, Peri'ackt, and the sight lashed him with emotions he could not contain. Here in the flesh was a reminder that death was the just reward granted all who betrayed their own.

"Shumak!" Mac's voice was sharp. They'd come too far to be undone now, but all he got was a croak of some word in Shumak's own tongue. *Shit!*

"Shumak!" This time he followed with a slap to the back, out of sight he hoped. The lizard blinked and tore his gaze from Peri'ackt. "Greet them, Shumak..." Mac hissed, the words pushed through clenched teeth. "Tell them we come in peace."

"I…" Shumak stammered, "Sssumakss deathss isss thre." He pointed to Peri'ackt, his arm trembling, "Iss Chiefss." As if that simple statement meant everything. To him it did.

Here now, staring him in the face, was the glaring flaw in Mac's plan. So caught up in the bigger issues, it wasn't until this very moment that it dawned on him how meeting the People would impact Shumak. Quite simply, he'd seen the lizard as a convenient means to an end, assumed the tool was to be used. But now, the normally gruff, normally belligerent Shumak was shaken. Mac knew the tale of how he'd come to the Rayattl, but the import of the action had not hit home. He quickly placed himself in Shumak's very large boots. The reptilian eyes matched his, but in them Mac saw surrender and defeat.

"Shumak! I will not let them take you." His words were sincere. "Listen to me. They are your people. But you are also a part of us." He grabbed a scaly arm. "Shumak! What you did, you did for your people!"

Shumak knew this was an un-truth because he knew his true motivations, and even Mac suspected them to be selfish. But this was far bigger than his selfishness, and lives depended on what he did now. Mac had to make him see it. "Don't think about the why or even the how! Think only of the future, Shumak." He pointed to Peri'ackt. "Your actions, back then and now, will make peace possible. You, Shumak. You will make peace possible. That's all that counts. Do your people not believe in fate, Shumak?" Mac searched for a clan word to match the concept and came up empty.

He tried a different tact. "Shumak, do you believe something good can come from a selfish act? My people do,

Shumak. Your actions, what you decide to do now, will save lives. The lives of your People and the lives of your friends." His grip was fierce, "Forget the past. I will protect you, Shumak. Think only of what is to come."

Shumak caught most of what Mac was telling him. Even tried to believe it. But it was not so. He knew what his actions meant, knew fully the consequences at the time, and did it anyway. Thus, his life was forfeit. Now he was here and there was no escape. Sighing, his shoulders sank. *What is meant to be... will be... and we can not change it.* An old saying that matched the words of the Drakil. He straightened his shoulders. *Perhaps,* he thought. *Perhaps my death will still mean something.* He looked at Mac, "Ssshumak wiiill ssspek."

Peri'ackt could not see clearly in the descending gloom and the glare of the flickering torch light distorted the features of those he faced. He could not know the visage of every member of his people, yet the one accompanying the clansmen was somewhat familiar. And he was holding conversation with one of them. *No! Certainly not captive.* But any other explanation defied belief. What possible hold could the clansmen have upon him? What spell? *Did the clans have sorcerers?* That was a fear he would not contemplate. Peri'ackt considered only a moment more. "Issat'l."

"My Chief?" The question was automatic.

"Dismount and bring one other!" Peri'ackt didn't wait for an answer, considering it may be an unfortunate beginning should he be required to behead his second in command for another outburst of incredulity. He himself dismounted, carefully ignoring the sputtering behind him, knowing surely that whatever they thought, Issat'l and one other would be following him as he strode forward to this unreal meeting.

Only three long steps had he taken when two things became very clear. The first was that he did indeed know the warrior standing with the clansmen, that recognition causing his bold steps to falter and his blood to boil. The second shook him even more because he was mistaken, it was not two clansmen waiting for him. One was something else, and he recalled a report given to him at the beginning of this disaster. The report, which began with the regret at the death of his son, alluded to a being like this and those like him that were chased onto his lands by the hated Aranu. Realization that both were true served to put him on emotional and very uncertain ground.

Love had not existed between he and his youngest son, but this, *What was his name?* Furiously he fought his memory, until finally it supplied, *Shumak!* This Shumak had presided over the disaster that killed Peri'il and the events that followed. Had abandoned his post and lost his entire command! *And now this! Oh how Shumak would pay.* It was a vow, and there was rage in his thoughts which transferred to a low grumble in his throat that was clearly audible, even to Mac many feet away.

With Herculean effort, he held his emotions in check and ripped his attention away from the traitorous bastard. *What of this new race?* Peri'ackt knew exactly how he 'should' deal with the clans, for they were inferior in all ways. But what of this one? Something told him he could not afford to underestimate this one. Peri'ackt had only to think of the white ones to realize a new race, no matter how inferior it looked, may hold great danger. He mastered himself. Mastered his first impulse to strike the head from Shumak, and in doing so, took the first step toward a new world for his people. But it would prove to be an incredibly difficult step, and the first words from Shumak nearly broke his newly discovered control.

"My Chieftain." Shumak's words were like salt in a wound and it was fortunate for all that Peri'ackt stood several sword lengths away.

He was livid. "You would dare use those words with me? I will not even name you!" The words spat from his mouth, their venom slapping Shumak. "Tell me why I should not kill the traitor that stands before me. Killer of my blood? Tell me why?"

Mac had no need to understand the words, he heard the threat in the voice. It was all hisses and clicks, but rage and incredible tension was visible on the beast in front of him. A man ready to visit all the woes that had befallen him and his people on one individual. The air between them was suddenly pungent with a musky milky reek, the smell of a lizard under stress. A smell that emanated from both Shumak and the Chief. This meeting figured to be short and bloody if Mac didn't do something quickly.

Mac practically yelled, “Tell me his name, Shumak!” He needed to distract and defuse them immediately. Yet Shumak did not respond. The hissing language continued and he tried again, “Shumak!”

Shumak broke eye contact with Peri’ackt then spoke in Clan, “Thisss iss Peri’ackt.” The name came out as a guttural spit, and Mac was not sure he could reproduce it even after a bad nights drinking. “Isss Chiefss all peoplsss.”

Shumak told Mac about his leader. Of the death of his son and as much of the lizard hierarchy as Mac could wrap his mind around. *Good!* he thought, we’ve got the top dog here. No go betweens.

Peri’ackt now cast his considerable gaze upon Mac. “Thisss onss deathhh,” he said, pointing at Shumak. “Iss minse!”

If Mac was surprised by the clan speech, it was a pleasant surprise. Especially since he spoke it better than Shumak. “Welcome Chieftain of the People!” Mac ignored the threat to Shumak for now, as well as the chieftains name, cursing the lack of wisdom he’d used in bringing Shumak along with them. Yet he could not have known Peri’ackt could speak Clan. *Well I could have! If I’d just asked Shumak!* Mental flogging was as pointless as it was unavoidable.

“I wish peace!” The statement was simple and to the point.

Peri’ackt looked at the being that spoke Clan even more poorly than he, and considered the words. *Peace?* The words continued.

“Long have the clans and the People been separate. That is no longer wise.” Mac waited for a response and received none. *Maybe I need to speak slower?* “We both have an enemy.” He waved beyond the trees toward the river saying, “We do not need to kill each other!”

“Needs no peass,” Peri’ackt spat, his eyes shifting to Shumak.

“Do you need more enemies?”

Peri’ackt went still as Mac struck the proper nerve. “Wee sstrng!”

“Yes! You are strong. But the white ones are many.”

"Not fearsss whit onesss." Peri'ackt had not been ready to concede he even knew about the white ones, yet the being in front of him made that increasingly impossible.

"Yet you flee before them."

Still he tried, "Fleess nothingss. Warirsss." *Let him think we are a war party. Let them fear us.*

"You flee the white ones!" Mac stated flatly. "I have seen it."

"Maksss warss on themsss!" Rage and uncertainty threatened him again.

"No! They make war on you."

Mac had to be careful now. Peri'ackt needed to protect his position and Mac needed to break it down, but very carefully. He tiptoed a line between truth and antagonism using a more brutal truth. "We know this is true. And you know they make war on us as well! This is why we are here. This is why you are here. The white ones have driven us, and we, like you, have nowhere else to run."

"Peoplsss not drivensss. Nver runssss!" The last was an extended hiss of anger.

Desperately, Mac tried to read the reptiles emotions. Judging how far could he go. How far he could push. "No, you do not run. You retreat. But you are driven. This is why your females and young are with your war party. You have been pushed from your home."

Peri'ackt was stunned. How could this one know about his females and young? He was sure they were unobserved as they crossed the river, his outriders had seen to that. And his refugees crossed last.

"You are refugees," Mac stated flatly and firmly. "You need our help!"

"Needss nthinss frm clnsss!" He said it, but was beginning believe it was an untruth. He and his were on the edge. Perhaps…

"I believe we need each other, Peri'ackt! Five of your warriors lay stricken with wounds and may yet die." He said again, "I have seen them! We can help you." Mac wanted to shake the Chieftain with his knowledge. Knowledge he couldn't have unless he had a spy in their camp, or, the arcane gift of vision. The truth lay in between. Mac had spies in the trees above his camp, and

Mac had vision. But if the Chief was surprised, he hid it well, so Mac pushed again. "Will you continue to run?"

This did hit a nerve. Peri'ackt spoke an epitaph in his own language, and it was powerful enough that Shumak flinched beside him. He then spoke in Clan, "Peoplsss no…." He was angry enough the words would not come, so instead he said, "Minss killlss all." The voice was harsh, and Peri'ackt waved his hand to indicate Mac and his warriors in the distance.

Mac kept his composure. It was very difficult though because Peri'ackt followed his threat with a half drawn weapon. Mac's voice was even and contemplating. "Perhaps!" he said nonchalantly, even though sweat began to trickle uncomfortably down his back leaving behind a stream of chill and fear. There was no turning back however, they were committed to the course. "You may kill all that you see," he paused looking sternly. "What will that cost you in lives?" Another pause. "And we that you see before you… are not all there are. Many more clansmen await you." Mac turned partially away and closed his eyes, as if seeing things no one else could. Abruptly he turned back, saying, "And you are not as many as you would have me believe. Even now your encampment is perilously under protected and this has your mind very worried. The young warriors that walk your perimeter are afraid and ill prepared for what is to come. The few that guard the ford look over their shoulders, wondering if battle will take them from behind as well as the front. What will you decide?"

Peri'ackt spit, but re-sheathed his sword, and Mac stared at one of the warriors behind him until that one too put away his blade. *First crisis over!* He'd combined what Saber had shown him with a good guess at the Chief's current mind and struck true. Now? The olive branch.

"Would you find yourself between two enemies when one would count you as friend?" Mac raised his hands away from his body. Away from his weapon. It mattered little at this point that he was covered by several bows. The dye was cast. Silence covered them then, and it became a palpable thing. Mac had done all the selling he could think to do. Now he simply stood there, defenseless. Waiting.

"Clansss ndsss hlp!" The answer was a statement and a hiss, as if the dawning realization of where this would end cost

Peri'ackt much. But he was not ready to give all. He would make it look like it were he that delivered the clans from certain death, not the other way around.

"The clans and the People need each other," Mac replied.

"Hlpsss Clnss," he nodded slowly, then, "Gvsss Shumak!" It was a statement and a bargain asked. The People and no war, for Shumak. Not that Mac believed his word would mean spit if he turned over his friend, nor was there any chance he would acquiesce to the demand.

Shumak stood beside him, stiff and awaiting his fate. Mac smiled inside, but wondered what his denial would cost. Would it mean war? What was the life of one friend against a hundred? Would it be different had Peri'ackt asked for the life of someone Mac didn't know? The answer was the same. He shook his head and stated flatly, "No!"

Mac knew enough of the lizard facial expressions from being around Shumak to recognize extreme anger on Peri'ackt. He hissed, "Shumak isss Peoplsss!"

Mac shook his head again, "Shumak is no longer yours. His life is mine to give or take!" Did he read surprise? "Shumak has passed the line of skulls! Shumak has gone where no other warrior of the People dared go. The Rayattl!" It came out as 'forbidden place'. The confirmation of what Peri'ackt was told many days earlier caused another sputter, though Mac had no idea what it meant, only that his statement caused a dribble of saliva to seep past the sharp teeth as Peri'ackt's lips pulled back in grimace.

"Himsss?" He said it as if the coward in front of him could not have possibly done what Mac said. Yet it was independently confirmed by the reports. As was the fact that Shumak and his son were chasing a group that contained a new race, one of which was now standing here, like an equal, negotiating with him! One that, if he could believe the same report, had also done the impossible, and survived as well. Plus, he had to consider the visions which somehow gave this being access to the unknowable, the predicament of Peri'ackt and his people.

"Yes!" Mac nodded in affirmation, as if reading Peri'ackt's mind. He placed a hand possessively upon Shumak. "His life is now tied to mine and you may not have it!"

The fight went out of Peri'ackt. He was without good options and had no more chips in the game. It seemed Mac offered a possible way out, a way to live another day. *Besides,* he thought. *There was always an after!* After the white ones were gone there would be another reckoning. Then Peri'ackt could dance on their ashes.

But his pride was still as strong as ever and he stated loudly, as if this were all his idea, "Peplssss no warss ws clnsss!"

Mac breathed a silent sigh of relief. Peri'ackt watched him a moment then looked directly at Shumak and hissed and clicked. Then he turned back to Mac, "Meetss whn ssun iss agin. Tlksss of whte oness."

Mac waved a hand, "It makes no difference now. You can go no further. The white are at the ford ready to cross the river behind you. You will either fight them alone or with the clans. If it is to be with the clans, we will welcome you. Come to the Valley of the Moon…" Mac pointed over his shoulder, "…when the sun is again in the sky."

Peri'ackt was now torn, having just been dismissed by this being, which aggravated him almost back to the point of rage. Though it would be an impotent rage with nothing but bad options facing him. He calmly stepped back. Though in truth it was everything he could do not to leap into his saddle and charge back to his camp, for he believed in Mac's gift of vision and feared the white ones were even now overrunning his people. Yet to do so would severely diminish his position and no war horns sounded in the distance. So he did what any diplomat would do. He excused himself, deferring to make his decision on the morrow. But as he turned to go, he spouted another dozen words in his own language, these again shot directly at Shumak.

They watched as the People moved away hearing the stomping of many mounts in the darkness. Only now did he allow himself to believe he'd live awhile longer.

"Is it true, my Drakil?" Zukal's voice was neutral, but his eyes showed the fear of a believer. "Have the white ones come?"

Mac continued to watch until the People were gone but he nodded the affirmative. Tawnee had confirmed it while they talked with the People, the enemy was at the ford and had begun their crossing. They were coming, and Mac was deep in thought. Zukal waited for more, but Mac dismissed him without another word, needing to have other conversations first. "My apologies, Shumak! I did not think of how this meeting would affect you."

Shumak looked at him but said nothing, and Mac wondered what was going on behind those alien eyes.

"What did he say to you there at the last?" Mac asked.

"Iss Peri'actl. My Chiefsss. Sssays whn nxt Shumak sse hm. Hiss wil cut Shumak'ss head frm hisss bdy." Shumak turned and began walking away, for he knew now, beyond all doubt that his people were lost to him. This was possibly worse than the death he'd expected to face this night. Mac could only watch him go, his heart heavy as his friend walked away into the dark.

Turning back to the others he ordered, "Let's mount up! It's a long way back to the valley. And the enemy is coming!"

Chapter 16

The slow moving expanse of dark water only slightly distorted the reflected stars as it sighed past the ghostly figure standing on the bank. Small lonely clouds created interesting shadows upon the ebony surface, partially obscuring both the stars above and those in the reflection, their patterns describing an intricate and fascinating story. A story only the True Leader could read. Altil stood statue still in the tall grass watching this play. Absorbing. Calculating.

Across the waters stood the encampment of the reptile men. Worthy fighters they had proven, yet The One was not among them. Still, this fact would not save them. Altil had closed the noose and the People were inside. There was no concept of mercy in the Chalgu, and an army must eat.

Night sounds gently buffeted his skin, the waves of disturbed molecules collected by the billions of sensors on his dermas. These sensors then pumped the signals directly to his brain in a system much different than the human ear. Quite literally, Altil felt the sound. The woosh of the wings of a diving bird. The chittering of rodents in the grass and the soft sway of that same grass as it bent and swayed in the soft breeze. All of these things he felt. As well as a presence.

You are here! Altil watched the patterns and the currents and eddies just under the waters surface. Bulging and swirling making the stars dance and shift. There a cloud shadow obliterated the stars signifying a battle fought. A battle won.

The surface of the river was like a living moving map to Altil. A map of the past. A map of the present, and most important, a map to the future.

It was this latter map which gave him pause. The past was written in stone. The present was here before you and only by deceiving yourself would it change, and only then in the mind, never in reality. It was the future that remained cloudy.

You are here, he said again. The currents painted a future with many possibilities. Such was the fate of a seer, to see the possibilities, then try to assess the probabilities. To choose the likely path from myriad possibles. Long ago as now, he'd chosen his path, the only one he could see that would restore his god. The loss of which was caused by The One.

He pointed, then changed his statement as the silvery sides of a water dweller broke the surface, slapping with a resounding splash and sending out surface ripples that were quickly swallowed by the currents. Ripples that focused one star more strongly that the rest. *You are there!* his mind told him. *You are within my grasp!*

Altil, satisfied that of the ten possible futures he'd seen that night, six would end as he wished, turned to the warriors gathered to witness. They stood as ghostly as Altil, unmoving and half concealed in the brush, the sliver and black of night blending their white bodies into grey obscurity. Altil flashed his orders directly into their minds. He could have used the whistling language of the Chalgu as that would be less painful to the recipients, but sometimes it was good to demonstrate his abilities. And pain tended to reinforce his words. He watched as they melted into the dark and only when they were gone did he allow himself to shudder, the tremble shaking his huge bulk. Not because he feared battle. Not because he feared the death of his warriors, nor even his own. No. Altil, True Leader of the Chalgu, shuddered because of the other four futures he'd just witnessed.

Mac lay in the darkness, desperately tired yet far from sleep. By right of conquest, he now resided in the great skin tent of the late Solonar. A tent that was the very center of life for Clan Briss'y. In the darkness lay the rest of those who called Mac friend, including Jehkal and Shumak. The only one missing was Den'al who elected to stay with his own family in the camp of the Paliece. Solonar would turn flip-flops in his grave if he knew his proud residence now housed humans, a lizard, and warriors of Clan Paliece and Clan Sar-too.

It certainly caused a stir with the warriors who now called him Chief. Yet Mac and, as unlikely as it was, Solonak, had come together thereby avoiding problems. The new Chief/Mac telling them the way it was to be. The Chieftain's son embracing the new paradigm. Solonak himself slept soundly not far away.

The furs were itchy and his body was filthy with grit invading every crevice. Plus he smelled to high heaven. How long had it been since his last chance to bathe? He sniffed again, *Too long!* Sounds in the night were small and indistinct, though with several hundred individuals camped in the valley, noise was inevitable.

One difference between here and a similar camp on earth was the lack of dogs. Mac didn't know why that particular fact stuck in his head, but it did as his mind ran from thought to thought. There was no barking. The only animal noise was the occasional far off scream of a skeel which scolded someone or something for some infraction unknowable to its bipedal masters. Yet none of these items held off sleep, instead the cause was the visions Saber and Tawnee continued to send him.

The enemy had indeed crossed in force behind the People, but not at the ford. Mac was struck by the vision of bloated white bodies as they floated or swam across the water then pulled themselves up on the bank. They looked like animated alien corpses newly released from the grave. Even more than that part of the vision, he was struck by the numbers. Mac had no idea how far away they were, but it sure as hell wasn't the other side of the planet. To make it worse, Tawnee was scouting the far side beyond the ford, further on than Saber. Even more enemy soldiers were massing there. The People would have a fight on their hands tomorrow, and Mac would have one as soon as the day after. Everyone was looking to him for a solution. For salvation. Thus his quandary, *What can I do?*

The question echoed in his thoughts. There was no escape. No escape from the battle that was to come and no escape from the responsibilities of the Drakil, the responsibility to his friends.

Mac considered the Drakil for a moment. A title bestowed upon him by Niloc. Unearned, undeserved, and unwanted. Yet it hardly mattered what Mac wanted anymore, hadn't since he'd met the Sar-too. He was the Drakil! In all that mattered anyway, because he was the Drakil in the minds of the clans, and, since he couldn't escape physically, he was the Drakil in fact and flesh. He set that aside. They, the clans and his friends, would look to him for leadership. For a way out. For him to save their lives. This was the nightmare that would not let him sleep.

What can I do? It was not asked in a self-pitying way, it was more a proper placement of the nightmare and precursor to tactical planning. He considered the questions that flooded his brain. *Break it down!* What were his assets? Clan warriors, fighters one and all. What was their training? Battle hardened and trained from birth to fight. He had direct experience with their ability, having fought along side both Niloc and Jehkal. Would they stick in the heat of battle, or run? Without doubt they would stick. The certain death of their families guaranteed it.

Having assessed this, there were still many many other unknowns. These various clans were at best reluctant allies. Never before had they banded together in common cause. Mac considered this facet of his multi-faceted problem. Would they take his orders? Would they act as a unit, or fracture into their clan and family groups? Mac suspected they would fracture and he had no time to train them. No time to build a cohesive force necessary for the coming conflict. He chalked that up as a major advantage for his enemy.

What about tactics? There were so many questions here. Terrain was a major factor. This was not the wide open prairie where the clansmen could use their mobility and the speed of their mounts to greatest advantage. Instead, this battlefield was strewn with man sized boulders and a forest of brush and small trees with only a few large openings. Great if you had modern weapons or even bows and could fight from cover. Then they could clear fields of fire and use that same cover to great advantage. Unfortunately, all he had to work with was spear and sword. When combat came it would be up-close and very personal. Clan warriors could fight well on the ground, and did so, but mainly in one-on-one combat. They had no concept of the foot soldier. They were deadly and far more efficient in the saddle. Arrayed against them would be an exclusive ground force on ideal terrain. Again, the advantage was theirs.

In a rush his thoughts turned to the enemy itself. Singularly hideous and individually formidable. Four-armed fighting machines wielding multiple weapons. They'd bested a small group of them, but that was only due to surprise and overconfidence on the white one's part. He remembered the loathing and fear the very sight of their bloated bodies had on him and the others. That factor alone could shake his warriors, most of which had not yet seen the enemy and were being fed rumor. Rumor that Mac thought fell short of the reality.

Already the enemy was winning the psychological battle. Mac saw a fear bordering on the supernatural dread settling upon his warriors. They tried to hide it behind their clan stoicism, but it was there and it was visceral. Mac wished he could capture one of the enemy warriors and put it on display. At least his warriors would know it to be flesh and blood. Also he wished there was a name to mark them. Calling them the 'white ones' or the 'white warriors' gave them an ethereal quality. Another consideration to set aside, for now. *What else?* They could narrow the battle field. Saber and Tawnee had scouted up river looking for an escape route, and there was a place they could do it.

He deviated a moment to think about the cats and contemplate their part in his new life, smiling genuinely in the dark. They were now a part of him, an extension of his 'self' and a comfort he desperately needed. He felt them constantly now and feared putting them at such great risk in their scouting, and feared for them even more in the battle to come. If he could, he would send them away. But he could not. They were connected on a level far deeper than he could understand, and they would defend him totally at the expense of their lives. This is perhaps the only thing in which they would defy his order. His only hope was that when he fell, and the connection was severed, they would flee. Of them all, the cats had the only realistic chance to survive and escape what was to come. He shuddered. Those thoughts led down the path to despair. Quickly his mind moved back to tactics.

Up river? In that direction the river bent in a great arc till it met the wall of the escarpment. Less than a mile beyond that another tributary plunged down from the plains above in an impassable cataract. In that direction there was no escape, but Mac could draw his forces from the valley and narrow his line of defense considerably. In the morning he would ride and see it for himself. *In the morning.* Closing his grainy eyes he calmed his breathing preparing his body for sleep, only then aware of a figure kneeling near.

"Rebecca?" His voice was low and full of question, but his body felt as if he'd just been gut kicked.

"Ssh, Mac?" she whispered, all too aware of the many others around them. He hadn't realized how loud he'd spoken and his next question was merely the confused, and he supposed, stupid look on his face, almost un-seeable in the gloom.

"May I?" Her voice was quavering as she pointed at where he lay.

Mac pulled back the covers and she crawled in beside him, nestling herself into the crook of his arm, her body shaking, but feeling warm and comfortable against his side.

"Rebecca, I..."

She shushed him again, "Not now, Mac."

Her words were a salve to his soul and the wounds he'd held open so long. He felt her fear. Her uncertainty.

She whispered so softly he barely heard, "Just hold me."

And so he did, until her quivering stopped and she fell into a deep contented sleep. No longer was he the Drakil. No longer a man with the weight of the world and the lives of hundreds upon his shoulders. That was for tomorrow. For now he could simply be a man holding and comforting a woman in the dark. It was cathartic for him as well, and in moments he followed her into slumber, dreaming dreams far more pleasant than those that plagued his waking.

Not everyone in the darkness slept, and other eyes watched as the two nestled together. Solonak was a young man with a fierce spirit who tried very hard to master his emotions. Yet his father was dead and not yet cold in the ground, and the deed was done by the hand of his new father. His mother was secluded and mourning, and he'd assumed his new father would have loyalty to her! It was not unheard of yet rare for a chieftain to take more than one wife. So the fact that the Drakil had brought a mate of his own did not cause Solonak undue stress. No! It was far more than that. The one called Rebecca was a devil that inflamed him. She had bewitched him and claimed his soul with her beauty. Never before had anyone seen such visions as the two females brought by the Drakil. Visions become flesh which stirred the blood.

This one had seemed unattached. Aloof and uncaring towards the Drakil. Somehow, in the mind of the young son of the Drakil, attainable! His heart would skip and his breath catch whenever she was near, and he'd dreamt of so many things. Until now. Now she shared the furs of the Chief of all the Briss'y. The furs of the Drakil! With his foolish dream shattered, it was Solonak who would not sleep this night.

Mac slumbered, more content than he'd been in some time, his dreams unencumbered with thoughts from earlier. The warmth of Rebecca's body a cathartic presence which served as potion for sleep, so he was unaware as a large form pushed through the tent flap and padded silently forward. Was equally unaware when Saber settled in against him, though he would have been amused to see the near dead faint of their young guide and the shock of fear on the face of Solonak. A man who'd just been sending threatening thoughts toward his new father.

Solonak knew the great cats faced the banner of the Drakil. Heard by rumor that the cats were a part of him and even served at his command. Yet few had actually seen them. Solonak himself killed one not two seasons ago, though in truth the animal was weak with age and could barely see. Certainly they were an animal to be feared and one that could never be tamed.

The young Briss'y stifled a scream as the animal entered the tent, and only the knowledge that the Drakil held them in thrall kept the cry from his lips. Solonak swallowed and pushed himself as far away as possible, his back up against the tent wall till he could feel the chill from outside, and still it was not far enough. Not nearly. Pulling his furs up around him he tried to make himself as small and hidden as possible, yet whenever he looked the cat's eyes watched, never once blinking and never once leaving him. They hovered in the dark, huge green glowing orbs, and he felt them even when he turned away, causing his skin to crawl. He dared not move. The cat made that clear. Each subtle shift by the young man eliciting a low menacing growl. *It knows what I'm thinking! Somehow it knows.* Solonak shivered, and it had nothing to do with the cold penetrating his back. It would be an uneasy life he lived from now on.

They came with the dawn like wraiths out of the mist. Sunlight streamed like an aurora in the eastern sky, but the earth lay in darkness, not yet kissed by the light. Fog drifted past as it wandered through the trees, stealing vision from the eyes, its passing leaving the skin clammy and cold like a touch of death. From this mist came the Chalgu.

Peri'ackt heeded the warning the strange one had given him. Heeded his vision. Thus, his warriors were waiting and his people were fleeing. Fleeing towards a promise from a being he could not fathom, to a safety that was dubious at best. Peri'ackt and his warriors would fall back before this enemy. Giving battle if he must, but buying time for his people at all costs.

Under him his Thalk rumbled, its voice a deep bass clearly felt through his knees. It could tell the enemy and battle drew near and fear was not an emotion it knew. Peri'ackt had once believed the same of himself, yet now he knew better. Now he feared. It was an intense emotion that carried one on a current almost impossible to fight. It tore at the edges of the mind like a pack of Parth worrying a carcass, and worse, it was insidious, leaching his confidence. Now he, the ultimately confident chieftain, questioned his every decision, and once they were made, second guessed until he felt a doddering old fool. But now it was done and he actually welcomed the coming of the enemy. No more decisions. Like a salve, action was what he needed.

The mist effectively killed all scent, but the Thalk needed no such warning, nor did Peri'ackt. He'd sent his scouts out into the night and these confirmed what Mac told him. Those that came back! The enemy was on the move and the tension in his warriors ran through their mounts.

The white ones were near and too soon they appeared in a line three deep from out of the fog. Peri'ackt waved his arm and a horn sounded signaling the attack. The Chalgu froze as if they were one warrior instead of hundreds, then presented their spears in a bristling hedge. A hundred warriors on a hundred mounts moved forward in a slow thunderous roll. A single charge had Peri'ackt ordered. Forward and attack then spin and retreat. Bloody them and make them pause. Show them the power of the People. Yet as he saw the enemy arrayed against him he knew the order to be suicidal. The enemy was too close and far too numerous. Thalk took a lot of space to build up speed and Peri'ackt counted on shear mass to break the enemy line. It would not be so. Three deep, the enemy would simply bend around his warriors and spear them from the saddle. He paused and caused disaster.

Peri'ackt pulled violently at his reins, willing his mount to stop as the warriors around him moved past, surprise showing on the faces of those nearest. The Chief of the People searched desperately for his signalman who'd fallen behind and nearly ran into him, his Thalk screaming its displeasure at the near collision. "Retreat!" Peri'ackt yelled to the warrior. "Sound the retreat!"

The horn sounded, its voice harsh in Peri'ackt's ears as it blared out its desperate order. Whatever weight, whatever cohesiveness the attack had, it died in that moment. Most of the warriors heard the call, but some did not. Those that did tried to turn their mounts or stop before contact was made. Some actually achieved it ramming those around them. Chaos reigned on the field as the Chalgu accepted their gift. Screams and the clash of arms ruled the mist, though the sounds were oddly deadened. Many warriors died in that moment, and Peri'ackt, the blood draining from his face, realized what he'd done. The fear gripped him again. From several directions and multiple horns the retreat continued to be called, yet the order was overridden by the hooting screams of the Chalgu as they sounded their battle joy.

Near to hand Peri'ackt was witness to carnage. Two of his warriors lay dead, their Thalk down and writhing in their death throws amid many dead Chalgu. Another of his warriors battled in a circle of the white warriors, hacking from side to side in a desperate attempt to keep the weapons of the enemy away from his body. It was hopeless and the enemy knew it, seeming to be playing with their kill. Rage overcame Peri'ackt. Overcame his fear and galvanized his heart. To Peri'ackt, this one warrior fighting for his life represented all that had happened to the People. Their desperation, and what he perceived as his failed leadership. Without a word he spurred his Thalk forward.

Peri'ackt's world narrowed to a single point and his voiced raged in a battle cry as his mount burst upon the circle of Chalgu.

So intent were they on their prize that his attack caught them completely off guard. Even hoots of warning from other Chalgu failed to penetrate the din surrounding the trapped reptile warrior, and Peri'ackt crushed two before they were even aware of their danger. Two long strides more and he burst into the circle, pulling up beside his besieged soldier, their eyes locking. But only for a moment as the eyes went glassy and the one he'd tried to rescue pitched slowly off the back of his mount, pierced or cut in a hundred places. Peri'ackt's eyes followed him to the ground, this final despair seizing his soul.

So intent was the Chieftain of the People that he was not aware of the enemy as they crowded around. Or perhaps he simply no longer cared. The Thalk of the fallen warrior succumbed as well, huffing and panting as its legs gave out, following his master on the last long march. This is the vision that held Peri'ackt, the rest of the world had ceased to exist.

His first inkling of his fate was a spear, thrust by the huge arms of a Chalgu warrior, that drove completely through his thigh and deep into the chest of his mount. Bright red pain coursed through him and Peri'ackt screamed in agony, his scream drown by the mortal bellow of the beast under him. Pinned now to a dying animal, Peri'ackt overcame his pain and swung his sword in a mighty arc with all the intent of his dying people behind it. Down came the blade, whistling through the cold until it met enemy. Bones in his arm cracked and the sword snapped as a Chalgu caught it, blade flat, on the boss of its shield, the broken blade spinning off to fall and disappear in the grass. Three more spears transfixed the Thalk, and though it raged and lashed out, its attack was as ineffectual as Peri'ackt's. In two more steps the beast collapsed, taking its pinned master with it and spilling Peri'ackt at the feet of his enemies.

White bodies crowded around him and so the chief didn't see the valiant attempt by his guards as they tried to rescue him. Didn't see them repulsed, nor hear their cries as they retreated in defeat. Peri'ackt heard none of it as he waited for his death. Ten blades hovered over him. Ten blades waited to taste his blood. Yet not one descended as a hush fell over the field, only the wounded and dying could be heard, and that only as a distant roar in Peri'ackt's pain racked mind. Slowly the ring of fighters pulled back, then a single warrior stepped in to stand over him. It looked down and stared. Rage and pain had driven his fear far to the back of his consciousness, diminished, but not forgotten. It rushed forward now to become his predominate emotion, for Peri'ackt looked up into those hideous eyes and saw more than death. He saw doom.

Altil looked down, and if the face of a Chalgu could have allowed it, smiled. "Bring him!" His voice echoed in the minds of those around him. He grunted once toward his captive then turned and walked away.

Peri'ackt screamed as the warriors grabbed him. One wrapped a fist around the spear shaft and broke it off just above where it protruded from the ragged bloody hole in his thigh. Viciously the beast yanked, pulling Peri'ackt's leg from the broken stump and freeing him from the still wheezing Thalk. His life blood poured from the wound yet no attempt was made to staunch the flow, it was not required. Those destined for testing had no need of such care.

Peri'ackt, with his final desperate act, achieved what he'd set out that morning to do. Like the young Clansman Hatchik before him, his sacrifice allowed his people to escape. It took several hours to test a living vessel. It took far longer to test one that was a leader of his kind. With the sun at its zenith the final ax fell. Altil held the hemispheres of the Chieftains brain and read the omens. Seeing there what only he could see. The vision excited the True leader! This vessel was not The One, yet it had recent contact with him! For the first time Altil *saw* his enemy. For the first time he truly *knew* him! Altil now knew beyond all doubt that his search was near its end. With that final meaty thwack, so passed Peri'ackt, Son of Peri'ac'd, Son of Theris, Chieftain of the People. His sons were dead or missing, and so with his passing, so passed the mantle of leadership. Falling to the highest ranking officer left alive.

Shumak wandered the forest just after dawn preparing himself for the next stage of his life. The final stage. He was shadowed by Jehkal and his brother and he knew they were there, yet ignored their presence. Now was a time of reflection, or recrimination. So much had happened in the last few turns he hardly remembered the brash Wilderness Captain who commanded and controlled his own destiny, living amongst his own kind almost as a king. Every one of his soldiers owing all that they were to him, including their lives. He'd been independent and free.

However, he knew himself. He'd commanded with an iron fist, feared and possibly hated by the warriors under him. He also knew, despite his dreams and scheming, he'd progressed as far as he could possibly could under the strict structure of the People. At that point in time when he'd made his fateful decision, he was all that he would ever be! *Was this why he'd braved the Rayattl? Was this why he'd thrown away his life?* He paused in his wandering, asking, *What have I gained by my actions? What have I gained?* Had he stayed behind he would now be under the direct command of Peri'ackt. Probably he would be dead because he'd allowed the Chieftain's son to go and get himself killed. So what was different? On the morrow Peri'ackt would come and demand his life. It would be the price of peace and alliance, and Shumak had no doubt the Drakil would comply. It was the only decision Shumak was conditioned to accept. It was the decision he would make were he in the shoes of the Drakil. *So*, he asked himself again, *What have I gained?*

Jehkal watched Shumak and considered his own obligations and emotions. He had only to look to his left to see his obligations. There stood Rahkal, wounded yet healing swiftly, and alive only because of the lizard they now protected. A protection required because many of the clansmen would rather see him dead, though the deed would be done in secret, his head would never grace a clansmen's tent. Most of the females feared Shumak would eat their babies, feared his look would render them infertile. Jehkal smiled because that's what he believed not so long ago. The young simply feared, and the warriors saw only an enemy in their midst. The Chieftains saw an alien tied to the Drakil tighter than they themselves and would like nothing better than to have him removed. Even so, Jehkal would defend Shumak with his life! Yet not just from his sense of obligation, it was because the Drakil was wearing off on him. The Drakil had great respect for Shumak, and Jehkal found himself liking the lizard more than he liked many of his own race. This was the curiosity he himself pondered as he watched the internal struggle his battle brother was going through.

Suddenly, Shumak turned and strode back toward the camp, pushing right between his startled escorts. The lizard chuckled inward. *This is what I have gained! I have gone where none dared go. I have learned of the larger world. I have learned that all clansmen are not the enemy. And they are not as inferior as we believed.* An image of Mac formed in his mind. *I have become involved and a participant in great things. I have found my place.* He'd also found the one thing he, as a Commander of the People, would have never found. Friendship! And should he die this day he would die content.

Mac too was content. For the moment at least. He'd awoken that morning in a panic, pinned in his furs by Rebecca on one side and Saber, who lay gently snoring seemingly oblivious to the world, on the other. More than a shock as he'd not expected the cat to be anywhere near, let alone inside his tent in the middle of a clan encampment. Early morning light streamed around the cracks in the tent flap, stinging his eyes but giving no further details from outside. Not wanting to disturb either sleeper, and with nothing else pressing him at the moment, he lay back and watched the dust motes as they drifted from light to shadow, half listening to the muted noises as the encampment came to life. Near, yet still outside the tent, so for now, a million miles away. The rest of the tent was empty and a moment of anger flared within him, upset that his friends would let him sleep when he needed to be up and dealing with the terrible events to come. Then a moment later he thanked them for the few moments of peace he'd been given.

Feeling movement, he looked back and met a green-eyed stare from Saber, the cat now awake and waiting. Mac would give a lot to know what was going on behind those alien eyes. Why did the cat decide to sneak into a camp where anyone that saw him would have tried to kill him? Or at the very least, screamed in terror and raised the entire camp. That brought the other question; *how?* How was Saber able to penetrate the sentries and several hundred pairs of eyes? Even in the middle of the night someone should have seen. Security must be tightened.

Back to the why? Mac couldn't ask Saber and the *connection* was not historical. He couldn't read the cat's mind nor plumb his memories. Mac knew Saber would not have come unless there was strong reason. Yet to look at him now he was just a typical lazy tabby, waiting for someone or some thing to relieve the boredom. Of course it was a tabby the size of a St. Bernard and sporting huge tusks, but…

Enough musing. He would just have to keep his eyes pealed. Saber came for a reason, and so Mac would be wary; heaven knew there were more than a few things to be wary of. He would count himself forewarned enough to be on guard, and, since Saber was here, Mac would use him to make a few graphically important points with the natives. *As in, you mess with me you get the cat!*

Mac turned his attention to the woman still sound asleep beside him, her face relaxed, the tension gone. *If only I could keep it this way!* She looked…peaceful. *That's all I want. For all of us!* The thought was just born when suddenly Saber tensed and a moment later there came a commotion outside. Saber growled low in his throat and Rebecca woke with a start.

"Mac?" She mumbled sleepily, then louder as the tent flap was thrown open and Niloc burst through, Cam on his heels. Going from light to dark, they couldn't see where Mac was so they simply yelled, one in Clan and one in English, both with the same message. "They're here, Mac/My Drakil! You must come."

Mac panicked, reaching for weapons that stood too far away while cursing himself for a fool. "Where" he stammered? "Where are they attacking?"

Rebecca scrambled up and crawled backward, clutching the furs to her body. Not from modesty as they'd slept clothed, but from sudden cold dread.

Cam looked chagrined, "Shit, Mac! I'm sorry. Not the enemy…It's Shumak's people. Couple hundred of them. Women and children mostly. But the clansmen are close to crappin their britches. Shumak and Jehkal are there and so are Sue and Demitri, but we need you now or somebody's going to do something stupid."

It had been a long while since Cam strung that many words together; the normally ebullient man had been silent, almost sullen for days. Now he was fairly overflowing, and Mac caught the sly turn of mirth at the edges of his mouth as he watched his friend scrambling. Mac ignored him, relieved no attack was in progress, though still shaken. Lives hung in the balance and only quick intervention would stop it. Maybe not even then. The clans made it very clear they wanted no part of the People. If he didn't do something quick, they may have more than a little part of the People! The lizards may well carve a bloody path right through them. Despite the orders of the Drakil, the clans may let their xenophobia get them killed. When he, the Drakil, was out of sight, he was most conveniently out of mind. Mac cursed, "I should have prepared for this."

Rebecca however, was vastly relieved. "Wait, Mac. I'll go with you."

She stood and gathered her own weapons, but Mac was already half out the door and didn't hear. He gave a quick command to Saber and strode away, followed by Cam and Niloc. Rebecca, sad, but now committed to her path, followed as quickly as she could. Mac needed her, even if he didn't yet realize it, and more importantly, she needed him.

Mac ran through the camp. It was not hard to know where to go, even from right outside his tent in the very center of the encampment, he could hear the raised voices and the bawling of Thalk and skeel rising in the distance. *At least there's no metal on metal!* So far it was just words.

Just ahead the ground rose toward a small ridge, the very place Mac had first come to the clans! The same place he knew the People would be. To one side jogged his friends with Saber loping along on the other, the cat lending a curious and terrifying quality to his little group as they burst over the lip. Immediately, Mac saw a crowd of clan people. A large group of the lizard folk stood beyond them, interspersed within verge of the forest and open ground. Between the two groups was a sight that turned him cold. Shumak and Demitri, flanked by Sue and Jehkal and two other lizard warriors, stood with weapons drawn, facing a much larger group of armed clansmen, all of which were shouting and waving their swords.

"Hold!" He bellowed as loud as he could. "Hold damn you!"

The yell was in English yet it carried all of the passion and power of the Drakil, rolling like a wave across the clearing.

Individuals paused to look, then pointed, gasping to see Mac striding toward them in all his righteous anger, Saber at his side, the true and living symbol of what they believed the Drakil to be.

Those nearest pulled away, stumbling into each other in their haste to get out of his way, if not out of his sight. Mac fell upon them, not caring if it were a warrior, a woman or a child that stood in his way. He and those with him pushed and shoved, yet it was like watching an axe split wood. Of its own will, the crowd cleaved in two, creating a path to the center. None dared block his way. Saber growled or snarled and both parties were in too much shock do naught but watch and wait what form the Drakil's wrath would take.

At that moment he was no longer Mac Crowe; it was the Drakil-at'sakaal that strode into the no-mans land between the groups, bigger than life and threatening more than death. A nervous calm fell as he turned; finding those facing Shumak included his son Solonak and several other warriors he did not recognize, though they were not all Briss'y. Thalk bellowed and the skeel shied at the smell of a Kraagen, but they were well back behind the crowd and all those around were on foot.

Mac turned and looked out at the People. Clearly these were refugees, not an invading army. Before him was the result of Mac's confrontation with Peri'ackt yesterday. It was a worn, tired and desperate group that waited and he saw that they'd traveled most of the night to get here, probably fleeing in terror. Peri'ackt had taken him at his word. Here indeed was the life blood of the People. Their females, their young, and their old, perhaps the last of a race. Certainly the remnants of Peri'ackt's and Shumak's tribe.

Mac looked at Shumak who stood unflinching, though the other lizard warriors had taken a step back at the sight of Mac and Saber, uncertain what he was or what he would do. They were also confused by Shumak. Here was a man called traitor by his Chief and with a death sentence hanging over his head, yet still he stood his ground, willing to die beside them to defend his kind. Even more shocking was the presence of Jehkal, a clansman, willing to face his people in defense of a race not his own.

This is what Mac saw in that moment. *Perhaps there's hope for us yet!* Mac thought. He rounded on Solonak. "What goes on here?" he growled.

However his words were lost on the young man. He ignored his father, ignored his Drakil. He had eyes only for Saber. Saber returned the stare calmly, his tail whipping back and forth, leaving no doubt who would be the first to meet his ancestors should the Drakil not be pleased.

"Saber!" Mac said. The cat broke the contact then lay down at his feet. Through hooded eyes he looked up, extended a claw and began to meticulously clean it with a raspy tongue.

"Solonak!" It took great effort, but the young man pulled his eyes from the cat and to the Drakil. The rest of the young warriors stepped back trying to meld into the pack, abandoning Solonak to his fate. Mac assessed the mood of the crowd as he pinned each one that retreated with a piercing stare. It had certainly changed, now wary and anticipating instead of on the verge of bloodlust. He saw Zukal and the other Chieftains pushing forward, conspicuously absent a moment before. They were willing to let the mob have its way, but now that the Drakil was here, they could not afford to be left out of the events shortly to transpire.

"Solonak!" he repeated, as calm settled. Even the Thalk had ceased to rumble. "What do you intend to do Solonak?" The young man was now fully abandoned by his friends and stood alone. He looked quickly behind for support and found none.

Solonak licked his lips, "My Drakil..." His voice quavered at first then strengthened and Mac found himself at least a little admiring of the young man's bravery.

"My father. The Briss'y will not allow these…." He searched for a word and found none to fit his requirement. "We will not allow them to soil our grounds." Strong was his voice, though it was lacking conviction.

Mac raised his own voice, controlled and demanding, "Who decides what the Briss'y will allow?"

Solonak looked uncertain, but at the moment Zukal and the other Chieftains stepped up behind him firming his confidence, solidifying his resolve. "The Briss'y…" he began, then stuttered to a stop seeing fire spark in Mac's eye.

"The Chief decides," he said. Mac thought that may end his defiance. It was not so. "But you do not understand our ways, my father."

Mac's rage cooled somewhat, replaced by cautious optimism. Then it flared anew as the young man continued. "The Briss'y…We have lost many warriors to these…these things!" He waved a hand at Shumak. "Many kin have we all lost." When Mac didn't respond he spoke on. "They deserve death. Let the white ones have them I say, or let us kill them."

They were brave and stupid words. Zukal stepped forward and made as if to speak, but what he would say would remain forever unknown because Mac exploded. "And how many of them have the clans killed?" he bellowed, and Solonak fell back a step as Mac advanced on him. "You want to kill them?" he said, waving a hand over his shoulder. "Look at them, Solonak. Truly look at them. They flee the same enemy you will soon face. That is assuming you survive the next few minutes."

Mac let the implied threat settle over all who could hear him not just Solonak, him he grabbed by the arm. Mac dragged him forward, taking an incredible risk by turning his back on the Zukal and the rest. He pointed at an infant clinging to its mother, cringing, it's scaled skin turned pale by fright. "Will you start with that one?"

Solonak tried to pull away but Mac's grip was iron. He pointed to a warrior standing by Shumak. "What about him?" The lizard was huge and held its sword in a telling grip. "Do you think you could kill him, Solonak?"

Mac didn't want the man's youthful pride to answer because no matter what, Solonak would say yes. Instead, he raised his voice even higher and waved an arm at the gathered clansmen. "How many of you will die trying to kill them?" Mac saw Rebecca push her way through the line and the sight of her helped to calm him. Again he looked over the clans, letting his eyes stop on individuals. Warriors, then their wives, mothers and children. Then they settled on Zukal, hoping to appeal to the other authority figures. To sanity. "Would you have them turn *your* children away were the situation reversed?"

His voice calmed, "We can kill them. We are many and they are few." It was true. The clan warriors could easily overwhelm this group as there were few fighters among the People, and Mac knew where their army was. What was left of it was fleeing toward them though far away. "But then I ask you…

How many of us would be left to face the white ones?" Mac stared at a particular that stood in the midst of a family group. "Who will stand to defend your family? Who then?"

He let that sink a moment, then released Solonak, purposefully abandoning him to make a decision. He was very near Shumak and must now be the first to strike or the first to retreat. Or make peace! Retreat for a clansman in personal combat was not an option, thus Mac had to give him an honorable way out, and quickly. The rash young man may still do something stupid before Mac could set this right. Shumak showed his anger and aggression and looked ready to gut the man, but he stayed his hand, knowing the ultimate outcome should any blood be spilled now. Yet that did not keep him from stepping forward with a snarl to intimidate.

Mac pushed between them. "No, Shumak!" he said. "I have decided he is mine to deal with."

Solonak's emotions were overloaded. He'd fully expected to die a moment ago, and now he seemed to be all alone against the People. All alone against his father, against the Drakil. What seemed so certain a few minutes before now seemed foolish, and far more dangerous than the killing he'd tried to incite.

Mac walked him straight back to Zukal, then, raising his voice to new heights he yelled, "You who would call me Drakil! Hear me now. I have promised these people my protection. Promised an alliance against the white army! Even now the warriors of the People do battle with them and soon it will be our turn."

Pausing, he stepped back and pulled his blade. "I tire of this!" he said, pointing his weapon at Solonak. "Decide now if you will be as your father was. Will you seek greater wisdom? Or will you cling to ideals that have no place in the new world to come?" Mac thought, *new world my ass. We'll be lucky to live a week!*

Solonak grasped at the straw Mac threw him. Sheathing his weapon, he crossed his fists over his chest and bowed his head. Mac nodded, then dismissed the young man, shifting the clav'ls' point to Zukal and the other chieftains. "An army can have many chiefs… But it can have only one leader! Will we fight together? Or shall I abandon the prophesy… leave you to fight amongst yourselves and watch the white ones finish what is left?"

Zukal was truly shocked by the words. "My Drakil!" he almost shrilled. "We of the Paliece heed your words." Zukal crossed his own fists, yet palm out as befitting a leader of his clan honoring another. One by one the others followed.

My God! How many times am I going to have to fight this fight? Through it all Saber had lain calmly yet ready to aid Mac in any battle he picked, the same for Cam, Demitri and Sue. The same certainly for Niloc. But Mac had Jehkal and his brother, and Den'al as well. And he had Shumak. Each of them a comfort that lay in the back of his mind. Knowing they were there allowed him to do what he'd just done. He turned, and there beside Shumak was Rebecca, her bow in hand and an arrow nocked. A smile sprang to his lips. *With an army like this we can't loose!*

Positive action was what they needed now and Mac began giving orders. The first to Saber, and, somewhere out there, Tawnee. *Scout!*

Squeals of fright followed as the cat went from prone to a flat out run in the blink of an eye, weaving between screaming Thalk for the simple joy of it. Mac watched him go, willing him to be careful. Closing his eyes he issued his mental orders. They needed information for the next step. A step he would take as soon as the People were settled. By noon he would call a council of war.

Chapter 17

Mac stood on the tallest rock he could find and threw back his coat to let the cold breeze wash over his body. It was good at times like these to feel alive and the cold was just the thing as it brushed against every nerve on his skin whether exposed or not, goose bumps pimpling his flesh. Refreshing and invigorating, thought it was tough to cast off gloomy thoughts while he continued his survey of the killing ground. Out front, the earth flowed down a gentle hill a mile or so till it reached the river which could be seen flowing wide and swift between the trees. From there the land rose sharply on the far bank where virgin forest marched away as far as the eye could see. To the right, the land along the bank narrowed where the river bent in toward the escarpment. His desire to go there and prove to himself there was no way out had been quashed by the near insurrection this morning, though even now Tawnee wandered there, confirming what he'd been told.

To the east, toward the ford where the enemy would be in force, the land was wide. He would love to know the outcome of Peri'ackt's battle and Saber was on the way to look, but even he couldn't have gotten there as yet. Saber would circle wide, avoiding any contact. Mac had *seen* that as the cat climbed through the rocks and scree below the escarpment face. There was no doubt that a battle had been fought though. Shumak's people told the tale. Peri'ackt had heeded Mac's warning, breaking camp and sending the non-combatants to the valley. They'd traveled most of the night to arrive this morning. Peri'ackt and his army would have fought their holding action sometime near the dawn. Mac had no illusions as to the outcome, the only question was the cost of the butchers-bill.

Mac dismissed that thought as he looked even further east. The day was cold and windy and the sun shone bright, but the far horizon held a dark line that promised a new storm. Mac didn't know whether to pray for another killer blizzard or not. Perhaps Mother Nature could help stop the enemy! *If wishes were…!* He knew full well that any storm strong enough to do that would equally devastate his own, so he wisely held back his prayer.

Looking behind and up, he studied each lip of the boxed canyon. Eying where they terminated then angled back along the river valley. Further back and deep in the valley, Mac tried to envision Cam and Jehkal as they struggled up the single steep path that was the only way out of the trap laid by the enemy.

It was their job to find an escape route, or at the very least, a secure hiding place for as many individuals as possible. Mac grinned remembering the discussion he'd had with the Captain. Cam had argued vociferously against it. His position being that Mac, like it or not, was their savior and should not be left unguarded. That meant by him! The Captain then pointed out the very same facts presented by the clansmen. They said the trail was impassable in bad weather and could only be traversed single file, and only then by those of great strength. The interpretation was that rock climbing was involved, especially in the last few hundred meters to the top. There was a trail, but it led to the Sea of Tears, and the only escape from there was, as far as Mac could tell from the description, many miles away. Mac argued back, pointing out that a clan warrior went nowhere without a skeel! Certainly they would balk at anything that involved leaving their mounts behind. They just couldn't trust it to be true. Perhaps there was a way out. At least for a few of them. He pulled Cam close and whispered fiercely, "I won't let Rebecca and Sue die damn it! If nothing else, find them a place to hide."

That had done it. Cam gathered some rope and Jehkal and left immediately, but not without cautioning Mac to do, "Nothin stupid," until he got back.

Mac laughed at his back, "You know me too well, Cam! I save all my stupid so you get to see it." His voice fell to a mumble, "Wouldn't be the same if I didn't." But Cam was already gone.

Watching a moment more he tried to imagine where they were. *Good luck my friend.* He tore his vision and his thoughts away. He'd shot that arrow, now he must forget it and let it fly.

Mac's eyes wandered back to the grounds in front, watching as every available hand in the village worked to clear underbrush and small trees, taking the debris to build defensive positions. Their plan was simple and straight forward. Build clear areas where the advantage would be to their mounted troops and build funnels toward defensive positions where the mounted Calvary could act as the hammer against the defensive anvil. Given time, Mac figured they could build enough defenses and create enough kill boxes to thoroughly discourage any enemy. Given enough time they would build pits and booby traps. He would use fire in pits and improvised grenades, and add a hundred bows to their defense. Given time they would make this little valley impregnable! Then he'd let those white sons-of-bitches bleed themselves dry.

Time? Only one of the many advantages he didn't have. The gathering he called 'the council of war' pointed out many other deficiencies, and confirmed many of his fears as well. Zith'al, Cal'dil, Paliece and Briss'y. These were the only clans that made their way here relatively intact. Five other clans were represented in smaller numbers, the smallest the Atch'ee with a single warrior whom Mac suspected of desertion. These warriors held no voice in the battle planning and would be integrated into other clan units, over very vociferous objections on both sides. They would be used, but he would certainly not rely on either their loyalty, or their courage to stay in the fight. Their chieftains were not here and it seemed it took a Chief to truly secure their pledge, even to the Drakil. Mac cursed their lack of individualism. But the clan structure was strict and these warriors would wait for Mac to prove himself to their satisfaction, or for their leaders to show up and tell them to pledge their swords. Still, they said they would fight. Little choice did they have. Each individual or group was picked by one of the four larger clans, using some arcane method known only to them. Previous agreements? Marriage? Common raiding alliances? Less hate? Mac didn't know what it took and didn't really care. He'd let Zukal and the others work it out, and they did, though he could still see sullen looks and distrust among them.

The Cal'dil and Briss'y fielded the most warriors, and this was their homeland. First blood was an honor demanded by the Cal'dil, and they would not stand next to the Zith'al whom they considered liars and kin stealers. A tense moment in the tent as Chief Lac'al of the Zith'al, and Chief Em'ac of the Cal'dil came nearly to blows for some perceived slight that was a mystery to the humans, and it was no small miracle a civil war hadn't broken out already. Add to this volatile mix Shumak and his people, as well as the fear of imminent annihilation, and Mac feared the white ones would have little to do when they arrived.

A shout to his right brought him back to the present. Jehkal was yelling at a group of Paliece youths that were not performing to his high standards. The party was working to build a palisade of rock and brush and with typical clan stoicism, they took his abuse, though his tirade had little if any affect. They would have to work on the man's management style because certainly he had none!

Off in the distance, Shumak was working at the edge of the trees. At the war council he'd represented himself and his people well. The only one of the lizard people with any command of the clan language, and the only one with any leadership experience. Two others accompanied him, but only Shumak gave any input, fortunately, sound and rational. When things got hot, Mac wanted him near.

A gust of wind caught his coat and nearly pushed him from his perch, his arms wind-milled to keep his balance eliciting a laugh from below. "Watch out o-great leader!" Rebecca stood looking up, Sue sitting nearby and grinning. "Wouldn't do for the Drakil to fall off a rock and break his neck!"

He grinned just as another gust caught him, this one driving him to his knees. They were here as his personal guard, each armed with bows and other personal weapons. In reality, Mac wanted all the humans near. Cam he'd sent way by necessity, but he needed the others close, both for security and for comfort, needing to know they remained safe. Saber's showing up in the middle of the night had him unsettled, and the looks Solonak cast at Rebecca reinforced his sense of unease. Every clan male looked upon the women as if Aphrodite had descended to walk among them! But with Solonak it was something more. Mac would keep them close and leave no possibility for them to be harmed, or possibly abducted and used against him.

"Ah, lovely lady! Should I fall you will certainly catch me, thus saving this unfortunate wretch the indignity of such a fate!"

Her laughter was lyrical and it filled him with joy, her retort just as he expected. "Should you fall o-great one! I will surely step back to see just how high a Drakil can bounce!"

His made to retort, but it died on his lips as a horn sounded in the distance. As he spun, a second sounded, both coming from the forest in the direction of the ford. Mac knew the sound. It was a signal horn of the army of the People. Peri'ackt was coming.

A small army sat arrayed on skeel or Thalk facing the forest and the oncoming horns. Several now sounded and, though Mac could not see them, he could tell the People were close. It was still two hours before dark, but the low angle of sunlight cast deep shadows, though the light was bright against the escarpment turning the sandstone and granite of the cliffs a distinctive amber.

Shumak sat his mount a short distance away, backed by seven warriors. All that had escorted the non-combatants earlier in the day. Mac had Demitri and Niloc beside him, and Rahkal sat his skeel beside his Chief not far away. Other than that there was little order to their lines, one clan mixed with another with much milling about as they tried to maneuver and regroup around the various Clan Chieftains. There was shouting and even more confusion as the ranks continued to swell with latecomers.

Mac was disgusted. "Shit!" he cursed under his breath. "A sizable cub scout troop could rout us right now!"

That disgust was tinged with no small amount of fear. The People were coming, but Mac had no idea whether they were chased. Would an army of white warriors burst from cover? He took a deep breath and looked to Niloc while waving his hand at the milling mess. "Tell them hold, damn it!"

Niloc was used to the mixture of Clan and English. The Drakil always interspersed words from his own language when severely displeased. Niloc signaled a warrior behind them and suddenly the blare of a single horn bleated twice. A long plaintive call, then a short blat. Soon other horns sounded the same pattern, and for the moment the lines stabilized with all eyes to the front. *Better,* Mac thought, and he was about to give further orders when the horns were answered from the trees ahead, yet horns blown by reptile lips not clan. *Very soon,* he thought.

A crash to his right brought him about as a clan warrior burst from the forest, colored strings bouncing in his hair announcing him as a warrior of the Paliece and one of the scouts Mac had sent forward.

The man rode up to Zukal and saluted giving his report, breathless and fairly shouting, “They’re right behind me!”

Who, what, and how damn many! That was no report. If the man had been near, Mac would have struck him from the saddle. Yet there was no more time to think about the idiot as the first of the lizard warriors crashed through the underbrush and pulled his Thalk to a halt. Even from fifty yards away Mac could see a ragged wound down his right arm which still seeped crimson around a blackened scab. Wild-eyed it stared across at the new enemy he now faced, prepared to charge or retreat as needed. Yet he was only the first. Mac could see more movement behind as three more, then ten stepped out. With the sudden appearance of so many Mac was afraid they would be unable to hold the clans back. He could see it up and down the line, in the face of every warrior. Here was something to attack. Something on which to vent their rage and fear. Something they could surely defeat!

Mac could give them no chance. “Shumak, to me!” he yelled, and spurred his skeel forward, holding his arms out wide and weaponless. By agreement, Niloc did the same as did Zukal! All others froze in place. They didn’t know the plan and there had been no time to spread proper orders to everyone. Mac could only hope his display would hold them. It did and an expectant hush descended upon the scene.

Forward went Mac and his group, and forward went Shumak. All others stood frozen in shock or uncertainty, this, fortunately, included the People. As they approached, Mac saw still more of the warriors. They held themselves back in the shadows waiting on the events to come. There was no sign of Peri’ackt, so Mac would deal with the messenger first and worry about the leader whenever he appeared. He rode forward as far as he safely could given the evolutionary animosity between a skeel and a Thalk, and halted. It was Shumak's show now.

Shumak heeded the command of the Drakil and the hasty plan they'd agreed upon. This was his part to play for the good of his people. He would confront his death when the time arrived, but until that time, he would try to insure that no war was fought here and now. It would be up to him to see that no People died at the hands of the clans, and that the People spilled no blood of the clans. These were his only thoughts as he rode up to the wounded soldier on his borrowed Thalk, and so it was to Shumak's great surprise that the young fighter, reading the insignia upon Shumak's coat, his eyes going wide, saluted as he would his Chieftain, intoning the ritual words. "Peri'ackt, the great Chieftain, and father to us all is dead… As are his sons and the captains of his court. By right of rank, you are now Chieftain!" He hesitated a moment in embarrassment. "My Chief, I would know your name so that I might proclaim it to your warriors. My Chief, we await your will."

With that the soldier cast down his eyes and waited, leaving a stunned and speechless Shumak to contemplate his future.

At that same moment, Altil sat and contemplated Peri'ackt as well, and the ruin that was the Chieftain's body as it lay in its various and bloody pieces in front of him. None arranged! That was the point. The ritual that caused his death was far more than an execution, for Peri'ackt had the honor of enduring the Seven Steps! Seven levels of pain beginning with the removal of the eyes by use of hook and knife, and culminating with the skull splitting and 'reading' of the gray matter. Tomás de Torquemada, Grand Inquisitor of Queen Isabella, could have learned much from the Chalgu. Each step of the rite carried out with precision, care and agonizing sloth. Each step designed to dismantle the soul one piece at a time.

The Chalgu believed in a soul. Believed it to be the ultimate connection to the gods, and that the soul would reveal the future if extracted, piece by ritualized piece, in the Seven Steps. The Chalgu believed the soul resided throughout the body, not in one place, and that it would flee the cooling flesh when the body died, taking with it all its secrets. They also believed that at the point of transition, that very moment when the body died and the bonds which held the soul were broken, all knowledge contained in the world, past, present and future, were bestowed upon it as it passed toward enlightenment. Yet if the soul was separated, split from the whole piece by piece rather than in a single moment, each portion would see a bit of that knowledge. If one were careful and the rite performed just so, the knowledge could be intercepted and passed to one still living; the priest conducting the rite.

The Seven Steps were nothing more than ritualized dismemberment and evisceration, each piece carefully removed in the most painful method possible, then cast aside to fall where it would. A bloody stump or gaping hole would be cauterized by fire. This would continue until the body could stand no more and finally succumbed to blood loss and shock. Some victims lasted only two steps, or three, and rare was the soul that was strong enough and unlucky enough to last until seven. Peri'ackt was one of the latter, his screams enduring until the final ax fell, his spirit finally clawing its way free, released to whatever the afterlife held for one such as he.

Altil sat in a bloody pool, smiling with the knowledge he'd gained, breathing in the coppery smell as he prepared to continue, for the Seven Steps only dealt with the soul and there was still more to learn.

Blue smoke from guttering tapers cast a dim ruddy light about the tent, their illumination flickering and flashing in the cooling blood. Shadows danced to the small flames, lending a macabre illusion of animation to those scattered hunks of meat and bone that in their whole, used to be known as Peri'ackt. Bloodied and weary, Altil sat cross-legged and watched the play. Much as the embers of a fire, or the play of star light upon the water could reveal a future that may be, the patterns left in the aftermath of the ritual also held many truths. For Altil, the question was *which* of those truths would he choose to believe?

As before, the many paths held possibilities that alternately excited, frightened, or petrified the True Leader, with almost every one of the truths revolving around one entity that shined far brighter than the rest. *He* was the one they sought. The one whose image was much clearer now that the lizard had been tested and the memories contained within the vessel carved away and revealed. Recent memories which held the knowledge Altil so desired.

He wondered briefly whether the one who lay before him would be pleased to understand that he now held a place of honor among the Chalgu. All who brought knowledge or the path to greater wisdom held this place, and it was such with those who passed through the Seven Steps. Their names chiseled in stone upon the column of holies in the Chalgu valley. Forever remembered. Altil's eyes passed over the halves of the lizard's bloody skull, the two eye cavities, empty and dark, now staring at each other. *No! The honor is lost on this one.* His thought was not made in humor, Altil held no such emotion. His reflection was calculatingly cold logic. Also, he supposed, had their positions been reversed, he himself would care little for the honor.

As his ordered mind moved on, he thought about his goal; the capture of The One and *his* ultimate trip through the Steps. The culmination of which would result in the return of Altil's deity. What the True Leader sought was so very close now. Both in proximity, and in time. Fulfillment was near, and soon he would once again commune with god! The thought caused thick layers of fatty tissue just under his dermas to quiver, sending literal waves of excitement rippling across his body. *Soon!*

Leaning back he calmed himself, as it was the mark of a True Leader to rein in ones emotions. Instead, he closed his eyes, removing the visual distractions as he prepared for his next journey. There was a base to his knowledge now. He knew what The One looked like, the shape of his face, the configuration of his body. Knew even the tenor of *his* voice. No lizard certainly, and not one of the hide-covered vermin! Not one of the clans. He was something new, something curious, and very dangerous.

Concentrating on nothing but the sounds of the guttering candles, he drew himself inward toward a trance like state. Once there, he cast! Not like a fisherman tossing a single line toward a hopeful ripple, but like that same fisherman tossing a net over a vast area. With the cast his awareness passed from the tent. Through and above the Chalgu sentries surrounding the camp, flying above the trees and out toward the Valley of The Moon. He cast wide, though seeking then finding a single point.

Altil called and the Nannites that coursed through Mac did as they were programmed; they answered. The Nannites that inhabited the bodies of the Chalgu were similar in technology to those passed to Mac when he'd bonded to Saber. Yet similar was not exact and to Mac it felt like a hammer blow.

Mac walked beside Shumak as his friend explained the death of Peri'ackt and his resulting, though in his mind, temporary appointment. Temporary because Shumak believed others of higher rank may have survived and simply not made it here yet. His mind would allow no other thought. But he was of the People and for Shumak, this was a chance for redemption, and possibly even salvation, so he would be play chieftain for as long as it lasted. And should one of those others suddenly show up? Shumak would be faced with the choice of stepping down or claim the right of personal combat. It was the way of the people.

Mac heard the words and tried to follow, knowing he couldn't begin to unravel what had occurred. Couldn't begin to understand the nuances of such an alien society. What he did get was that a battle had been fought, Peri'ackt died, and somehow Shumak had ended up their friggin Commander In Chief! It was not something he could fathom, but *what the hell!* It made the job of integrating the lizards into his fighting force so much easier. Now, only half listening, he thought ahead to the first confrontation with the white army.

Almost unbidden, one of the enemy warriors filled his vision, stunning in its detail. Thc pale bloated body sporting four huge arms, though curiously, these held no weapons. Internally he stared, not realizing he'd stopped in his tracks. Shumak took two more steps before noticing Mac no longer strode beside him, the small group that trailed them parting as Mac ceased to move. Mac, eyes wide and dilated, saw nothing but the stark white thing that now dominated his world. A strange and fascinating vision indeed, then it spoke. Its words like thunder.

You are the one I seek! The words exploded in his mind and would have been no louder had he stuck his head into the aft end of a throttled-up jet engine. Just once he screamed, then collapsed to the ground in a boneless heap.

Unprepared for the attack, Mac writhed in mindless agony as Altil lashed him with a hundred mental whips. The Chalgu raced about, digging into his memories, prying away the locks to his deepest secrets, violating him in ways he would have not thought possible. Nothing could be hidden from the onslaught, and in a few more moments nothing would be left but a drooling empty shell.

Two things saved Mac in those moments. Altil had merely sought to find him when he pushed out his thoughts. The connection came as much a shock to him as it was to Mac; almost. Altil's first instinct was to attack and attack he did. Fortunately for Mac, in those first seconds his own brain was overwhelmed by the huge amounts of alien information. Overloading and nearly overwhelming the True Leader as the two minds and their accompanying Nannites sought to sync. It was beyond his control and he was in almost as much pain as Mac. Viciously he pulled back. Not out, just back. A mere hesitation in the questions being thrown at the human. It was in that small moment of pause that Altil was vulnerable, and into that silent gulf came the snarling presence of Saber!

Mac's awareness came slowly back as the dual screams echoed. Saber's in rage and Altil's in terror! They rolled about in his mind and he watched the play between them as he recovered. The white warrior was falling back, its arms waving in a desperate attempt to ward off the cat. Saber pressing forward, immense and impenetrable, yet unable to fully prosecute his advantage. Altil was not without his own defense and he recovered quickly, throwing up a barrier that Saber could not cross. The resulting stalemate allowed Mac to gather himself and regain his wits. At that moment, the Chalgu, emboldened by his ability to hold back the cat, spoke to him.

I know you now! I will destroy you.

Mac's response was automatic, *You think you know me... but you do not. And you cannot kill me! If you try, if you come against me, I will destroy you. Utterly.* Then Mac smiled an evil smile, *It is you that is at risk my enemy, because now, I... know you!*

Altil was used to total obedience from anyone he spoke to, and Mac's challenge shook him to his core. Never had he been spoken to thus. Never had he been challenged. The Chalgu were overwhelming. Defeat was not conceivable.

Mac took this hesitation as a good sign thinking he'd put the damn thing off guard. Mac reveled in Saber's strength, his indomitable protection. It was the reason he didn't break the connection as he knew he now could. The pain had passed and with it the fear. *Why do you wish to come against me and destroy yourself?* His question was full of confidence. Psychological warfare was a discipline he understood, and sewing doubt was its most powerful lesson.

It was then Altil made his first mistake. He answered. *I must! I must destroy The One to return my deity.*

With the statement came a flood of images. Mac saw a moon hanging low and bright in the night sky. Saw a night when it writhed in blue lightening as if agonizing in pain. Felt the dismay and ache that flowed among the Chalgu when one night the moon did not return. *Chalgu!* Now he had a name to put to the enemy. A vast plain within a ring of smoking mountains filled his vision, the remote and hostile home of these warriors. He saw them muster to the call of their True Leader, and saw them march forth in their multitudes. These images and hundreds more flooded his brain as he beheld *their* undeniable truth! Only one event would stop their onslaught and that was the death of The One! Mac's own death, and the thought shook him. All of this was because of him! The killing and destruction, all in an effort to find and trap Mac. *How! Why? The Drakil and now this!*

Finally, he witnessed the sacrifice of young Hatchik and the Seven Steps of Peri'ackt. Saw it. Felt it. Experienced it fully. No, it was far more than that. It was his hand that held the ax. His arm that drew it back and slammed it forward. Saw the hollow eyes and felt the hot blood splash his face. He experienced it all, utterly! The weight of lifetimes fell upon him in mere moments. His psychological warfare had backfired and Mac knew despair. Overwhelmed, he broke the connection, yet as he did he heard a final command from Altil, a command to his troops. Mac pulled his eyes open and looked up into the concerned faces of the crowd bending over him. He blinked twice to clear his head, then croaked, "They're coming!" *And it's all because of me.*

It was a solemn group which met that night in the tent of the Briss'y Chief. Perhaps the last night they would ever see. Mac told them of the Chalgu and his experience with Altil. Told them what was revealed by seeing into the mind of the Chalgu leader. How the Chalgu had but one mission. He spared them the horrifying details of the testing and his visions of all that had died at the hands of Altil. That was a cross he would bare alone, and there was enough horror and fear as it was. They were stunned as well, and could tell he was not revealing all. Eyes glittering, Mac stared at the fire they were gathered around and his voice faltered. He didn't know what else to say.

Outside, in front of the clans, he'd been strong, informing the chieftains their enemy was on the move and that battle would come with the rising of the sun. The Chalgu were marching and with their goal this close, darkness would not stop them. Mac put on his bravest face and gave his orders. It would fall to the Paliece to defend the center and have the honor of first blood. The warriors of the People, led by Shumak, would hold the low ground toward the river. They and their massive mounts would either pin the Chalgu in place, or sweep their flank depending on the ebb and flow of the battle. And so it went. He gave his orders, placing the Briss'y here, the Zith'al there. By agreement, they held back many warriors so they would have a mounted light Calvary as a reserve, ready to prosecute any advantage, or to rush and plug any breach. Their plans were sound, and Mac read defiance and pride in their eyes. He conducted the meeting with all the professionalism he could muster, all the discipline instilled in him over his years of service. Yet internally, despair threatened to rip him apart.

Outside he'd seen the children, frightened, yet excited by all the preparations as they watched the warriors and their rituals. Preparing themselves to face imminent battle. One far bigger than they could ever have imagined. Small groups gathered, usually friends, men who'd faced death many times, and won. They shouted out praises to one another, extolling their deeds. Making all of the battles, duels, or fights that had gone before seem glorious. Proving to themselves they were invincible. Yes, the children watched with wonder while the women cried and held them close, and Mac died a little more inside.

Other memories from Altil haunted him. Villages destroyed, men women and children butchered. He couldn't help but overlay those visions upon the faces around him. So many had died! So would all of these. *For what and why?* But he knew the answer. They would die because of him! Because of religious fervor. Because the Chalgu wanted his blood in some bizarre and tragic attempt to bring back a damn moon! Because of him it was happening, and nothing he could do would stop it.

Yet this was only half the tragedy. As he walked among them the clansmen watched him with a mixture of awe and worse, belief. They saw him as the Drakil! The one their legends promised would save them! To them he was invincible, and tomorrow the clans would follow him to victory. Mac stared at the fire and saw only death.

"So many," he whispered. A voice cleared, and, his musing broken, he looked around the circle at the friends that were gathered there. Struck by the emotions reflected in each, and struck by the faces that were missing.

Shumak was with his People, and Mac thought how oddly that situation had turned out. *Shumak, traitor to his people, now their king!* Mac bit down on his bitterness. He had no right to judge. Shumak had made his own choices, and he was prepared to die at the hands of Peri'ackt because of them. Shumak was his friend, and his success was an incredible boon. They didn't have to worry about the People now.

He did have to worry about Cam, and his thoughts turned there. His best friend had not returned from his mission. He and Den'al were out there, somewhere up the face of the escarpment, in the darkness with snow beginning to fall. Mac worried desperately for them. Worried they were hurt or dead, and despairing that he would never know which. It was his fervent hope the mission would succeed and they would find a haven or escape. Now he just wanted them back here beside him.

"Mac!" Rebecca broke the silence to get his attention. "Mac…we're not dead yet. There is always a way."

He smiled but it was a weary droopy thing. "You're right Rebecca, we're not." He let a pause fall between as he looked at her and then Sue. "It was my intention to find a way out for you both. At least a place to hide till this is over." He left them do doubt which way he expected it to be *over* as he made his lame attempt to apologize for the situation.

Sue settled closer to Demitri. Rebecca spoke for both, "We knew what you were trying to do, Mac. We wouldn't have gone." She amended it slightly, seeing the flash of pain cross his face. "We all go together or not at all." she said, not wanting him to think he'd sent Cam off on a fruitless trek. One that could have taken his life.

"We talked to Cam before he left." She looked guiltily at the couple, then at Niloc. "We all agree on this! We won't be split up again."

Mac lashed out in desperation, but it came out as anger, "Even if it means you die!"

She stared him down, un-phased. "Especially if we die," she stated flatly.

Mac deflated, inwardly relieved, for which he felt considerable shame. He desperately wanted them with him, needed their strength. But it was a selfish emotion. He would still try to get them to go if a place could be found. Order them if need be or have them bound and dragged if he must. Yet he conceded that this was not a battle to be fought right now. Still, he couldn't overcome his sense of defeat. He'd seen too much, carried too much knowledge. Staring back at the fire, watching the flames dance among the orange and yellow embers, he decided to explain what he could. "It's me they want." His voice was barely audible over the crackling fire. "I would hand myself to them if it would stop this."

But he'd seen Altil's *Great Plan*. His path of destruction to return his god. Mac was the key and would be taken alive, as would as many 'living vessels' as possible. It would take great suffering and the blood of many to achieve Altil's end. The suffering and blood would be Mac's and his people's contribution. Altil was not at all concerned with the death of his own soldiers and would use his army recklessly, thus, it would be a single overwhelming non-stop attack. They would fight until it was done and he possessed the key. Ordinarily, Mac would use such information to his advantage. An opponent with no regard for his troops could be defeated. But this army was different. Mac had never experienced such discipline and single minded determination. Call it what you will, religious fervor or hive mentality. It didn't matter. The result would be the same.

Demitri's voice was deep and forceful, "No, my friend! You have told us that it won't matter. We came to this place together and we will face this together. We have already survived the improbable. This will be no different."

Mac's heart pounded faster. So this was it, they would follow him no matter what. Closing his eyes, he tried to think of something meaningful to say. Something to express his love and pride for these people. There was no chance as a clamor began outside. Suddenly, the skin that served as a tent flap was swept aside. Mac and the others jumped to their feet as Cam stepped through. He was covered in snow, and when he pulled back his hood much of it cascaded to the floor.

"Damn, it's cold out there!" He pushed past Mac and stepped to the fire, ignoring the stupid looks on their faces. "Jehkal'l be here in a minute. Went to check on his brother. Shit Mac! Don't send me out with him ever again." He shrugged his shoulders as if to cast off a great weight. "Can't climb for crap. Too much time on a horse, and he has zero humor. Guy is dry as ash!" He paused for affect then turned and winked.

"You wouldn't think a snowball down the back would piss a guy off so much." He decided to leave out his description of the surprise on the Clansman's face, though that was funny as hell, and how he'd stomped around sputtering in fury until he slipped and almost fell off a ledge, but he saw his story was lost on them. He sobered immediately, "We went up the trail… made it all the way to the top, Mac." He shivered a great birddog chill. "Met five people coming down. Two men, a woman. Couple kids. Called themselves Grouw-sul or some such. About shit when they saw me. Didn't know if any more of their clan was left." His sentences were more and more clipped. "Said there were white ones up there. Killed and killed. We made it to the top, but saw nothing. Miles and miles of nothing." His voice fell to almost a whisper, "No caves either, Mac." He'd failed. At least that's the way he felt. "With the storm… no way out. I'm sorry." He couldn't look at the women.

Mac was devastated, but he couldn't let Cam know that. "You tried, Cam. You did all you could and more. Don't worry."

His voice lacked conviction, but he said, “We’ll just find another way.” Then he brightened, “I’m just glad you’re back. Let’s get you something hot to eat and I can fill you in on what you missed.”

They spent the next two hours discussing many things. Talking of life and memories while avoiding talking about the future. Instead, they spent time just being human.

Later, deep in the night, Mac pulled Demitri, Cam, and Niloc aside. “I have something to ask of you,” he said, more serious than he’d ever been in his life, pinning each of them with his eyes. He ran a great risk with this. “None of us… I mean it. None of us can be captured alive!” The risk was that he may so shock them by giving them the reason that they’d become useless to themselves or those around them. In fact, he feared what he told them now would get out to the rest of the clans and completely gut his army before the battle even began. Yet he couldn’t risk the women being captured, or any of them. Not since he’d seen the Seven Steps! He told them now, all of it. Sparing no detail.

“My god, Mac!” Cam’s comment was the only one. The rest were speechless, doubtlessly imagining the visions Mac couldn’t help but see when he closed his eyes, knowing that whatever they thought, it didn’t come close.

“I want your promise!” His voice was quavering and full of passion. “None of us lives to experience that. Promise me!” He watched their struggle. Especially Demitri. He was being asked to murder the woman he loved and was balancing that act against the horror Mac just described. Finally, lips tight, he nodded once then walked stiffly away.

“You’re absolutely positive about this Mac?” Cam’s spoke quietly. He looked at his friend. Again Mac’s anger flared, “You think I could make something like this up? Or would!”

“No, Mac… I don’t. I’m sorry. I just…” His voice faltered, then, “My god, I can’t believe it’s going to come down to this.”

Mac sighed, “I want your promise, Cam. Whatever it takes. I’m asking as a friend. I’m asking as a brother. You’re the only one I can count on. Don’t let her go through that!”

His friend bowed his head in defeat, “I promise, Mac. If it really comes to that, I won’t let her get….” He could say no more.

Niloc stood to the side. Mac had spoken in Clan for all but his plea with Demitri and Cam, that was in English. So he had time to consider the Drakil's request, though then as now, he rejected it completely. Niloc had no doubt the Drakil had seen what these Chalgu could do. Fully believed that the enemy was as hideous and implacable as he described. Yet there was another answer. Another outcome.

"My Drakil..." he began.

Mac cut him off, "I want your oath, Niloc!" The clansman didn't know how to respond. The Drakil was ordering him to take an oath, yet the prophecy pointed to a different path.

"Your oath!" Mac was insistent.

Perhaps this is the way, Niloc thought. *How it must be. The Drakil must have his trial.* He crossed his arms in front and bowed his head. "I give you my oath to do as you order should I be in a position to do so. But know this, my Drakil! The thing you ask will not come to pass. You are the Drakil-at'sakaal and the legends will not… They cannot be denied. Tomorrow all will be revealed. I know not how, but tomorrow, the Drakil will lead us to victory."

This was the longest most passionate speech Mac had ever heard from the clansman, and he was touched and very saddened by his conviction. He grabbed his friend by his shoulders and pulled him close. "You have been true to your belief since the first day we met. I respect that, Niloc. But I respect you even more as my friend. I will pray that your prophesy comes true tomorrow with all my heart. Believe me, no one will be more happy if I truly am what you say. But please, should things not turn out as you hope, fulfill your oath. Do what I demand of you." His voice trailed off, "Do as I ask."

Niloc nodded, keeping his emotions in check, keeping the balance of his thoughts to himself. The Drakil asked and he had only one answer. He nodded, "I will fulfill my oath!"

Chapter 18

Fear! Cold, rushing, and clinging to him like a second skin. Chaos surrounded him as he spun, blades thrusting and slashing, seeking his blood. Enemies were there, just beyond his ability to see in the dim smoky light. Shadows that screamed and howled, dancing and swirling in the grand dance of death. Right he slashed, then left, his blade tip barely missing an indistinct form that spun close then back into the murk. Panic built within him. He slashed blindly, flailing like a windmill in a hurricane wind.

'Rebecca!' He screamed the name, yet it was lost in the cacophony. *Where is she? Where's Niloc? Cam?* Wild and desperate he attempted to penetrate the confusion, casting left and right till one familiar face drifted past. 'Jehkal!' he screamed again, as a blade whipped past his face so close he felt the air being cut just under his lips. 'Jehkal!' He screamed the name again and again until he was hoarse, but the clansman was gone.

Over and over he cut and slashed, feeling his blade strike nothing. Each slice followed by taunts and jeers at his ineptitude, at his inability to save his friends. His utter helplessness. In ever more futile attempts he tried to touch the enemy. Once more he struck over his small shield, feeling the sword finally strike home. Felt the blade sink deep as it stuck in the wood of another shield. With a brutal wrench, the weapon was torn from his hand leaving him all but defenseless against the hoard. Where before there was panic and fear, now there was mind numbing dread! Alone and defenseless against the shadows his vision changed. Again he witnessed the horror of Peri'ackt's last few moments in this life!

Mac screamed a sound so loud and so primordial that all other sound stopped. His enemy, frozen in place, gave him a chance. One chance! He turned and ran. It was futile, his legs felt like they were mired ankle deep in mud. He swung his arms and pumped his legs yet speed eluded him. Then a new sound drummed out of the darkness, thumping and throbbing. It was the echoing sound of his heart pounding wildly against his breastbone. Thumping and thumping until it physically hurt, yet that feeling was as nothing compared to the incredible agony a moment later when the tip of a spear pierced his back!

A spear in the back! Mac startled from his dream, sitting bolt upright and flinging away his covers. *A spear in the back!* Even now he could feel the entry point prickle his skin so real it seemed. Of all the things that frightened Mac, this was perhaps his greatest personal fear. Not that someone, or in this case something couldn't kill him, especially in a mêlée where a strike could come from any direction. That would be acceptable. No, Mac's roots were steeped in thousands of years of military system history. He amended that. The human military. His great fear was that when they found his body, all the wounds would be in the back! *I am not a coward!* He said the words almost as a chant, but the thought and the dream still echoed as he lay back down. *I am no coward!* he repeated, trying to shake his mind clear. It didn't work. No matter what he did he couldn't change what was to come, nor could he alleviate his fear. It was less than three hours till dawn and death sat his shoulder like a pirate's parrot, endlessly mocking him!

All were awake and eating a hot breakfast around a blazing fire, though none had much of an appetite, most simply picking through their food. 'All' included the chieftains as well as the humans, Shumak, and Mac's own clansmen, Niloc and Jehkal. Outside the snow fell. Not hard, yet constant, and a good two inches already covered the ground. Mac stepped outside earlier and was struck by the smell of it. So normal. So earthy. It smelled just like snow back home. That fact alone left him melancholy. It wasn't fair. It should have looked alien. Should have felt and smelled alien! That would have been *fair* on a day like today. Instead, the world he'd stepped out into could have been any earthbound wood. It left him with the feeling that all that had happened was but a dream. All he had to do was to play his part to the end, then he could wake up. Yet the cold and his nagging bladder belied that thought, and it became all too real as he relieved himself in a fetid trench latrine in the gloom.

Mac closed his eyes and listened to the dark a moment, steadying himself before reaching out. Saber was there, waiting, as was Tawnee, though *there* was relative. Saber shadowed the main advance and Tawnee circled wide, skirting the river. Other things he felt as well. Altil was a presence chipping away at his awareness. But Mac knew him now, and was able to hold him at bay, easily shutting out his attack. Yet there was something else. A new presence. Or perhaps several. Not frightening and somehow familiar. Familiar like Tawnee was familiar. He tried to attract that presence, but it slipped away like sand through his fingers. He tried to hold it, but could not. Another curiosity for another time.

Steadying himself, he blocked everything but Saber, seeing what the cat saw as he watched the steady advance of the Chalgu. They marched in columns two wide, and very long. The lines disappeared in the distance, obscured by limb and branch, by falling snow and darkness. They were utterly alien and incredibly disciplined. Mac had no idea how far away they were. That information would come with the scouts the clans had out. No, this information was more to confirm their numbers and abilities. To watch how they moved and see the structure of their command. Search for weakness, anything to exploit. He saw little. The warriors were cookie cutter similar, and he saw nothing obvious. Nothing to give him hope.

You will be mine today. The words pierced his guard like a slap. *It is foreseen. You and those with you... with your blood, will pave the way for the return. I have seen it.*

The words were guttural, literally scraping their way across his consciousness like nails across a chalk board. Mac shuddered once, but he was determined not to allow Altil the satisfaction of defeating. Not here, in his mind.

I know you now, Mac returned, his mind voice strong and firm. *And I know you have never faced one such as me!*

Altil's voice rode over him, *It matters not! I will have you. I must!*

I must? Did Mac detect a small hesitation? An edge of desperation? Uncertainty? He took a wild shot and struck home. *Know this my enemy! You may think you have seen the future. But which future have you seen I ask? Have you seen that I am not of this world? I have traveled between the stars, Altil! You yourself said I drove away your god... I did!"* His voice was like a cannon shot. *"Think, Altil. A single human had that power! Look at me!"* He demanded. *"I... drove away your god!* He felt Altil step back as if struck. Mac pressed on, his voice deep and commanding. *There are many futures and you cannot know them all.* Mac unwittingly struck Altil's greatest vulnerability. He *had* seen many futures, some of which he feared. Some he dreaded!

I too have seen 'a' future! Mac boomed. *You are not in it!* He released his anger and his pent up despair in a mighty rush. *If you come against me today... your god will truly be lost!* Mac's mind lashed out, augmented by the full weight of Saber. *Know this! I am death to you, Altil! You...* he spat in disgust, *and your god!* His last words were thunder, and as the thought echoed away Mac could find no more sign of Altil!

Son of a bitch! he thought, as the connection dropped away and he found himself once again outside his tent standing in the snow. *Round one to the good guys.* His elation lasted only a moment as he reviewed what he'd seen of their army. Yet the glow remained. The Chalgu weren't invulnerable. Mac still expected to die this day, but he vowed to do so on his own terms, and not until Altil lay shattered at his feet.

Altil stopped and went dead still in the darkness, his guards and aids stopped as well. He in fear, and the others in confusion, though the columns of troops merely flowed wider as they passed their leader, oblivious to anything but marching ahead. The One had touched Altil and struck a nerve. He, above all others, understood the fickle nature of the flow of time. The danger of reading the future. Reading the streams of possibilities, how they eddied, split or converged.

Each future was based on probabilities and Altil had analyzed each one. His current course of action held many possible outcomes, and one used all available information to predict the most likely path. His enemy was bottled up with no possible escape. Altil's warriors, bloodied in many battles and hardened by the Chalgu's special military training, were superior to any foe they'd yet met, no matter the numbers. Here was the convergence.

Two of his three armies could be brought to bear, and the Chalgu outnumbered the enemy seven or eight warriors to one. Even the weather fell in his favor. The One would be unable to manage this battle. Altil saw this in his mind. The One could not do what Altil could. Could not place his commands directly in the brains of his Generals. Altil would be all over the battle field, The One would see only that part the storm allowed. Altil had read the future and calculated the probabilities. The Chalgu were supreme. The Chalgu would have The One. Altil would have The One; before darkness touched this world again, his god would return.

Altil should have felt nothing but elation and anticipation. Yet The One had also seen the future. Altil had not read it in his memories, that part was closed, but the description was clear. The future his enemy had seen was one of the futures Altil had glimpsed when he'd watched the slow moving waters on a starry night not long ago. That future had left Altil cold, causing his current and certain trepidation. Altil succumbed to a rare emotion as rage slowly sparked to full flame. The vision was false and The One had succeeded in making Altil doubt! Rage settled quickly into grime resolve. He concentrated a moment and sent a mental command to each and every warrior. It was even more imperative now for The One to be captured alive. The battle had now become very personal, and Altil determined to add an eighth step to the ritual!

Mac was a different man when he reentered the tent. His resolve hardened, his back ramrod straight as he told them of his encounter with Altil. He gave it straight. Told them everything he'd seen through Saber. Let them know the odds. They deserved nothing less. Mac gave his final orders and, even as the horns of the Chalgu sounded eerily and frightening in the distance, he gave them hope. He addressed the clansmen, and Niloc swelled in pride as the Drakil's words rolled over them.

"Your prophesy calls for a great struggle. A time when things are so dark all seems lost. I truly believe this is that time. Your traditions say survival… and the birth of a new world… will not be possible without this sacrifice, and not without the one you call Drakil. You believe this Drakil will bring a miracle. Bring you deliverance. You believe me to be the one your ancient words describe." He paused and caught every eye, then said, "I believe it as well!" In their eyes and in their faces, he saw the change. Where before there was only fear backed up with forced bravado, courage new steeled within them, and what peered out was a growing flame of hope.

"Our sacrifice today will be great, and I tell you with truth, the odds against us are incredible. But we humans never give up! We have a saying. 'As long as there is breath in your lungs, there is hope.'" He took a deep breath and plunged ahead. "Your families are the cost of failure. Fight with them in your mind and we will not fail." Mac looked them over a final time. "Tonight, as darkness settles over the land, we will gather here once again and feast the clan's, and the People's, greatest victory!" The Drakil-at'sakaal and Lt. Colonel James Macintosh "Mac" Crowe, was rewarded by elated yells and a clashing of many swords on shields. And even though he believed much of what he'd just spouted to be *tripe*, even he felt a glow of hope.

Mac stood at the very center of their defenses listening to the advance of the enemy, easily tracked by the near constant hooting calls which rose up from the forest and from the low country near the river. Each sound blending into a single hideous symphony which echoed back from the cliffs behind. Dawn had come and gone, but the light was still dim. The clouds were heavy, gray and thick, and low enough to touch, the sky spitting a constant barrage of large gray flakes. Mac didn't know whether to despair of visibility that was little more than fifty or sixty yards, or welcome it. Perhaps the blinding storm would spare him the broader horrors to come.

Behind and around him stood most of his friends, together at the last. Briefly, his thoughts went to those who were not. Shumak was far to the right with his own people. Jehkal and Rahkal were nearer to his left with the Paliece. If he yelled loud they would respond, but still were unseen in the falling snow. Den'al was a mystery. Mac had no idea where he was. Jehkal said he'd given the young man an important mission, but became evasive when pressed. Mac had to trust that Jehkal knew what he needed to do, and he suspected the mission had something to do with family. So he let it lay, and instead gathered comfort from the presence of the others. Dare he say it, his own kind.

Cam was a rock beside him and Demitri a mountain, Sue very near, almost in the Russian's shadow. He looked at Rebecca who stood staring into the murk with her bow clutched in a fist, white crystals framing her face. A Valkyrie ready for war! Mac was stirred and proud of them all, yet his inventory was incomplete. Niloc stood out front in his self-appointed position as the Drakil's shield. Niloc the true believer. The man without a clan who would make of Mac something he never wished to be. Because of that alone, Mac would try to live and die as the Drakil the clansman thought him to be. His attention was again drawn to the front as the sound of breaking limbs proved the enemy was near. *Soon*, he thought, *Very soon.*

Almost on cue, Saber and Tawnee burst from the woods, causing the clansmen nearby to gasp in wonder as the cats rushed too Mac. Two cats? Further proof he was who they believed. Mac just wanted them here so he could control what happened. Of all of them, he believed the two cats could escape. Saber would not abandon him, even after Mac ordered it. But he figured that after he fell the connection would be broken and the cats would be free of him, free of their obligation. He impressed this on their minds. Either way, he would not know.

A scream to the right brought the first sighting of the enemy, and all too quickly there were more. Solonak and the Briss'y Guard stepped forward to join Niloc's position in front of their chief, though his *son* cast Mac a peculiar look. Solonak had a plan that was very different from his fathers. If the Chalgu came straight for the Drakil, Solonak would push aside and let them, for he held grand hopes of stealing away the human woman who so occupied and consumed his thoughts. Mac stared him down, not knowing why the boy chose now to challenge him and having no time to care, because the pieces were set and the enemy had arrived.

It was hard to tell where first contact came. The falling snow deadened sound and the cries from his right and left seemed far away, though they were likely only a hundred and fifty yards from his position. Though it mattered little where first contact happened. Within seconds their entire line, from Shumak's end near the river to the escarpment edge, was fully involved. From a tactical standpoint Mac would have been proud. The plan they'd laid out worked to perfection as the enemy pushed into the cleared areas, seemingly oblivious to the dangers. Their numbers became a hindrance when their lines were diverted around obstacles and pushed into ever smaller funnels. The shear weight of their masses became a liability as they were pressed together in ever thickening crowds, their own bodies defeating their ability to wield weapons. Clansmen all along the funnels took advantage of height, striking down with spear or sword. And the chant and cry that was heard was not of fear, but of triumph as the enemy first milled, then began to push back as their losses quickly mounted.

That was the cue for the mounted Calvary. Roaring their battle yells as they swung through prepared gaps and fell upon the enemy. Whether clansmen on skeel, or reptile warriors on their great ugly steeds, the outcome was the same. The slaughter was complete. Each pocket was cutoff and wiped out. Reeling, the Chalgu army pulled back, streaming away in full retreat. Mac would have been proud! And horrified. In war, success was born on the blood of the victor and the cost was high. Many a clan warrior and many soldiers of the People died in those few minutes. The victory was heady, bitter, and short lived. They had defeated the Chalgu! But only in part. A part that was a fraction of the whole, and now the enemy knew their defenses.

Mac heard the cries screams and the clash of arms. But not those of the battle general, because all that and more unfolded directly in front of him. Mac stared into the gray as the hoots of the Chalgu drew closer, clutching his clav'l in one hand and a knife in the other. His bow was slung over his back to be used for targets of opportunity only. Their few arrows would mean little against this foe. Everyone tensed and waited, imagining and fearing the fight to come. Mac knew the fear would bleed away as the adrenaline of battle took hold, but it was this waiting and imagining that was hardest to bear. Unfortunately, they had not long to wait.

They came as a dream. With snow falling as thick as fog, the first he knew they were there was a ghostly movement not thirty yards away. As bare as the day they were born they came.

The Chalgu had stripped their furs despite the cold and their naked white bodies were ethereal, seeming to float toward them, the only real color the black tips of their spears and the tan of their shields. The defenders stood mesmerized, watching as death flowed toward them like white vapor. Gone was the cold. Gone was the wind, and for Mac it was like staring into the center of a snow globe. Artificial and unreal. At twenty yards the details became clear yet still they stared, and would have for some time more had one of their precious arrows not interrupted the scene.

He felt the whip of the arrow when it passed by, hissing as its fletching cut the air, his eye catching the flight as a fast moving blur, tracking it right to the target. The lead Chalgu warrior had a look of great surprise when, as if by magic, a wooden shaft sprouted from his chest. It howled in rage and pain as Rebecca's arrow knocked it from its feet, the shocking contrast between white and suddenly flowing crimson adding deadly reality to the ghostly scene.

Broken from their reverie, the clansmen and humans sprang their trap. Mac surged forward behind the Briss'y just as the screams of skeel sounded the flanking attack. So sudden and so unexpected was the assault that the Chalgu milled in confusion. Just as in the other kill pockets, the battle was short, fierce, and deadly. Chalgu fell beneath clan swords and clansmen fell to spear and sword. In moments the snow was churned to bloody ruin, the screams of the dying overriding the calls of the victors.

The Drakil was merely an observer caught up in the maelstrom, unable to strike and unable to retreat as the press of bodies moved him to and fro. Screams of rage and pain and the hooting battle cries of the Chalgu became one unending sound blending with the clang of metal and thunk of sword chopped wood. At one point amidst the chaos, he thought he heard his name called by a voice carrying high across the killing ground, but he was unsure of who or where, or even if. Then, suddenly, the clansman in front of him lurched backward, a spear thrusting through him and out his back. His assailant cast the body aside, spear and all, then advanced on Mac, sword and shield swinging wildly. Mac was surprised and unprepared for the attack as the four white arms sought him. One swung a sword high and over in a downward chop. Another pushed at him with a shield, and two more, bare handed, tried to grasp and hold him firm so the steel that sought his life could split him it two. He pushed backward and swung his own weapon, striking and cutting deeply into one bare arm, though if it bothered his opponent at all it showed no sign. Mac dropped to his knees as Chalgu steel whistled by, barely missing his head, then flew backward onto his back from the smack of the shield. His landing was soft, cushioned by three inches of slushy snow, but pain quickly followed from the blow of wood to ribs. A one armed slash that had brutally tossed him limp as a rag doll, knocking the air from his lungs with an audible whoosh. Dazed, he looked up, seeing death. The Chalgu stood over him, his sword a spear point poised above his chest. Then it was gone.

There was a flash of tan as two bodies crashed into the warrior, carrying it, arms flailing wildly, over onto its back. Mac rolled in time to see the fallen warrior eviscerated by Saber. Then Tawnee, closing her jaws over the white throat, pulled away with a jerk of her maw, leaving nothing but red ruin behind. The already dead body quivered and shook, flinging even more blood into the red watery slush. Mac rose shakily to his feet in time to see the last of the Chalgu die. At least those caught in the trap, for beyond he could see many more streaming away in defeat.

Jeers and shouts of joy chased the Chalgu, as did several mounted clansmen. Quickly, Mac yelled out calling for the signal to re-group, a clan horn blaring two short and one long over and over again. But two of the mounted warriors could not, or would not, hear. They didn't heed the call as they charged into the trees. In moments their battle cries changed to bellows of pain. Only one skeel reemerged and without its rider. It stumbled forth and made it halfway back to their lines before collapsing, slashed and stabbed and cut to ribbons, blood flowing from its wounds in rivulets. A final call issued from deep in its chest as it died, then a weary hush replaced the pandemonium from a moment before. Weary and now subdued, the victors viewed their work, and its cost. Many went to their knees, grim faced at seeing friends and brothers lying lifelessly on the field, others attending their own injuries or assisting the more gravely wounded.

As in a dream Mac stood and stared, seeing everything and nothing. Numb, yet steeling himself for the discovery of who had died and who still lived, walling off his emotions as a Commander must. There was much to do before the enemy came again and he must prepare his people. With a sigh he began.

So ended the first battle for the Valley of The Moon.

Chapter 19

Mac slogged back up the gentle slope, assisted by a gore covered Cam. All of it the enemy's and all gathered proudly by the young Captain. He'd killed two Chalgu himself and gave an 'assist' on a couple others. "My God, Mac! We did it! We beat em!" Cam was elated, Mac less so. Especially as they stepped past a dead Briss'y warrior, his skull neatly split leaving his mind open for all to see. Many others lay wounded, moaning, or looking about in bewilderment. Mac reached down to help one young man, a boy really, with a stab wound in the thigh back to where he could be cared for. Others had to be carried, still others would need to be buried. But only if anyone was left to do the job after the next battle.

"Yea, Cam. We beat em." He tried to grin but couldn't, looking at each body, yet not, deathly afraid to see a familiar face.

Niloc stepped up beside him, taking the wounded boy in his arms. "My Drakil! This is a great victory." The Sar too was cautiously elated, but elated all the same.

Mac flashed in anger. He spat, "Look around you man! Does this look like victory?"

This battle field was no worse than any other. Dead and wounded of both sides littered the ground, but the images were much more startling because of the alien bodies and the bright sprays of blood on virgin snow. The image was indelible. "This isn't victory… This is just death…" Mac pushed past, leaving Cam and a confused Niloc behind.

"Cheer up, Niloc!" Cam's mood was cheery. He was on the verge of battle madness and it flashed in his eyes like a berserker of old. "He's just mad cause a big white guy dumped him on his ass and almost killed him." Cam patted the alien on the back, then winked at him wickedly, "He'll get into the spirit! Just wait till he gets mad." Cam walked away following his commander, leaving Niloc behind to, for the hundredth time, re-evaluate everything he knew of human behavior.

Mac was amazed at how far he'd actually traveled from the start of the fight to the place he'd been knocked on his butt. And Cam was wrong. He would not 'get into the spirit!' Killing was a business to be conducted as coolly and methodically as possible. The most dangerous fighters killed without passion, and Mac was very dangerous. Right now he needed to find out how the rest of his line fared. And how fared his friends. Casting left and right he forced himself to study each body, praying not to see a familiar face staring glassy eyed into space. Thus distracted and with his guard down, Altil pushed into his mind.

Prepare yourself human! I come for you. Now! Mac stumbled physically, then lashed out with his mind. It was like swinging for the fences and missing the ball, for Altil was gone.

Come to me you son of a bitch and I'll put your stinking maggot head on a pike! He cast out the words with such mental power and violence that Saber and Tawnee howled in the distance, pained from the assault. But whether Altil heard or felt Mac would never know. His vision cleared only to find Demitri standing on the rise, yelling and waving frantically.

"They're gone!" His voice was anguish as he rushed forward grabbing Mac in an iron grip. "Hurry, Mac! They're gone! He took them!"

Mac dug in his feet in sudden panic. "What are you talking about! Who…"

"No time, Mac. The women. They're gone. We have to find them before…"

Demitri was dragging him now, pulling him back toward the village. Mac's dread and turned into an icy cold sweat. But he couldn't run blindly and he physically pushed Demitri's hand away. "Who took them damn it!"

The Russian's eyes were wild, "Solonak! Solonak took them!"

The surprise was complete. Mac pieced together the look the young man had given him just before the fight with someone screaming his name during the heat of battle. Suddenly it all made a sick sort of sense and he cursed because for having not seen it coming. "Why…?" But he knew why, and it frightened him more than death. His mind was working in overdrive as he considered possibilities and actions he should have and now needed to take. Yet it was not to be. His thoughts and desires were interrupted by the one thing that could take precedence over this crisis, the return of the Chalgu army.

Solonak was hunted! He knew that now, and knew his folly. An error the he and the five warriors with him would not survive; a fact that made him desperate. The plan had been elegant in its simplicity, and perhaps that was the problem. Like his father, his *real* father, his emotions had overcome his good sense and he had not thought through his actions. Not foreseen all possibilities. Unknown to his new father, there *was* a place to hide. Solonak spit as he thought of the alien who now held that position. There was a cave in which to hide. One where even the Chalgu might not find them. The very cave where his mother waited out her days of mourning. Remote and hidden. Solonak made sure by adding all the camouflage he could last night. There they could hide; emerging after the carnage was over and the Chalgu had moved on. *Alive!* It was a simple and selfish plan, and one that would have held a high percentage of success. But only if the Drakil had not won the first battle!

Solonak and his compatriots counted on failure, and it was inconceivable to them that the Chalgu could be stopped. As the battle was joined, they pulled out of their places and moved behind in the confusion. When the Drakil and his guard rushed forward to meet the enemy, they'd left the two goddesses alone and unprotected. And why not. They were behind the line and among *friends*. Quickly Solonak and his friends rushed them, grabbing the two women and clubbing them into unconsciousness. Their struggle had been brief and violent. The one called Sue dodged the first blow, delivering a strike against poor Sa'sool that would certainly leave him childless, and, as he folded upon himself in agony, she'd screamed out the hated name of his father. Solonak himself delivered the blow to render her unconscious, but the damage was done, they'd been seen.

Even that problem would have been rectified quickly had the Chalgu not been less than imagined. Their defeat was a surprise that still shook the young man as he huddled inside the cave, waiting with the others. *All* were now his enemy. Clan, human or lizard. If they came near they would have to die. Solonak shook in fear and frustration. He would now die, and his fate may well be shared by his mother and young brother who waited in the dark behind him, tending his unconscious and gravely injured captives.

Grimly he watched the ministrations, wondering at his foolishness, but then a smile softened the line of his lips. Placed there by hope, because in the distance he heard the unmistakable sound of Chalgu battle horns. The enemy was back. *Maybe,* he thought. Maybe they would complete their task, thus saving young Solonak from his fate.

Shumak lay against a large rock, propped there by two of his warriors. A position from which he could watch the end. His wound ensured he would not participate in the fight. Ensured he could not run. Ensured his death would be swift when the enemy broke through. An event that would unfold shortly with the enemy massing and ready to surge. He sighed, knowing there would be no surprise this time. The Drakil had bought them a longer life, but only a very small portion.

He watched as his soldiers prepared, feeling great pride and equal sadness. It was not so long ago he'd begun a journey, a personal and selfish search, unwittingly leading him to this precise point in time. This place, and what he now considered his destiny. The Wilderness Commander who'd deserted his people only to become their king! He smiled inside, *I could become a parable.*

Wincing, he shifted in an attempt at comfort that was not to be. The hole in his chest wheezed from a lung that was punctured when a Chalgu spear had taken him, lifting him several hand spans from his saddle before the shaft broke then depositing him in a bloody heap on the ground. Only the great strength of his race allowed him to survive, though even now he felt his life draining slowly away. Yet there was enough left in him to see the end. He would allow no other option.

Sad he was to see the bodies of his dead. Another reflection. In years past the sight would have left him indifferent.

Those beneath him were a tool. His to employ and, like a broken sword, discard when no longer useable. But now...now was different. They fought for him. Were truly his. And the pride of their skill and great strength was awesome to feel.

Far more of the enemy littered the ground, and Shumak would pit any five of his against ten or fifteen of theirs. This was not just pride speaking, the evidence and proof cluttered the field. Unfortunately, all their advantages would ultimately avail them little, for there were easily twenty or thirty enemy to those same five. He would watch his soldiers die and then the females and young would follow. But Shumak smiled a pained reptile smile. Yes they would die, but they would die in glory.

As if to echo his thoughts, the hoots and calls of the Chalgu assault screamed and echoed up from the trees. They were coming. Shumak coughed, feeling a fresh spurt of blood trickle warmly down his chest as he watched white shadows move in the distance, knowing the end would not be far distant now.

Altil strode forward with his troops, his position in the center opposite where The One stood like a beacon in the distance. He was too close to his goal to have the object of their efforts killed by mistake. His orders were explicit, delivered firmly and painfully to each Chalgu mind. No warrior was to engage The One… no matter what. Without doubt he would live to undergo the steps, as would as many others as could be efficiently spared. It mattered not if *warriors* accompanied The One on his final journey, Altil would be just as happy to sacrifice the young and old. Their blood and pain would equally suffice.

Another mental command from Altil began the assault and he nodded in satisfaction as the hooting calls answered, preceded the rush. He himself followed in the wake of the great white wave as it foamed against the defenses, pushing against, into, and then through the clansmen. A smile caressed his mind, followed by a prayer formed of a single thought built with care before being thrown skyward. He watched The One and spread his hands to the sky. *Soon!*

Den'al, followed by his small band of fighters, crept up the slope of the hill, careful to keep hidden as they approached the hidden cave. One so well hidden he wouldn't have guessed it existed had he not watched Solonak disappear inside a few minutes earlier. The young man was torn, his loyalties sorely tested. He was here by the command of Jehkal who somehow knew this fool of a Briss'y, this false Chieftain's son, held evil intent toward his father and covetous eyes for the Alt-sul. Jehkal had felt that Solonak's evil would play out against the Drakil personally, and Den'al had prepared himself to prevent patricide, watching from a distance in case the Briss'y attacked the Drakil in the heat of battle. Therefore, he and his men had been out of position when Solonak struck the women, and he'd cursed vehemently. With no good options, as the first battle raged, he'd abandoned the fight, shadowing the traitorous Briss'y. Desperately afraid a direct confrontation would cost the lives of his friends, Rebecca and Sue. The village, as they passed through, was deserted, the inhabitants not in the fight fleeing to the very back of the canyon where they huddled to await their fate.

Now, as he moved in to surprise Solonak, the battle below was renewed. Den'al's orders lay here, but his heart was ripping in two, torn between friendship and loyalty to his friends, and an overpowering desire to be with his clan. To die with them battling the white ones. A crash of arms, and the bellow of horns and skeel and Thalk, sounded in the distance, echoing and reechoing off the canyon walls. He listened only a moment, then Den'al closed his eyes and dismissed his misgivings. Though they would *all* die in the next few minutes, or hours, he was determined that Rebecca and Sue die free, weapon in hand and with honor, not trussed, wrapped and lying utterly helpless. With a silent nod to the others, he drew his clav'l and rushed the cave.

Mac's anguish was complete as he stared at his Russian friend. The very two he was most desperate to save were the first to fall, and to an enemy within.

Demitri was desperate grabbing at him and yelling, "Come! We must go! We must find them. Sue…" his voice trailed off in a moan.

Mac hesitated just a moment as he stared back over his shoulder and into a rushing tide of enemies. In their midst was a sight that froze him in place. Making time for that single instant stand still. There he spied the architect of all that had befallen them. All the woes of the clan and the People. All the woes of the humans. *Altil!*

"Mac!" Demitri yelled in his ear and spun him sideways, almost throwing him from his feet. "What the hell is wrong with you! We have to go after them." His voice cracked and strained with emotion, and Mac had never seen such desperation on any face, human or otherwise. But he knew it was too late, and knew his next decision would haunt him for the rest of his very short life.

"I can't..." Demitri staggered as if struck. "Go, Demitri. Go find them. I must... I have to stay here."

Demitri pulled away in disbelief, eyes wide. The Russian gave him the most hateful and accusatory look he could muster, and Mac heard a single muttered word as he staggered away, though it echoed in his ears as if shouted by a hundred voices, "Bastard."

Mac watched him disappear. Then, closing his eyes and wishing his friend all the luck in the world, he did the only thing he could possibly think to do. He sent a command to Saber.

The clash of arms brought him back around. Clansmen beat against the rising tide, flinging themselves bodily upon the enemy, only to be thrown back bloody, bruised, and stunned. Mac watched in amazement and despair. The Chalgu warriors, borrowing a page from the ancient Romans, locked shields and formed a wall three lines deep as they advanced. Each counter attack was met and repulsed, yet as Mac watched, he saw it was almost without loss of life.

The Chalgu were using the heels of their spears, the flats of their swords, and the wood of their shields to batter and beat back each attack. They were not killing! They were herding or disabling. Any clansman unfortunate enough to be heavily wounded was dispatched by a quick slice to an exposed throat. The lightly wounded were flung back against their brethren, and the unconscious were grabbed and passed hand over hand behind the Chalgu lines where hundreds of other eager hands gathered them up and carted them away. Mac was chilled to his marrow knowing the reason. This was not war. It was genocide.

Once again, his despair turned to rage. The roller coaster of his emotions threatened to drown him, but the figure in the distance was galvanizing. Mac pulled the bow from his back and nocked an arrow. Reaching his arms high, he drew the string to his chin, his entire world narrowing to a single line drawn from his outstretched fist to the center of Altil's chest. At that moment it could not be more clear. Mac would make him pay. The clouds drew back and the snow slowed as if nature herself conspired to help him. He took one breath then two, held the last a moment, then let his fingers relax. The arrow leapt from the string, whipping the air as it flew, a dark blur winging its way across sixty yards.

Niloc, Jehkal and Rahkal fought side by side, a living wedge forcing their way into the Chalgu wall as they tried to reach Cam. In front of them, a line of white bodies two deep separated them from the human and three other clansmen. Only a moment before, the Chalgu had swarmed forward cutting off the small party and their attack was merciless. Already two were down, clubbed senseless, and Cam and one lone Briss'y fought back to back as the press continued. Even as Niloc charged, both went down, eager white hands grasping and pulling them toward the rear and a fate the Drakil had described in such terrible and livid detail.

With roars of rage and the battle cries of their ancestors on their lips, they clove into the Chalgu ranks, the shock of their attack cutting deep. Niloc slashed left, removing the arm of an adversary, rewarded with a gush of hot blood that sprayed him from crotch to chin. He pushed further, killing the same warrior with a slash to the throat. He heard battle around him, but for him it ceased to exist. His eyes held only one goal.

Cam lay just beyond his outstretched hands and with a final push, Niloc burst through the line, rushing forward to stand over his friend. Then he turned and knew despair, for their rush had not been as devastating as he thought. The Chalgu had not been beaten, they'd parted to let them into the circle, and like a wave, the Chalgu flowed back into the gap, completely surrounding the three would be rescuers. Niloc took a huge breath and prepared himself to die, knowing he would never let them take him alive. Looking back at their line, he was just in time to see the Drakil loose his arrow. *Gods speed*, he thought, as the white wave began to crash upon them.

The arrow was like a living thing. A small god of war, brought to life by the energies stored in limbs of wood, bent nearly to the breaking point by a string of catgut, the engine of the energy, the warm flesh of a human body. The strain on shoulders, back and fingers, was enormous as the stored potential screamed for release. It was as simple as relaxing those same fingers to set it free, and that potential had only one place to go. The shaft of the arrow accepted the power in full, flexing from butt to tip, converting potential energy into kinetic as its speed went from zero to 175 feet per second in half the blink of an eye. Its passage from the bow marked by the rebounding hum of the string and a small puff of ice crystals blown loose from the feathers.

Stately and swift it carved its ballistic arc, knowing not its destination nor deadly purpose. Sharper than a knife edge the tip cut the air, splitting even snowflakes as it passed, the serrated point whistling a tune none could hear. As it passed over Niloc it hit the top of its arc and gravity bent it to its will, pulling the arrow over and down in a curve towards the broad white chest of Altil, True Leader of all the Chalgu. The aim was true as the shaft of alien wood delivered a gift from earth! The point, fashioned from a chipped heat tile off the ill fated Atlantis, slammed home with enough force to knock Altil from his feet, but not before carving a bloody path clean through him from breast to spine. The arrow, most of its energy now spent, burst from his skin in a fountain of crimson. Then on it passed, burying itself in the snow five feet behind, disappearing a full second before Altil hit the ground.

Shock and pain and outrage pounded through Altil. Somehow The One had reached out and struck him. His vision blurred and he felt the heat of spilled blood mingling with the quickly melting snow underneath him. Felt the runnels of fluid rolling down his chest, staring at the small hole and watching in fascination at the play of red on white. Then, incredibly, he rolled over and stood up. Had he been human he would have died almost instantly. Had he been of the clans or even Aranu, he would have died. But Chalgu were internally different, and the arrow missed his vitals, causing great damage but not death. Leaving in its wake, volcanic fury.

Each breath was agony, each movement a reminder of how dangerous his opponent was and thus, the necessity of his death. Even now Altil felt his own life literally dripping out of him. His wound was devastating and would kill in time, yet his death would benefit the greater purpose and he would be that much quicker to his god. But his will was great as well, and he vowed to live long enough to serve the Steps upon the living carcass of The One.

Altil stumbled slightly then closed his eyes, no longer worried about being struck by another dart as a wall of shields stood impenetrable in front of him. His thoughts reached out to his warriors. They felt his pain, many gasping and many hooting at his agony. Touching each of them, he gave new orders. With his wound the battle was taking too long. Their stratagem of capture rather than kill would no longer suffice. From this moment they would turn their blades to edge and kill rather than capture. Death to all not already subdued and passed into captivity. Death to all that remained. All except The One. Weakened by loss of blood, he fell to his knees and finally submitted to a healer.

Den'al was first through the mouth of the cave, crouching and thrusting his blade forward to clear the expected counter attack. Pushing in blind was akin to placing your head on a chopping block, but no one impeded his way. Inside he stood warily, swinging his sword from side to side as his eyes adjusted to a gloom lit only by dim flickering fire light, the inside far larger than he expected.

"Hold, Paliece! Or the humans die." The words were delivered as if the speaker were casting something distasteful from his mouth. But Den'al also heard the unmistakable tinge of fear at its edges. The speaker was beyond the fire, yet Den'al knew the voice and he could see its owner standing over a wide-eyed Rebecca, his clav'l pressed to her throat. *Solonak!* Another warrior held a knife to Sue as well, though she lay as limp as the dead. A clanswoman and her child huddled behind in a dark corner, as did two more Briss'y warriors, blades bare. Den'al pushed the rest of the way in, stepping to the side and allowing his friends room to enter, until all stood arrayed and ready, though swinging a sword in the closed space would be an equal danger to friend and foe alike.

"Release them, traitor. Provide no more dishonor to your house!" Den'al's voice was deep and emotion filled. The hostages were as much his friends as his charges. He and they shared much.

Solonak bristled. He was afraid certainly, thinking he could have survived, instead being found out. Now, with the battle rejoined, it was possible they could still see this through with their lifeblood still flowing in their bodies! But only if they could kill these before him, and the Paliece's words struck like a whip. "You dare call me traitor!" His blade wavered at Rebecca's throat, and her eyes widened even more as the edge drew a thin line of seeping blood. His words dripped venom, "You who brought that abomination among us!"

"That abomination is the Drakil! And *your* father." Den'al spoke in a deliberate and slow voice, using the time gained to push ever so slightly closer and to bring rage and rash decision to the Briss'y.

"*My father!*" Solonak spat, "That alien thing killed my father!"

Den'al saw the clanswoman flinch at Solonak's words. So here was Alegna, former wife of Solonar, now wife to the Drakil. Solonak's mother.

"Your father… The over proud Solonar, brought his death upon himself. He was a fool, as obviously he raised his son. Your mother must be very proud."

Solonak snarled, knowing he was being baited but not caring. "This fool," he slapped his chest, "Will have your heart." He waved his clav'l in signal, springing his trap. Then sprang forward to meet Den'al.

Den'al saw the signal but was unprepared for the suddenness of the attack, or the scream to his right, impossibly loud and echoing in the rock chamber. A young Briss'y, hidden in a dark corner, lunged out, taking a Paliece warrior in the chest, the weapon punching out his side. But Den'al's shock lasted only a moment as Solonak rushed him. He blocked the first thrust and stumbled backward before swinging a counter. By then the rest of the Briss'y had joined the attack, and Den'al and his friends could only fight for their lives.

Demitri stumbled past huts, abandoned campfires, and the detritus left behind by people rushing to, or fleeing from battle. He was delirious with emotion. Sue was lost and Demitri could not find her, and Mac had abandoned them. Abandoned him! Demitri heard the battle joined again behind him, and perhaps at some level he understood Mac's decision, but that realization was superceded and drown by his other fears. He ran forward toward the edge of camp, past the pen that held the skeel herd that included Shorn and Baron. The animals raising a cacophony of sound as they assaulted the barrier, excited to desperation by the sound of war and the smell of blood. A desperation fully shared by the human as he ran past.

Demitri ran faster, passing beyond the corral and into the jumble of rocks that marked the edge of the scree field under the escarpment wall. He slowed to a walk, hindered by rocks and brush and a lack of breath. Below and behind he heard the ring of sword on sward, their echo rebounding from the mass of rock to his front. Staring at the snow, he sought to make sense of the crisscrossing tracks left by many feet. Here someone paused, a yellow stain indicting the need. There someone ran up the trail, and several other tracks entered from a point further on, impossible to tell who or when. *Think damn it!* he scolded himself needlessly, then closed his eyes in frustration. It was then he realized the sound of sword upon sword was much nearer than the valley below. Though muffled, it came from just ahead. Adrenaline flooded his system, lending steel to his failing strength. Demitri rushed forward, finding a trail of trampled snow that led to the mouth of a cave he would never have seen had the sound not drawn him. Caring nothing of the danger or what lay beyond, he bent over and rushed inside.

Five remained in the fight, Den'al and four of the enemy. The last of his compatriots lay dead and Den'al was pressed into a corner, fighting in desperation. Solonak may be a fool, but he was a skilled fool, and two other swords now pressed in from the sides. Den'al had mere moments to live. The fourth warrior abandoned the fight and walked back to Rebecca, his intent unclear. Solonak stepped back and out of the fight, allowing his friends the room they needed to finish it.

"Who's the fool now?" The words were full of confidence and triumph.

"You are!" The voice behind Solonak was deep, full of hatred, and utterly alien. He turned in shock as Demitri straightened and lunged forward in one swift move, his clav'l slicing across Solonak's arm, drawing first blood. The young Briss'y pulled away and parried, nearly taking Demitri in the knee as the Russian jumped back.

His eyes were fire as Demitri stared his hate, "You dared harm one I love and for that I will show no mercy." But his vehemence failed and his sword tip dropped as he saw a warrior with his weapon to Sue's throat, his despair falling over him like a cloak.

Solonak smiled, once again in control, and he made to reply thinking to plant a barb before he killed this alien. But for him it was already too late. A brown streak entered the cave followed by a roar and a scream that deafened him, the sound like a physical blow. Saber needed no orientation to the dark. He hit the floor at full speed, taking a single bound that put him right in the chest of the man holding Sue. The screams were the clansman's terror and final breath. His yell accompanied by Solonak's mother and younger brother who shared his terror as well as a bath of the dead man's blood. Tawnee was only a step behind, spinning in the closed space and passing in another streak behind Demitri, taking down both Briss'y facing Den'al in a wild tumble of fur and flesh. Another even more terrible scream beating the chamber.

The Russian ignored the carnage around him. He now had eyes only for Solonak. Like an avalanche he fell upon the Briss'y, and what he lacked in skill he made up with shear strength and rage. He beat at Solonak's guard, pushing the clav'l up and out of the way.

"No!" Solonak screamed, flinging up a warding hand only to lose it as Demitri swept it away with a cross cut. The Briss'y stared at the stump in dismay and shock. But it was short lived as Demitri reversed the cut and stepped in, the blade taking the traitor in the side of the throat, thus ending anymore foolish words as well as the life of the Drakil's oldest son.

Demitri didn't even watch the body fall as he rushed to Sue, cradling the woman in his arms. The bitter fight was over, but the cost was heavy. Den'al stepped to Rebecca and Saber to his fallen mate. Tawnee lay panting her last breath, impaled by a sword from a clansman who'd simply raised it in terror. It was a mournful howl that rose from the earth as the big cat announced her passing. The sound rolled out of the cave and held on the wind, only to be overwhelmed by a new sound that could not be contained within the great cleft known as the Valley of The Moon!

Mac was overwhelmed with sensory input assaulting him from multiple sources. He was of two minds, his awareness split, his reality fractured. He saw his arrow strike Altil, and saw the Chalgu fall backward only to stand back up again a moment later. The elation he felt thinking he'd killed the enemy leader quickly turned to dread because he *heard* the order Altil gave his army. *Kill them all except The One!* Saw the change as weapons now cut to kill. Mac stood in a sea of death and he was the center of a maelstrom.

At the same instant he *saw* Saber rush a strange clansman who was holding Sue at knife point, a moment later he witnessed the same warrior's bloody death. Around him he witnessed more clansmen falling, his lines breaking and the Chalgu pouring through the gaps. He saw Niloc and Jehkal surrounded, with Rahkal sprawled on the ground beside an unmoving Cam. He saw Tawnee's death and felt Saber's mournful howl. He saw a crowd of Chalgu as they reached for him, sensing as did he, that this was the end. Closing his eyes, he waited for the enemy to reach him, hearing them approach, waiting to lunge out with his sword hoping to kill, and in that act, force them to kill him. He heard the crunch of heavy feet and felt the first brush of a white hand graze him. Then the earth jumped under his feet and the sound of a thousand thunders slammed him to the ground.

The battle had passed Shumak. His lines were now somewhere behind him and the field was packed with Chalgu who streamed around and past him, somehow ignoring the wounded lizard propped against a tree. He looked into the sky, watching the gray clouds and the play of snowflakes as they drifted toward the ground. As a game, he would seek a single crystal and watch it fall toward him till it lit upon branch or ground or his outstretched leg. Then he would select another and repeat this mindless task as his life drained away. Thus it was he who first saw the clouds change. The gray began to foam and twist, the clouds beginning to twirl then twist into a growing vortex. He watched in fascination as the gray coalesced into ever brighter white and pulsing blue, turning faster and faster, silent lightening flashing deeper in the clouds strobing the sky. *What...?* his question died along with the silence. The lightening froze momentarily, then it lashed out in blinding thunderous strikes, cleaving into the Chalgu lines and tossing the enemy around like leaves in a stiff wind. The very earth heaved and groaned from the assault, turning Shumak and his world upside down.

Mac pulled himself to his feet, shocked to his core at the billowing explosions rocking the valley. The Chalgu around him remained prone as if pinned there by silent command. Mac stared. Where the lightening struck great gouts of earth rose skyward, and only one thing he'd ever seen in his life came close to what he witnessed. An artillery barrage. One that was methodically ripping the Chalgu to shreds. The rumble of it was felt in the chest, the sound a physical thing rolling on and on until, as suddenly as it had come, the attack ceased. And it was an attack, Mac had no doubts, nor did the Chalgu. Stumbling a step forward, Mac stood and stared at the sky, watching the play in the clouds just as Shumak did, thankful for the respite but not knowing what new peril may now befall them.

All fighting had ceased across the field, and those still living cast their terror filled eyes skyward. The vortex continued unabated, but when no more lightening descended several Chalgu rose up intending to grab Mac, their orders still clear and resounding in their minds.

Niloc saw them and yelled, "Watch out, Drakil!"

Mac spun, holding out his weapon as two rushed forward, but they'd made only two steps when a single word boomed down from the sky as if from the lips of God himself.

"Hold!" it ordered. Mac heard it in his mind as well as through his auditory sense, his mouth falling open in shock. The command came in the language of the clans, in the hissing speech of the people, the clicking of the Chalgu. And... in English! Everywhere across the field of battle, no matter their race, stunned warriors heeded the word from above.

All except one. Altil, True Leader of the Chalgu, was delirious from loss of blood and the onset of shock. His brain was confused and in his confusion he mistook the thing above for the presence of the thing he desired most. His god. Returned but ethereal, not quite crossed back into this world. His god called to him, needing something more, and Altil knew what was required to sunder the final barrier. The death of The One. He drew himself painfully to his feet and pulled a spear from the grasp of one of his soldiers, then, stumbling forward, he braced to hurl it at Mac.

"Hold!" Again the word thundered across the valley, but Altil was far beyond hearing as he drew back ready to cast.

Mac heard Altil in his mind and turned to see him struggle forward, blood streaming from the hole in his chest. *I must kill you!* The Chalgu leader pulled one of his arms back, preparing to throw a spear. Mac stood frozen, waiting for the flight of death. Then he blinked closed his eyes as a single bolt of blue lightening shot down from the sky. It engulfed Altil, covering him from head to toe with hell fire. He writhed in momentary agony then he was gone. The True Leader was incinerated in an instant. Mac opened his eyes and saw nothing but ash and a smoking hole to mark where once Altil had stood.

After the fall of Altil, a series of hoots and whistles, sounding impossibly loud, fell from the sky. The Chalgu warriors heard and obeyed. They began to move backward, dropping their weapons. In moments they were streaming away back toward the forest, most stumbling as they watched over their shoulders, wondering if more death would be visited upon them. But the entity in the sky seemed content with their flight. Mac ignored them, not questioning the end of the battle, just thankful. He rushed down hill to where Niloc stood. The clansman staring at him in wonder. Mac ignored *him* as well, falling to the ground beside his friend.

"Cam!" He grabbed the Captain by his shoulders and was rewarded with a groan, then a flutter of eyelids as he opened his eyes.

Cam looked up at him and smiled, "You look like shit, Mac."

His voice was weak, but Mac beamed at him, "I though you were dead!" Cam tried to sit up but Mac held him down. "Just lay there while I check your wounds."

"Forget me, Mac. I'll live. Just a bump on the head. Hurts like hell but… What about the others?"

What indeed? Jehkal sat nearby, Rahkal cradled in his lap. A gash ran the across the boys forehead, but his eyes were open and Jehkal nodded in confirmation. He would be ok. His thoughts of the others bored a hole in his heart. Tawnee he knew was gone. What of the others? He braced himself for a connection to Saber, but Niloc's voice stopped him.

"My Drakil! Look!"

Mac did, looking up where Niloc pointed, seeing a huge mass drop from the clouds. Not totally surprised, Mac watched as an ship fell below the cover to hover above him. No lights now, just an oblong shape easily as big as his own ship Atlantis. In near silence it moved, creeping slowly toward a clear area where it settled to the ground, coming to a rest on three protrusions that seemed to flow from the skin as it neared the ground. It ceased all motion, simply sitting there, a gray shape that was no shape, as if the skin flowed and changed as you watched.

Mac had lived so long as a barbarian he'd almost forgotten about UFO's, he simply watched. Not so the clansmen. They backed away or prostrated themselves, not knowing if the wrath of god would be visited upon them as it so recently was upon the Chalgu. Mac had no such qualms. He stood as an opening in the skin of the ship irised open, disgorging two figures of human proportion. Each dressed in one piece silver suites, including the helmet, seamless and shimmering just like the ship. One stepped forward until it stood only five paces away. Mac saw his own reflection in the spotless silver globe of the visor, struck by his image. The ragged bearded face, long stringy hair, and hollow sunken eyes. Patiently he waited; this was the spaceman's show. Like a bubble bursting, the helmet fell away, disappearing completely into the neck of the suit, revealing a perfectly ordinary and human face. Mac knees almost buckled, now truly stunned.

The face, Mac noted, was vaguely familiar as the spaceman snapped a salute as sharp and crisp as an academy graduate, then spoke, "Commander Mac Crowe!" It was as much a statement as a question; the speaker possibly disbelieving Mac's bloody disheveled appearance.

"You may not remember me. but we crossed paths a few times… back in the world." He stuck out his silver covered hand and grabbed Mac's. "We played hell finding you…" A beaming smile broke out across the man's face. "I'm Commander Samuel Rodgers, 'Buck' Rodgers, at your service! We're here to bring you home."

Conclusions

Mac, clean, shaven and clothed in real clothes, sat in the antiseptic whiteness of the med bay on the strange alien ship, sipping a quite ordinary, though truly extraordinary cup of coffee. Yet the ship was alien only in its strangeness, because it was now a ship of earth, the Victory II, so named after the huge mother ship from which it originated. The very ship that inadvertently began their odyssey so long ago. Mac listened to a tale enthusiastically spun by Buck and Cal. A tale almost as strange as his own!

As he listened, Mac realized that many of Dr. Gordon's suppositions were golden. The great alien warship had orbited this planet for close to two thousand years, damaged in a battle that rendered it cold, dead, and useless. The same battle that resulted in this planet being bombed back to the Stone Age. Then, somehow, something had revived the ship. Revived was an accurate description because the ship was, at its core, an artificially intelligent brain. Feeling and thinking and unbelievably advanced, though incredibly damaged, not even able to remember the entire name it was christened with. Calling itself Vi-t-ry instead of Victory. "Of course, that's the English translation, Mac." Buck said. "We couldn't begin to pronounce it in their language."

Mac smiled, *I could.* He spoke clan and it was almost a match to the language of the ship.

It was Victory's flawed search for his home system that resulted in the Unity and the Atlantis being brought to this lonely end of the galaxy. A simple, yet incredible fluke!

Mac was devastated to hear about the events its arrival caused back home. "I'm surprised WWIII hasn't broken out," Buck said, "Still not sure it won't. Lot a politicin happening back in the world."

Amazingly, the *world* in general was ignorant of the mission to Victory, their contact with the ship, and the resulting partnership. Vi-t-ry/Victory was aware of and sorry for the damage he'd caused, and he'd offered his knowledge and technology to help correct it. The ship also knew it could do much in the future, but little without human assistance. It required warm blooded help to continue its repairs. A bargain was struck. Humanity would help repair the alien ship and in return, Victory would provide technology and history and myriad advances. A thousand year technological jump forward. Even now the first humans were crawling around the great vessel. Scientists, engineers, archeologists. As Cal said, "if it ended in 'ist', there was at least fifty of them up there sifting through all that Victory had to offer. The first active installment on Victory's side was sending Buck and Cal as a rescue team to find the lost crews. An act of faith so to speak. So here they were, the Calvary arriving just in the nick of time.

Mac had a thousand questions, each answer incredible, or improbable, or both. Primary on is list was, "How the hell did you find us?"

Buck smiled a smile that would shame the Cheshire Cat. "You can't believe the technology, Mac! Almost completely based on nano-tech. They have self-replicating Nannites that get into everything. And I mean everything… including you and me!"

"Me?" In a day of surprises this was just one more.

"Yeah, Mac. You. We would have found you anyway because this beauty," He patted the ships bulkhead lovingly. "...she could search every individual on the planet by DNA signature. We programmed each of your DNA into her, and she painted and compared people… well not all are people… from orbit." He paused a moment in poignant silence.

"We found the graves, Mac. I'm sorry. I'm just glad we didn't find any more." He was referring to the graves of the first three members of Mac's crew to die on this planet, so many months and a lifetime ago.

"Anyway, we knew we were close, but the DNA proved unnecessary. It was you, Mac. You were blazing like a beacon!"

They showed him a screen that showed he was. The Nannites coursing through him responded to inquiries from the ship, screaming out his position. Not only his, but Saber, Tawnee and the entire Chalgu nation, particularly Altil. All carried the mechanical creatures.

Why not the others? Why not Cam or any of the other humans? There was no answer to that, even the computer on the rescue ship didn't know. Not that it really mattered. What really counted was that beyond the impossible, they were rescued.

Mac sighed in wonder, dismay, and partial disgust. *The rescue certainly fulfilled Niloc's damn legend!* But the rescue was bittersweet as well, evidenced by the beds in the room in which he sat and the patients they contained. Shumak, Rahkal and Rebecca, lay attached to medical equipment Mac couldn't begin to describe. Each had wounds that may have killed them had it not been for this ship, as would many others. Even now there was a steady stream of wounded receiving care, though it took the bravery of Jehkal carrying his brother into the ship to finally overcome the fear and religious awe of the clansmen. They were wary and wide-eyed, but they came.

There was skin glue to close wounds, antibiotics, and an injection of Nannites for most, mechanical surgery for others. Still, a level of care far beyond any earthbound hospital. The only real problem was volume. It would take two days to see to them all, and for some that help would be too late, though they made every effort to triage effectively.

Mac's heart lurched as he sat with Rebecca, her hand in his, waiting for her to wake from a drug induced coma. The deep sleep was designed to help her bruised brain heal. How would he explain his decision to stay in the fight and not rush to her rescue? This haunted him.

Then there was Demitri. The look on the Russian's face would haunt him as well, perhaps forever. Mac had only to close his eyes to relive the moment Demitri appeared at the top of the hill. Slowly and mechanically he'd walked to Mac, and then past, never looking up as he carried the body of the woman he loved down to the Victory II. Her wounds were grievous and only time would tell if she would live. She lay now in a stasis chamber in the room next door. It was hoped that perhaps the larger facilities on Victory, and the knowledge buried in his databanks, would provide hope. Until then, Demitri would stay by her side, ignoring Mac completely.

That was hard to accept, but Mac allowed himself a small smile and bit of hope. Soon Victory II would take her home, and he had every confidence that in time, Sue would be well.

Many other burning questions were answered as well, things debated by campfire now confirmed. The Aranu were indeed the original owners of this rock, and so, as much victims as anyone. Their world, this world, had been a galactic Switzerland; part vacation retreat, part galactic banking central, and a neutral go between for a federation of systems known as the Collective, and its trade partners and many adversaries. In the language of the Collective it was known as Sul-Anroth. The Aranu called their home Nacoltchee, and it translated roughly into English as a world known as Paradise!

Niloc and his kind were Prime, or *first* members of the Collective. The reptilian People were Collective as well, though *second* members, and they were not *The People*, but were known in the databanks by the name of their home star; Scillian. Why they had changed the name to People was anyone's guess. Shumak certainly didn't know and it would take an army of archaeologist to find out. Shumak, though, was intrigued with the name. In the future they would be known as the People first, but Scillian second. Shumak the Scillian, Mac told him it had a nice ring to it.

The Chalgu were but one of the Collective's more reluctant and disgruntled partners. It seemed there were many that fell into this category. Mac had yet to meet any of those, and by the look of their pictures and descriptions, didn't care to. Who really started the war that consumed them all is a mystery still locked away in Victory. Or perhaps the answer could be found somewhere here on Paradise. Buck told them the planet was a virtual honeycomb underneath, the entire civilization operating underground, leaving most of the world pristine. This was why the surface held so little, so few cities and so few clues. Another adventure? Perhaps, but it would in fact be a minor one. Man had just gone from scratching the edge of space to a technology that could open up to them the entire galaxy, possibly the universe. Incredibly, Mac would live to be apart of this new and grand adventure!

Mac stood well back, reveling in the sunshine that competed feebly with the cold still air of morning, thankful to trade in his furs for hi-tech protection. Nearly indestructible and warm. His new suit of nano-skin was an incredible gift provided by the Victory II. Saber sat beside him in cat like disdain at the proceedings, but the crowd at his back was enthralled in total. Mac saluted, and with incredible grace and a total lack of noise, the Victory II rose into the clear green sky. She circled the field once, then, with a burst of speed that was impossible to follow, disappeared over the escarpment, headed north and up to where she would rendezvous at a single and specific point in orbit, and time. From there, the mother ship would reach out and bring her home. There would be only one shot at the recovery because the energy required would leave Vi-t-ry exhausted for weeks to come. Yet they would be back. And Mac would be waiting. The Commander of the lost Atlantis was now a man of two worlds, and right now this one needed him more. There were alliances to form and a world to explore.

Rebecca squeezed his hand. “Ok, my Drakil! What now?”

Mac snorted, “Don’t start with that Drakil crap! It’s Macintosh Crowe! Illustrious and Grand Ambassador of Earth! And I’ll thank you not to forget it.”

“Quiet, Mac. The natives are listening.” Cam placed upon his face a most cherubic smile. “I just hope they bring some women when they come back.” It was a wistful statement, and one that let Mac know his friend was once again, healthy and truly ok.

“My, Drakil!” This time it was in Clan and very formal, including a chest salute and lowered eyes. “The Chieftains await your presence.” Niloc at least, would not let him forget his clan title. A title that, now that he had gained a little history on it, shocked him more than a bit. There was a Drakil-at’sakaal of a sort listed in the Victory II’s language databank. Buck had translated it with a curious look. Even more curious after hearing Mac’s full tale. Drakil-at’sakaal was in reality a conglomeration of words. Clan and the Peoples tongue. Drakil, or Draka’il was Clan for *Light*. At’sakaal, or Ata slsakal, was the name of the People’s home world, the mostly desert planet that orbited the star, Scillian. But there was more. *Light* for the Collective religion also referred to a mythical being. *Draka'il, the One awaited,* so said the records. Broadly interpreted, the name Drakil-at'sakaal meant savior, or more literally, Mac was thought to be the *Light of the Home World!* Religion and technology mixed long ago into a prophecy, or a legend of hope. Probably long after the various races were stranded here by war and falling quickly into the chaos of subsistence survival. Who knew what the original saying was or how it had changed over the ages, falling eventually into the mantra of Niloc's faith. The One, the Kraagen, and the serpent. The lost moon? Technology and religion combined, and… who could know what other *entities* played a part? *Home World* was literal. This was their home world. The Clan's, the Scillian's, and now Mac's.

He sighed and looked to the sky, thinking of friends departing. Shumak and Jehkal would go far beyond anything they could have ever imagined, ambassadors of their world and their peoples, to Earth. Demitri and Sue… he gave a silent prayer for her recovery… would go home and tell their story, and he fervently hoped they would return as well. Silently he wished them the best, then waved Niloc to lead off.

"Come on then. Let's not keep them waiting."

Mac's eyes were not they only ones watching the departure of the Victory II. The Quinllius scout ship which orbited beyond the planet's moons also noted the event with great interest. Moments after Victory II disappeared, it too blinked out of existence, heading for its base. Vi-t-ry's poking into other systems when he'd searched for home had alerted the Quinllius hive, and this scout followed that poking back to its source, arriving not long after the huge wounded ship had left for Earth. But the robot scout was patient, content to wait for events to manifest themselves. It recorded the Victory II, her arrival, search, and her exit. The message was clear. Something stirred in sector 9-027-A. Something not sensed in more than two thousand cycles, and it tasted suspiciously like the long dead Collective! A decision was made by the Central Authority. This system bore careful watching indeed.

Books By
Gregory J. Saunders

Visit: www.gregoryjsaunders.com